Madness On The
ORIENT
EXPRESS

Also from Chaosium:

Madness On The

ORIENT EXPRESS

EDITED BY JAMES LOWDER

CHAOSIUM
INC.

Madness on the Orient Express
is published by Chaosium Inc.

Madness on the Orient Express and Introduction
©2014 by James Lowder.

Cover illustration © 2014 by Victor Leza

www.chaosium.com

This book is printed on 100% acid-free paper.

FIRST EDITION
10 9 8 7 6 5 4 3 2 1

Chaosium Publication 6057
Published in December 2014

ISBN-10: 1568823991
ISBN-13: 9781568823997

Printed in the USA

To Lynn Willis,
for getting the train rolling.

CONTENTS

INTRODUCTION
James Lowder

As Agatha Christie's Hercule Poirot famously notes in *Murder on the Orient Express*, "The impossible could not have happened, therefore the impossible must be possible in spite of appearances." Odd as it may seem at first glance, H.P. Lovecraft might have agreed with the fastidious Belgian sleuth on this. It would be in the definition of *the impossible* where the two formidable intellects would find themselves in for some spirited debate—and in describing just what an encounter with the newly expanded *possible* would mean for the human psyche.

Lovecraft was no mystic. Neither did he distrust science. As a young man he wrote a number of essays on the subject, particularly on astronomy, for newspapers such as the *Pawtuxet Valley Gleaner* and the *Providence Evening News*. Throughout his career he maintained that science was a valuable weapon against the forces of ignorance and superstition. Fellow foe of charlatans Harry Houdini (who makes an appearance in this volume, courtesy of Christopher Golden) even hired Lovecraft and C.M. Eddy, Jr. to write an entire book bashing superstition. Sadly, Houdini's death led to the project being abandoned.

For all that he championed science, though, Lovecraft recognized its dark side. The horror in his stories is not derived from the discovery of the impossible, the intrusion of the unreal into the mundane, but rather from the realization that the universe contains truths far beyond humankind's comprehension. And science sometimes plays a vital role in that awful realization. It's in the "piecing together of dissociated knowledge," as his narrator notes at the start of "The Call of Cthulhu," that the scientist "will open up such terrifying vistas of reality, and of our frightful position therein, that we shall either go mad from the revelation or flee from the light into the peace and safety of a new dark age."

Which brings us back to the Orient Express.

In real life and in art, trains have often embodied the promise—and peril—of technological advance. Like much of the innovation firing the Industrial Revolution, the train unlocked new opportunities for wealth and travel, but also created incredible chaos, uprooting populations and blighting landscapes. By the late 1860s, for example, the California Board of Agriculture estimated that fully one third of the state's forests had been harvested, much of that for use by the railroads. In this anthology, stories such as Geoff Gillan's "The Lost Station Horror" and James L. Sutter's moving "The God Beneath the Mountain" explore the idea that work on or around the rails might lead to unwelcome discoveries, while Ari Marmell's "Engineered" pulls back to examine the implications of the rail system as a whole.

Along with unrestrained scientific endeavor, the most certain path to uncovering some unwelcome truth about the universe in a Mythos tale is for a character to venture beyond his "placid island of ignorance" and encounter a foreign culture. "Searchers after horror," notes the narrator of Lovecraft's "The Picture in the House," "haunt strange, far places." Here, the Orient Express serves as a perfect vehicle for such excursions, designed as it is to bridge the West and the East. This movement into mystery forms the central action for many of our stories, most notably Penelope Love's "Daddy, Daddy," Lucien Soulban's chilling "Black Cat of the Orient," and the aptly titled "On the Eastbound Train" by Mythos legend Darrell Schweitzer.

As is sometimes the case with the anthologies I edit, *Madness on the Orient Express* came about because of a casual comment at a convention—Gen Con, in this case. I was chatting with Chaosium owner Charlie Krank about the way in which publishers were using Kickstarter to fund anthologies, and Charlie revealed that he was, indeed, looking into launching the company's next projects through the crowdsourcing platform. He was hoping for a positive reception, and we left the possibility open for me to put together a related anthology, should any of those Kickstarters take off.

A couple hundred thousand dollars in Kickstarter support later, here we are.

Specifically, this anthology was created as a stretch goal for the campaign to fund a reprint of the classic *Horror on the Orient Express* roleplaying campaign for *Call of Cthulhu*. So thanks are immediately due to all the backers who got behind that project and allowed us to create this collection of original stories, and to the folks at Chaosium: Charlie, Meghan, Mike, Nick, and Dustin. Thanks are also due to the designers of the original *Horror on the Orient Express* campaign and to Chaosium editor extraordinaire Lynn Willis.

The designers for the first incarnation of the *Horror on the Orient Express* adventure grew out of the thriving Australian convention scene of the 1980s. As Mark Morrison explains in an article for the British fanzine *Dagon*, the lack of a game manufacturer presence meant the local cons were very much focused on getting enthusiasts together to play. Morrison and a growing circle of friends—known as the Cthulhu Conglomerate—became ambassadors for the *Call of Cthulhu* RPG, and eventually published designers in their own right. After turning down a proposal for a Europe sourcebook from Morrison and Christian Lehmann, Lynn Willis countered, as was his wont, with a brilliant alternative: an epic adventure set aboard the Orient Express. No fewer than eighteen people contributed to the original published adventure, including Cthulhu Conglomerate founder Mark Morrison and horror fiction legend Thomas Ligotti, and two authors you will also find represented in this anthology: the aforementioned Love and Gillan.

Whether in a roleplaying adventure or a short story, the nature of rail travel makes it amenable as a setting for storytelling. Train travel takes time, and the train itself is structured so that passengers can get up and move around. This gives a storyteller some room to pace a tale out, and to grant her or his characters some changes of scenery along the way to the resolution. There's also the motion, a fact that continues to make speeding trains a standard trope for adventure stories in all media. The only limitation placed upon the writers for this collection was that their works somehow involve the

Orient Express and the Mythos. Our authors have taken full advantage of all this freedom, exploring both the inner working of the
train (Elaine Cunningham's "A Great and Terrible Hunger") and
the mystique attached to the Orient Express itself (Kenneth Hite's
"La Musique de l'Ennui"), with other entries ranging in tone and
approach from Cody Goodfellow's two-fisted pulp yarn to Joshua
Alan Doetsch's surrealistic nightmare.

The last warning whistle has blown, and we need to get underway. So please have your tickets at the ready and settle in for a journey across unexpected landscapes to a destination that—well, we'll
just let you see it for yourself when you arrive. We can promise this,
though: murder will be the least of your problems on this trip
aboard the Orient Express.

THERE IS A BOOK
Dennis Detwiller

THE BOOK WAS WRITTEN BEFORE it could be written.

Before the dominance of any single life-form on Earth, the book *was* already, waiting for a hand to transcribe it. It hovered, before the first sludge crawled from the oceans, before the Earth cooled and the sun lit and the worlds upon world were spat from a rip in the nothing.

It was *there*.

The ideas it contained were a primer for this universe. The things for which it was messenger had long arrived at their places in the beyond, and waited for it to herald their coming in the existence that would be.

It is hard to describe something that transcends the world it finds itself in, but the book is this. A puncture through, a hole to the labyrinths of alien thought beyond the veil of this transient edifice of order.

The book was an agreement between inhuman powers; which might come first, which would come last. Because to them time was merely a measure of patience. All was visible before them; time and order nothing but a vast field of movement that hovered and shifted and shifted back, and beyond it—what they longed for— absolute freedom.

The book manifested on Earth because reality is *thin* there; it's a cosmic sinkhole, a place where things congeal like clots of blood drawn to the edge of a drain. The entire universe beyond it, ready to despoil and ruin, is blocked to powers beyond, so they circle and wait for the way to open.

Their plans were laid before the Earth's mantle cooled.

For eons, millennia, epochs, the book was nothing more than a series of thoughts waiting for a mind, a series of movements waiting for some dumb limb to make them, a series of actions waiting for bodies to execute.

Then, man.

Humanity, the winner of endless biological conflict, crept across the face of the globe like a stain. First as ape-men that crooned at the moon and smashed each other's heads in, then crawled through the jungles and stacked rocks and cried to the sun in worship, piling bodies in great mountains.

Then those that slept in high grass and ate seeds and berries and meat, when they could find it, hiding from marauders with skull-painted faces who hunted them, leaving bleached white bones gnawed clean in their path.

Then the snows receded, the Earth warmed, and the minds of men grew. It wasn't long until man discovered they could sow seeds wherever they went, that the seeds could be carried, inter-bred, harvested. Food became plentiful, and men knew leisure for the first time.

Time passed. Buildings came, and then the stories.

The clock that was the book ticked away, counting, waiting. But even the things beyond grew impatient. The book grew impatient too, wanting to serve its function. It saw man as a blunt instrument, a method to fashion an escape for those it awaited, something with which it could pry the locks on the blue world and complete its purpose: the release of those it served into a universe ready for ruin.

Its first attempt to transcribe itself was in a fertile place, where men worked metal, burned children alive for luck, where they tracked the stars for the first time and scribbled notes down on clay tablets that baked in the sun.

There, it found a man named Asu, leapt through his hand onto the tablets and left him reeling. By the end, after the pictures came,

Asu was a madman, his mind scorched by the secrets of the keys and gates that held the powers waiting beyond.

The tablets grew in notoriety, a disease of ideas that crept out and infected hundreds and then thousands of men. War and slaughter and hatred followed. Before the rituals from the book could be enacted, Asu and his followers were hung from gibbets and cut open. A campaign to destroy the tablets and all copies was undertaken.

The book had acted too soon. The plague it started spread too fast and collapsed upon itself, leaving only bodies, ashes and death.

But clay tablets are small, they are resilient.

They are easily overlooked.

❖   ❖   ❖

Not all the tablets had been smashed. Once, a man raced through the streets of a city, pursued by the king's guards, carrying a pail with a set of the tablets, spilling them as he ran. Three nights before, he had inscribed markings in the dirt, seeing signs and portents that showed the truth in the letters. His face and arms were covered in the dried blood of his family, whom he had murdered and then devoured, and his eyes were mad.

When the guards cornered him, he was run through by spears and fell into the well at the center of town. Later, they would fish his body out and, eventually, the pail. But the tablets—nine of them—would remain at the bottom.

Nearly two thousand years later—the span of a blink to the things beyond—a young man crawled through the ruins of Babylon with a spade and books of his own. He was a scholar, a peaceful man concerned with the study of the past and the meaning of man's future. He was a man of letters, someone ahead of his time, who saw mankind's ascent from the dirt as assurance of some meaning, the first steps toward a grand enterprise in the future.

He was wrong.

As he had done many times before, he dug the artifacts up from the dry well. Before, the tablets he had uncovered were lists, receipts of centuries-dead merchants, a glimpse into another time. Not this time. This time he uncovered the nine tablets. Long he had worked on the language of the ancient peoples of the world. In the city of peace he had stitched together earlier learnings to translate the new-found tablets.

Finally, in Sanaá, he scribbled down the first words of the translation in a finely made book of linen and goatskin, and as his hand placed them on the page, it shook. The ideas of the tablets opened the gap in the world, and the rest of the book came through. The young man was changed. When he finished, the book was scrawled in smears of ink and drawn in gouts of his own blood. For the first time since the assembly of the ideas of the book, its full concept had transited into the world.

What followed was madness.

❖   ❖   ❖

Alhazred was his name, though some also called him mad, and his book entered the hive of knowledge of the city of peace just like any other book; it was a place that valued knowledge and ideas as things separate from reality. Something to be considered and stored and looked to. This was before they realized an idea alone could kill, that a concept was a weapon, that a thought could mean death.

In Baghdad, the book was copied, like any other book, and it spread to hundreds, and then thousands, and finally tens of thousands. Within a year, it had moved through the centers of knowledge, and Alhazred meant prophet or criminal to all.

His version of the book, the *Al-Azif*, was synonymous with death and madness.

His list of offenses had grown too vast to be ignored by the Caliphate, and they moved to eliminate him. Possession of the book was designated a crime. Tens of thousands who read it rose up in orgies of murder and debauchery and in turn were suppressed or killed. The book was burned, but through followers it mutated into codes and cyphers so it might be hidden in plain sight and spread farther. Different versions were produced to foil the censors. From nine clay tablets it had bloomed into nearly eight hundred different volumes, scrolls, and manuscript fragments.

Alhazred died, but the book to which he had given form remained. Finally, it had found its way permanently into the world.

In all their machinations, the things from beyond never before considered the possibility of something working against them.

They could see the vast expanse of time at once. A field of existence that unfurled and spread and was drawn taut around the world. There, in the darkness as their plans through the book rose and crumbled, they began to suspect they *might not be able to see everything after all.*

That something else might be involved.

Despite the success of the *Al-Azif,* and the book's spread beyond the Caliphates to the foreign West, and finally to the East, the moment never arrived; the time when the humans would descend into fits of madness in such numbers that could allow the gates to swing wide. Every time release seemed close, something happened, some turn that pulled the rift back closed.

By then, most copies of the book were known under a singular name, despite various editions: *Necronomicon.*

The shop was old by human standards. The building it was in had been constructed a year before the crusaders seized the city, and was used as a field headquarters for a madman in steel plate who wore Muslim fingers in a loop around his belt as a prize. He died in the building, a few years later. A fifteen-year-old boy cut his head from his shoulders in one clean swipe.

Later, during the civil war that followed, it served as a larder, holding boxes of goods. A cadre of men with hooked pikes stood guard while the city burned, so the rich could eat, while the poor rioted and starved.

When the Ottomans seized the city, the building fell within the lands of some secondary clark, and its lease was auctioned to a family of some note. Later, nearly two centuries later, it would become a bookstore, run by an insignificant second cousin of this family. This bookstore was a place where old tomes found their way, a sinkhole itself with a painted green door, simply called The Bookstore, and known to all in that area of the city.

It sold nearly nothing, and its owner subsisted on the dwindling fortunes of his family. At night he pored through the books and made his notes and made the signs and sigils that showed him the gates and the keys to the gates.

It also was, by happenstance, the only place in the world that a complete, perfect copy of the *Necronomicon* remained.

The man stepped from the train in Istanbul, his face set, his eyes behind folding spectacles a bright, clear blue. In his long jacket, he had a hunting knife and a small automatic pistol fastened to him, just in case. Just two years before, in 1925, he had been stabbed in New York City with a weapon called a *pranga*. The wound it left in his chest was like the hole from some giant lion's tooth.

He had shot his way out of the hotel room there, bleeding, and killed four men in ceremonial robes. During his escape, he stumbled over the entrails of his dead friend, splayed across a bed in some sick display of worship.

Today, his group still tracked those involved, and it was that grail that had brought them here, on the train, on the Express moving from the west and to the east. They fought all over the globe and closed the gaps that the cult opened. They found the gaps. They located and killed the men who attempted to fumble at the locks to the powers beyond the world.

But the man was weary. It was only recently that he had begun to see the true sprawl of history, and how the horrors stretched over it, a theme that covered everything, maws clamped closed beneath every human act—a seeming foundation that was waiting to snap open. Nothing they had done, in the many years he and his group of compatriots had hunted the worshippers of these powers, had made a single difference in the final outcome. It was just a matter of time.

He was fragile and weary and old. What had filled him with purpose once—the preservation of the world of men—now filled him with dread.

He had recruited, fought beside, and lost too many people along the way, and maybe, he thought for the first time, he might be on the wrong side of this fight.

When he stepped from the train into the old city, this thought felt like a truth. A reflection played across his glasses, a green door across the plaza, past a gate. As he watched it, the green door opened, showing a black hole in space.

He began to walk toward the green door, and a thousand gibbering things in the beyond roiled in their pleasure.

THE LOST STATION HORROR
GEOFF GILLAN

I HAVE NOT LONG BEFORE that malevolent shifting thing I glimpsed in the volcanic depths of the earth beneath southern Bulgaria comes to claim me. The angles of this cell alter each time I close and open my eyes and the arm I no longer have itches and writhes, a fulcrum trying to twist my whole body no matter how I turn. I pray that at least I might have carried this madness with me and that nothing still lives in that wilderness to bring ruin on the world; pray that once I have gone all trace of its evil will depart from this world. I know I will not live long enough for the guillotine's blade to be my end.

I have written repeatedly, warning the directors of Brand and Company to cease their construction, expunge the whole site, and trust nothing that comes out of it, but they ignore me. I have heard that the chief engineer spits when my name is spoken. They doubtless all consider me an insane monster. Well, I have not long to brood on any shipwreck of my reputation; greater evils than calumny await. My last hope is that this is considered a dying declaration, and might spur them to seal up the way to the entire plateau and find some other route through to Sofia.

But I doubt it. The Orient Express will have its way.

Damn their train and their progress.

This was the opposite of my opinion when I arrived at the town of Z——, a young engineer basking in the privilege of joining in one of the great engineering feats Europe has seen: the construction of the first continuous train link through Bulgaria from east to west, forming a line across the whole of Europe. The recent success of the Compagnie International des Wagons-Lits's fabulous Orient Express ensured it wished to offer one continuous journey by train, from Paris to Constantinople. The current journey had to be made by coach beyond Nisch in Serbia, before the passengers could again entrain at Tatar-Bazardjik in Bulgaria, a wearisome trip through often mountainous and hostile terrain. Nagelmackers himself had accompanied the surveyors laying down the new route, and a great part of the line fell to the Bulgarian State Railway to construct. Its success was a matter of great national import to the now-independent Bulgarians, freshly liberated from the Ottomans and determined to show their worth.

My task was to work on a railway station in the hinterland, whose construction had recently run into trouble. The Bulgarians knew that to simply throw down rail lines was not enough. The track had to be maintained and repaired, the engines and rolling stock serviced, the whole new rail artery through their country kept alive and pulsing. Even if the Orient Express was to make few stops in Bulgaria, other local services must use the line, or else the cost would hardly be worth it. For this a series of stations at strategic intervals must be planned and erected. It was to one of these, in the Pazardzhik region of Bulgaria, around Belovo, that I was sent.

The Bulgarians had contracted my services through the German firm of engineers for which I worked. The Ottomans had established a tradition of using European expertise, especially German and Italian, and the new Bulgarian king was a German princeling, so our two countries' links were strong. I was dispatched to the nearby village of Z——— to assist the chief engineer. I was one of the new breed of practical rather than scientific engineers. At thirty I had eschewed wife and family to focus utterly on my career. My friends thought me single-minded and even dull, but now I was vindicated surely, in being hired as assistant engineer on one of the age's most ambitious projects.

The chief engineer met me in the town of Belovo with reports and instructions. He was an inspiring and energetic fellow I had long known by reputation and greatly admired, and he promised me an assistant in the village. The construction of the station had begun on a plateau beyond a newly blasted tunnel but recently a subsidence had bought the entire thing down, even cracking some of the nearby rock. A new building had been commenced farther along, on what was considered more stable ground, but there were rumors of tremors and other movement. I needed to determine if the new station would be sound. It would be costly and difficult to reroute the line over such rugged country—more tunnels and bridges would be needed to avoid to steep a grade in the lines—and someone senior among the Bulgarians was determined to create a station here instead.

"Perhaps he is from here originally. They are not a people who forget their roots," the chief engineer suggested.

"What am I to do then?"

"Find a solution that is practical. The geologist's report has been little help. They tell us the area is volcanic and might experience tremors. Well, you could say that about the whole place. Maybe there is something more here, or some deficit in the station's design. We've started the second foundations but we need an answer fast."

He paused for a moment and moved his jaws as if chewing over his next words. "Your predecessor Hartz was lost when the wall of the first station fell in."

"Lost? You mean killed?"

"I mean lost. Perhaps he fell into a crevasse that later closed. We never found him."

Then he gave me a hard and appraising look that, I must admit, made me uncomfortable. "Don't listen to the wild tales some of the workers are telling. We have had deaths; all engineering projects of this size have deaths. But some of the men are spooked. We've had threats of violence—so many that we've had to hire a private firm to put down some of the unrest. It has all been very regrettable."

"Have they some strange fancies about what we are doing? Surely the tremors alone would not lead to such behavior."

The chief engineer shrugged. "The region's folklore says it was created when God got tired of carrying a bundle of rocks and let them fall onto Bulgaria and lie there. Strange fancies are in the air. But the workers have been toiling long hours under impossible conditions and they are, perhaps, overwrought. Just don't get drawn in. That's my advice to you."

He would himself be drawn in no further on the subject but

promised to come and check on my progress in a few days, after he had attended to other problems farther along the line. I was left to continue my journey to the village of Z—— alone and spend my first night in a modest hostelry in fruitless speculation.

By morning all that had seized me was not dread or even apprehension, but an intense ambition. Might I be the one to solve the dilemma halting our progress and make a name for myself in the company—or even, more widely, in my profession? I was entertaining these jejune fantasies while shaving, when came a knock at my door. This was my fateful meeting with Orrin Lester Leacock.

He stood in the doorway, a slender figure wearing rugged workman's clothes and a green Tyrolean hat, carrying a canvas bag bulging with instruments and brimming with rolled-up plans. He was fair and his face was narrow with a shallow forehead and long nose that gave him a thrusting appearance. The hair under his hat was dark blond. His eyes were muddy blue, as though some tainted substance had mixed with their natural color. I noticed, too, that his pupils were always dilated and incredibly wide, like an animal's. He confessed later that, as a child, he had stared too long at the sun, causing this strangeness, but it leant him an intense and discomforting appearance. He stood awkwardly, tilted at an angle askew. I don't believe I ever saw him straighten, I recall now with a shudder.

Leacock introduced himself in German that was clearly English accented, though solid enough. My own English was fluent so I proposed we converse in his native tongue, which pleased him. He was a young man, hardly twenty-five, but his appraising gaze seemed knowing in a way that belied his years.

We passed a few pleasantries and over breakfast at the hostelry went through the geologist's report. Leacock's enthusiasm for his work was strong, his energy and excitement exceeding my own. The light of some greater purpose lit his eyes when he thumped the table to make a point, and he was full of intense speculation about drilling into other areas of the rock around the plateau to resolve the issue. He expounded a strange theory that the angles of the digging were important and would somehow liberate us from our dilemma.

"Don't you think there is a plan to the world, an arrangement of angles and joints like there is any colossal structure?"

"You mean God's plan?" I smiled indulgently. It seemed a silly question.

"Not that. A plan to the universe itself. A blueprint of connections and portals that would lay this universe bare—lay it open to other, greater places—if only it could be discovered."

I let him ramble on a bit longer, but my mind had drifted back to the engineering problem at hand. I confess I paid scant attention to the details of what he said, more fool me. It seemed, at the time, the kind of mad fancy the young dream up before experience and knowledge teach them otherwise.

A train whistle summoned us to the temporary rail that had been built outside the village where a small locomotive was used to transport supplies and the workers billeted there back and forth to the work site. The village had a rough-stoned, red-roofed peasant charm. I wondered how much it might retain once the rail brought the world to its door, but such is the price of progress.

We quickly left the village behind and toiled up the grade to the site, via a new tunnel that had been only recently blasted, and which some suspected had caused the previous cave in. Muckers were still at work in the tunnel clearing the loose dirt and debris, and some scaffolding still remained, but we passed through smoothly enough. The geologist's report did not support the digging here was to blame; certainly I noticed no cracks or fissures in the tunnel walls, which even lamplight would have shown, had they been serious enough.

Once out of the tunnel we came onto a broad plateau, an expanse of rock and wild bush that commanded a breathtaking view across the hilly country beyond. The station was designed to sit on this plateau, and the open stretch after the tunnel was wide enough to allow good visibility, paramount in railroad station design for the safety of passengers and workers. The original station works slumped at the northeast end where it has collapsed against a massive spur of rock rising from the ground, as if leaning drunkenly against this great stone wall for support. The new station foundations were being dug to the northwest. Past this, the smoothness of the plateau broke down and the dummy rail ran through a long gulley to where a new bridge was being erected to cross a small creek and maintain the grade of the line to a tolerable degree.

The locomotive stopped near the original station and we alighted. On closer inspection I could see it was a complete ruin. Considerable work had been done on the foundation and exterior walls, but now the foundation cement—a mixture of concrete and aggregate of stone in these parts—lay cracked like a broken and discarded bowl. The walls had tumbled all in a northerly direction, so that the northern wall had fallen into the natural spur of stone, which sat high and broad above the plateau. A jagged rend gashed the rock vertically, either from the impact or the initial movement of the earth. It was almost wide enough for a man to pass through. The whole place had an evil aspect, as if some superhuman malignancy had smote the earth and work of man alike.

The now-broken station walls had been constructed of granite and local stone, and I could see sheet metal had been prepared for the roof. This was unusual: most of the stations I had passed on the line were simple wooden affairs, lucky even to have a warehouse or a siding. This had been planned on a grander scale, with a large central passenger area, a supporting warehouse for baggage and goods, and a separate siding granting access to a maintenance shed and water tower, for the upkeep of trains. Immediately I was reminded of the chief engineer's assertion that some powerful person was lobbying behind the scenes, for such a remote village station should normally not expect so grand a station. Perhaps the Orient Express was intended to stop here.

Leacock interrupted my speculations by introducing me to the foreman, a doughty Bulgarian named Dimova. He was an older man with the florid beard and mustaches of a runaway pantomime devil; he reminded me of pictures of the ancient Bulgar warriors that drove the Byzantines before them in the forging of their medieval empire. Brusquely he showed us around the site and explained our presence to the men. Leacock seemed well known by everyone. I remarked on this and Dimova noted that the man had been my predecessor's assistant also.

Leacock and I spent a week investigating every aspect of the station collapse and the site, including the tunnel- and bridgeworks nearby and the surrounding geology. There seemed no obvious reason for the violence beyond freak chance or act of God. No immediate tunnel blasting or tremor was felt prior to the splitting rock and the station's collapse, which had happened in the small hours in the morning while a skeleton crew was on duty. While work had progressed digging a foundation trench for a new building little effort had been made to reclaim parts from the lost station. For days I wondered that it had not been cleared away. As the men came to know me better, and seemed pleased when I demonstrated my rudimentary Bulgarian, they revealed why.

No one wanted to go near the area around the collapsed station. Over the last few weeks there had been eleven deaths. All major constructions have deaths. They are regrettable but the dangers of the work are too great to avoid them. These were different, though. First, the sheer number in that amount of time, especially when they were unrelated to the initial station collapse, was unusual. Second, all the deaths had occurred within a few hundred feet of the lost station. And third, perhaps I should call them disappearances or, to use the chief engineer's word, *losses*, since not one single body had been found. This tally included Hartz, my predecessor. I tried to draw them out on what had happened. No one would speculate, but there was a lot of frightened mumbling and signs to ward off the evil eye.

Most strange of all were the repeated sightings of what they called "a man of angles." Shifting and twisting and never standing straight, it seemed to appear at the corner of one's eyes only to vanish when one turned to look at it. No two people had a common description of the thing, except that its shape was impossible to determine, for it was never static, and that even the most fleeting glimpse left the viewer overwhelmed with a sense of revulsion.

After hearing these stories, I began to sleep poorly. My dreams were plagued by visions of the thing that the men had described. Like them, I remained tantalized; even in my dreams, it stayed out of focus and just at the edge of my vision. One night, having given up entirely on sleep, I walked out of the village and up to the camp. The night was cold and seemed to magnify the stars. I felt insignificant under their myriad stare. As I stood shivering I became aware of a sound that resembled a chant, repeated over and over, coming from within the broken rock at the work site. I thought at first it was the men of the nightshift, but this sounded like no work song in any language I had ever heard. The syllables were alien and guttural, the rhythm impossible to predict, even with repetition. Worse, when I remarked on the sound to a man tending one of the mules near the camp, he replied, "What sound?" in honest confusion.

I know not what answer I gave, only that I flew back to my room in terror. Only Leacock's urgings in the morning drew me out.

From then I determined I needed to learn the secret behind these strange stories. My hope of sanity seemed to demand I solve it for the no-doubt mundane mystery it had to be.

Since the collapsed station lay at the heart of it, I went to give it a closer inspection. I told no one lest they try and dissuade me, since there was a suggestion it might yet be unstable. It was easy enough to go alone, since the workers avoided it always. I sent Leacock a spurious message about my whereabouts and climbed onto the rock itself, from which I could lower myself into the fissure.

Bulgaria is rich in natural caves, many unmapped, and I wondered as I moved in the dark if the station fall had not opened access to a heretofore-undiscovered one. The way was almost entirely blocked but I could step down into the darkness and found that a crude passage opened before me. I had to squirm between rocks to navigate it. I went as far as I felt I could go and then turned to look back out and see how far down I had come. Suddenly I was seized with a strange vertigo. The rock's angles were skewed by the light of my torch. Standing there and looking back along my path, it was as if the rock bent in toward me, and around me what was left of the broken station walls sloped this way and that, not upright and skewed exactly, but both and neither, as if it were a mad scarecrow in a breeze, with arms akimbo that twisted first one way and then another. The odd sense of movement was not all. It was as if the parts of the station and the rocks that I could see were merely a façade, a curtain separating me from a place beyond that obeyed no human laws. This sensation, combined with a sudden and most unprecedented sense of claustrophobia, unmanned me. I shrieked and scrambled for freedom and air.

I wanted no more to do with that rock beneath the station. Instead I would turn my attention to the station itself. I went in search of the original plans, for the chief engineer had wanted me to see if there were an inherent flaw in the station's plan, but also because I was curious to see if some aspect of its initial design could help me to comprehend some of the strangeness around the site.

For some reason I felt compelled to keep this activity from Leacock, though I could not say why. I waited to the end of the shift and went to the small office in the village. The company had set it up to handle some aspects of the job and manned it with clerks to keep its papers and plans for the region. It was already late and so I was trusted to stay and keep searching while the clerks went home.

I went through the plans, starting with the most immediate—including the new design for the relocated station—and working back to the original design for that first station. It was in all ways exactly like any other architects plan: a simple building with some engineering considerations for its role as a station, such as train egress and water supply.

I rose from the filing cabinets and boxes I had been rifling to see a succession of lights coming from the direction of the work site. Going closer to the window I could see it was a group of workers, all holding lanterns, marching down to the village. As they got nearer, I could see they were headed toward the office. I started out to meet them, a sense of alarm and panic already gripping me.

"We have found them, we think," one of them cried.

"Found whom?" I asked. "The missing men? Which one?"

"We don't know for sure. There was another subsidence at the old site, and the crack has opened wider. No one will go down without a manager, and we can't find the shift man. Will you come?"

I said that I would, of course, and sent a worker on horseback to find the chief engineer and the senior company official near Belovo, to rouse them and bring them to the site at once. When he set off on his mission, the rest of us went back to the railhead and, on handcarts, sped up to the tunnel and through to the plateau and site. Had I known what awaited me, I should have stayed where I was, or in a cowardly fashion offered to get the officials myself.

Around the collapsed site a small knot of men awaited. I was surprised to find Leacock among them. He appeared exhausted, drained even. All of his youth and energy looked to have fled.

"Where are they?" I asked.

The foreman Dimova took me aside and we climbed up the

original crevasse, which was now wider. Other cracks and fissures ran through the rock. He held his light up and I could see the passage I had initially traversed. It had opened up farther, creating a black road into the earth that spilled down into what looked like steps. Unlike earlier, the rock appeared to be steaming hot.

"There was no one working here, but we can make out what we think is a body. The men won't go down."

I had no desire to go into that place again, but my duty insisted. "Will you come with me?"

Dimova nodded numbly. I took him with me as I started out, pausing only to determine that the new heat was not dangerous. Leacock followed, too. We crept down into the fissure. Leacock and I carried lanterns. Dimova knew where the body had been seen. As we climbed I noted his clenched teeth and trembling jaw. The thought of descending here seemed to fill him with complete dread.

We came upon the body a few minutes later. It was at the base of these crude steps and lay on a raised piece of rock, a natural platform, with a drop beyond. It was indeed a vast natural cave system we had uncovered. I believed I could also see light coming from another place in the east. Unnatural heat and steam rose up here and wilted us. But I scarcely noticed. I think someone could have applied a hot iron to my forehead while I beheld that body and I would have barely flinched.

The thing no longer resembled a human, not in its general shape. Oh, it was a man all right; it was impossible to argue otherwise. It had limbs and features of a sort and hair and the other human traits. What robbed it of its humanity were the *angles* into which its form had been twisted. Do not misunderstand that I am speaking here of bent limbs and spine or those mundane breakages that can cripple or kill a man in a cave in. His very flesh had been made over into something else, so that the fundamental shape of his being no longer conformed to humanity's template. It was as if someone had used a human body as the building blocks from which to construct something else: a collection of angles and lines so utterly inhuman, as to dispense with the body's humanity forever.

Worse, these angles and lines shimmered and moved. The poor man was clearly dead, but there could be no doubt some alien force was animating him. As we watched with horror, his head, if head it can even be called, rotated and twisted and spun as the body below and beside it twitched and writhed.

The patterns the thing formed were hypnotic, so fantastic that I could not pull myself away. The others had wildly different responses. Dimova lurched to the side sobbing, then threw himself over the gap past where the body lay. He fell shrieking and, more alarming still, singing all the way down. Leacock arched his body back and roared out a laugh—a gust, a gale of a laugh that had malice and triumph and no humor in it at all. "It has come! It has come at last!" he hooted. He bent and somehow scooped up the broken shimmering thing. With inhuman strength and speed, he lurched up the natural stairs and away.

The removal of the body brought me back to my senses. Had it been up to me I would have left the thing where it was and used dynamite to bury it forever. Surely no good could come of Leacock's flaunting this twisted horror to the men. As I turned to go after him, I realized I had already lost him. The stupor had held me in its grasp too long. I would never catch him in the struggle up the rock.

Then I noticed that, in his haste and madness, Leacock had dropped his pack, the one stuffed with books and plans he always carried. On the curled underside of one the rolled plans a heavy pencil mark denoted the site I had earlier been seeking information on. I should not have recognized it had I not seen its notation recently in the mundane version in the office. I plucked it out.

The plan was covered with eldritch writing and arcane symbols. It described some great cosmic pattern overlaying the site and the architectural plan that made my mind reel to contemplate it. Worse, this plan was not the only one. His pack contained similar plans for other, older structures, some going back years.

I made my way back toward the opening. Some shreds of lucidity and reason must have remained to me then, for I scooped up the pack as evidence, before I went.

At the site I could not guess at the horror that awaited me. If Leacock had some of the crew previously in his allegiance it mattered not now. The sight of the twisted man must have driven them all insane, for all stood behind him, raving and gnashing their teeth like maddened beasts, as Leacock leapt and cavorted in front of them. He crooned to his terrible gods and promised these mindless men favors from powers that, as far as I could discern, would care little for their existence, let alone their prosperity. I called to the men to come to their senses; they parted around Leacock and came for me. It was the warped thing itself that stood now and thrust out its hand—and bid its mad disciples bring me down.

The workers began to ring around me, blocking my way across the plateau to the tunnel and any hope of escape back to the village. Then I recalled the lights I'd seen from the east while in the cave the first time. Perhaps I could scramble back there and escape in the direction of the tunnel. I looked wildly about in the flickering lamplight and dived back into the crevasse.

I clambered and slithered along, hoping desperately to find another passage. Hands snatched at me to drag me back, and I felt a backward lurch. But they had only Leacock's pack. I let it drop behind me and scrambled on. The difficulties that impeded me I hoped would now slow my pursuers. I pushed myself into hollows of rock and gaps between boulders I would never have attempted to navigate otherwise. It was in suffocating darkness that I plunged into the strange passage.

I crawled and pushed ahead farther than I had dared before. Before me was light, the light of that other passage, I hoped—for what other light could it be in this desolate place? As I drew on toward it, the small point of light, about the size and strength of a lantern glow, expanded and bent. The light came rushing to me and accelerating away simultaneously. One part of my mind knew I was trapped in the constraints of a recent rock slide while the other wholly refuted this, for before and around me the walls and floor and ceiling bent and angled in preposterous, giddying ways. I cried out and tried to shield my eyes. Nothing I beheld made sense, as the laws of all normal physics suddenly exploded into imbecility. Yet this was not the worst of it.

The strange surroundings I found myself in were but a portal to a great chaos of surfaces and angles, turning and meeting and shimmering into infinity, another world beyond this one. Then I saw the angled man, his body twisted and tortured in cruel and alien ways. I saw by his eyes he was not sane and that he felt every twinge of change and wrack I could see him perform. Nor was he alone. Dozens of his fellows, all twisted to conform to the vertiginous properties of this world, danced and swayed around him. I felt myself pitched into that fathomless existence. It was as if I flew below my previous vantage point yet looked down on it at the same time. Far below, clawing up yet right above me, gibbered another form. The place was alive with these gigantic, squamous green-gray beasts with an elongated, obscene head and flaccid, drooling mouth, whose barbed and gnashing teeth poked through its own flesh. Even as I watched, this monstrosity grabbed with ridged talons for an angled man, tore him apart, and stuffed large, bleeding chunks of him into its maw.

I was seized with an insight that must have blazed with the last of my sanity fled. The angular men were the workers, prepared for this harsh environment so they could traverse it successfully. But not as equals, explorers, or even mere denizens. They—*we*—were also being shaped into food, raw sustenance for the titanic beasts that dwelt here.

With even greater horror I felt a tearing pain in my right arm, and looked down to see it being twisted and warped in the same way as the flesh of the angular man. I screamed, but no sound could be heard in those strange climes. Then a beast turned its baleful yellow eye upon me. Never had I experienced such evil intent coalesced into one look.

A rush and booming echo surrounded about me and I was pulled out of the clutches of that thing and back into my own world. A rock wall had collapsed and uncovered the original passage I had sought to the light. I had not totally entered that alien world after all.

Maddened and shivering, my arm an agony, I clawed my way up and out into the gaping rock east of the fallen station. Suddenly there was light: real light, not the unnatural effluvium of those visions that had assaulted me while I stumbled through the black. I could hear the men roaring behind me. Ahead of me sat a foreman's cabin, a rough affair of wooden stilts and canvas. Next to it was a handcart on the rail track that led to the tunnel, the same kind of cart the men and I had ridden up there. On it was strapped boxes of dynamite.

I no longer cared for my own safety. That may have been mad, but I suspect now I was beyond sanity at that moment.

Grabbing up the top box of dynamite, I hurled it at the men approaching me out of the crevasse. The box split, enough for me to see the sticks of dynamite poking through the wood. I lit a stick from the second box and pitched it at the first. My attackers apparently cared as little for their own safety as I did for mine and came rushing on, right over the dynamite at the point of detonation.

Even now I am not certain I ever heard the blast. The pressure on my ears and the percussive thrust that smashed me back into the makeshift cabin and brought the whole thing down upon me dominated my senses.

I lay in a mess of rock, canvas, wood and limbs, painted with the gore of more than a dozen men. How long I was there I cannot be sure. When my senses cleared I struggled to my feet. Nothing moved around me.

The dynamite blast had also brought down the whole original spur right onto the station structure, the entire thing now a ruin. My eye detected movement as I surveyed the wreckage. Among the scrum of fallen men, Leacock crawled slowly and painfully. He must have been shielded from much of the blast by the bodies of his allies, or simply by the vagaries of chance. The rock fall had injured him more. I stood over him, a wrench in my hand. I must have grabbed it from the worker's cabin but I do not recall picking it up. The police did not believe this claim.

As I watched, his bones and flesh shimmered and twisted, conforming to angles unlike any the human body ever took. I struck out at him without hesitation or remorse. It was as if a dam had burst. Again and again I smashed the wrench into his head. Even when he no longer writhed or screeched, I continued to smash at him. When I was done, I could find no sure sign of his head, just a glutinous mass above his now-red collar that showed shards of bone and some teeth. A single eyeball swaying by a long red sinew hung off the wrench when I pulled back that mortal implement. Perhaps I fainted then. I cannot say I felt guilty; that would be a lie. But the intense swell of violence and hatred that electrified me also overwhelmed me. When I came to my senses, Leacock still lay bloodied at my feet. His body was normal now.

Voices sounded beyond me. The engineer and manager I had sent for must have come up during the earlier part of the ordeal, only to be turned back by the blast. I heard someone shouting orders. I sat down on the broken rock to await them. While I waited, I found a workman's hacksaw for hewing beams for the scaffolding. They tell me I was laughing as I cut the twisting, disobedient flesh of my arm from my shoulder.

They attended to my wound and turned me over to the police when they found the dynamite and the dead men and the murdered Leacock. Leacock's plans, of course, along with any peculiarity in the original station, were destroyed. I imagine they will also blame the missing men on me, too, despite the fact that they were missing long before I arrived.

As a German national working for a German company, I was sent home for justice to be dispensed. My story alarmed the locals in Bulgaria and they were glad to be rid of me rather than have me repeat my claims in open court. The German authorities lost little time finding me guilty of Leacock's killing, guilty, too, of sabotage and base treachery against the company that had hired and sustained me. Once the verdict was in, they could do little else but sentence me to death by guillotine.

The company has continued with the station at the new site, damn them. They have moved farther out onto the plateau and shifted the rail line just a little. They are praying, I suspect, for no tremors.

Soon the Orient Express and other trains will run regularly through that benighted place. I cannot believe they will escape unscathed. Something unnatural and unpitying waits deep under the earth to devour at least some of the unfortunate souls that pass within its grasp—and we have allowed it egress to our world.

I would write more, warn you of the other things I saw in those plans I took from Leacock's pack for stations all across Europe, but this will have to be enough.

Already my one hand is twisting out of true.

BITTER SHADOWS
LISA MORTON

THE DOOR TO THE COMPARTMENT burst open just before midnight. Georges looked up from his Paris newspaper, startled, heart thrumming in time to the tracks beneath the train.

A young woman clutching a bulging carpetbag ran in, panting, slamming the door behind her. She saw Georges eyeing her and whispered, in English, "Please, sir, I beg of you: a few moments of sanctuary...?"

Georges was briefly thankful that he hadn't undressed for bed yet; he was still fit for his sixty-one years, but he preferred not to alarm the lady any further, if possible. He stood, put his finger to his lips, and moved to the compartment door. Cracking it open slightly, he risked a glance out.

What he saw caused his heart to nearly shudder to a stop: three men, each so tall that they had to stoop in the train's hallway, were coming toward him. Georges had never seen their like. In addition to their unusual size, their skin was excessively pale, nearly the color of Georges's snowy mustache and beard; their long hair was silver; and each bore a strange, swirling mark in the center of his forehead. For a moment he thought them actors, perhaps ogres in a cinematic fantasy like those he had made decades ago. Then he saw their forehead marks were neither makeup nor tattoos, but were burned into the flesh, a nightmarish brand. Each kept one hand beneath his ragged jacket, and when Georges saw a flash of metal he realized they were attempting to conceal knives.

As he watched, they tore open one door after another, looking within the individual sleeping compartments with no regard for the hour or the privacy of the passengers. Shrieks and protests followed behind them. One angry man stepped into the corridor, but ran when one of them snarled and partly withdrew a blade.

Georges promptly eased his door shut again and rushed back to the luxurious bunk. Without comment, he threw his coat over the young lady's bag, sat, reached out, and pulled her to him. "Sir—!" she cried out, as Georges hugged her.

The door banged open and one of the scarred giants looked in. Georges turned only his head, not moving otherwise, hoping he hid the woman from view. Summoning his best sense of outrage, he shouted out, "*Excusez-moi—!*"

The savages peered at Georges, and he hoped they didn't see the way his hand trembled beneath the woman's sleeve, but after another breathless second they moved on. Georges waited to be sure they were gone, then stood, looked outside to watch them retreat, and closed the door again, doing what he could to secure it.

His visitor remained seated, looking up at him in gratitude. "Thank you, sir," she said with an elegant British accent. "I believe you've saved my life."

Georges examined her—and her half-open carpetbag—then asked in French-accented English, "May I ask . . . did you know those . . ."

"Brutes," she supplied. "No. They were horrible, weren't they?"

"They were not pursuing you?"

"Oh, they were indeed, but I've no idea why."

Georges considered. He didn't believe her; as a professional in the arts of magic and cinema, he was skilled in recognizing fellow deceivers. Her hand fluttered alluringly, even seductively, at her collar, and Georges knew misdirection when he saw it. Still, she was easily the most interesting thing he'd encountered so far on the famed Orient Express. "Well, Mademoiselle, you are welcome to stay as long as you'd like."

The woman nodded. "You are very kind. Your name, sir?"

With a flourish, Georges reached toward her head and appeared to pluck something from behind her ear. He took in her appreciative smile as he handed the finely printed calling card to her. The name

Georges Méliès appeared in bold letters in the center, above two addresses, one in Paris and one in Montreuil.

"Monsieur Méliès..." She peered at the card for several seconds before looking up at Georges. "I feel as if I should know you."

"I concur, Mademoiselle."

She looked away, and Georges was charmed by her youthful shyness and beauty; she reminded him, in fact, of his one-time mistress Jehanne, whom he'd been missing a great deal of late. Lovely Jehanne, with her wry smile and hourglass figure, had been his muse a quarter-century ago, when movies were still silent toddlers; together they'd given birth to great cinematic wonders, all forgotten now

"Your name is familiar—"

She broke off as her bag, neglected during the entrance of the sinister pursuers, fell from beneath Georges's coat to the train's floor with a heavy thump. It spilled out a passport and a large object, wrapped in oilcloth. The woman started to reach forward, but Georges retrieved the passport first and flipped it open. She was indeed a British citizen, named, "...Helen Smythe-Whittington?"

She batted her lashes and Georges was even more charmed. "Helen, please," she said in a soft purr.

Georges returned the passport to the bag, then hefted the heavy object. It was about the size of a cannonball, but as Georges turned it in his hands the oilcloth fell away and what he saw caused him to forget his lovely guest. The thing was some sort of squatting figure, instantly repellent, with a malformed face that included tusks curving up nearly to a trio of deepset eyes; the arms ended in hooked pincers, the legs in hooves, and membranous wings sprouted from the bent back. The sculpture was the hue of a stagnant pond, and was vaguely slimy beneath his fingers. Georges couldn't imagine the nature of the material. "*Mon dieu—*"

He broke off as he peered closer at the head and saw the swirling symbol there—the same one that had been branded into the brows of Helen's three pursuers. The symbol seemed to be moving, drawing him in; the sides of his vision fell away, and something dark and huge loomed before him—

Helen draped the oilcloth over the carving and took it from Georges, and he realized he had no idea how long he'd been staring at it. His fingers felt numb, his gaze heavy as he looked up at Helen. "This is quite clearly what your peculiar friends sought. What is it?"

Méliès felt some dreadful weight lift from him as she returned the wrapped figure to the carpetbag. "I don't know very much about it, I'm afraid. Georges, if I may . . . my experiences since I came into possession of it have been simply terrible. My beloved Aunt Hilda died last month. On her deathbed she made me promise to personally return this piece to a one-time suitor who had given it to her in her youth. I'm on my way to see him in Istanbul, but those . . . *things* started chasing me on the Channel Ferry. I can't imagine how they got onto the train."

"Why on earth, I wonder, would anyone have given your aunt such a thing as *that*?" He nodded toward the bag.

Helen's smile twitched only briefly. "Oh, my aunt was a very eccentric woman. There were those in her village who thought her a witch."

"What village was that?"

"Are you well-traveled in England, Georges? Because I'm quite sure you wouldn't have heard of it otherwise. It was very small."

In his youth, Georges had spent time in London, investigating cameras and projectors, but he couldn't rightly claim to know much of the English countryside. "You are right, Mademoiselle Helen. My time in your homeland was spent almost entirely on business in London."

"And what is your business?"

"I am a filmmaker." Georges was lying now. He hadn't made a film since 1912—had it really been eleven years ago?—but he'd never been able to refer to himself as a *former* filmmaker. It was too precious a vocation.

"How exciting! I love the pictures. Do you know any of the great stars? Charlie Chaplin? Or Clara Bow? I've had a few friends tell me I look like her."

"Alas, I have made films only in my native France. My last was called *The Conquest of the Pole*."

"It sounds quite dashing. Did you go to the Pole to film it?"

"No, I recreated the Pole in my studio, along with a snow giant that ate several intrepid explorers."

Helen laughed, and for a moment Georges forgot the strange

circumstances of her arrival. "Mademoiselle, might I suggest that you stay here, in my compartment, until this trouble is over? If that's not improper."

"Not at all, Georges. That's very kind of you, and I accept." She moved the bag near her feet on the floor, and Georges remembered the unease that had washed over him while holding the idol. He'd spent his life trying to frighten willing audiences—his films had presented both real-life cataclysms and fantastic, startling tableaux—but he knew he'd never succeeded in provoking the kind of dread the carved monster had produced in him.

Georges ceded his sleeping bunk to his guest that night, leaving him to curl up beneath a blanket on the padded bench. He barely slept, and yet he dreamt. He saw hordes of the huge, branded savages genuflecting and wailing as something unseen approached, a mountain of shadows that plucked one man from the tribe and consumed him. Blood from his crushed chest sprayed down on the pale skin and hair of his brethren. Georges wanted to look away, but instead he tilted his head back and back, trying to take in the immensity of what he saw. The thing—he heard the name "Shaurash-Ho" whispered—loomed over the cowering tribesmen, and their demise seemed certain; then one of them, a priest-mage, waged a war with the god and finally captured its essence in the small carving, which was placed within a sacred altar saturated with magicks. The priest-mage took his place at the altar and was soon joined by others, a ring of devotees whose only duty was to keep Shaurash-Ho imprisoned.

Georges's eyes snapped open to gray morning light filtering in beneath the compartment's shade. He remembered everything about the dream, and as he stared at the bag on the floor, he realized: In his dream, the savages had *protected* humanity, especially when the fury of the Great War had roused Shaurash-Ho. Was it possible Helen's pursuers sought the idol to restore order, to save mankind from the terrible thing imprisoned within the green stone?

He shook his head. No, it was ridiculous. He of all people should know better than to trust a dream. His dreams had all failed him.

His daughter, Georgette, had given him this ticket in the hopes of rescuing him from those failures. A wealthy friend had purchased the ticket and then fallen ill, and Georgette had given it to Georges. "Escape yourself, Papa," she'd urged him, along with a kiss. "Travel to new places. Eat, drink, enjoy the world. Let the trip restore your spirits."

His daughter would have been pleased to know he'd met a lovely woman, although the circumstances would undoubtedly have troubled her.

He thought of the night's terrible dreams and was abruptly anxious to be among company again, away from his guest's dreadful possession. Helen continued to sleep, so he slipped from the compartment and made his way to the dining car.

The hour was still early, but other passengers already populated the car, and Méliès was calmed by their presence. A waiter, Gaston, led him to a table. "Tell me," Méliès asked as he took his seat, "was there any sort of disturbance on the train last night?"

"Oh, yes, Monsieur. Three men attempted some sort of robbery."

"Were they apprehended?"

The waiter looked around anxiously. "I—I am not sure."

"Could you have a senior conductor brought to me?"

Gaston nodded. "Of course." He turned and left.

A few moments later, a uniformed man carrying a notebook bound in metal approached Georges, asking how he might be of service.

"Last night, three strange men—"

The conductor smiled. "Ahhh, yes. I do apologize for the commotion, sir. The men were captured this morning, attempting to steal this—" he waved the notebook with a flourish "—the master passenger list. They apparently sought to rob one of our guests, but rest assured the situation is under control. We at the Compagnie Internationale des Wagons-Lits take our obligations to our passengers most seriously. We will be making a small unscheduled stop shortly to hand them over to local authorities."

"That's good. May I ask if you show a passenger named Helen Smythe-Whittington on that list?"

The conductor frowned, flipped through pages, and shook his head. "I'm sorry, sir, but we have no one by that name on board."

Georges was about to thank the man when an unearthly howl sounded from the rear of the car. Startled, he turned and saw the three savages being led through the doorway by half-a-dozen men. The silver-haired ruffians were tied with heavy ropes. All bore cuts or bruises on their heads, but so did several of their captors. As the struggling trio was led through the center of the dining car, other passengers gasped and involuntarily slid chairs back. The official blanched and begin to argue with the guards surrounding the savages. "*Non, non, pas de cette façon!*"

The group approached Georges and the brutes abruptly dug in their heels and fought against their bounds. Their noses twitched, heads tilted back, like dogs catching a scent. They turned toward Georges and one broke away and started toward him; the filmmaker shrank back as the savage shoved the table aside and looked beneath. The conductor cried out and intervened, grappling with the brute for a few seconds. The savage broke free and finished scanning the area around Georges, until, finding nothing, he sagged and was easily shoved back into line. Georges straightened himself, and to his surprise, the savage turned a look on him, but it bore no malice or threat; instead, it was an expression of dismal failure. The three barbarians were then quite easily led from the train.

The conductor turned to Georges. "Are you quite all right, Monsieur? My most sincere apologies. My assistants should have thought to clear this car first."

Georges rose, his thoughts jumbled, rationality nearly forced out by images of white-haired priests guarding a divine monster. "I must return to business elsewhere."

He pushed past the perplexed conductor, left the dining car, and made his way to his compartment. After a polite knock on the door, Georges entered to find Helen awake and seated by the window, peering out.

"Do you know why we're stopping?" Helen gestured outside, and Georges realized he hadn't even been aware of the train slowing down. "A sign identified this place as Friedensdorf, but I thought Munich was the next stop."

Georges lowered himself to the bench. "They captured the three who chased you last night. I believe they're removing them from the train here."

"Oh." Helen abruptly leaned back, and Georges realized that she feared being seen.

"Mademoiselle," Georges began, "you have not been truthful with me."

She looked at him innocently, and for a heartbeat Georges hoped he was wrong, but that hope soon fled. "There is no Helen Smythe-Whittington on the passenger list, to begin with," he said.

"I thought it prudent to travel under an assumed name."

Georges fixed her with the most serious look he could muster. "Mademoiselle, I'd like to tell you about myself, and hope you will indulge an old man."

"I somehow can't think of you as 'old,' Georges," she said, and the smile she gave him made him want to believe her; but the memory of the night's dreams caused him to continue.

"There was a time when I was a famous filmmaker. I invented my own camera and made hundreds of films that were shown all over the world. Thomas Edison stole my film *A Trip to the Moon* and made a fortune showing it in America, but I remained undaunted. I kept making movies full of wonder and tricks. *Mon dieu,* but I loved my little lies!

"Then the War came. My films were melted down to make soldiers' boots. My Paris theatre was demolished to make room for a street. And my studio—my beautiful studio in Montreuil—was taken because I could no longer pay my debts. My wife and mistress both left me, and now I have nothing but—" Georges gestured at the luggage rack overhead, where a pair of leathered-covered boxes attached to wooden legs were nestled next to a single suitcase "—that old camera, a few feet of raw film, and this trip.

"Now I have told you all the failures of my life. Please, Mademoiselle, do me the courtesy of not causing my trust in you to become another of them."

Helen returned Georges's steady gaze, but added a half-smile. When she spoke, he was startled by her flat American accent. "Show me your camera and I'll tell you the truth."

She was stalling. Georges almost shouted, "We don't have time," then realized he wasn't even sure why he'd almost said that; time was the most honest thing they had together. "You will tell me everything, including what that carving is?"

"Everything that I know."

Georges pulled the crates down, staggering slightly as the train started up again, chugging forward as they left Friedensdorf. He found his balance and arranged the wooden legs to open into a tripod. The camera itself was about half-a-meter tall, with a lens on the front and a crank and covered eye-hole on the back. The second box, the film magazine, sat atop the camera.

Helen's eyes went wide, and she tentatively touched it. "This is a movie camera. . . ? I've never seen one."

"Yes." Georges was surprised to realize it still gave him pleasure to demonstrate his art.

"Is there film in it?"

"There is." Georges pointed to the magazine. "The film is held up here. It passes through the camera down here." He moved up the cover over the eye-hole. "Look in here."

Helen did, and saw the world beyond the train in blurred shades of gray. "It looks so strange. . . ."

Georges adjusted a small knob next to the eye-hole. "You're looking right through the film. We can adjust the focus here."

The image took on sharp definition, and Helen uttered a delighted laugh. "So this is how the camera sees life."

"Yes."

"You could actually make a movie with this right now?"

By way of answer, Georges swung the camera on its tripod head until the lens was pointed at Helen. He examined her portrait in the eye-hole, then began to turn the crank.

"What are you doing?"

"I'm recording you for posterity."

Her blush was natural, her laugh delicate. "Oh, don't waste your film. I'm no star."

"You are definitely an extremely accomplished actress."

He kept cranking as she dropped to the bunk, glancing out the window at the passing scenery: thick forests edged right up to the tracks, the curtain of greenery punctuated only by the occasional river or road. There was no longer any sign of human habitation, not even fields or grazing cattle.

"My name is Helen Harrison. I'm American by birth, but have been working in Europe for several years."

"And your profession?"

"I'm a thief."

He wasn't shocked; he was, instead, pleased that she was at last confiding in him. "A very particular kind of thief, I'd imagine."

"Yes. I work only for select clients, who pay me well to deliver special items."

Georges looked up from the eye-hole and nodded at her bag. "Like that relic."

"Precisely. I was hired by a collector in Istanbul to steal it from a cult in Greenland. Those three men who pursued me . . . their clan is very old, dating back to when their land was known as Hyperborea. Their god has a strange name."

Helen struggled to remember, and Georges intervened. "Shaurash-Ho."

"Yes, that's it. How did you know?"

A chill crawled over Georges's shoulders, an icy spider. "I heard it last night. In a dream. I know that's impossible, but—"

Helen interrupted. "It's not. I've seen many strange things on the jobs I've performed. When I took this piece from its altar, I saw something I can only call a living darkness. I almost understand why the other name for this god was 'Bitter Shadows.'"

"'Bitter Shadows' . . ." The name slotted perfectly into both Georges's dreams and his own life; it felt like an apt description of the films that had nourished Georges for so long, but so long ago.

He nearly stopped cranking as he struggled to rise above his reveries, stumbling over his words. "I am a rationalist. I do not believe in magic, except that which is created by trickery."

"Haven't you felt something since we've been on this train? Something shifting." Helen rose and paced, and when she held his gaze again he saw realization there. "Georges, I think I've been deceived as well."

"How so?"

"My client, he paid me three times my usual fee for this job, and now I suspect that was to buy my complicity. What if his intention all along was that I release something dreadful?"

Georges looked up from the camera, confused. The image he'd seen on the film had been darkening, as if something were filling the compartment. "I don't—"

He broke off as he tried to look at Helen, and she simply faded from his view.

Alarmed, he returned his attention to the camera's eye-hole; he saw the sides of the train dissolving like one of his camera effects. The train had stopped moving. It was surrounded now by a dark and mist-shrouded forest.

He kept turning the handle, advancing the film; he sensed that what was happening was more than all the hundreds of recordings of storms and laughing couples and horse-drawn carriages he'd made, even more than the monsters and devils of his imagination. This was real.

Through the camera's lens, he saw neither the train nor the woods, but an alien plain populated by amorphous shapes that writhed with some sort of organic energy. The gaseous pools were coalescing into something with solidity. This new mass was dark, huge, winged—

Shaurash-Ho.

Fully formed, the eldritch nightmare lumbered forward, moving closer, but Georges swallowed back his panic, forcing his attention to stay on his task as cameraman. This was no mere puppet of wood and cloth, but a *god*, captured on film.

Shaurash-Ho stood before him, surrounded by noxious yellow gases and scorched pits full of corpses, dead fingers still curled around knives and guns; the god stood over the hell of the Great War, bloated but never sated. Georges tilted the camera back and up, trying to capture its size on his film. The god looked down at him, blinked its three eyes, ground its tusks into something that might have been an obscene smile—

Georges staggered back as something struck his eye. He lost his hold on the camera, one hand instinctively flying to his face, anticipating blood or pain . . . but there was none. His heart hammered, but finally slowed as he realized he was alive, still whole.

Shaurash-Ho and the otherworld were gone, and, lowering his hand, blinking, Georges turned to see Helen beside him, her eyes wide, mouth agape.

"What—?" She seemed to be unable to form words.

Georges, remembering, looked at the footage counter on the camera. He had used virtually the entire magazine.

"I did it."

Helen looked at him, perplexed. "Did what"

"I filmed it—Shaurash-Ho."

Sagging onto the bench, Helen's fingers moved as if trying to capture fleeting thoughts. "But there was only mist."

Georges gestured at the camera. "No, there was more, and the camera saw it all! It *was* here, and now it's on my film."

"You filmed Shaurash-Ho?"

"Yes. Do you know what this means? I have captured something on film that no one living has ever seen. When I share this with the world, it will change *everything*." As the full import of that settled on him, so did exhaustion. Utterly drained, Georges slumped down beside Helen.

"Something else happened to us, Georges."

If she said more, he didn't hear.

Georges awoke to find the train conductor standing over him in concern. "Do you hear me, Monsieur? Ahhh, good, you're coming around."

He was on the bench in his compartment, leaning against the window of the train. He shook himself and sat up, looking around; the camera was still there, but Helen was gone, as was her bag.

"What happened?"

"We seem to have passed through some pocket of gas. Possibly an unexploded bomb of some sort left over from the War went off and released something. If you'll excuse me now, Monsieur, I must check on the other passengers."

The conductor left, and Georges tried to remember. His recollections were disorganized and fuzzy, but one thing floated to the surface: the camera. He had filmed the manifestation of a god.

He was about to rise when he heard a crinkling sound under his fingers. Looking down, he saw a small scribbled note, written hastily on the reverse side of a Compagnie Internationale des Wagons-Lits menu.

My Dear Georges,

*I apologize for what I have taken from you, but I am going
to be in need of funds if I am to seek revenge on the former
employer who used me. Yes, I understand completely now:
He had no interest in the carving as an* objet d'art, *but only
wanted it removed from the safety of its altar in order to release the evil it contained. I'm not sure yet what exactly I've
done, but I fear the consequences of my actions and so I
mean to do what I can to make amends. I am truly sorry,
Georges. I know you have no reason to trust me, but I hope
you will believe me when I say that I wish we'd had more
time together.*

Yours,
Helen

His heart in his throat, Georges Méliès crumpled the note as
he leapt from the bench, but he saw immediately what he'd missed
before:

The film magazine was gone. With Helen.

He felt it, then: the particle of Shaurash-Ho that now resided
within him. That was what had struck him as he looked through
the lens—or perhaps it had already been there and was merely
awakened now by so direct a vision. The Great War had made an
opening and the freed Shaurash-Ho had filled it, leading them all
into a new age of darkness. He wondered about his own place in
this new reality: Had he given his audiences a speck of hope by
delighting them with whimsy, or had he laid the groundwork for
centuries of empty cinematic spectacle? Was this the true failure
of his life?

Georges disembarked from the train at the next stop. He took
his clothing, but left the camera. He neither knew nor cared where
he was; he only understood that he would catch the returning Orient
Express back to Paris. He wanted nothing so much as to burn the
last copies of his old films, the ones he'd held onto out of some vain
hope of becoming a filmmaker again. He would spend his remaining

days fighting the grain of despair blossoming blackly within him, and questioning the part he'd played in unleashing a grim, violent future.

A future of bitter shadows.

LA MUSIQUE DE L'ENNUI
Kenneth Hite

CORYDON: Then, sister, you have seen the face of Truth.
CORDELIA: Glimpsed—only glimpsed. For just one moment,
the Mask slipped and I gazed upon the void.

—*The King in Yellow*, Act 1, Scene 1

THE TRAIN WINDOWS SHOWED NOTHING but streaks of mist and blackness, and the Wi-Fi had been dead since Budapest. Kristie looked at the blank face of her phone and sighed. It's not as though she had any one to call anyhow, but she would have liked to update her blog. "Daaé and Night" was the best Phandom blog in Canada, maybe in North America, and she had spent months teasing—and, yes, taunting—her readers with promises of posts from the exclusive Orient Express "Return to the Phantom of the Opera" tour. Six cities! Four nights! Everything authentic and high-end! Including, apparently, authentic 1910 Wagons-Lits railroad cars with authentic 1910 Wi-Fi connectivity and cell reception. The cars were beautifully restored, it was true. Mahogany and marquetry wood paneling, real leather and period fabrics instead of printed vinyl. Aubusson carpets and Lalique screens, brass fittings and warm yellow light erasing the memory of off-white fluorescents. While the train moved, especially while it moved through the night between cities, Kristie could imagine herself back in 1910, back in the Belle Époque, without even closing her eyes. That part of the trip was living up to the promotion.

The two stops so far, on the other hand, had seemed weirdly slipshod for such a grandiose package. The locomotive lurching forward in sudden clouds of pale steam, too old or cranky to crouch stable at the platform. Busses delayed or idling, taking strange routes through cobbled streets with high concrete or low brick walls to either side. Lots of standing around in empty squares and bridges at weird hours of the day and night, winter leaves or dusty newsprint pages she couldn't read blowing around them in circles. Everything had to be coordinated around train schedules, she guessed, and that was throwing things off. Maybe it was just the way those countries were—Kristie was from Montreal and had never been east of London until this trip. But even when the bus finally arrived and then dropped them in front of the correct strangely alien façade, she couldn't escape into the Phantom's world the way she wanted.

They were supposed to start with the Joel Schumacher movie, shown in Bucharest's best cinema palace. Maybe it was, but it seemed echoing and cavernous, and smelled like something had died there a long time ago. Worse, the movie was a Romanian print, with Romanian subtitles—Kristie supposed she should be thankful nothing was dubbed—and she found the long strings of utterly foreign words distracting. *În somn uoht cântat, în vise yhtill venit*—who could pay attention to the singing with that alphabet soup there? The projector or the lighting faded the costumes, too; they looked like tinsel and motley. Somehow even Gerard Butler seemed pale and distracted on screen, something Kristie would never have thought possible.

In Budapest, they saw a performance of the Andrew Lloyd Webber musical in the Madách Theater. Kristie knew that this was supposed to be a rare "non-clone" show, with different direction and sets and costumes from the standard production, but what was that Child doing in the story? The singing was all in Hungarian, so she couldn't tell. Nor could she tell if Christine and Carlotta were supposed to be sisters in this version as well as rivals. In fairness, the Madách had magnificent acoustics, the sound somehow enveloping her in a way that even the Pantages couldn't manage. The Hungarian Phantom, too, drew her in, beautifully singing lyrics she couldn't possibly understand even though she knew them by heart.

She hummed the music under her breath, feeling her pulse and heartbeat match the rhythms. But again, the lighting was weird. They used a gel that washed out the Phantom's Red Death costume completely, leaving it looking a dirty yellow-white instead of full-blooded scarlet.

After the shows, when she tried some good-humored nitpicks out on her supposed fellow fans, they just stared at her or changed the subject. Nobody else agreed things were sloppy or off-kilter, or maybe they were too easily faked out to admit it, the phonies. Kristie had read these same people arguing online about the minutiae of Ramin Karimloo versus John Cudia for hours on end, but now they just gushed like tourists about how wonderful everything was. It was as though being on a real, live—and beautiful—train was draining their judgment even faster than it drained their checkbooks.

Which was, she knew well, pretty fast. When Kristie had first read about the Orient Express *Phantom* tour, she couldn't get it out of her mind—the vision of gowns and china and wineglasses and the Paris Opera House at the end of the line. She spent three weeks of blog posts talking it up, sending in links and hoping for a free ticket from the organizers. She heard nothing. Then she panicked, worried that the tour would sell out and she would have to beg for updates from other blogs, that "Daaé and Night" wouldn't be part of the greatest *Phantom* experience since the Royal Albert Hall twenty-fifth anniversary performance. She just had to go. She had her grandmother's money still, and her retirement savings account, so she could just barely afford it after all the taxes and fees and air-fare. After she hit *Purchase* she drank too much chardonnay and posted an entry headlined *That's why they call it "life savings," isn't it?* and that got retweeted a lot and then she really had to go.

So she went, to sit alone in a century-old railway car while people chattered and babbled about a play they apparently hadn't even bothered to really watch. Kristie drained her glass. Money, stress, jet lag, the weirdness of apparently not really knowing anyone from the Phandom world she'd spent her life in. It would all be worth it, still, if she could just see the Phantom for real, if this Europe could get its act together and show her something perfect that she hadn't seen five hundred times before, if being here meant she could just touch his world of romance and doomed love and opera cloaks.

If that stupid bitch Carla Hotchkiss would shut up for ten minutes.

Carla hadn't just been *at* the Albert Hall performance. She'd been *in* it, in the chorus but on stage, and she didn't let anyone forget it for a minute. Although she was born and bred in Fayetteville, Arkansas, she put on a fake English accent and drawled anecdote after anecdote about her time "in West End, don't you know" and about "dear Sierra, she was all nerves but you could never tell unless you'd seen her backstage" and about "the divine Mister Crawford, he asked us to call him Michael you know, so giving." Her blog was like that, too, and because she knew people in the trades, she got some plum interviews and some exclusive pictures.

Kristie had to link her, but she sure as Hell didn't have to listen to her. Not tonight, on their first social night in the legendary saloon car of the Orient Express. Not after eating coq au vin off bone china plates, plates in which kings and emperors had seen their faces. So instead, she avoided her fellow bloggers and her friends and readers, who might not, she had realized in a distant epiphany, be either of those things. She drifted toward the bar, toward two thirtyish men who hadn't let themselves be drawn out of alcohol's orbit by the promise of first-hand anecdotes about "dear Sierra." The taller of the two looked nothing like a *Phantom* fan, but the slender idler next to him had more than something of the musical theater aficionado about him. Kristie kept her opening line anyhow. "Do you suppose the Orient Express turned the Wi-Fi off so nobody could email them to complain that their Wi-Fi sucks?"

The slender one turned his brown eyes to her . . . yes, to her satin Pinet reproduction shoes first. Bingo. "Actually, you should write your email to SFB. They're the bloated hospitality-entertainment conglomerate that currently battens on your alienation. Eldon here can give you their address. Or you could just take his card."

The taller man, who wore an aggrieved look and a tailcoat slightly too old to be rightly period, took a pull of his wine and scowled. "Jesus, Lee, save some for the article."

"Can't do it, I'm afraid. Too much truth, too few column inches, even online."

The tall American looked at Kristie's tits first, but covered well enough. "Eldon Bryant." He gestured with his glass. "I'll be your cruise director. Please hesitate to ask. This is Garrick Lee, who will spell your name wrong in the *Guardian* after the tour is over."

Lee seemed just as in love with himself as Carla, but at least his English accent was real.

Kristie handed him her card. "As long as he links my blog, he can spell my name any way he wants." She gave another one to Eldon, who actually looked at it before putting it in his vest pocket.

Lee gestured airily with a fresh drink. "So you sublimate your alienation by sharecropping in the Andrew Lloyd Webber factory greenhouse, do you?" The light tone only took some of the sting from the question.

Kristie began her well-rehearsed reply. "Actually, I first met the Phantom in Fisher's Hammer film, and then I read the Gaston Leroux novel and found out how wrong Hammer got it." Then her frustration took her off-book. "Between them, Andrew Lloyd Webber and Terence Fisher certainly make the case that the British just can't read." Eldon smothered a laugh in his glass as Lee narrowed his eyes and she continued, warming to her subject. "Webber's music, though. It doesn't need to fit the novel, because somehow it fits the novel's meaning, and its time. It's not ashamed. It fits the atmosphere . . . it's like the novel and the music come from the same alien world, the same beautiful alien world of this train. And if it's alienation to want to go there, well. . . ."

Eldon interrupted with sudden energy. "That's the same thing Fisher does with his *Dracula*. He just tosses the book aside and goes right for the real meaning of the story, the cruelty and power of this foreign aristocrat, this stranger who brings death with him." He briefly seemed to remember a plan to remain uninterested, and his voice softened before gathering speed again. "*Dracula* is my real line. I just finished the Orient Express *Dracula* tour last week: London to Innsbruck to Budapest to Bucharest to Varna, all the stops and everything first class. We recreated the exact menu from Harker's meal at the Golden Crown. We had Elizabeth Miller, and in Munich Werner Herzog showed us his cut of *Nosferatu*."

Kristie didn't know who Elizabeth Miller was, and only had a faint idea that Herzog was a director, but she resented his enthusiasm anyway. "Well, you didn't manage to get us Joel Schumacher in Bucharest. Or even a very good print of his movie."

He shrugged and slugged from the fresh wineglass that had appeared at his elbow. "I didn't plan this tour. I don't know jack about *The Phantom of the Opera*. I was supposed to get a month off in Romania. I'm only on this train because my bosses at SFB made me ride shotgun to save a few bucks."

"You mean, because nobody planned this tour," Lee interrupted, his tone far from light now. "They had to run the train they've leased back to Paris anyway and decided to throw a random playpen of cultural detritus together at the last minute, a bento box of nostalgia rattling quaintly along an irrelevant siding. They just pack extruded pop product into retro hipster railway cars, and set it up to drug the sensibilities of people gullible enough to spend a year's wages on tickets to a lowbrow musical they've seen a dozen times—a musical with no real connection with the Orient Express except its appeal to the same infantile brand-name fake history."

Eldon began a half-hearted apology, or maybe it was corporate sloganeering, but Kristie rolled right over him, raising her voice and glaring at Lee. "Apparently the *Guardian* research budget doesn't even extend to a library card. Read a book for a change, not just a book review. Gaston Leroux was a Paris reporter on the Balkan beat. He covered Turkey and wrote firsthand reports of Armenian massacres. He rode this train both directions for years, writing his copy on the train desks. Maybe he wrote stories in this very car. Then, in 1907, he suddenly gave up journalism and wrote his first bestseller, *The Mystery of the Yellow Room*. He kept riding this train, though, maybe from superstition, or maybe because he—" Kristie took a ragged breath "—he, too, thought it was something special, an escape to inspiration."

Lee put his drink down on the bar with a too-audible *clack*, and paused momentarily. "You can't escape on a train. Much like a *Phantom of the Opera* enthusiast, it can only go one place. I, by contrast, am going elsewhere." With that, he stalked off, heading for the knot of admirers around Carla Hotchkiss.

Eldon handed Kristie a full wineglass. "You deserve that, after that speech. Look, I'm sorry about Lee. You *Phantom* fans are all right, I guess."

Still fuming, Kristie drank without tasting. "You should put that on the brochure."

Eldon held up a hand. "No, seriously, it's refreshing. You all dress nice, and you're way better than the Agatha Christie people. Every one of them is eighty if they're a day, and they all have special food requirements, and they tip like it's 1930 and so the staff hates them, and that's even before they start pretending to be murdered. They all think they're hilarious. God, I hate that tour. It's like a rolling Alzheimer's ward. We do get to use the Thirties cars, though, instead of these. Makes for a change."

He had another refill, and his voice raised a bit. "Now, the Graham Greene fans on the *Stamboul Train* tour are pretentious dicks like Lee, but they know how to tip. They know how to drink, too. They also cheat on their wives and get depressed, just like Graham Greene narrators. They probably blame the train. The Ian Fleming wannabes on our *From Russia With Love* tour don't have wives, of course—or they don't bring them—and we don't stock sexy SMERSH honey traps, more's the pity. They want it to be 1960, or at least they don't want to believe they're seventy. They all dress like early Sean Connery and look like really late Roger Moore. They do insist on the high-end drinks, though, so we can charge a premium and I don't have to drink this swill."

He scowled at his glass and held it up to the light, gold shining in its ruby depths. "This swill is the *Phantom* special. We forklift on six-dozen cases of cheap Shiraz, because none of you can tell the difference. We can just say it's French and everyone is happy as long as they don't take off its mask. Nostalgia wholesale at four euro the bottle."

Kristie snapped her head back as though he'd slapped her. "Sneer all you want, but if it hadn't been for the Phantom, for him, your precious *Dracula* tour would have been empty."

"Bullshit! Stoker wrote *Dracula* fourteen years before—"

"Yes, but it was only after Universal made a million Depression dollars by re-releasing the Lon Chaney *Phantom* with sound that they realized horror could still sell tickets. That was 1930, and that was the year that Universal greenlit *Dracula*. Stoker's only good book didn't sell for beans. Leroux wrote a dozen bestsellers."

Eldon just stared at her. She felt cold, and alone again. "It's all because of the Phantom. All because of him."

Kristie suddenly found herself choking back tears. She dropped her wineglass and heard it shatter behind her as she fled the saloon car. She played the Japanese original cast recording in her cabin all night, eagerly falling into the music behind the alien words while the train wheels beat out the percussion.

In Venice, a stagehands' strike meant they couldn't even tour La Fenice, and the planned performance at the opera house of songs from the 1976 musical had to be canceled. Instead they watched the 1943 Universal *Phantom of the Opera* on a flatscreen in the Sofitel's biggest function room. The sound and lighting seemed fine, the projector behaved. Kristie could easily accept Claude Rains—no Gerard Butler, he!—as a pale nonentity. She chalked that up to the script, not the DVD. Kristie had seen the film plenty of times, so she tuned out the weirdly altered plot— What kind of publishing house keeps acid on the desks? The Phantom is Christine's father? Why Circassian dances instead of *Faust*?—and focused on the occasional production slips. She smiled when she realized that Nelson Eddy's hair dye turned bright blond in one scene, and once more saw the famous "extra shadow" in the basement.

According to film legend, that was the shadow of Lon Chaney, Jr. The alcoholic Chaney was angry he didn't get the chance to play the Phantom, his father's great part, so he would show up on set unannounced. Both that legend and the screenplay of the Universal version seemed to emphasize weak heirs and destined roles, as though the Phantom were part of some hidden royal lineage, a king as well as a masked stranger. Kristie pondered the strange family echo of what she thought she had seen in Budapest, with the rival singers as sisters and the intrusive Child. She thought that would make a good blog entry, if the Wi-Fi ever came back on.

She saw Eldon on his cell phone—his worked!—but after he hung up he didn't say anything to her except "Sorry it wasn't the Hammer version. Couldn't find a copy in Venice. Out of print in region two or something." Kristie didn't reply. He probably didn't have time to talk. He was scrambling for something else for that evening's stop in Milan. If the stagehands struck La Fenice, they were striking La Scala, too, and there went their one-night production of *Phantasia*.

Instead, it was back to the cinematic well. But this time, Eldon really came through. The busses still seemingly took forever to travel from the train to an auditorium outside the city center. A college building, surrounded by some kind of half-frozen canal, she thought. There was a genteel English scholar there to greet them, somehow connected to the silent film festival at Pordenone. In his soft voice he explained that Mussolini's government had suppressed this cut of the 1925 *Phantom of the Opera* shortly after its premiere in Naples. The "Yellow Cut," he said, had only recently been rediscovered and the festival or someone had restored the film stock and score. The government crackdown had been so complete that nobody knew who had originally recolored it and assembled its soundtrack. Indeed, nobody quite knew exactly when the Yellow Cut had been made, or even when it had opened, but it was probably after Universal struck the 1930 "international sound version," because it had a synchronized music track. Instead of the usual Gounod score, this print played to a selection of works by the Neapolitan baroque composer Benvenuto Chieti Bordighera and the Russian modernist Alexander Scriabin—both of whom, the Englishman noted, died very young, and insane. Scriabin had a powerful "mystical chord" experience in 1907 that convinced him that all musical keys had innate colors. 1907, Kristie mused, the same year that Leroux suddenly abandoned journalism. The pieces in this film, apparently—she found it hard to make out the almost-whispered details—were in D, which was yellow.

This cut of the film definitely kept the eerie atmosphere of the other versions she'd seen. The title cards were in Italian, of course, but Kristie knew the story well enough to follow along. Bordighera's strings picked and whined, introducing the strange figure with the lamp, who stands on what might be battlements or cellar arches, and invites the viewer inside. The strange letters come insisting on performing a specific "dramma," Christine sings to an invisible voice, the fall of the chandelier removes her rival. Then, with the sudden advent of color footage in the Bal du Masque scene, Scriabin's music breathed into the film.

The yellow tint showed up not on the Phantom, as Kristie had half-expected, but on people who would soon meet him: the stage-hand who gets hanged, on the Comte de Chagny—called the Comte de Castaigne in this version—when he leaves the box, and, of course, on Christine. The violins and pianos moaned and dueled beneath the Phantom's arrival at the ball, and shrieked at the inexplicable sight of the skies above the Opera House shown in photographic negative, with black stars in white space. They groaned at his unmasking and throughout the dreamlike voyages into the hidden chambers beneath the Paris Opera House. The film's unknown editor must have liked the negative effect because he repeated it nonsensically in the Phantom's grotto, on the ceiling above the Black Lake.

The story concluded abruptly, not with the usual desperate chase to the Seine but with the Phantom enthroned on his organ bench, Raoul "Castaigne" and Christine before him on their knees, pleading for Raoul's life. A final minute or two of footage, which Kristie recognized from the 1925 original ending, showed Christine giving the Phantom a ring. But the scene had been recut in this version from its original intent—a regretful departure—to become something like a proposal of marriage. The film rattled out and the screen went dark in the silent room.

For once, Kristie realized distantly, not even Carla said anything.

She remembered nothing of the bus ride back to Milan Central Station, heard only Scriabin and Bordighera. She got off the bus in a daze and pushed her way past fans whispering and milling around the platform. The train's steam vaporized freezing rain, and Kristie saw the station bathed in a gray projector light streaked with pale fire, as though the film still rattled around her. As the minutes crept by, building another unfathomable delay, her fellow tour members began to murmur and buzz, and Scriabin faded. Any minute now, Carla would bray something, and the moment would be lost.

The train pulled forward, then backed on its haunches. They weren't letting anyone board for some reason. Kristie spotted Eldon, talking to Lee at the far end of the platform. Just before she set about shouldering her way toward them, the train gave a lurch and the wind blew a blinding wave of sleet onto the crowd. There was a scream at Kristie's left ear, and a spasm of motion, and a grinding noise like shearing crystal, and a whistle, and a splash of blood that fanned out on the locomotive. At first Carla was nowhere to be seen, but Kristie soon saw where she'd gone.

The crowd shrank back from the scene instinctively, the fear of death overwhelming even their tourist urges. They pulled Kristie back with them in their undertow, the last notes of Bordighera lost as the shrieks died down and became babble. She somehow heard Lee's nasal tenor clearly: "Now there's an idea, Eldon. An *Anna Karenina*-themed train tour."

Kristie still hated Carla. If she'd been the center of attention before, she dominated every conversation tonight, a night that was supposed to be the tour's Bal du Masque, when personalities melt away. This was supposed to be a night to talk about, to invoke, to live in the world of the Phantom, here in this perfect Art Nouveau décor, this cloak of the Romantic past. Most everyone was dressed in period costume, a slow mingling dance of bold blue and purple and green gowns from Worth or Doucet or the Web equivalent. The men got off cheaper, mostly in black tuxedos accessorized with the occasional opera cloak and half-mask. The lamps reflecting off the wet train windows turned the bar car into a chamber of mirrors, an endless Impressionist sea of color, filled with yellow Monet light.

Even dead, though, somehow Carla still managed to spoil things. If there was anything worse than Carla going on about how wonderfully, completely devoted and involved and connected she was, it was everybody else doing it, competing to share Carla stories and recall every detail of her conversation from the night before. Kristie wouldn't have minded the worst kind of one-upmanship, or the most tiresome recounting of an Emmy Rossum sighting in Los Angeles. She wouldn't even have minded yet another argument about whether *Love Never Dies* was heresy or homage, if it didn't have to be about Carla's opinion of the sequel. Why couldn't this night be perfect? Why couldn't everyone just agree to talk about the Phantom? Why couldn't these people just *listen* for a change? Kristie felt as though some obscure bargain, made for her benefit, was being violated with no concern for precedent. She had listened to the music, hadn't she? She had taken her steps in the dance, hadn't she?

She looked desperately around for anything that was right, true to the night she had spent everything for. A bearded man in a brown-gray suit caught her eye by not catching her eye. He wasn't darting glances everywhere. He was just writing in a notebook with a fountain pen. He was playing it very cool. He was fortyish, and a little on the heavy side, but not so much for a fan. He'd trimmed his beard, maybe even waxed it a bit. He wore gold-rimmed spectacles and a starched collar. Kristie moved toward him. Even with everyone else distracted by Carla's accident, she couldn't believe he hadn't drawn an audience. Every detail worked.

His sack coat, that of a moderately successful middle-class gentleman, was authentically Parisian cut. She'd seen a hundred like it in the Belle Époque fashion books she pored over during late nights in the costume library at the Clarke. It was also authentically frayed, threads parting over shiny brown cloth. It looked like he'd worn it regularly for weeks, not like he just put it on for a con weekend once every six months. Lying on the table, his satchel was the same way: leather, with just enough mileage on it to be a real piece of luggage, but without the powdery, almost moldy sheen of a century-old antique. The three books inside looked period, too. They were bound in yellow paper, not pre-printed dust jackets.

Kristie moved closer and peeked over his shoulder. He was writing in French, of course. She read a few lines: . . . *barbouillé de notes rouges. Je demandai la permission de le regarder et je lus à la première page: Don Juan triomphant.* It was, of course, a page from *Le Fantome de l'Oper*. She must have made a triumphant noise of her own, because the writing man stopped and looked up. For just a second, Kristie thought she saw stark fear twist his placid features, but he composed himself quickly enough that she decided she was mistaken.

He stood and, in French, offered her a seat at his table. Grateful as she seldom was for those endless school lessons, Kristie thanked him in the same language and introduced herself. He made a slight bow. "Delightful to meet you, Mademoiselle. Permit me to give my name as well; I am called Gaston Leroux."

Even though she had expected it, the name still thrilled her and she decided she could play along. "Oh, but this is incredible, Monsieur Leroux. I'm a great devotee of your works."

He lit up with real interest, as his shrug showed he had heard such things before, of course, and dismissed them. *What an actor*, she thought, *even his writer's mask was perfect.*

"Can you tell me what you are working on now? Some new thrill, perhaps?"

Instead of bragging about his new masterpiece, as Kristie expected, he looked down, not so much shy as apprehensive. She followed his gaze to the pages under his left hand, which were spotted liberally with crimson. He had apparently drunk a considerable amount of the Shiraz, she decided.

He came to a sudden decision, perhaps made bold by the wine. He looked up and met her eyes straight on. "I am working on an exorcism, Mademoiselle. I saw a play, some years ago, staged after hours at the Opera by a coterie of—well, do you recall that business with de Guaita? No? No matter. Providentially, a light exploded and the counterweight of the chandelier fell and the play was left incomplete. For ten years I thought to purge it from my mind, although I must have dreamed it a thousand times. I traveled all over the world, on this train, on ships, to outer Siberia trying to escape. And then Huysmans died, his face rotted away by unnatural cancer. That was three years ago, and I knew I had to exorcise that vision or meet his fate. My first attempts were partially successful, but I must lance the poison soon. I do so here, perhaps hoping the iron of the rails or the constant motion of the carriage will contain it."

He reached across the desk and into his bag. Again Kristie saw that lightning glimpse of terror in his eyes, as though he had touched some venomous thing in the satchel, but when he looked her in the face he had once more mastered himself. He held two books bound in yellow paper out to her.

She read the titles: *Le mystère de la chambre jaune*, or *The Mystery of the Yellow Room*. *Le roi mystère*, or *The Mysterious King*.

"My first two attempts. Both worthwhile in their way, but useless to me now. But perhaps you, who are devoted, as you say . . ."

Kristie tried to demur.

"No, but I insist. You should have them. You especially. I am sure of it." He bent over the books and scribbled first in one, then the other.

She looked at the books, riffled through the pages. They smelled new, but somehow richer than even new paperbacks. When she looked up again, four or five fans drew her eye as they stumbled toward her, only to camp out on another table and begin talking loudly about Carla. She turned back to say something arch in French to the writer, but he was gone. She craned her neck and scanned the car, but could see no brown suit, no sign of him.

"What have you got there?" It was Eldon, holding out a glass of pale golden wine to her. "This is the Tokay. The good stuff. Like in the novel."

Kristie accepted the wine and, she decided, the implied apology. "*Merci*. They're books. Gaston gave them to me . . . I mean, the Leroux cosplayer. He was over there."

Eldon looked blank and, after a cursory glance in the direction she pointed, passed the volumes to Lee, who hovered in the background. "I can't keep track of everyone here, sorry. For all I know or care, we've got freeloaders on board. The head count never matches. I just thank God I don't have to take tickets."

Lee was paging carefully through the books. "These are first editions. They're in really good shape, too. Probably pull a good price on eBay, especially autographed like this."

"What? Autographed by a cosplayer? That doesn't make sense."

"That ink is brown. It's dry. It's old. And your name's not . . . what is that? Camille? Cassilde? He pretended to 'autograph' them to mess with you. Playing." He held the books out toward her, languidly dismissing them already.

Kristie took, almost snatched, them back, then held them up like a pair of aces. "Why would he play a prank on me with two expensive antique books?"

Lee didn't quite sneer, but he didn't try to keep the condescension out of his voice, either. "He probably just wanted to get in your pants. Or crinolines, or whatever. He'll ask you for them back at the end of the trip, tell you it was a joke. One super-fan to another." As Kristie stalked off, she could hear him say in that same tone, "Shame you didn't think of it first, Eldon. She might have shagged you just to spite Carla."

That night Kristie cued up her bootleg recording of the final Toronto show on the iPod, Halloween 1999, the one with Paul Stanley of KISS as the Phantom and Melissa Dye as Christine. But the battery kept cutting out or something as the train syncopated around her. What came through her earbuds as she drifted into sleep sounded more like the saw and whine of the Scriabin she had heard in Milan, over the bass moan of the wooden Wagons-Lits cars hurtling through the wind and dark.

On the fourth night, Kristie finally experienced the Paris Opera House in person. She had seen pictures, of course, and the sets designed to duplicate it in movies and on other, lesser stages. She had posters of it on her walls and owned whole coffee table books devoted to the building. She had seen it in dreams, she now realized, almost all her life, and especially for the last three nights. The tour ended here, at what was now called the Palais Garnier, after its architect, Charles Garnier. She remembered from her books that he had built a villa in Bordighera in Italy, in the native town of the mad composer whose work she had heard as a soundtrack in Milan. His *palais* had once held prisoners of the Commune in its dungeons; it now held not the opera but the Paris ballet. Tonight, thanks to some hidden machinations behind the scenes by SFB, it was again an opera house, staging Gounod's *Faust* to climax the tour in a spectacle of sound and scenery.

The Orient Express had carried her here, like an ark floating on the flood that followed the ruin of the Belle Époque in madness and war. It had carried her and only her. None of the rest of them had noticed the signals on the track. Like Lee and Eldon said, they were just ignorant puppets on a fancy stage set. She lost count of how many chandelier jokes she heard, and soon tuned the clacking of the tourists out entirely.

The trip from the Gare de l'Est to the Opera took no time and all the time, Kristie floating past the glowing balls of street lamps in the fog. She supposed she got on the bus and off again, but she could barely see the ground. The ice left it slick and black, the streets like canals running toward some enormous ebon lake. The sky was mist and clouds and snow, lit dirty white from below, with patches of darkness barely visible.

The fog parted once, revealing a full moon so close and so large that it seemed to block the Eiffel Tower behind it.

Against the backdrop of the crowd dressed again in their finest garb, Kristie flowed up the steps into the crush room, then up the grand staircase to her box, number five. She heard an unpleasant sound, tenor complaint, but it faded to insignificance. She looked out at the swells of Paris society, applause crashing below as the overture started, and wished for opera glasses. She so wanted to see the faces of the performers, but they blurred with distance and delight.

During the third act, as Marguerite sung her ballad to the King of Thule—reading *Thale* in the misprinted program—Kristie got up from her seat and moved into the corridor. At a specific turning, she remembered a scene from the film in Milan and pressed four gold ornaments that together made up a certain Sign. When the door swung open, she heard the brief moan of Scriabin's viol. Then she descended the staircase within, all the way to the fifth sub-cellar.

There, surrounded by the Black Lake, stood the Phantom, his face invisible behind a smooth surface of pallid ivory or porcelain.

Kristie desired only to cross the Black Lake, and she dropped the two slim books she carried into its inky waters in her haste to do so. She did not know what craft had carried her to her Phantom, but her feet were dry when she approached him, the mystical chords of Scriabin pounding in her brain and filling her eyes with yellow light.

She reached out her hands and grasped the pallid mask, inhaling the rot and mildew that poured off the Phantom's tattered robes and offered up the smells of a century or more in Garnier's deepest, most secret places. She breathed deep and pulled.

She pulled, and then stumbled back and screamed.

The figure wore no mask.

A GREAT AND TERRIBLE HUNGER

ELAINE CUNNINGHAM

TOMAS BUSTLED INTO THE KITCHEN car, a smirk on his too-handsome face and a full dinner plate in his hands. He slid the rejected meal onto the service ledge in front of me and announced, "From the viscount."

A moment's silence fell over the bustling kitchen. Even the *chef du cuisine* ceased his grumbling long enough to eye the flawless presentation. Of course there was no fault to find. The salmon had been impeccably prepared—poached in wine and resting in a small pool of *sauce verte au pain* beside a *mélange* of tiny buttered vegetables. Viscount or not, sending back the fish course all but untouched was an insult I could not take lightly.

"What reason did he give?"

Tomas performed one of those expressive Gallic shrugs. "He is a viscount. What reason does he need?"

Emile, my fellow subchef and the bane of my existence, dipped a spoon into the rejected sauce and touched it to his tongue. One eloquent eyebrow rose.

And so, it must be said, did my hackles. "It is a classic sauce, properly prepared!"

"Bread soaked in vinegar, blended into an emulsion with olive oil, tarragon, garlic, and a pinch of salt," Emile recited in a bored tone. "I can even tell which vinegar you used. Doubtless you assumed a vinegar infused with dried tarragon would deepen the flavor of the fresh herb, rather than muddy it."

I could refute none of this. "The sauce is correct."

"Most certainly, if by 'correct' you mean it is a dull and lifeless copy. Where is the moment of discovery, the lingering delight of an elusive melody? Taste this."

He thrust a spoon at me. I took it from his hands and sampled the green sauce. For a moment, irritation succumbed to pleasure. Without a doubt, the foundation herb was sorrel. Nothing else could duplicate that particular not-quite-lemon tang. Emile had contrived a sauce with a pleasantly rich mouth feel—a spoonful of *crème fraîche*, perhaps?—a hint of sweetness beneath the sour, and a fresh, bright note I could not identify. Delicious!

Infuriating.

"Lime," he said, clearly enjoying my reaction. "Sorrel and lime. Inspired, don't you agree?"

"It will do." The chef, a bear-sized Burgundian, spoke without looking up from his work. "Sauce a turbot filet and send it out."

"Already done." Emile slid a newly prepared plate onto the ledge.

Tomas cleared his throat.

The chef huffed and began over-salting the contents of a square metal box. "Well? What is it?"

"The maharajah requires lamb curry again for tomorrow's dinner. For him and his wives."

Finally the chef glanced up. "All of them?"

"All."

The Burgundian threw both hands high and shook them in wordless supplication. "I ask you, what sane man keeps seven wives? And such women! They look like sylphs but eat like sows."

I'd heard much about the Indian rajah's beautiful wives, but of course I had not seen them. The subchefs had no occasion to enter the dining car during meals. Neither did we venture into the sleeping coaches at any point during the journey. Only the most highly ranked staff—the *chef du train*, the *chef du cuisine*, and sometimes the *maître d'hôtel*—rated a compartment, and only when the train was not fully booked. The rest of us slept in hammocks slung between the racks of the restaurant car, rising before dawn to replace beds of canvas and hempen rope with the finest damask and porce-lain and crystal. A necessary transformation, but of course Emile liked to mutter about the unearned privilege of the wealthy. He is a fool in all matters except food. The train's passengers had purchased the right to expect luxury, and it was our job to provide it, flawlessly.

"There is insufficient lamb," I said.

"Of this I am aware." The chef reached for the pepper mill and cranked it with grim enthusiasm. One of our English passengers refused to eat anything prepared on the train, insisting upon "au-thentically Oriental" meals from the Pere Palace Hotel in Constan-tinople. The chef, naturally, took insult—not only at the slight to his art, but also the indignity of serving reheated food. In a small act of vengeance, he seasoned each boxed meal to the point of ined-ibility. So far the Englishman had found nothing amiss.

"What shall we do?" I asked.

The chef slammed down the pepper mill. "A man cannot think in this kitchen for all the chatter! We will purchase more lamb, of course. Surely there are sheep near Ploesti. As for the other thing," he said, looking meaningfully from me to Emile, "you two will make an end to this rivalry before we reach Vienna, or one of you will not continue on to Paris."

We murmured respectful assent and I applied myself to the frantic pace of dinner preparation. But when a task has been per-formed many times, the hands remember and the mind is free to roam. There was much to ponder, for the chef's ultimatum troubled me. Try as I might, I could think of no circumstance under which I might be reconciled with Emile. Neither could I devise a plan that would guarantee his ouster. Perhaps his thoughts followed similar paths, but nothing more was said on the subject until we began to plate the cheese course.

"I propose a simple contest," Emile said.

"Oh, do you?"

"I assure you, the rules of the game are entirely in your favor. I have made certain observations—one might even go so far as to call them insults—about your ability to cook with originality and inspi-ration. If I cannot prove my words, I will withdraw them and make public apology."

This, I had not expected. The man's arrogance was boundless—

he was French, after all—and our rivalry permitted no such concession. I was skeptical, certainly, but I will admit to a certain curiosity.

"Go on."

"You will create a dish of your choice. I will reproduce it precisely, and then I will improve upon it. If I fail at either task, I will name you the better cook and seek other employment in Vienna. But if I succeed—"

"It will do," the chef said. "Dietgar accepts. I will judge his dish and Emile's response to it."

The rest of the kitchen staff applauded. Later they would probably lay bets. I had little doubt how the odds would fall.

We two had similar training, similar experience. I am Belgian, which would count against me in some men's eyes, but Emile's primary advantage lay in his uncanny ability to name the ingredients in any dish he tasted. It is said that the great Mozart once attended the performance of a symphony and after the concert wrote down the music, entirely and precisely, from a single hearing. Emile is no Mozart, but his gift was formidable enough to inspire a moment of dread and doubt as I pondered the wager.

But only a single moment. I knew myself to be the better man, and the desire to prove my supremacy burned in me like a fever, like thirst, like lust.

So I smiled at Emile and said, "You will enjoy living in Vienna, I think."

We reached Ploesti around eight o'clock the next morning. The station was tiny, but the town itself boasted two impressive buildings: Pilishor, the summer residence of Rumanian boyars, and Castel Peles, a newly built monstrosity well suited to the king and queen who inhabited it.

Grandiose but strange, the castle resembled something a giant child might build from mismatched blocks. Here it resembled a medieval German town, there a French chalet. One wall boasted classical marble pillars, another flaunted a modern expanse of glass. Many spires rose into the sky, ranging in appearance from English clock towers to an Oriental minaret. On a fair day, this monument to hubris and lack of taste was almost amusing, but a storm was brewing over the Carpathians, and under the strange yellow-gray sky the castle looked distressingly like a monster stitched together from many parts.

While a few passengers took in the dubious sights, two porters sought out a local butcher shop where, according to the stationmaster, excellent lamb could be had. Since it was my task to pack the meat in ice, I paced the platform as I awaited their return. The porters made short work of the errand and came back at a run, arms laden with packages and eyes casting uneasy glances at the lowering clouds.

As we left Ploesti we passed several tall wooden derricks—rigs of the wells sunk deep into the earth to obtain the oil that the Americans call petroleum. I hate the sight of them, and not only because I can never pass one without envisioning gallows awaiting a hangman. Some nights, when the chorus of snoring handymen and baggage handlers keeps sleep at bay, I think of those wells and wonder what other things, either treasures or terrors, they might unearth. Mind you, I am not a fanciful man, but there is something about Rumania that inspires dark imaginings.

The next stretch of the journey was usually the least pleasant, with the possible exception of the Black Sea crossing. Nearly two hundred miles of track threaded through a narrow defile between the Miroch range of the Balkan Mountains and the Carpathians. The track ran very close to the Danube here, built on piles of rock—remnants of cliffs and outcrops reduced to rubble by blasting. Small avalanches were not uncommon. Progress was, of necessity, slow and halting.

So it came as no surprise when the train screeched to stop during the breakfast preparation. Chef sent Giles, the youngest of the waiters, to fetch details. The lad scurried back in moments, shrugging off his tailcoat as he came.

"A landslide ahead," he said. "Can't tell you how much of the track is blocked—can't hardly see my own boots in this fog. The *chef du train* wants every man you can spare to help clear the way."

"I see you have already volunteered," the chef said dryly. He tipped his head toward the cleaners. "Take Yves and Victoir. Oh, and Dietger, you may go as well."

My wellspring of outrage threatened to overflow, but I schooled my face to professional calm. "Since there is no other man here by that name, am I to assume you are speaking to me?"

A sour expression crossed the chef's face. "Mind your tone, Dietgar. And you, Emile, stop smirking. Dietger is bigger and stronger, that is all. To work, all of you!"

There was nothing for it but to leave the train and do as I was told. I took the leather gloves one of the baggage handlers gave me and stood for a moment to watch the men hauling away stones. I was somewhat mollified to note that nearly all the staff shared my assignment, but my pride was pricked by that fact that I was consigned to unskilled labor and Emile was not.

The main pile of rubble stood a few scant feet from the engine, but more rocks littered the track ahead. How far the damage went, I could not tell, for the rails curved before disappearing into the deepening mist. I picked my way westward, thinking to begin at the farthest end of the landslide so that I might work alone, at least for a short while.

But I was not the first to choose solitude. The mist swirled to reveal small, dark-clad figure. As I drew nearer, I realized to my surprise that the worker was a woman wearing the habit of an Eastern Orthodox nun.

She bent to pick up a large stone. Being a man of proper sensibilities, I rushed to take her burden from her. As her eyes met mine, I observed that she was young, certainly no more than thirty, yet she wore the garments that proclaimed her a *stavrophore*—a nun who has reached an exceptional level of piety and discipline.

She tossed the stone aside and gave me a smile of unexpected charm. "Oh, was that the rock you wanted? I do apologize."

"No, Holy Mother, I—"

"There are many more," she said as she reached for another. "Perhaps, in time, you will find another to your liking."

"I was going to say that this is not work for you. You are—"

"A nun, yes," she said with a hint of impatience. She hurled the second rock. "And as such, I am no stranger to hard work."

"I was *going* to say," I repeated in a tone firm enough to forestall further interruption, "that you are a *passenger.*"

"Ah." For a moment, the merry light in her eyes threatened to push back the fog. "Now *there* is a holy state indeed!"

I could not decide whether or not she was mocking me, so I responded only with dignified silence.

The nun's mirth faded away. "Perhaps you think my presence on such a train incompatible with my vows of poverty?"

"I would not presume to have an opinion on that matter, Holy Mother."

She tossed another rock with more force than was strictly necessary. "I have no shortage of opinions, on that matter or any other. Not that my opinion is of any consequence. I travel with the permission of my order, and in the company of my brother. It is all very proper, I assure you."

The bitterness in her voice puzzled me, but it was not my place to ponder its source. "I did not mean to imply otherwise, Holy Mother. My only concern is your wellbeing, and of course you are the best judge of that. But at least let me give you these gloves."

The nun smiled and showed me her hands. No doubt she was born of good family—any brother who could convince an abbess to give leave to one of her nuns must be a powerful and important man—but the *stavrophore*'s hands were as rough as any peasant's.

"Keep the gloves for yourself," she said kindly. "Hands are an artist's most important tools, and I judge by your clothing that you are one of the artists responsible for the meals my brother has been enjoying so heartily."

I pulled on the gloves and started working beside her. "And you? You do not enjoy these meals?"

"It is still the Lenten season," she said. "I will not eat meat for another week. But the bread is very fine, the vegetables fresh, and bottles of mineral water are a luxury to which I could happily become accustomed."

"Surely you eat more than that! What of the fish? The cheeses, the desserts?"

Humor danced in her eyes. "I see I have committed sacrilege."

"That, I very much doubt."

"Not by the tenets of my order, perhaps, but what is sacred to one is not sacred to all. Take my brother, for example." She picked up two fist-sized rocks and hurled them into the gorge. "Like many men of wealth, he worships Mammon. Or would, if he had a soul to sell."

"Forgive me, but that seems harsh."

"Does it? I assure you, if the maharajah wished to add me to his collection and offered sufficient recompense, my brother would sell me in a heartbeat."

Her tone was now lighter than my best soufflé, but I could not fail to notice the faint, lingering note of bitterness beneath the jest.

I looked about for something to divert the conversation and noticed a rift in the rock wall. "That looks to be the entrance to a cave, does it not?"

The nun studied the rift for a moment, her brow furrowed with concentration. "Do you hear something?"

A frisson of dread raced down my spine, and I knew sudden, fervent regret over my choice of diversion.

Everyone, I suspect, has a secret fear, something that returns again and again to haunt his dreams. For no reason that I can explain, I have always feared caves and the things that might lurk in them. Did the avalanche unseal such a cave? Could it have unleashed one of the deeply buried terrors my imagination so often conjured as we passed through this gorge? Unlikely, to be sure, but the mere possibility rooted my feet to the track.

But the nun wandered closer, her face suffused with stern purpose as she picked her way across the rubble. She stopped suddenly and folded like someone who'd taken a fist to the gut.

I thrust aside my fears and hurried to her side. As I bent to help her rise, a terrible cloud enveloped me.

You must understand that this was no natural cloud. There was nothing one could see or touch or smell—no mist or haze, no scent or sound, no color or light or darkness. There was not even a Presence, not in any sense that I would use that word, nor anything approaching any emotion I could name or understand. The closest I can come to describing what I sensed was *hunger*.

Nausea rolled through me, but I managed to raise the nun to her feet. We leaned on each other as we staggered away from the rift.

We got as far as the track before she fell to her knees, retching. I backed away, determined to give her some small measure of dignity and privacy while retaining what I could of my own.

At length she wiped her eyes on her sleeve and turned to me. "There was a voice. A call for help, I think. I heard it . . . *before*."

I did not need to ask what she meant. Some moments, a very few, have the power to turn a page in a man's life. I had not realized until now that one single moment could rip away all the preceding pages and send the shreds spinning away into a maelstrom of confusion. The terrible hunger I sensed in that cave overwhelmed all other truths. Everything that came *before* no longer made sense to me. I felt utterly adrift—unable to think, uncertain of what I should do.

The nun had no such doubts. She pushed herself to her feet and staggered toward me, her so-expressive eyes ablaze with fervor.

"We must help that poor soul!"

I thought I had known fear beyond bearing, but the prospect of entering that cave, confronting that Hunger, dragged me into new depths of terror.

"Madness," I murmured.

"Sacrifice," she said firmly. "We must emulate Our Lord in this, as in all things."

She spun away from me and headed for the rift.

The prospect of a nun—a passenger!—putting herself at such risk shook me from my lethargy. I pushed past her, drew in a long breath of relatively wholesome air, and squeezed through the narrow rift.

To my relief, the cave appeared to be small and shallow. It would take but a few moments to explore the shadows for the source of the mysterious call. I suspected there was nothing to find. Surely the nun had only heard one of the workers. The dense fog played strange games with sound, that was all. Nothing more. Surely not.

Before I'd gone a dozen steps, my ankle turned on a loose rock and suddenly I was tumbling down a steep incline.

Several bruising moments passed as I flailed about for a handhold—anything to stop my fall. Branches—or tree roots, more likely—lashed at my face and I managed to grab hold of one.

For the space of several long, ragged breaths, I clung to the roots and waited for my eyes to adjust to the darkness. To no avail—the blackness was total, with no hint of light above or below me. Not trusting the roots to hold my weight for long, I sought a foothold and found, to my great relief, an expanse of solid rock.

"Hello? *Monsieur le chef?*"

The nun's voice sounded very far away. I tried to call back, but my dust-choked throat could manage no more than a croak.

"Courage, Monsieur! I will bring help."

But she would not. She would flee this place and not return. I knew this in the marrow of my bones. And in truth, I could not blame her.

I settled down among the rocks and wrapped my arms around my body, partly for the slight comfort this offered and partly to ward off the cold. Afraid to move for fear of falling deeper still, afraid to speak for fear of what I might awaken, I sat and rocked and rocked like a child, or perhaps a madman.

Time passed. How much, I could not say, but at length my thirst overcame my fear. I forced my chilled limbs to move and crawled so very slowly through the rocks.

My seeking hand found flesh—colder than my own, and horribly sticky. I recoiled, shrieking in terror at the image flooding my mind.

Blue-gray hide, tentacles, many slack mouths ringed with curved fangs...

There was more, much more, but my mind could not absorb it. As horrific as the creature might be, I did not get the sense that it was any great size—probably not much bigger than a man. It lay still and silent, to all appearances as lifeless as the tumbled rock surrounding it.

I prodded the creature again. It did not move, but I could not be certain that it *would* not. If I fled, I would be easy prey in the darkness.

So reasoning, I settled down beside the thing and felt around until I found a stone shaped remarkably like a knife. Having armed myself, I found enough calm to ponder the thing.

What was it, and where had it come from? Was its origin some alien world, or a hidden pocket of the world I thought I knew? And what of that terrible cloud of hunger that overcame the nun and me? Was this creature the source of it, or an unconsumed victim of some greater horror?

Such thoughts occupied me as hours stretched into days. I dared not leave the creature's side, because in all this time it did not putrefy. Not in the slightest. No scent of decay rose from the carcass, if such it was. For all I knew, it only slept.

Hunger brings its own sort of madness. When I could bear it no more, I cut a bit of flesh from the creature and did what I must to survive. The revulsion I expected did not come, nor did the paroxysms of poison. Indeed, I felt much revived. Whatever the thing was, my body recognized its flesh as food.

And why should it not? Was not man master of the world, and in the end, does he not turn everything to feed himself? There is an order to life, not unlike the proper running of the train.

The train!

For the first time in days, I thought of the Orient Express, and I remembered the contest that would determine my future. I was suddenly struck by inspiration, a notion as brilliant as it was terrible.

The flesh of this creature, artfully prepared, would be a dish Emile could neither identify nor reproduce!

"Dietgar! Can you hear me?"

I could and did, but several moments passed before I could remember the speaker's name. Tomas, the waiter.

Light flared above me, blinding in its intensity. I quickly turned away and cut a generous collop of flesh from the creature.

"Dietgar?"

"I am here—have been here, all these days," I called back as I hurriedly shrugged off my coat and wrapped the meat. "Have you a rope?"

A thick length slithered down the rock wall. I tied the coat and its precious contents around my waist and grasped the rope. Climbing was easier than I expected it to be, given my long ordeal and weakened state.

Strong hands helped me climb free of the pit. The blinding light turned out to be a single oil lantern, and the rescue party consisted only of Tomas and the nun. The holy mother, it must be said, did not look well, but her face was a most welcome sight.

"You came back," I marveled. "After all this time, I'd given up hope."

She sent me a strange look and leaned closer to peer into my eyes. "He must have suffered a knock to the head," she told Tomas. "Help him back to the train, and see that he does not sleep for a few hours."

I had many questions, but the look of alarm on the nun's face when I asked the date silenced me. We walked in that silence back to the train. It stood where I last saw it, which was a matter of no small concern. Certainly, I was glad of my rescue, but the thought that my misadventure might have disrupted the schedule—not just for hours, but days!—filled me with unease.

So absorbed was I with these thoughts that I almost missed the mushrooms growing in a small patch of weeds. Most were white cylinders, oddly scaled, but a few had opened. I picked one and studied the gills. As I suspected, they were pink.

And with that revelation, my triumph was assured. Shaggy ink cap mushrooms were a favorite childhood delicacy, but I doubted Emile knew of them and was certain there were none on the train. Though wholesome when young and freshly picked, they dissolved within hours into a disgusting black mass. I had perhaps six hours to make a broth that Emile could not hope to duplicate.

If one unknown ingredient was good, two could only be better.

The mountain passage was worse than any I'd experienced in my four years of service. The train lurched and bumped until even the most amiable staff members grew surly, and the stories filtering into the kitchen proved that the passengers were no more immune to the unpleasant conditions than the staff. Indeed, a sort of madness seemed to have settled over the train.

The maharajah, not content with a mere seven women, had enlivened luncheon by making lewd suggestions to the wife of a Turkish diplomat. Shortly thereafter, a Greek businessman was discovered in the viscountess's compartment, his pockets bulging with her jewelry. The Greek insisted that he had entered her compartment by mistake. He also insisted that the viscountess was already dead when he arrived. I wondered if this might be the nun's brother, and allowed that I might have dismissed her opinion of him too hastily.

Few of the passengers wanted dinner, and those who did ordered vast quantities of food delivered to their compartments. I wondered if some of the strange miasma that had so sickened the nun and me had crept into the train and spread over the course of the last few days like a summer fever. Whatever the case, most passengers stayed in their compartments, more than a few of them making wretched use of the vases supplied for privy purposes.

And so it was that dinner was finished earlier than usual, despite a short-handed kitchen. Most of the staff who'd helped clear the track were afflicted with the illness, and they'd been crammed into three vacant compartments in second class until they were fit for duty. I had the kitchen entirely to myself, as well as the chef's blessing to begin the contest with Emile.

Starvation adds a rare savor, one that no art can duplicate. To my relief, a sliver of the creature's meat, sautéed in butter, still tasted delicious. I cut the collop into thin slices and put the meat in a marinade of wine and oil while I sautéed the shaggy ink cap mushrooms. This mushroom releases a great deal of liquid, which I reduced into a sauce flavored with white truffles. By dawn, the fragrant dish was ready. The chef entered the kitchen car, closely shadowed by Emile, just as I finished garnishing the second tasting plate.

Without comment, I handed one plate to the chef, the other to Emile. They reached for forks, tasted, considered. Tasted again. I waited, hands folded and face serene with confidence.

"How much of this did you make?" the chef asked. "Is there enough to serve with the brunch?"

This was high and unexpected praise! "Not enough for all, but for some, yes," I said. "Unless, of course, Emile can duplicate the dish before noon."

"You had a full night to prepare, and the kitchen to yourself," Emile snapped. "I demand the same."

"And miss a night's sleep? Perhaps you would rather concede now."

Some feral thing stirred behind Emile's eyes. I stood a full head taller than my nemesis, but it was all I could do to stand my ground as he took a quick step closer.

"Do not mistake me," he hissed. "Do you truly think me incapable of doing all that you did, and more?"

❖　❖　❖

The dish I created was well received. Only a few passengers attended brunch, but Tomas, the only waiter who felt well enough to serve, assured me that everyone who tasted it had seemed pleased.

"That one Indian woman? The one with the . . ." He cupped the air several inches in front of his chest and looked at me inquiringly. I'd never seen the woman in question, but I nodded to show that I understood his pantomime. "She all but licked the plate."

I sent a sidelong look and a smug little smile in Emile's direction. "Tomorrow morning, no doubt she will be unable to refrain. You have, I trust, decided how to improve the dish? After you reproduce it, of course?"

"It is well that you speak German," he snarled. "You'll have need of it in Vienna."

His intemperate response pleased me—it was a gratifying departure from his supercilious airs—but the chef snatched a dish from the worktable and hurled it at Emile.

The crash and clatter seemed to echo in the shocked silence. Work ceased as the kitchen staff stared in astonishment at the chef.

"Enough!" he howled.

Before I could savor this delightful turn of events, the chef threw his hat to the floor and stalked into the restaurant car, kicking the fallen dish as he went. I noticed that the dish was square and metal—one of the boxes that held the Englishman's packaged meals—and realized that Emile had not been the target of the chef's ire.

The sounds of battle—albeit a battle fought with porcelain—rose above the chef's screams and curses and the Englishman's outraged shouts. In the short time it took me to reach the dining car, the fight had progressed to cutlery and blood. It took every member of the kitchen staff to drag the chef off the half-conscious passenger and confine him to his compartment.

The dining car was deserted when we came back through. After directing the waiters and cleaners to tend to the battle's aftermath, I returned to the kitchen.

But here, too, chaos reigned. One of the ice chests stood open, and several pieces of meat lay unwrapped on the floor. An exotically beautiful woman sat cross-legged on the floor, holding a large piece of raw meat with both hands. A trickle of blood ran from one corner of her painted mouth.

"I wanted lamb," she said, as if that explained all.

Tomas entered the kitchen, muttering as he fingered a tear on the thigh of his blue velvet breeches. He jolted to a stop, and a delighted leer spread across his face as he beheld the woman who was, I suspected, the curvy beauty who'd so enjoyed her morning meal.

The Indian woman returned his gaze, her eyes dark with female knowledge. Her lips curved in a smile of devastating power and promise. "Will there be more lamb, after?"

"Entire sheep, as many as you like," he said as he reached for her raised hand.

I planted myself between them. "There will be no 'after.' She is a passenger, and the wife of Indian nobility!"

Tomas pushed me aside and reached for the woman. I seized a skillet, lofted it with both hands, and brought it down hard on his head.

He turned to face me, an expression of astonishment on his face. I hit him again, and this time he went down.

The woman wriggled out from under the fallen waiter and, after extracting from me many promises of lamb curry and erotic delights, deigned to grab an ankle and help me drag Tomas into the pantry. Luncheon preparations would begin soon, and the kitchen car was small enough without a supine waiter taking up most of the floor.

I offered to see the woman to her compartment, but not for the reason she surmised. According to the passenger list posted in the kitchen, her compartment was next to the nun's, and the holy mother held the answer to a question of great importance.

The train was eerily silent. No passengers gathered in the parlor car, none walked the narrow halls. From time to time I heard the faint sound of weeping coming from a sleeping compartment, so soft and despairing and full of impossible longing. I cannot tell you what words accompanied this scattered chorus, but I recognized the music of frustrated desire.

The heartbreaking sound only strengthened my resolve. This was not a song I intended to sing.

The Indian woman began to shed her clothes before I could open her compartment door. I pushed her inside, ignoring the feel of fine silk and warm brown flesh beneath my hands. In moments she was entirely naked, a sight that surely would have riveted me

had there not been one far more compelling beyond her compartment window.

The train had stopped. How had I not realized this?

We had cleared the gorge and entered the foothills. An expanse
of meadow flowers carpeted the hill that rose toward the skyset
clouds. And on this hill perhaps a dozen passengers gamboled like
sheep or strode purposefully in various directions. Three young
women—by their simple gray gowns, I judged them to be ladies'
maids or governesses—were viciously stoning a stout matron. The
maharajah, as naked as his faithless wife, chased an equally unclad
English beauty who did not look averse to being caught.

I shook my head in astonishment. This was madness. Why
would the *chef du train* order an unscheduled stop?

The astonishment on the Indian beauty's face as I backed out
of her compartment would have been amusing, had I time to dwell
upon such things. I shut the door a heartbeat before the she hurled
herself against it, shrieking like a scalded cat.

The noise did not rouse the nun, nor did she respond to my
knock. The sleeping car attendant was soundly asleep, three empty
bottles of an excellent pinot noir at his feet. I liberated the key ring
from his belt, but this was not necessary. The nun had left her
door unlocked.

For a long moment I stood in the doorway and gazed at the red
scene beyond. The *stavrophore*, this most pious of nuns, lay on her
narrow cot, an expression of beatific joy on her bloodless face. A
long knife impaled both her bared feet. A smaller knife had been
driven hilt-deep into one of her outstretched palms.

She was dead, of course. She might have survived the self-
inflicted stigmata, but not the knife that opened her side.

I closed my eyes and breathed a long, heartfelt sight of relief.

It was Lent, and a woman so pious would never taste meat. The
madness infecting the train was none of my doing. I'd feared it
might be, after seeing the insanity of those who'd tasted the creature's flesh: the chef, the Indian woman, probably Tomas.

Upon consideration, this made good sense. After all, I, too, had
eaten the creature's flesh, and I was in full possession of my senses.
I hoped the same could be said of Emile—at least, until our contest
played out to completion.

He was in the kitchen car, of course, sharpening his knives with grim efficiency. As the Holy Mother had observed, what is sacred to one man might not be revered by another, but Emile and I worshipped the same gods.

"I know your secret," he said as I entered the car. He slammed a bone cleaver into the cutting board hard enough to send wooden chips flying. "I know what manner of meat you used this morning."

This was impossible, of course. He couldn't know what sort of creature had yielded the collops.

"Who was it?" he demanded. "Victoir? Giles? Perhaps one of the passengers?"

I stared at him, not believing I heard him aright.

"Did you not understand the question? Very well, then, I will put it to you more clearly: *Whom did you kill this morning?*"

Now I knew that Emile had lost his wits. I had been trapped for days. The creature had been dead for days before I butchered it.

Hadn't it?

"I suppose it's of no consequence," the madman muttered. "One beef tastes much like another, does it not? It's all in the sauce."

He wrenched his cleaver from the cutting board and pushed open the door to the pantry.

Tomas lay as I had left him. Whether or not he still breathed, I could not say. Really, how could I be sure of anything?

No, that was not entirely true. I knew beyond doubt that I had won and Emile had lost. I knew that which I desired above all things would be mine.

No one would believe Emile's story. He would be disgraced, discredited, cast out. The man might be many things, but when it came to food, his integrity was absolute. He would be forced to admit that he could neither identify nor duplicate the taste of shaggy ink cap mushrooms. Whatever tales were told of this trip, I would be recalled as the better chef.

As the cleaver flashed down, I drew in a long breath, savoring the remembered fragrance of that elusive, delicious sauce.

INSCRUTABLE
ROBIN D. LAWS

ADOPTING A MODE OF ADDRESS he fell into with comfortable regularity, Sir Russell spoke of Phut as if he were not present. "Time and again, he's proven himself damnably useful. However off-putting his aspect. Hah, Phut?"

Phut held the stolid expression that tamed a face men otherwise found unnerving. For the benefit of Sir Russell's traveling companion, he essayed a minimal nod. Between master and manservant an economy of communication prevailed. The need for overt response from Phut to any of Sir Russell's statements or requests had long since been set aside. What Phut was required to do, he did, and that was all.

As was his habit, Sir Russell had chosen the dining car's earliest midday sitting. He tucked into his veal stroganoff. Across from him sat Stephens, who had ordered the roast chicken. Before Phut sat a plate of lentils, overlaid with buttery asparagus spears. Though indifferent to food, Phut assumed from the bright green coloration of the stalks that they had been expertly prepared. Sir Russell and Stephens made subdued sounds of pleasure as they ate. They raised their glasses of claret.

"To halcyon days," said Stephens.

"Indeed," nodded Sir Russell.

Sir Russell, Phut gathered, knew this man from a place called Eton. He understood this to be an indoctrination center, where boys were molded into masters of empire. In this it resembled the youth

barracks of Sparta, or the madrasas of Syria's *hashishin*. Caste mu-
tuality permitted Sir Russell to allude indiscreetly to his true business in Turkey. Stephens's position, whatever that was, in turn
allowed him to infer that Sir Russell's trip had nothing to do with
lepidoptery, but was instead undertaken at the behest of Whitehall.
They spoke of the matter in an oblique way, mentioning stickiness,
a thorn in Earl Curzon's side, and a necessity for discreet removal.
Phut had yet to suss out the full details. He would do so, as he always
did, before it mattered. Which in this case it might not, given what
awaited in Istanbul.

Sir Russell returned to his subject: his own cleverness in retaining Phut as a factotum. "Never has a good deed so repaid itself than
on the day I saved him from that mob in Selangor."

Stephens turned his head sidelong, so he would not appear to
be staring at Phut in all of his spectacular, mesmerizing ugliness.
Phut was barely four feet tall, his skin weather-hardened and dark-
complected, his fingers stubby and tipped by immaculate, lacquered
nails. His unblinking eyes burned like brown fire. A sparse mustache sprawled obscenely atop his thick upper lip. Jagged yellow
teeth poked out from a pronounced overbite.

Stephens noted Phut's charcoal-colored wool suit, correctly sus-
pecting it as the handiwork of the Savile Row man both he and Sir
Russell used. Superbly fitted to his irregular frame, it minimized,
but could not conceal, an assortment of humps and bulges.

(What Stephens could not guess was that these adjustments to
his malformations also hid the modifications Phut had made to
the lining of his jacket, to hold pouches of powders, along with less
subtle weapons of his trade.)

Sir Russell twisted noodles around his silver fork and speared a
piece of veal. "What taboo he'd committed to so rile his countrymen he'll still not speak of."

Phut was not, in fact, from Selangor, or for that matter from any
part of Malaya. Like other of Sir Russell's misapprehensions about
him, it suited Phut's purposes and took no effort on his part to sus-
tain. Phut belonged to a people scattered widely across the globe,
united by ancient blood and an older language, spared the degen-
erate taint of mere humanity. Neither was Phut his real name—
though it would do for the time being. As presently configured, his

own vocal apparatus could muster only an approximation of the necessary sounds.

"For the price of a few well-placed revolver rounds, I earned his constant fealty," Sir Russell told Stephens. "I saved his life once, he saved mine—how many times now, Phut?"

Phut neither spoke nor gestured.

Sir Russell counted on the fingers of his right hand. "The boar in Andaman. The knife-man in Bombay. The hotel fire in Honduras. That skirmish with the tongs in Tsimshatshui—that counts as two separate incidents. And if you number Sarajevo as a legitimate ambush, the total comes to six. Not a bad arrangement, hah, Stephens? Perhaps you should look into getting a native valet."

"The cost of acquisition seems parlous," Stephens said. Though roughly Sir Russell's age, his slimmer build and milky-smooth fingers marked him as a man of inaction. "And truth be told, I lack your propensity for needing my life saved."

"That is just the icing on the cake of such a fellow's utility." A serveur appeared to refill Sir Russell's glass. "That visage of his, that implacable mask of a face. One can neither help but stare at it, nor allow oneself to be seen to stare. A magnificent distraction he is. To put a negotiating partner off his stride, all I have to do is introduce him to Phut beforehand. Throughout our discussion, Phut's countenance plays at the mind, haunting, vexing. It took me months to get used to it, myself, hah, Phut?'

Phut made no response.

"In his ugliness there is great profundity. A majesty, if you will. A living paradox sits before you. You'll not soon forget him, now that you've seen him, will you?"

Stephens muttered an embarrassed demurral into his wine goblet.

"Don't worry about Phut's tender sensibilities. I assure you he has none. Isn't that right, Phut?"

Phut nodded.

"That is the second, and deeper, of Phut's ineffable qualities. Even more so than the conventional Asiatic, his inner musings remain impenetrable. Drawn from a deep well of understanding, I dare say, one that, perhaps, eclipses our flat-footed questing for practical advantage. Though he is an unquestioned master of the train schedule, of the hotel reservation, of launderers and suppliers, within his stolid chest resonates the heart of an instinctive man. A mystic in an age of accountants. There is something boundless in him, wouldn't you say?"

"I daren't venture to gainsay you, Beaky. On this or any other matter."

Sir Russell swirled his Bordeaux and inhaled its aroma. "Or mayhaps he thinks not at all, and forces us to project our own doubts onto those impassive features—that great crag of a brow, the appalling graveyard of teeth. But as the yogis would have us believe, in the absence of thought enlightenment lies. So perhaps to be limited is in some sense the same as being limitless, hah?"

Phut leaned forward to cut an asparagus spear into bite-sized chunks. He sipped from his glass of still water. Sir Russell never offered him wine or spirits. The slight mattered not. Since his awakening, Phut had been staunchly abstemious, allowing himself nothing stronger than the occasional solitary lager in the heat of a tropical day. Alcohol affected his people more strongly than it did humans, clouding the intuitive senses. Dulled awareness risked defeat. Manifold forces converged, and mistakes made now could redound for an aeon to come.

Sir Russell lowered his voice. "I'll confess this to you, Stephens. As odd a duck as Phut here is, as illimitably alien as his consciousness might be, there are a dozen of my dearest friends I'd leave on a sinking ship, rescuing him before them."

"Present company excepted, I hope."

"Naturally so, old chum."

Sir Russell straightened himself against the plush back of the dining car chair. "In my peregrinations, I'll frankly tell you, I have unlearned more than I have learned. One certainty after another has fallen away from me, when confronted with the deuced mystery of existence. Yet if there's one nugget of wisdom I can claim to have acquired along the way, it's this—loyalty is preferable to friendship. Infinitely so."

"Can a friendship not also be loyal?"

"Not in the same way, Stephens. Like a plant, a friendship requires constant watering. A marriage even more so."

"How is Cecily, by the way?"

Sir Russell waved the question away. "The same, Stephens, the same. But you deflect my point. With admirable cheek, but deflect it all the same. A friendship is a constant exchange, a *quid pro quo*, provisional by the moment—"

"That's a grossly cynical view of human relations, Shepstone. You—"

"Let me complete the thought. Loyalty draws from a deeper well. It is allegiance devoid of tit for tat. It does not weigh itself. It merely is. Hah, Phut?"

Phut raised his water glass to him. By Phut's standards the gesture was unusually expressive. Sir Russell flushed, a broad grin breaking across his face.

The interior of the dining car darkened as the train rattled through a tunnel. As it cleared the opening, a shaft of sunlight flashed through the window, highlighting a diner seated on the other side of the car. Phut had seen the man before, as he had surveyed all of the dining car's inhabitants.

But now the flash of solar illumination afforded Phut a second chance to perceive him, this time less with his eyes than with the intuition of a sliced and slivered instant. Insight wriggled between Phut's vertebrae like a parasite, alerting him to a troubling kinship.

Phut took pains to conceal his reaction. He gazed aimlessly through the dining car. (As he would have been, absent this distraction: they now spoke of proposed reforms to the civil service and how they might be derailed.) In quick snatches, Phut took the measure of the alarming figure.

Unlike Phut, this diner did not, or could not, disguise his interest in his quarry. He gazed at Sir Russell with a frank relentlessness. Phut could not place his ancestry. He could pass for a national of any of the Mediterranean or Near Eastern lands. Yet something about his physiognomy contradicted that. Beady eyes glared out from beneath a thick ridge of bone. His jaws thrust forward, and there was something indefinably odd about the angle of his ears. Still, in contrast to Phut's, this man's ugliness was unremarkable. He looked somewhat brutish, but would not seem out of place in a souk or on a pier.

Here, in a luxury dining car, he seemed to regard himself as out of place. Bullets of sweat ran down his neck and soaked into his starched collar. He tapped uneasy fingers on the white tablecloth. His loin chop and potatoes sat all but uneaten on the plate in front of him. With hairy fingers he reached for his glass of white wine and downed it in a single gulp. The serveur materialized over his shoulder to refill it, startling him. He clutched reflexively for a bulging object concealed under his jacket, over his chest, then, as quickly, withdrew his hand.

Though Phut did not glimpse it directly, the man quite evidently carried a pistol.

Tickets on this train were expensive. This was not his world. He would have been sent. An agent of others.

His interest in Sir Russell might mark him only as a cat's-paw in the workaday schemes between nations. Sir Russell was meant to sweep a pawn from the board, to remove a small thorn from the foreign minister's side. This man could be working for him. That would be the parsimonious explanation.

Yet, Sir Russell's prophesied role meant that other possibilities had to be considered. Phut's people were not the only ones who meant to shape the nature of the next cycle. Phut had rescued Sir Russell many more than five times, from forces whose very existence eluded him. A man with a gun staring at him en route to Istanbul, on the brink of the alignment, might easily be a piece in the greater game.

Who he represented might or might not decide Phut's countermove. The train's confines limited options for attacker and defender alike. Still, as Phut waited, and studied, there was nothing to be lost by enumerating the possibilities. Phut had surprises sewn into the lining of his coat. If this man was of the cosmic battle, he might also wield unexpected weapons. It would be better to be ready than not.

Phut ruled him out as one of the sea people, those who yearned for a flooded aeon, with cities thrown up from the ocean floor and the seven continents sunk beneath the waves. A part of the gunman, he sensed, bore the blessing of inhuman blood, but those features were neither fishy nor frog-like.

Neither did his motions match those in the ninth planet's thrall. His muscles flowed properly, with no particular lag between thought and action. Phut had never heard of a possession by the clawed ones that would pass prolonged inspection in a well-lit location.

The gunman's evident volition also argued against other forms of possession, whether by sorcerers or by long-dead races welling up through the joins of time.

An answer nagged at him, as from behind a gauzy curtain. If he stopped trying to force the revelation, maybe it would come to him. He strove for calm, reminding himself that in time all would be revealed, and he would know what to do. The prophecy demanded it.

"Phut!" Sir Russell exclaimed.

Grimacing, he snapped his attention back to his master.

Sir Russell chuckled. "It's not like you to be lost in thought."

Phut positioned himself to keep the gunman at the periphery of his vision.

"All that talk of consciousness, was it? Had you daydreaming, did it? Some day I would like a complete accounting of your philosophy. A bracingly taciturn series of dicta, I wager."

Mimicking patience, Phut folded his hands and placed them in his lap. Whatever his point was, Sir Russell would return to it eventually.

"The festival of the dead we attended in Sarawak," Sir Russell said. "Was that a Dayak ceremony or Iban?"

"Iban," Phut said.

"And what did they call it? It's on the tip of my tongue."

"Gawai Antu," said Phut. In the details of that ceremony he had glimpsed hints of a forgotten treaty with the corpse-eaters. He had kept the observation, like so many others, to himself. Mustn't let the mask slip.

"To be honest, I've never been one for anthropology," said Stephens. "Even a Morris dance arouses in me an inexplicable revulsion. As if we're half-remembering things we rather ought to forget."

"You lack adventurous spirit, Stephens, and always have."

"I'll toast to that."

A dining partner joined the gunman. Phut tensed. The strap of a shoulder holster made itself barely visible beneath the man's thin suit jacket, which was at least a size too small for him. Dark hairs jutted from his collar, running all the way up to the hairline. The ears, too, matched the first gunman's. They might be brothers. Or the spawn of the same nest.

Two adversaries multiplied the complications. One might draw him off, leaving the other to ambush Sir Russell. It might be time to alert him to the danger. But if they were players of the cosmic game, that risked much. Phut had invested too much in the cultivation of his master's ignorance to let him see the real battle now.

He reached into his jacket's false lining for a leather pouch. Carefully counting the number of beads sewn onto the pouch's surface, he confirmed it as the one containing the green lotus powder. Phut hopped down from his chair, replacing its extra cushion, and weaved down the aisle between tables toward the WC. The gunman watched him approach, kicking his companion under the table to alert him. In a show of contemptible amateurism, each let his hand hover near his jacket lapel, ready to thrust in and grab his gun.

Phut maintained his dead expression as he drew alongside their table. He covertly flicked his fingers, now coated with the green powder, to which he had long ago built up an immunity. He continued along to the WC. Once inside, he closed the door, performed his necessaries, and then exited, weaving his hasty way back to Sir Russell's table. The gunmen were still in place, engaged in a *sotto voce* argument too quiet for Phut to discern. A bruise-like rash already spread across the first gunman's wrist.

Phut retook his seat as the serveur asked Stephens and Sir Russell for their pudding orders. He declined the offer of sweets; Stephens chose vanilla ice cream; Sir Russell, a lemon tart. The serveur moved off, allowing Phut a clear view of the gunman's table. His victim's skin assumed an ashen tone. The skin below his eyes drooped, revealing red rims. He trembled, heaved, and then was up the aisle, rushing for the WC. Moments after he stepped inside, the unmistakable sound of copious vomiting emanated through the dining car. Serveurs and the *chef de brigade* gathered in dismay outside the door. They surveyed the discomfited diners, several of whom grew visibly nauseated.

The rest depended on the standard of the service, which Phut knew to be supreme. As expected, the *chef de brigade* waited for a break in the emesis and tapped firmly on the door. It opened; two serveurs escorted the would-be gunman, a linen napkin held over his mouth, down the aisle and out of the dining car. The gunman's worried companion followed, snarling at Phut as he passed. Phut hopped down, thinking that there was something not quite right about the interior of the man's mouth.

As expected, the serveurs ushered the sickened gunman to the WC in the adjoining baggage car, where the sounds of his distress would not further disturb the guests. Phut waited at the threshold between cars. About now an acrid stench would be wafting from the poisoned man's pores. He peered in—yes, the serveurs and the crewmembers who'd been sleeping in the baggage car's berth were exiting the car at the other end, to the fourgon beyond. Their exodus left only the second gunman by the WC door, hand over mouth, color draining from his face.

Phut slipped into the car and pressed himself against a luggage rack. The entire length of the car separated him from his enemies. After fishing into his pockets for the weapon he would need, he hauled himself into the lower rack, squeezing his diminutive frame into the foot or so of clearance between its suitcases and the shelf above. He wriggled atop the nearly even row of suitcases, sweating and wincing, crawling by inches toward the foe.

The gunman sniffed the air; his head swiveled to Phut's location. Phut muttered a curse in the ancient tongue as the man slowly advanced, revolver ready.

How reluctant would he be to fire? Shots fired now would draw opposition. The two of them would be killed or captured before they had the opportunity to complete their assignment. But men with guns in their hands could not be counted on to reason well. The attacker's darting looks and queasy pallor afforded scant confidence.

Phut let him draw nearer before firing his blowgun. The dart landed true, in his target's bulging jugular. The gunman clapped at the dart with his free hand, letting his weapon-arm fall to his side. He pulled out the dart, squinted at it, and goggled in panicked recognition. Phut waited; it would take a few seconds for him to collapse.

This the gunman did not do. He stumbled back, dizzy, but did not fall. His partial resistance to the toxin confirmed Phut's suspicion: not all of him was human.

From the WC behind him, his confederate loosed another awful heave, followed by a rush of splashing.

The attacker lifted his gun-arm, pointing wildly at the upper luggage rack. Phut crawled free of the suitcases and thumped into the aisle. Without stopping to regain his footing, he barreled at his opponent. The gunman was twice Phut's size. Surprise, and whatever toll the toxin was taking on him, would have to compensate. Drawing a small, curved blade, Phut reached up to slash at his enemy's weapon hand. The gun hit the floor and bounced. The gunman stared at his slashed wrist, roared, and clouted his adversary with the back of his other hand. Phut slid back, banging his skull on the luggage rack. The gunman kicked at him; Phut ducked below his swinging leg and cut the Achilles tendon. With a groan the man slid to the floor.

Phut leapt on him with the knife; the attacker grabbed his forearm and squeezed. He drew Phut's arm, still holding the blade, toward his mouth. His protuberant jaws transformed, extending themselves farther, exposing absurdly large, yellow teeth. Phut glimpsed inch-long canines just before they sank into the meat of his forearm. Seizing the knife with his free hand, he punched it down into the gunman's eye. After a moment of resistance, the blade piercing through bone to enter the brain, he twisted it. The gunman's jaws relaxed as he shuddered and died. Phut pulled his arm free and reeled over to the pistol, jamming it into his belt with his good hand. He drew a second, matching knife from the lining of his jacket and made his way to the WC.

He tested the door, found it unlatched, and kicked it open. The second attacker lifted his head out of the toilet bowl. Phut first attacked what he could easily reach: in turn, he severed each of the man's ankle tendons. He dropped the knife, pulled the gun and thrust it into the sickened man's open, protesting mouth. Like his comrade's, this, too, was endowed with the massive teeth of a gorilla. Phut pushed the gun deeper into his throat, to best muffle the sound of the coming shot, and pulled the trigger.

He checked the corpse for an exit wound, confirming that his careful angling of the barrel had ensured that there was none. This would aid the clean-up considerably. Only a thick dribble of blood escaped the side of his victim's jaw. None had sprayed onto the walls, or onto Phut.

His bitten arm throbbing, Phut exited the WC and removed a

steamer trunk from the luggage rack. He used it to bar the door to the adjacent fourgon. Then he stumbled down the aisle to do the same at the opposite door. When this was done, he removed his jacket and stripped off his shirt to examine the bite. It consisted of four deep punctures connected by rows of bruises where the front teeth had dented but not pierced the skin. If the bite of an ape-man was anything like that of an ordinary ape, the saliva would carry all manner of deadly infection. From his jacket Phut fished out the pouch containing powder of the red frond and poured it liberally onto the wounds. It hissed efficaciously. As he let it work, he poked open the lips of his first victim to examine those curious teeth.

Phut remembered now the rumors of a city of white apes. In the Belgian Congo, was it? French Africa? Whichever it was, Sir Russell had been there, and alluded to trouble, trouble so curious Phut's meager brain was not meant to encompass it. Sir Russell's account accorded with certain whisperings. These had it that there were men throughout the world who did not know they were not entirely men, that they descended from the residents of the city. As far as Phut had heard, they played no role in the cosmic game. It was not impossible that they were entering the contest now, when it was surely too late. More likely, their designs on Sir Russell arose from a completely separate affair. Revenge for whatever Sir Russell did to them in Africa, decades before Phut had found him.

Perhaps he might spur his master to reminiscence on his past activities in Africa.

Phut teased open the jacket compartment containing his emergency first aid supplies. With needle and thread he puckered the four wounds shut, wrapped a gauze bandage around his forearm, then clipped it shut. Given the potency of the red frond distillate, he anticipated limited seepage.

Straining against the dead weight, he dragged his second victim by the heels into the aisle, to rest atop the first. Working quickly, slashing at the fabric with his knife as needed, he stripped the corpses of clothing, gun-belts, and other possessions. These he rolled up and tossed from the baggage car window. Then he sprinkled them with salts of Leng, taken from another of his pouches. After a few seconds, these azure crystals catalyzed with the tissues of the slain men. Skin blackened and flaked. Muscle bubbled and liquefied. Organs evaporated into a vapor, at first red and later yellow. Bones crumbled into a paste that in turn became a dust. After a few minutes, only tangled orange strings of organic matter remained. These were the nerve networks, which for elusive reasons the salts of Leng could not fully break down. Phut gathered up the strands, rolling them into a gummy ball. It, too, he ejected from the fourgon window.

A banging came at the door. The *chef de brigade* shouted, first in French, then in English, inquiring after the sickened man. Phut yelled back, in Han Chinese, to confuse him for a while. With a second repair kit—this for tailoring problems—he crudely closed the holes in his jacket sleeve. He put his shirt back on, then the jacket.

The spot where the Leng salts had devoured the remains of the two men was now marked only by a clear, damp stain, as if water had recently been spilled there. Phut went to the door no one was knocking on and removed the steamer trunk blocking it. He then did the same at the far door.

His sudden appearance flustered the *chef de brigade*. The man asked him what had happened to the two men. Phut pointed to the door. In response to the further, obvious questions, Phut gave him only a series of shrugs, the incomprehension of a stupid foreigner.

In the end, Sir Russell was drawn in, and Stephens, too. The brigadier-postier, in charge of the baggage cars, had his own questions to ask, and then the conductor went through it all again. Phut eventually allowed Sir Russell to pull from him a simple tale—that he'd gone to offer a native remedy, only to find the two men leaping from the train.

"He is a dab hand with the remedies, I can attest to that," Sir Russell chimed.

As to their reasons for fleeing the train, Phut took care not to venture so much as a guess. He shrugged, as if the motivations of all save himself were irredeemably cryptic. Eventually the inquiry lost impetus for lack of new questions. Sir Russell, Stephens, and the conductor all agreed that there was something awfully rum about those fellows, and that what they had been up to might never be known. An Italian army colonel on leave intervened in the discussion to say that he thought one or both of the men wore shoulder holsters. Sir Russell proposed that they must have been bandits, that the one man's sickness resulted from nerves, and that they had risked injury over discovery. The authority of his reconstruction carried, and the colloquy broke up. Sir Russell returned with Stephens to their table for a round of cognacs, Phut trailing behind them. Uncharacteristically, Phut signaled his desire for a drink.

"Cognac, Phut? This is a day of wonders." Sir Russell nodded to the serveur, indicating his assent to his manservant's order.

When the drink came and Phut brought the glass to his lips, he saw that his hand trembled. He reminded himself that, if the calculations were to be trusted, only a few weeks of this remained. Sir Russell would be diverted from his petty game in Istanbul, then conveyed to Urfa to be inducted into the great one.

As *aqol-pazh*, he could only be an unwilling participant in what was to come. It would hardly console him to understand that, of the possible outcomes of the dawning alignment, the one Phut pursued was the most amenable to human goals. If Phut's people won the reconfiguration, there would still be humans—of a sort. That Sir Russell would take such a long view was not to be expected. To attempt to impose this perspective upon him would, Phut had decided, constitute a cruelty. The Englishman's ordeal could not be softened, but there was no call to gratuitously worsen it.

It was Phut, as the one who knew him best—as the *aqol-aqol*—who would have to mete out the torments. After geometrically precise placement on the altar beneath the hidden ruins, Sir Russell would receive the lunar salve, to keep him conscious and fully sensate throughout the rites of disassembly. He would be pumped with the milk of the black earth goddess, to preserve his life far past the threshold of ordinary endurance. Then the ceremony proper would commence. Over the first five days his skin would be slowly teased from his body, the muscles beneath packed with Dead Sea salt to amplify the agony. Then would come the five days of bone removal—the left foot, the left hand, the right foot, the right hand. The flautists would be summoned to feast then on his pain. Finally, the last five grueling hours, for which Phut had prepared since the cradle yet still regarded with faint apprehension. Every flick of the scalpel demanded unswerving precision. Yet, however great the rigors of his task, Phut was certain he could accomplish it.

There was no choice. The other outcomes were without exception too appalling to entertain. Yet in a way the prevision of Sir Russell's fate disturbed him.

Despite all, he was coming to like the man.

ENGINEERED
ARI MARMELL

ONE LONELY DROP IN A torrent of humanity, I boarded the train from the Gare de Lyon. That station is among the finest in Paris, but with eyelids heavy and luggage dragging behind me, I was in no position to appreciate it. Exhausted as I was, I'd scarcely even noted the magnificent arches, the soaring clock tower; nor had I allotted any time to seeing the sights of Paris. This was hardly my first experience of that city, but on any other visit I'd have taken an evening or two.

Not this time. Too many travels yet ahead of me.

For all my preoccupation, though, I couldn't suppress the tiniest frisson of excitement at the sight of the rich blue and gleaming gold of the sleeper cars, the sharp uniforms of the staff, and, of course, the name itself, emblazoned proudly for all to see.

If I must spend more time aboard a train, I could at least take solace in the comforts and luxuries offered by the renowned Orient Express.

"Might I assist with your baggage, sir?"

A hint of an Eastern European accent drew my attention to a dark-haired, thickly moustachioed fellow in a porter's cap and vest. I was fairly sure I could place said accent as Bulgarian, although that particular region has never been one of my specialties.

"Second car," I told him, fumbling at my ticket to assist my fatigued memory. "Room, ah, seven."

With a "Very good, sir" and a tip of the cap, the porter hefted my ponderous trunk as though it weighed nothing and set off down the corridor that ran along one side of the train. Allowing myself a much more leisurely pace, I followed.

It took little time to settle, as the bed was already folded shut, transforming the room into a tiny study. Everything was neat, squared away, ready for use. As I required.

Also as I *preferred*. I can't abide untidiness. Or at least, at the time, I couldn't.

I rested my eyes, leaning back in my chair, until the train was on its way. The world shuddered and clacked and swayed, by now a most familiar sensation. Doors thumped opened and shut, I heard the sound of passengers assembling and conversing as they waited to be ushered into the dining car, and I knew I must be about my work.

In a procedure now as automatic as fastening my own tie, I snapped open the trunk and removed the familiar bundle of maps and papers. In the same order as a dozen times before, I began to spread them out across the minuscule desk, and once again resumed the Sisyphean task of pinpointing one man in the whole of the continent.

I'd not bothered to do any further investigating in Paris, even though one of his last telegrams had originated there. Some of his *earliest* communications had come from there, as well, and I had already made three separate attempts at tracking him down in that city. The *gendarmes* were, I am certain, well and truly sick of my inquiries.

Paris. Liverpool. Budapest. Salzburg. Odense. Warsaw. Nantes. Berlin. Venice. And dozens more. They glared at me, mocked me, from the envelopes, the telegrams, and from the map where I studiously marked them all. As I had so many times before—so often my nail had left imprints in the map—I attempted to trace any route that made sense. As I had so many times before, I gave up in searing frustration. Some cities appeared but once; some two, three, even up to five times, at wildly differing dates. A contact from Strasburg might be followed by one from Sofia, very nearly across the continent, and then one from Zurich—less than a day's journey from

Strasburg! If there were any pattern to his movements, or any schedule to his communications . . .

Well, I could no longer deny it, for all that I'd spent weeks
avoiding this conclusion. There *was* no pattern here. No logic.
Whatever mad theories he pursued, his movements offered up no
discernable clue. To judge by the deteriorating contents of his mes-
sages, there was little even remaining of Harold that *could* aspire
to logical behavior.

I began to meticulously unfold the first of those letters, already
so worn from countless re-readings that it threatened to come
apart entirely.

Said task was interrupted by a voice from the doorway. "Your
pardon, Mister S———. I just wished to see if you require anything.
Assistance in folding your bed down for the night, perhaps?"

You'll have to forgive my decision to conceal my family name,
hackneyed as you may find it. I do not much care, at this point, what
people read or think of me; I've no standing or career remaining to
damage. My brother, however, deserves to be remembered as the
kind soul and mechanical genius he was, rather than—but I get
ahead of myself.

The speaker at the doorway was that same porter, the Eastern
European. He had not knocked, nor was this the first time he had
appeared, unsolicited, to inquire whether I needed anything. A man
doing his duty is one thing, but this had grown tiresome.

"*If* I need anything," I told him—somewhat coldly, I admit, "I
am perfectly capable of seeking you out." *Or one of your compatriots,
more probably!* I thought, but did not add.

He said nothing more, merely tipped his hat and departed,
though he did have the grace to shut the door behind him.

Again I started to open that letter, but I found myself in no state
of mind to face Harold's deterioration. With a muttered curse that
would have been dreadfully rude in anyone else's presence, I rose
to stretch my legs and perhaps have a spot of supper.

Once ensconced in the dining car, I lingered over my meal, a
remarkable pheasant prepared in a thick red wine reduction that
would not have been out of place in any Parisian restaurant. After
that, of course, nothing would do but a small snifter of brandy,
and after *that*, a nervous energy had me pacing the train for some

few hours. We had departed Stuttgart before I finally returned to my room.

Someone else had gotten there first.

I've developed something of an eye for detail during my genealogical researches, but I believe I've made it pretty clear how fatigued and distracted I was at the time. So I will note without undue embarrassment that, once I had settled in and taken my seat, it took me a few moments to realize that my stacks of letters had been knocked slightly askew, my notes disturbed, my map improperly folded.

To say I was enraged would be severe understatement. I shot back to my feet, nearly upsetting my papers far worse than the mysterious intruder had done. I confess that my first suspicions all pointed to that steward who had been so overly—let us, for the sake of decorum, say *solicitous*. I would very probably have confronted the fellow, had my search for him not been interrupted nearly the instant it began.

"You are Herr S——, *ja*? Timothy S——?"

One hardly required any depth of expertise to identify *that* accent.

My new acquaintance stood in the doorway to my private room, which at this juncture felt rather less than private. He was tall, thin of features and of hair, wrapped in a long coat. His hat and shoes were meticulously cared for, despite being of a flagrantly inexpensive make.

One wondered how he could afford to set foot on the Orient Express.

"Perhaps you ought to identify yourself first," I growled, "seeing as how you are the man currently invading my private space."

A curt nod, and then he displayed a badge of a sort I'd seen before but could not immediately place.

"Ritzler," he announced. "Detective Otto Ritzler, Bavarian *Kriminalpolizei*."

I acknowledged then that I was indeed who he believed me to be.

"You should collect your belongings, *mein herr*. You will be disembarking in Munich."

"You're mistaken," I replied. Honestly, I strongly suspected he intended to offer me no choice, but my pride—and my distaste for having my schedule disrupted—demanded a protest. "I've paid for passage through Istanbul."

"*Nein*. Even were I personally inclined to allow it, many *polizei* of many nations watch for you. As neither Bulgaria nor Turkey are signatories of the International Criminal Police Commission, you would never be allowed to pass beyond Budapest. As it was I who found you, you'll be disembarking within my country's own borders. No, *mein herr*. Munich is as far as you go."

The notion of fighting never even crossed my mind. I am not a violent man, and I certainly wasn't about to engage in fisticuffs with an officer of the law. Instead I merely slumped back into the chair. Ritzler took the opportunity to step fully into the chamber, leaning against the wall opposite me and lighting a cheap cigarette.

"Would you at least be so kind as to tell me," I asked him, "what this is about?"

He offered me a sneer that, in my experience, only Germans and Austrians can manage. "You pretend not to know this?"

"I do not pretend. I honestly don't know."

He studied me for a time, then—as I was beginning to feel less suspect than specimen—he spoke. Possibly he believed me, though I think it more likely he humored me, hoping to learn something.

He glanced at the door—I assume confirming that it remained shut. "You are aware of the threats your brother has made against the railroads?"

I'd known it was foolish to imagine he was here for any other reason, but still, I'd hoped that this wasn't the cause of his intrusion.

I winced to confirm any suspicions of Harold, but as Ritzler had already sifted through my papers, he'd probably know if I lied. "Surely the railroads receive any number of threats from people: unsatisfied customers, partisans of hostile countries."

He glared at me as though I were the worst sort of imbecile, and I cannot say I blamed him.

You must understand, Harold was a man heavily involved with the expansion of the railroads across the continent. His specialties included—but no. As I stated earlier, I would prefer not to offer any means of decisively identifying him. Suffice to say, if you have taken passage on a train in Western Europe since the turn of the century, the odds are high that you passed through or crossed over a route to which he contributed.

Ritzler knew all that, as he proved when he finally spoke again. "Your brother, unlike any random instigator or criminal, knows precisely how to carry out any threats he might make.

"Last year," the detective continued, "his behavior turned eccentric, *ja*? Public outbursts. Visits to the boards and investors of multiple railroads, first to request, and then to demand that travel along certain lines be halted. *Und* from there, threats to interrupt the lines himself if no one else would stop their use. With this, too, you are familiar?"

Again, he already knew the answer. Harold's letters and telegrams would have confirmed everything the police had already learned. They clearly showcased his deterioration, from the earliest missives, in which he eloquently if vaguely expressed his growing doubt as to the wisdom of so intricate a transportation network, to the last, written in fragments, declaring his intentions to protect us all from the "arrogant, blasphemous miscalculations" for which he held himself and his compatriots responsible.

It was during this apparent breakdown of his faculties that he had done his seemingly random traveling, crisscrossing the continent time and again before ceasing all contact. Utterly disappearing, for all intents, and prompting me to begin my search for him.

Ritzler leaned abruptly forward, perhaps trying to startle me. If so, he failed. "Such behavior would appear suspicious at any time, but now? In the months leading up to, and then including your brother's odd behavior, the number of missing persons reported along the major lines has increased. Measurably, throughout multiple countries."

I hadn't heard that, and it worried me that I hadn't. Was I so focused on my task that I was missing important details?

Ritzler was still talking. "Even if we leave aside the immediate damage your brother is capable of inflicting, consider today's political climate. Sabotage at the wrong place, at the wrong time, could instigate open war. Do you wonder why we are so determined to locate him?"

"No. No, of course not."

"Then you cannot possibly wonder that it might attract official interest when the man's younger brother suddenly behaves in a similarly alarming fashion—crossing borders and making stops along the railway at seemingly random intervals. What are you two involved in, Herr S——? What do you plan?"

It was my turn, now, to lean forward, hoping to emphasize the point. "Detective, my movements appear random as my brother's because I'm searching for him. I can make no more rhyme or reason of his trail than you. Besides, my background is in history and ethnology. Even if I wanted to sabotage a train, I'd barely know where to begin!"

"So you say." The detective shifted against the wall, trying on a more comfortable posture, and stubbed out his half-smoked cigarette. "Assuming this is true," he continued, clearly assuming nothing of the sort, "then your detention by the *Kriminalpolizei* should prove brief. For now, though, you *will* be disembarking with me, so I suggest, again, that you gather your belongings. We would not wish you to leave evidence behind, *ja?*"

Aggravated but lacking in options, I complied, opening my trunk and then reaching for the papers he'd so clumsily manhandled. Ritzler's eyes were on me; mine were on the documents I was scooping into my arms. So when the door to my room flew wide yet again, we were both equally startled.

"I'm afraid I must insist that this passenger be permitted to reach his ticketed destination."

It was that same porter yet again. This time, however, while his expression remained as solicitous as ever, the squat revolver in his fist suggested that he might not be in as considerate a state of mind. He was also not alone. Half-concealed by shadows in the hall behind him stood a second man in identical uniform. He wasn't armed, so far as I could see, but his presence held a suggestion of menace.

Ritzler tensed, and I saw his hand dart into his coat, but he clearly thought better of the notion—and wisely so, in the face of the porter's pistol. He settled, instead, for a vicious scowl.

"I am an officer of the Bavarian *Kriminalpolizei!*" he snapped. "Do you understand what you interfere with?"

"If you will kindly join me in the next room," the porter replied, "you can explain it to me in all the detail you wish. In the meantime, however, we must leave these gentlemen alone to talk."

The German radiated frustration, but again, knew better than to argue with the revolver.

"Do not fret, Herr Detective." It was the second porter who spoke now. "You'll not be returning home empty handed."

I failed to note Ritzler's reaction to that curious pronouncement. I was too busy reeling, almost stunned, at the sound of that voice.

He was far thinner than I remembered, sunken, even sickly. Although his face was clean-shaven and his hair neatly trimmed, there was something haggard about him. It was in his stance, in his expression, even if no longer in his upkeep.

"My God, Harold!" I could barely choke the words out, giving him plenty of time to slip inside and shut the door. "How can. . . ? You. . . ?"

I might have stammered on—however unlike me, though, the reaction was—had my brother not fiercely slammed both fists on the desk. The gesture shocked me back into silence.

"Why are you here?" he demanded, voice wavering as it struggled to break into a genuine shout. "God damn it, Timothy, I warned you! I told you very specifically *not* to come searching. Did you think I—?"

By then, my brain was working again.

"I received no such message. I heard from you often, month after month, chronicling your travels and your . . . concerns—and then nothing."

I swear that Harold grew paler than the paper of his letters. "Nothing? Not one warning?"

"Not a one."

"I sent five. By telegram and post. God . . . it knew. It wouldn't permit my cautions to reach you. Only my earlier writing, only what might draw you in. . . ."

I rose from my chair and guided him to it. Only when he was seated, and I had taken his—and Ritzler's—former spot against the opposite wall, did I say anything more.

"Harold, for Heaven's sake, speak clearly! You're raving as wildly as in your last letters! If you require a doctor—"

My brother's laugh seemed mad enough to belie the shake of his head. "No, Timothy. My problem is not one that medicine can address.

"People disappear from the trains," he said softly, after a minute. "All across Europe, and I would assume beyond."

"People disappear everywhere," I replied. "Foul play. Accidents. Or they're hiding from their former lives. It's hardly—"

"Oh, spare me! Do you think me ignorant of that fact? Mine was precisely the same reaction, when I first heard mutters spreading amongst the railroads' upper echelons. It was clearly nonsense! Just standard misfortunes, blown out of proportion by the rumor mill.

"But the stories grew stranger. Whispers of men vanishing between the train and the street outside the station. Entire sleeping cars hired out by peculiar groups, who greatly disturbed the other passengers even with minimal contact. Cars from which railroad staff swore they overheard strange, pagan chants! On one particular occasion—you won't have heard of this, it was kept from the papers—an entire train disappeared for almost two days! It simply wasn't on its track anymore, and then it was again."

"That's hogwash, Harold! You can't believe it."

"I didn't at the time, no. But all of it together? I figured it wouldn't hurt to look into it. Nobody else seemed to be."

"That was when you began your travels," I hazarded.

"Indeed. I won't tell you precisely who my sources were, in my search. You would find the very idea disturbing. But I *did* begin to figure some things out. I—How's your geography?"

Taken aback a bit at the nonsequitur, it took me a moment to reply. "Fairly good. When one's studying history and—"

"Yes, good. Picture a map of the continent."

I actually had a map of the continent, but I had put it away while packing under Ritzler's orders, and it didn't seem worth the effort of retrieving if memory would serve as well. "Right, yes."

"Good. Now, suppose a man were to travel from Zurich to Berlin."

"Very well."

"Then Berlin to Vienna."

"Seems a bit out of the way," I commented.

Harold scowled, but continued. "Vienna to Luxembourg. Luxembourg to Krakow. And from there back to Zurich. What do you see?"

I struggled, trying to view it all in my head. Finally, "A very rough, uneven—oh, you can't be serious?!"

"Of course not!" he insisted. "The pentagram is far too simple a glyph to actually mean anything, religious beliefs notwithstanding. I use it to illustrate my point only. But we sketch more complicated sigils every day, and never even know it. Yes, most travelers go from here to there, and that's the end of it, but those whose journeys are far longer? How many roads have run across the face of Europe for thousands of years? How many trains, today? Between how many stops, including towns and tributary lines you've never heard of?

"Those form patterns! Unseen by most human eyes, incomprehensible to human minds, consisting of shapes and geometries unlike any we have discovered, but patterns nonetheless! And patterns hold power!"

"Harold, you're not well. Come home. We'll get this mess with the police cleared up, and—"

"I tried to convince them to shut down some of the lines, at least until we could puzzle through. Then I thought I might make them! But I can't. It's too late. *It* won't allow me to, even if *they* would."

It was horrifying, and not a little depressing, seeing my brilliant sibling reduced to this. I began to speak again, but he was not finished.

After a deep breath to calm himself, he said, "There are others. Men and women who have come to understand as I do. Some have even seen more proof than I. The more superstitious-minded of them believe humanity has called to something. That the unseen patterns in the roads and rails—and the wires, the trails people walk from home to car to boat, and so much more—sang out to senses we cannot begin to imagine. And that something heard us."

"God, Harold!"

It was nonsensical, ludicrous. And yet . . .

People were disappearing, along stretches of the railroad connected only by the fact that they *were* along the railroad. Something had kept Harold's warnings from reaching me. Had it been only one note, I'd have said it was lost in the mail, but multiple?

"It could well be a human intelligence, though," I muttered. "A conspiracy of some sort. With war possibly looming . . ."

I didn't even need to look at him to imagine his expression; I probably wore one much like it. No, that made no sense either. A conspiracy to do what? Abduct random people and make a few lunatics believe a monster did it? To what possible end?

I was certain I must be slipping into my brother's delusion. Sane or not, though, my mind had grabbed hold of his logic's track. There was nothing to do but follow it to its conclusion.

"Why now?" I asked, thinking aloud. "Assuming there's any truth to what you say, if mankind *were* able to call on—demons or spirits or what have you—via accidental patterns, surely it should have happened long ago. The railroad can't possibly offer any patterns that roads and paths haven't."

Harold nodded approvingly, as he'd done in our childhood when he'd managed to help me understand some mathematical conundrum. "Right. And so?"

"Something to do with the technology itself?"

Again he nodded, and again my mind tore off down this new track, seeking connections I'd never thought of before.

I had always viewed scientific progress as a good thing. Something to make the world better. More comprehensible. More orderly.

Was it only that, though? Mankind was acquiring new knowledge, new technologies, faster than we knew what to do with them. Europe was poised on the brink of war, despite our 'War to End All Wars,' in part because our many advancements had made killing *too easy*. The world was shrinking, shoving civilized man and savage together, each alien to the other, and in almost every instance the result was hatred and violence!

Progress was orderly, progress followed patterns. Yet in the end, what did it bring into the world? Chaos. Entropy.

I shook my head, even forced a laugh. Clearly Harold had gotten to me. Yes, I could see how it all made a twisted sense, but still it was only the raving theory of a diseased mind.

"You're suggesting," I said eventually, hoping I'd misunderstood it all, "that it was the clash of order and chaos intrinsic to progress itself that called to this entity?"

"Who can say? Perhaps we called to it. Or perhaps we *created* it!" He was beginning to lose his composure. His voice shook, his jaw trembled. "In either case, it is here now! The railroads are its veins, the telegraph and telephone wires its synapses! We gave life to the pattern, and we gave it thought, and now it sees us! *It sees us!*"

Brakes squealed a banshee's cry, and the entire car shuddered. We had reached Munich.

"We've no more time!" Harold shouted. "If we hold Rintzler beyond his stop, if the German police believe something's happened to him, it'll only bring further troubles down on us later. I wish I could have spared you this, that my warnings had gotten through. But they did not, and you have traveled long enough in searching for me that you, too, may now well be part of it.

"*Listen!* Svetomir will take care of you until you've adjusted. He and I have become close. *Do not stop moving.* Do not leave the train unless you must, and then only briefly. Once a man has become part of the pattern, it takes note of him far more readily when he breaks it. Not immediately, not always; sometimes we have moments, sometimes days, but never, I think, any longer than that."

The whites of his eyes burning with their own light, he rose. "Be well, Timothy."

I felt more than dizzy, as though my body were running a fever to ward off my brother's madness. "What . . . what are you—?"

"It's my fault you're here. I can, at least, spare you an even worse fate."

He pulled the door shut behind him, and I heard something click. He'd locked me in!

This being my room, I obviously had my own key, but it took me a moment of fumbling to find it. By then the hallways were bustling with passengers departing or boarding. Of my brother—or, for that matter, Detective Ritzler—I found no sign. The porter, however, whom I now presumed to be Svetomir, found me in the crowd.

"Where are they?" I demanded before he could utter a word.

"Did Harold not explain?" he asked sadly. "He agreed to place himself in the detective's custody, if you would be left alone. Ritzler may certainly renege in the future, but for now, as Harold is the man the railroads consider the true threat—"

I shouted something at him, though I've no recollection of what, and was already shoving my way through the throng. Down the steps, knocking over baggage and elbowing disembarking passengers, utterly oblivious to the shouts and remonstrations I must surely have evoked. Steps to platform, platform to lobby. Where space opened up for even a few paces, I ran; where it did not, I continued bulling through by sheer force.

I wonder now what sort of sigil my haphazard course might have etched across the crowd.

In such chaos, in such a throng—and in a structure with so many exits—I should never have found them. Through chance or fate, however, I spotted them atop a set of squat, broad stairs. They were passing through the station doors at the very instant my brother was *noticed*.

I've no idea what Detective Rintzler saw. I know only that, when I departed, he was collapsed in the doorway. Before the concerned citizens gathered about him, I saw the glazed and empty stare of what, at best, must have been catatonic shock.

Nobody else, of all the myriad men and women whose business took them to or from the station that night, appeared to have seen anything out of the ordinary. They reacted not one whit, save to the fainting policeman; their oblivious, uncaring faces were a hideous counterpoint to the scene through which they passed.

Perhaps it was too drastically removed from their own patterns for them to recognize.

I can only describe what I, myself, saw. Or what, at any rate, I *think* I saw.

From the grumbling and growling traffic in the street beyond, a motorcar pulled up to the curb nearest Harold and his unwelcome companion. It was no make with which I was familiar, in a metallic hue some vague point between silver and steel. By the reactions of everyone around, it was just another vehicle, a driver arriving to collect a fare.

I, however, saw something else entirely. Much is lost to me. Although I'm certain I saw it quite clearly, I couldn't begin to say what drove the vehicle—only that it was by no means a man! I'm not entirely certain whatever it was didn't sprout from the car itself.

I have but a moment of clear memory, and I can only hope it was more hallucination than truth.

The rear door swung wide, stretching a thin membrane that

appeared to connect it to the car. Within, a gaping maw of darkness, a void that seemed to fall away forever. Only sporadically, when the lights flickered just so, could I make out any more, and nothingness would have been preferable. A slick palpitation, easily missed, suggested some great orifice, flexing, swallowing. Protruding through that split, black flesh, if flesh it was, were an array of . . . tarnished iron teeth? Gears? I couldn't tell, knew only that they appeared to rotate, tearing with each revolution, dripping fluids organic and chemical, grinding against unseen obstructions.

And Harold. His posture stiff as any corpse's, his hands held before him—palms upward, as some reluctant supplicant—Harold strode right up and *fed* himself to it, allowing those rotating jags and half-seen limbs to haul him inside. The door slammed behind him and the car was gone, just another part of the nighttime traffic.

I said nothing to Svetomir as I slouched back aboard the Orient Express, nor he to me. He merely guided me, an arm around my shoulders, to the private room I had taken. There, sitting folded upon the tiny table, was a porter's uniform.

I knew precisely what it meant: *Do not leave the train.*

Slowly, I removed my coat. I gazed at it a long moment, turned to hang it up—and then dropped it to lie crumpled on the floor. I threw open my trunk, reached inside, and many of my possessions followed the coat. Toiletries. Clothing. Letters.

I wanted no neatness around me, no order. Not anymore.

Only then did I reach for the waiting uniform.

"One of Harold's," Svetomir said then. "It should serve well enough until we can acquire some more properly fitted to you. It is an unrewarding position, but it gives you reason to be here, and that is paramount. We will ensure that all the necessary paperwork and forms are on file. Nobody of import should notice anything amiss about you."

I nodded dully. It sounded to me an unpleasant life, eternal service and drudgery—even if I could restrict myself to more luxurious lines such as the Orient Express—but after what had been done to Harold. . . .

Yes. Done *to* him. You see, as that one terrible memory grows slowly clearer, I have come to realize that I misspoke when I said he "allowed" himself to be taken. In that last moment before he vanished into that monstrous thing that was no car, through blurring eyes and broken nerves, I would have sworn I saw cables, wires, ripping through his skin like veins given life, reaching upward into the impenetrable dark, where some malevolence *steered him*, limb by limb, a living marionette, to whatever nightmarish, unfathomable hell awaits us all outside the pattern.

BLACK CAT OF THE ORIENT
Lucien Soulban

THE AGENT'S SMILE NEVER WAVERED, not when Jack Andrews pushed the leather folder back across the table with a "no thanks," and not when the black-haired man tilted the folder open to flash him the banknotes. The powder-blue print, stamp, and signature marked it as Banque de France tender, and the five hundred-franc stencil made Jack hesitate. A flash, and the notes vanished under the leather cover, too fast for the other tables to see. The agent's crooked smile widened under those wire-framed spectacles, and he echoed Andrew's thought.

"*Oui*, it is a small fortune for a man in your—" he looked at the stained and aging bricks of the basement pub before concluding "—position."

"I was going to say you got some kind of brass, flashing that much money in here." Nobody else seemed to notice, though. The other patrons sat with stooped shoulders, trying to auger something in their beers. The strangled light from the gaslamps on the walls kept the meeting to a comfortable anonymity and the man closest to them slept face down on his table, a thin line of spittle pooling on the wood.

"I didn't catch your name," Jack said. He reached for his cork pipe in the ashtray, willing his hand to sobriety calm, but the whiskey tremors rattled his fingertips and his tongue rasped in his dry mouth. In the distance, the war drums pounded in his head. Soon they'd reach the gates of his temples.

It's been too long. A couple of hours at least since my last swig, he reflected.

"Monsieur Henri du Lac."

"All right, so, Henry," Jack said, sucking on the pipe and drawing in a calming measure of the earthy smoke. "This isn't a good idea and let me tell you why. The money's pretty and all, and I am partial to blue, but, I'm a bit of a—"

"Bad luck charm?" Henri concluded. "A black cat, yes?" He pulled something out from his striped jacket's pocket and dangled a rabbit's foot at the end of a silver chain. "I am prepared."

Jack had to laugh, and yet Henri disquieted him with his gaze scalpel-like under those spectacles. A man like that, Jack suspected, always noticed the details, including the ones you kept buried. "Like I said: brass. So what would a gent like yourself want with the likes of me?"

"To hire you, of course."

"Nah," Jack said, pushing away from the table. "I wouldn't feel right, robbing you like that. You go on and find yourself a better breed of bad luck."

"I've already hired them, Mister Andrews. Black cats like yourself whose brush with the unknown has turned them into magnets for the supernatural. None of them, however, have your penchant for misfortune."

The man at the table next to them started from his drunken sleep, screaming and thrashing, trying to ward off some nightmare clinging to him. His glass shattered on the floor and he fell backward, scrambling away from his table. Everyone shot up from their chairs, except for Henri. The man on the floor gasped and clutched at his own dirty shirt. He was breathing at a sprint, his eyes too wide and too awake.

Henri remained smiling and pushed the folder forward, this time flipping it open with the cover blocking the pub.

"You see?" the Frenchman said. "I know people who would pay to hear your story. An experience like that—?" He trailed off.

Jack understood. The five hundred-franc banknotes and the promise of what all that money could buy made him wet his cracked lips. No more basement pub swill and piss. Maybe a bottle of strong golden Kentucky bourbon. Or Maryland rye. Just so long as it'd been poured from home. The eggshell envelope also stared at him, stamped with two heraldic lions clutching the company crest of the Compagnie Internationale des Wagons-Lits et des Grands Express Européens. But it wasn't the words on the envelope that made him hesitate. It was the words he knew were inside the envelope, on the ticket.

The Orient Express.

The man on the floor was still gasping as others helped him up. *Constantinople.*

The man's eyes remained wide. Jack knew the look of terror well. He'd seen it in the faces of friends, but unlike them, this drunkard could drink the nightmare away and dull his senses until he remembered nothing, felt nothing.

Back to where it all started.

Jack picked up his button-down canvas haversack from the side of his chair, his worldly possessions in one hand. Du Lac continued smiling and Jack wondered if going back there might finally bring it all to an end or if he was lying to himself yet again.

No train could match the Orient Express in opulence and comfort. *Hell,* Jack thought, *it's nicer than any lodgings I'd ever had on either side of the Atlantic.*

The two four-wheel bogies made the ride as smooth as a skater gliding at the Glaciarium. Jack kept expecting the white-jacketed waiters to spill some of the red they poured for the passengers, but their steady hands matched the train's sure footing and the dining car's white table cloth remained immaculate.

Jack nodded for another glass of red from the mustachioed waiter heading to the back of the car and continued half-listening to the conversation at his table. Rizzo Bianco made being a black cat sound adventurous, thrilling even, to the couple at their table. Rizzo's peppered mustache danced on the roof of his thin lips and his eyes sparkled as he spoke with an Italian lilt that Jack was sure women found romantic.

". . . as Miss Marjorie, protesting loudly, distracted the museum guard away from me and the display case. . . ."

The couple at their table of four, the Braithwaites, listened in rapt interest. Mrs. Braithwaite's mustard-gloved hand hovered over her young, pouty mouth as she stifled a shocked titter. These were Henri du Lac's clients, rich couples and bachelors living vicariously through the adventures of black cats like Jack and Rizzo.

Their fortunes made them bored with the world. Now they're looking to escape in our stories and damned if we aren't looking to escape from ours.

The other tables likewise sang with their own music. To Rizzo's baritone came the bass of the corpulent Nigel Hughes from the two-person table across the carpeted aisle. The large man spoke in Oxford tones both informative and dry on the subject of the Arabian Peninsula and the time he glimpsed the sands unearth the strange lights of Ubar.

Behind Jack another black cat, Miss Constance Ford, held court at a table of three bachelors and another two across the aisle with an enthralling, earthy alto. Jack had to admit, her tone intoxicated him in a way that made him feel young and old at the same time. He'd forgotten he could feel that way, but he couldn't see her returning the sentiment once those pale blue eyes fell on his weathered face with its fissure-deep wrinkles and nose scarred from booze. *Heck,* he thought, *I can barely keep the dirt off my sleeves and she keeps herself immaculate.*

His own table had gone silent and Jack turned to find the Braithwaites and Rizzo staring at him expectantly.

"Pardon?" Jack said.

"My lovely wife was asking what turned you into a black cat," Mr. Braithwaite asked, his face a ruddy ruby in the white setting of his trimmed whiskers and hair. His starched collar was high and tight.

"Oh," Jack said, shifting in his seat. "Not much to tell. I was never a lucky man to begin with. Guess the Good Lord decided I could stand to shoulder a bit more misery."

The smile wilted on Mrs. Braithwaite's lips when she realized Jack wouldn't be as forthcoming as Rizzo had been. Jack could see their disappointment, could hear it when Mr. Braithwaite cleared his throat and smiled politely.

"The trip is long and my friend, he is saving the best stories for later, eh?" Rizzo said quickly.

"Of course," Mrs. Braithwaite said, excusing herself as she and her husband left their seats on their side of the table. Rizzo watched them leave with a polite smile before the look soured.

"Are you *stupido*, my friend? Or *idiota*?"

Jack studied the man, wondering if he should just punch him in the jaw, but they were fifty hours shy of Constantinople and that was the closest Jack had been to the seat of the Ottoman throne in years. Already, the pressure tightened the screws to his temple, but he couldn't afford to turn back now. He was committed, mind and body.

"Why?" Jack said, his voice low. "'Cause I won't cater to these folks or their bored lives?"

"Bored, *rich* lives," Rizzo corrected. "You heard about the train robbery last year? On the Orient, eh?"

"You mean that Greek fellah? So?"

"That filthy Greek bastard derailed the train, punched his own man who shot one of the passengers, and freed the hostages with five gold coins each. That is what these good people want: An adventure. A story like this, eh?"

Jack leaned forward, his elbows on the table in a manner he figured most civilized folks would likely have found shocking. "They don't got a clue what adventure means. I been listening to you, making it all sound pretty, but I didn't hear mention of how many people died on your escapades, or worse. Tell me something. You ever see the shadows slither? Or see those bastards with eyes like goddamn fish?"

Rizzo's Adam apple danced with a hard swallow, the color draining from his flesh. He no longer seemed in his mid-thirties, but much, much older, his eyes retreating into the back of his skull like that would help him un-see the things that haunted him.

"*Si*," he admitted, his voice a soft croak.

"Then why are you lying to these folks?"

"Because," Rizzo said, his voice choked on whatever temple dust still coated his windpipe, "they would never believe us. And I would never stop screaming if I did." With that, the Italian scuttled from his seat, his olive skin a decidedly paler shade.

Jack caught the looks from the other tables. Nigel barely paid Jack a glance as he went back to describing some Pre-Sumerian ruins in Jabal al-Druze. Constance, however, seemed to be scrutinizing him carefully. Jack wasn't sure what to do with her gaze or the extra hammering it put on his heart. Flustered, he went back to drinking, the world down to just him and his glass. Drunk, he wasn't much company, but sober he remembered things far too well and made others share that, too.

Night found them in the foothills, somewhere in the fertile river lands of Baden-Württemberg. The train rolled along at a steady clip, and Nigel kept pace with his deep snores. Jack sat on a white recessed couch clothed in fleur-de-lis stitching, in the junction of the split corridor that ran down either side of the car. Even here, Nigel's snorts followed. As though understanding his plight, the occasional sleeping car attendant with his pillbox hat who wandered by was sure to offer Jack a sympathetic smile.

Fatigue chased Jack to the edge of exhaustion, his mind numb and dizzy. Constantinople lay within reach, and each hour closer to the City on the Seven Hills made the hum in his skull grow louder. He was safe in Paris, safe from the effects of his ordeal, but out here, he was taking so many risks and it was becoming more difficult to keep the situation from unraveling. He needed to keep it locked up inside, but Constantinople had a way of unscrewing his head and letting the genie out.

Farther down the corridor, where the shadows made a wall, a door opened and clicked shut. Jack cocked his head, listening, watching. A delicate scuff of slippers against the patterned carpet whispered to him. The darkness shifted around the emerging silhouette like India ink bleeding into a water droplet, unsettled and effluvial, reaching out for purchase with its tendrils. Jack squeezed his eyes shut before opening them again. The chimera vanished and the figure materialized.

Constance, Jack realized. He straightened up and pulled his legs in. "Ma'am," he said, but she stopped him from standing with a raised hand.

"Your poison?" she asked, her accent a lilt from the Midwest. She nodded at the flask pressed like a bible between his two gnarled hands. "Or your salve?"

"Both. Irish whiskey," he said. He tipped the flask at her, but she demurred with a sluggish shake of her head.

"I prefer opium."

Jack instantly saw it in the dreamy glaze of her wet blue eyes. He supposed he should have raised an eyebrow or acted surprised, but the fatigue weighed too damn much for him to shrug off and muster anything worth a damn. "Does it help?"

"Some nights," she said. She motioned to the cushion next to him, and Jack pulled the haversack down to between his legs as she took a seat. Her shoulders slumped, her mouth slightly open, her eyes fixed on the wall, or beyond it. Jack thought the latter as he sat again.

"Not tonight, huh?" he said.

"No," she whispered. "I'm haunted, Mister Andrews. Haunted by that man's snoring."

Jack chuckled and her smile deepened as Nigel snorted loudly in his sleep.

"I'm in the cabin next to his," Jack said. "Never trust a man who sleeps that deeply."

"He does sleep rather well for a black cat."

Jack nodded in agreement and took a swig of the whiskey, quick as that, but not quick enough. Constance stared at his chin and touched under her jaw. She moved languidly, her voice tarred. "That's an unusual scar," she said. "It looks like a star."

Jack rubbed it, the skin smooth and dead to the touch. He had wanted to hide it, but no hair would grow there. It looked more conspicuous when he tried.

"A souvenir," he allowed.

"Constantinople."

Jack turned and studied the woman. Friends, when he'd still had them, told him he had the sort of gaze that made most folks uncomfortable, but Constance had obviously seen its like before. She could probably even throw one back with the best of them; most true black cats could. Facing the unknown had a way of killing something inside you. Or maybe it was the opium that made her indifferent. "Pish," she said. "Even if I weren't acquainted with Major Sumter, you're not beyond the reach of idle gossip, Mister Andrews."

"You know the Major? Is he—?"

"Alive? Or sane? I saw him at the Ridges," she said with a shrug. "At least it's not Bellevue. Such a terrible, terrible place. All that madness, you know. It comes out. No matter how tightly you cork the bottle. It still leaks."

"I guess," Jack said, staring at the floor. "What'd he tell you?"

Constance seemed to consider her answer before nodding to the flask.

"Only if you call me Jack," he said, offering it.

She nodded with a smile and took a delicate swig, wiping an errant droplet from her chin with her knuckle before handing it back. "Pardon," she said. "He was so far gone, it took a while to piece his story together. He told me that a shop owner was expanding his basement when a hole opened up into some ruins."

"A well. That's right," Jack said. "The Major was in good with the sultan or a minister, so he got us a look."

"A look," she said, her voice pulled to a strange distance and distorted by harrowed memory. "It always starts with a look or some trifling curiosity. I suppose that's always the rub. Well, after that, the Major's story becomes a little vague. Something about a Byzantine chamber and twelve urns capped with—what did he call them again—figureheads?"

Each word took a hammer to Jack's mind, breaking whatever flimsy walls he'd managed to erect to hold back the memories. He could still smell the dust and stagnant water of untreated centuries as he was lowered down the dark well, the rope cutting into his hamstrings; then the chamber beneath, its barrel walls covered in serpentine shapes that were at once body and limb all rolled into one. There were also the holes in the walls that swallowed the light of his lantern. Beyond them, the whispers and sloughing, wet sounds of movement and the stench of swamp sulfur.

"What did the Major say about me?" Jack asked, clearing his throat.

"Some good, some bad. It depended on how lucid he was."

"Then it's probably all true," Jack said, smiling despite his leaden muscles.

"He said you saved them."

"Did I?" Jack responded, whispering. He stood with a groan,

suddenly eager to depart Constance's company and the conversation. "Then how come nobody's left but me?"

Standing cost him more than he realized, and he swayed. Enough for her to steady him with a hand on his hip. The heat took to his head. Had it really been that long since someone touched him? "Ma'am," he said with an awkward tilt of his head.

"It's Constance, Jack."

He shouldered the haversack. "I think it's time I got some sleep."

"Jack? Why on earth are you going back?"

"Unfinished business," he said.

"Our lives are unfinished business," she said. "Some by choice. Some not. Leave yours to choice, sir. Please. The Major told me what happens when any of you approach Constantinople."

"I got a lot of regrets," Jack admitted. "Least I can do is lay some to rest." He staggered back to his room, more drunk on fatigue, but he did look back once, just to see if she were still watching him, just to see if he had her eye. She smiled at him, sadly it seemed, but at that moment, Jack could live with it.

The dreams came, as vivid as ever, and there were times in his compartment that Jack could see them with his eyes open. When the dreams first began, years ago, he thought they existed to haunt him, and then to taunt him. He watched and rewatched, powerless, as the remaining explorers dropped into the well and down into the ancient chamber beneath it. He should have warned them, begged them to pull him back up when he laid eyes on the place. His intestines crawled in his gut like maggots in a bag. Everything about the place felt wrong: the chamber smelt of brine and urine-soaked rock and the sulfur of swamp rot; the serpentine walls seemed to squirm, and many holes stared back at him.

Eventually, over the years, he realized there was nothing personal in the nightmares. The wasp that paralyzes the spider and impregnates it with larvae doesn't hate the spider no matter how horrible the fate. And what happened to them in Constantinople, down in that chamber wasn't vengeance or curse or retribution. The terrible dreams continued, but he didn't see them as torture, but as theater of the witness. Only in hindsight, from this vantage, did Jack realize that the serpent walls of the conical chamber looked more like tentacles, that the almond-shaped holes were eyes belonging to faces he could barely see crushed under the mass of uncoiling limbs, that the so-called well was in fact a forgotten stairwell stripped of its steps.

But he couldn't see any of that at the time. None of them could. They only saw the twelve bronze canopic jars atop the pedestals that ringed the room. Here was no collection of baboon-, falcon-, and jackal-headed guardians. The figures that topped the urns were mockeries of nature, creatures decidedly more alien and monstrous—and far older than the dynasties of the Nile.

Jack had come to realize that what happened in Constantinople was them falling prey to the wasp with all its indifference. That was little comfort, though; indifferent as its attacker may be, the spider is still consumed alive and from the inside out. Its fate remains horrible all the same.

By the time they'd left Vienna and were racing along the rolling green hills of Hungary, the mood on the train had soured. Jack drank alone, slumped over the table with his elbows holding him up, the conversation having moved away from him to other tables. Lively chatter had filled the dining car and smoking room last night, but in Jack's compartment, Rizzo tossed and turned behind heavy curtains, softly moaning and mewling in quiet terror. Even Nigel's snoring in the adjoining cabin had stopped, given to near derisive snorts of startling dreams.

This morning, the empty gazes and uncomfortable hush betrayed all. Red cradled Mrs. Braithwaite's eyes, and Rizzo offered flat, reassuring smiles whenever she glanced at him. When she didn't, his mouth drooped and his eyes sank back to the nightmares plaguing him. Mr. Braithwaite watched these exchanges between black cat and wife with tightly crossed arms. Meanwhile, Nigel's dry analysis and dissertations on the various empires of the Fertile Crescent fell on numb ears, not that he seemed to notice. His chatter had become a mania.

Constance, pale-faced and hollow-eyed, chased the food

around her plate with her fork and never seemed to catch it. The three bachelors who sat at her table nervously tried to fill the slack with questions and conversations, but their hearts weren't in it either, and they soon fell silent.

Almost nobody made eye contact with Jack, and their gazes squirmed away when they realized he was looking at them. Jack couldn't say he blamed them. He was sure all this misery was his curse leaking out of a widening crack in his soul. Being so close to Constantinople made his skin itch. The buzz in his skull electrified the nerves in his scalp and set them to dancing. He couldn't sleep, felt too impatient to eat. Now everyone felt the same way.

It was all happening again.

Something caught Jack's attention. From the table behind of him, two couples—the white-haired Beckers and the Kleins, who dressed in all the audacity of morticians in mourning—spoke in quiet tones. Jack caught the softer lilt of Austrian German and an opportune word here and there. Jack took a hard swallow of his remaining wine and turned to face them.

"I'm sorry for intruding, but you good folks are getting off at Budapest?"

The Kleins looked annoyed at the imposition, and the heavy-bosomed Mrs. Becker blushed in embarrassment, but Mr. Becker nodded and smiled thinly, making an effort to look at Jack. "No," he said over halting English. "But the Kleins say to go."

Jack didn't hesitate. "Listen to them. You're not safe here anymore."

"We pay good money," Mr. Becker began. Jack cut him off politely as he could muster.

"What'd you pay for? The promise of stories about the otherwordly?"

This time, it was Mr. Klein who nodded. "*Ja.* Herr du Lac promised us—" He hesitated. Was it a loss for the word or embarrassment?

"Promised what?" Jack pressed.

"He promised—" again the hesitation, but Mr. Klein pushed through it "—he promised a look at . . . *Leben nach dem Tod*?" he said to his wife.

"The afterlife?" Jack said. Then it struck him. "You're all spiritualists?"

"We are," the Kleins said in unison, but Becker shook his head.

"We just wish for proof," Mr. Becker offered. He patted his wife's hand. "We are not so young"

"You're not gonna find it here. All you'll find in our yarns is a reason to doubt your faith. Get off at Budapest and don't look back," Jack said, standing up. He made to leave, but everyone was looking at him now. They'd overheard him, his voice louder than he intended. Their expressions weren't so much neutral as they were reptilian and so familiar to him.

"This goes for all of you who got no reason to be here," Jack added. Constance shook her head; a warning, he saw, but he didn't stop. "Get the hell off this train, 'cause it's only gonna get worse." But everyone stared back in a way that felt like someone had ripped their humanity out by the roots.

Jack stormed past the tables, grabbing the bottle of red wine from the startled waiter on the way out of the dining car.

He hated getting drunk off red wine. It colored his teeth the losing side of an ugly brawl and he never had time to ease into his inebriation. It overtook him. Right now, though, they were rolling out of Budapest, the train lighter by a dozen rumps, and all he wanted was to wake up in Constantinople and . . .

. . . and do what?

He didn't know, but there had to be a reason why he couldn't stay in Constantinople after what happened. Why he and others were forced to leave. The mob that chased them out of the city and the flashes of violence that harried them across Eastern Europe were not stewed in anger or rational thought. It was as though the body of humanity were trying to violently expel anything unclean, and Jack and the others were certainly unclean.

Jack took another swig of the half-empty bottle of *vin d'Avignon* and felt his thoughts swim in the stew of his brain. He sat on the bunk of his sleeping compartment, the patterned curtains blurred behind the haze and the dreams that came to him even while awake. The chamber's wall seemed to lie just inches from his fingertips, the Major and the others echoes that surrounded him and bled into the darkness. The wine did nothing to stop the memories anymore and did nothing to dull the influence of Jack's curse over the other passengers. Not this close to Constantinople.

He could see the Major, his great gray mustache a skirt under his hawkish nose, his brow crinkled in delight as he approached one of the canopic jars. The squid-head atop the urn stared back with a flat gaze of carved bone, and the lantern light played across its porous surface.

Jack sighed. *Go back to Constantinople and do what?* he wondered again. Go back down that well, back into that chamber? Maybe the clues had been there all along, there for him to see after the fact, in the theater that replayed the performance again and again until the audience knew the lines and parts as well as the actors.

Their stage had been the chamber—a cage, Jack suspected, set within a larger chamber like those Russian nesting dolls. Or perhaps they stood within the heart of some god deep beneath Constantinople, buried back when it was Byzantium; something ancient impaled by Byzas of Megara with the foundations of the city to keep the ancient leviathan trapped. That's what the Major thought afterward, as his sanity escaped him.

The only thing left unanswered was the part each had been assigned upon that fateful stage. Was he the tragic fool for not telling them to run after they first set foot down the well? Or was it Hendriks, the Dutchman, who peered through a hole in the cage and leapt back, shrieking in terror and knocking an urn off its pedestal. The vulgar vapors that leaked from the broken insect-headed seal glowed with greasy light, a rainbow drenched in fish oil.

How that bulldog Morrow had screamed when he reached for the fallen urn and that wisp of light darted for his fingers. His skin turned to rot, the sudden rents in his flesh flowing with thick tar that Jack knew had once been blood. Then Morrow's hands and face sloughed off as the rot overtook him. What was left of him dissolved as Hendriks, still mad with animal terror, scrabbled and clutched at the rope like he'd forgotten how to climb.

Something outside the cage moaned and creaked, an ancient ship in a starless sea, and the whole chamber rumbled at their intrusion. Another jar tumbled and shattered, spilling effluvial vapors that reflected colors skipping madly along a dark spectrum.

Perhaps, in that moment, it had been the Major who played the part of the fool when he grabbed the squid-headed urn and shoved it into his worn haversack.

Jack nudged the aged haversack with his feet, to remind himself it was there, the urn, unbroken and unbreakable, as though hardened by the Major's theft of it. So then, what would he do when he reached Constantinople? Return the urn to its rightful place? Beg forgiveness from something that didn't see with human eyes?

Maybe that wasn't the point. Maybe—the terrible thought suggested itself to him—maybe your curse is so pointless as to be cruel.

He tipped the bottle toward his mouth and a trickle wet his lips. He left it on his bunk as he pushed the curtains aside. The other bunk lay empty, Rizzo gone and no longer bothering with the pretense of sleep. Or perhaps Rizzo couldn't stomach Jack anymore. That was part of it, too, part of being so close to Constantinople that people's indifference turned to hostility, turned to murder, turned to all-consuming, gibbering fear.

Outside the compartment window, night escorted them, but the countryside was one he couldn't identify. He only knew their location by the press of "that city" in his thoughts. *We're closer than ever*, Jack admitted before the wine finally put him to sleep.

❖   ❖   ❖

Boom.

Jack drew the hammer back with his thumb and fired the Colt Paterson a second time. The murky tentacles wormed their way through the holes in the chamber walls.

Boom.

One of the tentacles exploded into a meaty stub and snapped back into the darkness. He aimed at another tendril snaking for the Major, who was dragging Fahd away from the broken urn. Fahd clutched his fissured face, but he'd taken less of the vapor than Morrow or he, too, would be dead; Fahd's screams suggested he wished he were.

Boom.

The chamber shook as the thing beyond the walls pitched and raged against their cage. Jack's next shot went wild and more tendrils slid through the many holes like blind snakes that probed the air wildly. The Major made to grab the rope, but Hendriks shoved him away and screamed for the men upstairs to winch him to safety. The rope lurched, yanking the Dutchman up a handful of feet. As the Major went for the rope again, Hendriks kicked him away with a rabid fury.

Jack raised his pistol and took aim at the Dutchman.

Boom.

And again: *Boom.*

Too many shots, Jack realized as he snapped awake.

The thunder of yet another shot echoed through the train car, chasing the sounds of Hendriks's screams from Jack's head. He bolted out of the compartment and found them wrestling in the corridor before an open cabin door. Mr. Braithwaite held a pistol and one of the sleeping car attendants struggled to take it from him. The gun discharged again and blew another hole in the ceiling. The pistol then clicked empty; Jack rushed forward and punched Mr. Braithwaite in the jaw, collapsing him to the carpet.

A glance inside the compartment told him the entire story. Rizzo and Mrs. Braithwaite lay there, dead, arms wrapped around one another. Each had been trying to shield the other from the shots that spared neither of them. The skinny attendant picked up the pistol and looked at Jack like he was trying to remember something, something like *shoot Jack*, even though he couldn't understand why.

Jack stumbled away.

The bronze urn sat atop the dining table. The squid-head was carved of bone. No chisel marks marred its surface. Its mouth tentacles flowed down over the barrel shape of the jar like thick droplets, its almond eyes flat and dispassionate. Something about it looked more human than animal, the way the bone hinted at neck and shoulders before the strange cap melted into bronze and unfurling tendrils.

Jack brooded alone in the dark of the empty dining car, taking swigs of whiskey whenever the buzzing wormed its way back in. The scar under his chin itched.

"You have to leave," a soft voice said. Constance stood at the end of the table, her blue-eyed gaze constantly flitting to the urn. "Is that it?" she whispered. "The Major mentioned—"

Jack knew the power it held on the uninitiated, and even more the siren allure to black cats. He'd spent enough time in its company to resist displaying it in the open. Mostly. Instead, he rested his hand on the octopoid crown. Constance blinked and looked at Jack.

"The . . . others. They think you're responsible for their nightmares," she said.

"I am. You know I am. You've been sharing my dreams, too."

"Your nightmares, you mean."

"Can't be nightmares when that's all you got left to dream about." Jack slid the urn back into the haversack. Voices grew louder in the adjoining car. Angry voices. Constance glanced over at the door before looking back at him, almost pleading.

Jack had no reason to rush. No reason to be frightened. Old fears got washed out in the presence of more ancient ones. "If I drink, I can keep the curse down a good deal, but this close to Constantinople," Jack explained, "damn thing gets to where I can't hold it in. Won't be long before the other passengers come after me."

"Then why are you here?" she demanded.

"'Cause I gotta end it. I'm just so damn tired of moving around all the time. And—" He took another swing with the flask.

"And?" she said helplessly.

"And I thought we'd be in Constantinople fast enough. Maybe I was being foolish, or maybe just plumb desperate, but I tried by ship. Steamers. Carts. On horseback. On foot once, avoiding all the main roads. But they always came after me, like the smell of me gets stronger the closer I get. And the closer I get, the more people want to rip me limb from limb, though they can't figure out why. On the outskirts of the city once, there was a wall of them. Just waiting. That was the closest I got that time."

"How do you live like that?"

"I move around. France is a safe bet for me. It's far enough away that I can drink the hum into silence and French folk figure they don't like me on account of them being French," he said in a soft chuckle.

"They're coming," Constance said, looking at the door. "Please, you must leave."

"I got no place left to go and this thing's stuck to my hip." He nodded to the haversack. "That's why the Major's committed to the Ridges. I took it from him thinking I was relieving him of some burden and now everyone involved in that fiasco's a raving lunatic. Except me."

"They'll kill you!"

Jack looked at her. He hadn't heard that kind of concern from anyone in a long time. He slid out from the booth and cupped her chin between his rough forefinger and thumb. "Ain't we a pair?" he said. "You ain't scared of me like them, are you? Is that because you care, or because of the drugs?" She made to answer, but he touched her soft lips with his thumb. "Don't. You'll break my heart either way."

The door at the other end of the dining car burst open. Nigel and Mr. Becker stood ahead of the tired-eyed waiters, sleeping car attendants, and a few of the bachelors who were courting Constance's favor not a day ago. They wore an expression he'd become accustomed to, one he'd seen a dozen times before.

Constance pushed him, screaming at him to run. He saw the gun come up in Nigel's hand, his eyes runny and sagging under the nightmares. The gun was aimed at Jack, until Constance stepped in the way.

How Jack wished he could have warned her, told her he wasn't in danger, but there wasn't time. The bullet caught her in the back of the head and sprayed her blood and her brains onto his shirt. He caught her dead body as it fell into him, her blue eyes frozen wide in surprise. Another shot rang out, shrieking past his ear.

"They can't kill me," he would have told her. "I done worse to myself than shooting. It won't do no good." Then he would have pointed under his chin, against his scar, and cocked his thumb like a hammer.

But it was too late for all that now. Constance slid to the floor without another word, and another of Nigel's shots went wide. The mob pressed in, eager to rip out his throat. Nigel stumbled under their feet with a cry as they stampeded over him. Bone snapped loudly, and Nigel shrieked again.

They couldn't hurt him, but they would kill each other trying to get at him. Jack knew that, and cursed himself for thinking it'd be different this time. He turned and jumped atop the dining table, his feet almost slipping on the tablecloth. Reflected in the window was the waking dream—of the Major screaming and pulling at Fahd, at Hendriks falling from the rope, of the tentacles reaching for them as . . .

Jack threw himself at the memory with a cry of anger, haversack clutched to his chest, out the window in a shower of broken glass. The wind screamed at him and he tumbled into the darkness, his body breaking on its way down the rocky hill. To Jack, though, he was falling back down that damn stairwell again.

Jack came to, howling at the pain of his bones knitting back into place and the suturing bite of what felt like a thousand needles stitching his flesh together. His hands shot out over the gravel bed, fingers clutching sharp rocks until he found the cloth strap of his haversack. He pulled it to him and wept as the whistle of the Orient Express faded to silence in the distance.

Then he was alone.

Again.

For God knew how many more years, decades, centuries to come.

When he could finally feel his fingers again in that dark ravine, he sat up and fumbled for the haversack's flap and opened it. He couldn't see anything in that darkness, and even Constance's face was already fading under the weight of the chamber and the faces of the Major, Hendriks, Morrow, and Fahd. His fingers touched wet clothes that smelled of spilt whiskey, before closing over the cold bone and metal of the urn. He pulled it out and in one stroke, clubbed it on the rocks between his legs, and hammered again and again, trying to break the seal, trying to remember Constance's face, trying to destroy whatever kept him imprisoned in this cage within a cage.

"Come out!" he screamed at whatever vapors lay trapped within the urn. "Come out and kill me, God damn you!"

He stopped when he broke his third finger against the rocks and the urn slid, undamaged, from his numb hands. And there he sat, in the cold, in the dark, forever trapped in the chamber alongside the other men: Hendricks and Morrow dead and likely pulled through the grate of small holes by the tentacles. Fahd, he'd heard, was a hermit who clawed his eyes out every night in some cave in Arabia Felix, hoping that tonight would be the night they didn't grow back. The Major was entombed in the Ridges, babbling about prophecies and the rise of the Old Ones. And him, custodian for an urn that didn't want to return to the one place it belonged.

Jack stood up, his bones aching and his skin tingling from its fresh scars. It was time to go. Maybe this time he'd find Henri du Lac and ask him some pointed questions, like why the black cats had been invited into this fiasco. Was Henri really a broker for his clients, or was he an agent of Chaos or something else entirely, something that wanted to see this misery played out? Jack figured the answer would trouble him more than help, however.

So maybe instead, he'd travel farther away, back to America with his banknotes, and wait to see what the twentieth century would bring. He'd already seen the steamship and modern steam train, and there was talk of airships now. With a bit more patience, perhaps he'd see the rise of something new that would get him inside Constantinople, back inside that chamber. Maybe then he'd know peace. Maybe they all would. Jack knew he had years left before that time came. Years of lonely patience.

Like a black cat, he slunk off into the night once again, praying he wouldn't lose patience again and try to reach Constantinople before he was absolutely certain people wouldn't die in the process. Praying the next time, it would finally be different.

THE FACE OF THE DEEP
C. A. Suleiman

The insignia gleamed like a dying star, and in that moment it seemed to Alfred Pendleton that never in his life had his eyes beheld anything quite so magnificent.

That the man from whom it dangled, Sir Roderick Ulman, was Pendleton's superior in their corner of the labyrinthine bureaucracy that was the British Raj only made it that much more striking to look upon. The two grinning men on either side of Sir Roderick were dressed normally for what had proven itself a bitterly frigid "cold season" in this part of Eastern Europe, but in place of his usual dark suit, waistcoat, and derby, the knighted man between them was draped in a set of elaborate vestments: a mantle of blue satin lined with white silk; a golden collar patterned with alternating lotuses, roses, and palm branches; a cross-body sash weighted by a pair of hand-stitched tassels. And, of course, the insignia itself, a sunburst of gold with a central ring that housed a five-pointed star decorated with brilliant diamonds.

"Gentlemen, I'm afraid I—" Pendleton began, but stopped himself short when his eyes fell upon the legend emblazoned on that insignia. *Victoria Imperatrix*, it read. The reality of the scene began to swim into focus…

"By *Jove*, I—" blustered one of the other men, his cheeks ruddy in the lamplight of the railway carriage.

"Wait for it, Blakely," the middle man interrupted, and then, back to his guest: "Pendleton, do you recognize this? Blakely here seems to think you do."

"I believe so, sir," he replied. "That is the crest of the Order of the Indian Empire."

"The *Most Eminent* Order of the Indian Empire, my good man," Blakely corrected, offering an accusatory poke with his glass. A drop of brandy spilled over the frosted lip and splashed on the floor of the private salon car.

"Quite right," said Sir Roderick. He stood up straight, chin out, upper lip stiff as the Queen's corset.

"Of course, sir," Pendleton said, nodding, "But why wear your order regalia here? Now?" While decorum demanded the question be asked, he was certain he knew what answer was forthcoming.

"Blakely here thinks you already know. He thinks you ask out of modesty." At this, the inebriant nodded his support; a bead of drunken sweat clung to the corner of his mustache.

Pendleton cast a sidelong glance at the third man—Algernon Coffin, his name was—who had thus far said nothing to him, neither in this car nor earlier in the day, when the two met while boarding the train. Taller than the other two, Coffin had pallid skin and a form to his features that was both overly angular and drawn-out, as if some troubled creator had been overcome by a desire to combine all the most striking characteristics of a draft horse and a piece of courtyard statuary. Now that he actually looked *at* the man, Pendleton observed that he too held snifters of brandy, one in each white, distended hand. The openly celebratory air in the forward salon of the Express was as evident as it was unsettling—at least to Alfred Pendleton.

"I cannot say I do, sir, but at a guess . . . well, it appears that you are considering nominating me for initiation into your order?" A statement, but framed in the interrogative.

"Not 'considering,' no," Sir Roderick corrected. "And not 'nominating,' either. No."

"Love for two, old boy!" Blakely hooted and spun himself around in place, twice, taking one gulp from his glass at the conclusion of each rotation. When he was finished, his glass was empty and his face was, impossibly, even redder than it was before.

The mantled Knight Commander continued undeterred. "No, Pendleton. All the considering was done weeks ago. You're not being nominated. You're being initiated."

Pendleton's mind raced. "B-But," he stammered, "one must first be nominated by an existing Knight Commander or Grand Commander, no? And I—who nominated me?"

Sir Roderick smiled. "Your appointment came from the top down, old fellow. The formal initiation awaits you when we arrive in Paris, but we wanted to break the news early. You are now a Knight of Her Majesty's Most Eminent Order of the Indian Empire."

Pendleton stared again at the twinkling insignia. "I don't know what to say, sir."

Blakely leaned forward and, with a stern aspect and a tone of dire portent intoned, "Say that you'll drink with us. Like a *proper* Englishman." This he followed with a wink.

"Of course," said Pendleton. Apparently, Blakely found this reply amusing; he broke into an unbridled chuckling fit that persisted the better part of a minute, during which time the tall man handed out fresh snifters for all. For his part, Pendleton spent the interval resuming his marveling at the Knight Commander's regalia.

"It's the vestments you like, isn't it?" Sir Roderick's voice was low and somehow conspiratorial, and he rubbed his sash with one hand as he spoke. "The insignia. The *sign*."

Pendleton found himself blushing, and it confused him terribly. "I grew up watching men of the Order bear it proudly, sir. The Duke of Cambridge was himself a Grand Commander, and never has a man struck a figure of such English grandeur as he did, especially decked in the full ceremonial dress of his lordly station."

"Well, then you'll be happy to know," sputtered Blakely, halfway through his eighth finger of brandy, "that your own impending regalia travels with you. Every precious thread sits in an upright storage trunk in the rear baggage car, and if you—"

"Cambridge, you say?" Sir Roderick interjected. "If I'm not mistaken, Pendleton here matriculated himself at Cambridge, did you not?"

Pendleton nodded. "Indeed I did, sir. At King's College." The glass of rich brandy looked almost as good as it felt in his hands.

"Another pasty Eton boy?" Blakely howled. "What in God's

name sent you to *this* far-flung corner of Her Majesty's global estate?" The fact that they were all now speeding through the frozen highlands of Tcherkesskeuy, and no longer in, or even anywhere near, the Empire of India, was immaterial to the jubilant Briton.

Pendleton looked up. "To be perfectly honest, I just wanted to make a difference."

All three of the men before him laughed. The sound was sudden and humorless.

"That, you have," said Blakely. "That, you most certainly have." Blakely raised his glass and took a drink.

"Just so," Sir Roderick agreed. "And that's why today, you join the ranks of the august."

The Knight Commander raised his glass and took a drink.

Mr. Coffin, the tallest man, said nothing but raised his own glass as well, and together, the four men drank to the Order and to the Queen, and they drank to empire.

The news was so unexpected, so suddenly exhilarating, that even if he hadn't gone on to consume so much alcohol, Pendleton doubted he would have remembered much more of what transpired in the private salon car they had arranged to be attached to the Express back in Bucharest. Dim and already fading were his recollections of brandy, the vociferous regalement of tales of life inside the Raj, and little else, thanks to his state of mind.

For ease of transfer—and probably for nod to station—the car had been slotted near the front of the train, ahead of the first baggage car, and the newly minted member of Her Majesty's order stepped shakily from its rear vestibule now, his head swimming. His own compartment was in the last sleeping coach, also the penultimate car, down at the other end of the train. The walk would do him good, no doubt. It wouldn't merely clear the cobwebs and help him get his train-legs back underneath him, but it might also pump some much-needed blood to the cogitations of a mind that had grown restive of a sudden. There was *so* much to consider now. This appointment would change everything for the man whose mother called him "Little Alfie."

When he first started back, Alfie intended to simply to get to where he might put his feet up, perhaps with a stop off at the dining car. (Some cravings rose only as sobriety fell, he'd found.) Halfway through the forward baggage car, however, a notion took root in him. Blakely had said the regalia that would be awarded him was already on board, and after watching Sir Roderick stroll around in *his*, nothing would suit Pendleton better than a quick peek before bed. If only just to see it, to *touch* it, for himself . . .

Just the one time.

Something sinister stirred when he made the decision to follow his enthusiasm to the back of the train, however—subtle at first, the phenomenon soon grew into a waking fever dream for Alfred Pendleton. It began with a sound: a slow pulse, a low thrumming that resounded like the beat of a skin drum in the back of his mind. This he took for the opening salvo of a headache he suspected he would regret come morning (as he always paid a price for his dalliances with brandy), and thus thought nothing more of it. At least until the distortion crossed into the realm of the visual.

In the dining car, he passed by a woman sitting alone at a linen-covered table. She wore a green feather boa and sipped tea from a decorated porcelain cup. As he neared her, he watched as her boa appeared to slip down from around her shoulders, away from her raven tresses; on instinct he leaned forward to rescue the expensive item from the floor, but as he did, the boa transformed into a writhing serpent. Feathers flattened into scales before his eyes, one end rising cobra-like into the air as if to strike him dead, and he pulled up with a start. When the woman looked at him, alarmed, he found that all he could do to acquit himself was to say, "Madame, you've dropped your boa." With an awkwardly polite smile, she informed him that she had not worn a boa this evening.

No sooner had he escaped the swirling oddity of that experience than he found himself passing through the pair of long sleeping cars beyond the dining car—no disturbance in itself, but in God's name, the *people*. Each of those he passed wore the clothes of his day and culture, but all articles hung over skin that was waxy and yellowed, as though jaundiced from an early age. Not a soul registered its ghastly appearance to him in any way, and the first time he saw one's face, pressed nearly into his own as both maneuvered to pass in the cramped corridor, he had to struggle not to cry out.

The person standing before him had lost every distinguishing human feature. What had been its face was now little more than a yellowed oval of skin stretched drum-like over a skull bone. The same was true for each of those who followed; some half-dozen before the long and nightmarish walk through the sleeping cars was done. Although featureless, the faces he passed somehow reminded him of those he had seen while working under the Raj in India. Faces he never knew existed until he looked upon them with his own eyes. Faces he would now never forget.

When he arrived at his own compartment door he stopped to consider briefly whether his state of mind might be indicative of a larger, as yet undiagnosed problem, but he decided that even if it were, he would find no answers in the cramped little room beyond. If his mind was reacting poorly to something in the moment, then it could only benefit from taking the opportunity to lay eyes on his new regalia for the first time—an act that would surely solidify his place in his world. Perhaps even help justify the things he had done. Pressing his passkey back into his vest pocket, Pendleton forsook the warmth of his pull-down bed in the name of discovery and of pride, and continued on down the hall.

By the time he pushed through to the rear baggage car, with the help and gratitude of a handsomely rewarded attendant, he could no longer feel his own tongue. He could still *taste*, but that taste came insensate, carried through no vessel of flesh. Even pushing the meat of his tongue between his jaws and biting down produced only the one-way sensation felt in his gums and facial musculature, though he certainly tasted his own blood well enough when it finally spilled out. He was dimly aware of the pain, and of the drum that still sounded in his head, but none of that mattered now.

He was here, arrived now at the end of the line.

The last car on the westbound Orient Express was dark and filled to bursting with parcels of varying shape and size, which lent him as he entered a feeling not unlike being trapped in a lift during a loss of power. A lone valiant bulb above the entryway did its best to illuminate the proceedings, but its light was meager and washed out, fading within a few feet from the door. Pendleton wished he'd brought a lamp or at least a candle from his compartment, but he hadn't, and there was little sense in going back for one now. He knew what we was looking for and it couldn't rightly elude him for long.

Between the rows of shelving used to accommodate the smaller and lighter suitcases spanned a clearly delineated aisle, its purpose even called out in the floor decoration, and he was confident that if he stayed true to its course he needn't worry about his footing. In shuffling steps he made his way down the aisle, feeling all around him as he went: Here, some gentleman's luxury steamer trunk; there, some gentlewoman's travel chest. Nothing over which he ran either his hands or his mostly useless eyes matched the description of the thing he sought, and for one horrible moment he considered the idea that Blakely had misspoken and that the cabinet was in the *forward* baggage car all the while.

The prospect of having to go back now, past his own sleeping compartment, to where this all began made Pendleton's temples throb worse than ever before. He set one hand atop a nearby trunk and pinched the bridge of his nose with two fingers of his other. Never had he reacted this way to alcohol, and if *this* was what it meant to celebrate to excess with Sir Roderick and his kind, then he must make sure to never again repeat the mistake. Indeed, Pendleton now felt so ill at ease that he presently considered abandoning his mission here, despite fruition being so close at hand, in favor of the nicely elevated confines of his bunk. He wanted so desperately just to see his symbol of office, to *hold* it for himself just once before his rightful ordination, but . . . perhaps it was time to turn around.

That's when realization swelled in Alfred Pendleton's mind. And when it did, the bewildered Englishman wondered how he could have been so foolish. Blakely had said that the trunk was large and oriented *upright*, as a proper cabinet rather than the wide-based trunks the wealthy often used for long-distance travel. This meant that what he sought was effectively a trunk lid that was set against a wall.

In other words, a *door*, at least after a fashion.

Stumbling now, Pendleton abandoned the mundane luggage all around him and hobbled straight for the far wall. That part of the coach was lost to a blackness that was all but complete, but even as disorientated as he was, the Queen's newest Knight needed no light to find a handle. He waved his arms out in front of his body as he neared the wall, sweeping them in wide arcs before him. When his fingers fell by chance onto the handle, a thrill ran like a live current up his arm and swiftly through his body before dispersing as a lingering warmth beneath his feet.

None can say what Alfred Pendleton saw when he opened that "cabinet" door. It might have been the very object of his heart's desire: those glittering vestments of his newfound station. The simplest answer is, after all, the most commonly correct one. He might have actually seen them hanging there, seamless perhaps and bathed in a reverent light, beckoning him to reach out and lay at last his hand upon that golden seal.

Or it might have been a god he found beyond that door. Back home, those who knew him best would whisper that he was haunted by Kali, death goddess of the Hindus—that he secretly feared her like he feared nothing else, and that it was she who called to him that night. And that when he opened that door he saw her framed in terrible glory: hips swaying, black tongue lolling, her white eyes burning, two of her four hands clutching blades dripping with blood, the other two cradling his own severed head at her breast.

While none could say for certain, those who knew the *circumstances* best would whisper something altogether different, when they spoke of it at all. Such dangerously learned men suggested that it was neither gleaming regalia nor radiant divinity that Pendleton beheld beyond that door, but an otherworldly window, and that upon that dark horizon sat the source that was the *true* voice behind the call. Above a sea of faceless faces It floated, that giant proboscidean head atop that anthropoid torso and massive columnar legs, those legions of ashen disciples singing soundless paeans in Its name; how Its slick gray trunk must have ended in a flat disk of a mouth that opened and closed like a lotus flower, fine rows of teeth fanning out like blades of gleaming grass, opening and closing, opening, closing. Such dangerously learned men might suggest that Its vast and pitiless elephantine bulk was all that *ever* awaited Alfred Pendleton at the end of the line.

What is known for certain is that when the railway attendant entered the baggage car some time later, he found the room un-occupied and the back door flung wide open. Frigid air blew through the coach, carrying swirling eddies that covered all the cases and trunks in a fine dusting of snow. Of little Alfie Pendleton, Knight of the Order of the Indian Empire, there never was a sign. The attendant would later swear that in the time it took him to again secure the door, the rear baggage car was filled with the screams of a dying man. When told that this sound was merely the play of wind and temperature in the exposed enclosure, the attendant was heard to reply, "Not the wind." He never stepped foot in the car again.

DEMONS DREAMING
Cody Goodfellow

THE SUN SPARKLING OFF THE waters of the Golden Horn was twice the sight they said it'd be. The asparagus-hued estuary turned to molten gold and the city dissolved in a solution of light and took one away from the seething knots of beggars, pickpockets, and worse that crowded the streets of Constantinople, which was exactly what said unsavory citizens hoped for. No one showed any designs upon the tall, white-blond Welshman in a spotless ice cream suit or the florid, bullet-headed Scot in red sergeant's tunic who stood beside the wheelhouse of a ferry packet tied off on the Kadikoy wharf, looking nothing like the pirates they were.

"We'll give him a few minutes more, then, Gunn," said Captain Glendower. "Our lad always did cut it close."

"Och, ye daft bastard," Sergeant Gunn growled, "an' ye take that scunnerin' janus to your broch, doon a-crye when he bites yeh."

"Whatever else he was," Glendower said, "he was no traitor." *As for what he is*, the Welshman thought, *we'll see soon enough.*

He passed a few more oddly cold coins to the ferry captain and closed his ears to the din of the other passengers' bleating for the boat to put off. Across the vast strait—on what one couldn't help but think of as the European half of the city—the Simplon Orient Express at the Sirkeci terminal added its steam to the unseasonable soup of ominous clouds over the capital of the newly defunct Ottoman Empire. Its engineers would be less pliable than the ferryman and it would not wait for them.

For his part, Captain Glendower was at loose ends about the whole business. Studying the baffling myriad of bare and veiled faces, of fezzes, kepis, turbans, and wide-brimmed hats passing on the road, he could kick himself for not having a better sight-picture of his quarry. His old friend would not look the same, if the rumors among the old regiment had it right. But all of a sudden, he knew just where to find Lieutenant Roland Morrison.

He had only to hearken to the breaking wave of screams and baffled echoes of pistol shots from across the plaza to the steps of the nearby Haydarpasa train station. The sky cracked with a concussion like a thirty-pounder with a fouled barrel going up, like a great calling card writ large in black smoke and shrapnel, then hoisted up above the market stalls and the motley mix of mansard roofs and minarets that made up the Constantinople skyline.

Glendower nodded to Sergeant Gunn, who saluted and notched his revolver in the ferry captain's navel. "We'll shift for ourselves, won't we, laddie?"

Reminding himself to have a talk with the sergeant about his coarse manner, Glendower leapt down to the stone quay and thrust himself into the tide of terrified travelers, many of them European tourists utterly out of their depth even without the imminent peril of getting trampled or shot. Glendower turned into the shallow plaza before the train station's railhead and found the source of the smoke, at least. A private salon railcar of the type used by heads of state was engulfed in flames, and redolent with the rank, rich stink of burnt flesh.

A thickly bearded Turkish conductor approached him in haste and, catching his eye, led him back around the corner toward the street. The conductor surprised him more than he should have by removing the beard and a false nose.

"Damn shabby, Morrison," Glendower said, but the grisly slash of his mouth attempted a crooked smile.

"It's hardly over, old man. Look there."

A patrol of English infantry trotted across the platform in their cardinal-red tunics. They were searching the crowd and might not have noticed them at all, had Glendower not stopped in mid-stride and waved to them. "Something off about that lot. . . ."

Morrison's sidelong glance looked like he was telling a corker of a joke. "They're not soldiers of the Crown, old boy."

As if he could hear them, the color sergeant went for his sidearm. His trio of privates shouldered their rifles like a firing squad. With no cover in reach, Glendower turned sideways to the expected enfilade and went for his own revolver in its tricky shoulder holster under his damnable vest buttons, but he knew there would be no time to draw, let alone return their fire.

Glendower swiftly made his peace with a soldier's death, when suddenly, as if it had always been there, the sergeant had the naked steel of a knife jutting from his mouth. The dead man's spoiled shot went into the cantilevered canopy over the platform.

The riflemen fired just as Glendower went down with a stiff hand in his back. On his knees, he kept hauling his revolver out of its sheath and got off three shots. One soldier fell with a third eye, and the others were off and gone into the panicking crowd before their mate hit the ground.

Snarling, "Let's bloody well have at them," Glendower started after the fleeing imposters, but the man in the train conductor's uniform pulled him back and ran at a pace that left no breath for curses and questions.

Now Glendower took the lead around the inlet from the train station to the ferry wharf. "We're going to miss the train," Morrison called out, "unless you're game to take a boat by force."

"No need," Glendower panted. "The boat should wait for us, even if the train won't."

The mob in the street seemed actively to push them back, but across the sea of faces, he saw Sergeant Gunn leaning on the wheelhouse of the ferry, studiously stoking the embers of his briarwood pipe.

"They're damned tenacious, Captain," Morrison said.

Glendower said, "Well, they'll be easy to spot," just as Morrison picked up a freshly trampled cardinal-red private's tunic someone had only just dropped in the street.

"*Sanctaidd ffycin cachu!*" Glendower snarled in his ancestral tongue, the sibilant curse like a bullwhip. "What have you done this time, you mad bastard? Who are they?"

The bodies pressed ever closer, strange, fearful faces crushed against their own. Morrison slipped through the cracks in the wall of Turks, while Glendower bulled through every obstacle.

"Anarchy, chaos, and pagan idolatry," Morrison tossed over his shoulder. "They're bloody fanatics, old boy."

Glendower drew his revolver, cocked it, and fired twice into the air. "And I'm not?" The terrorized crowd evaporated. Nothing more interrupted their hasty retreat to the ferry, which untied and beat all ahead full against the choppy, wind-lashed Bosporus.

"Your boyos weren't all that quick," Glendower said, taking out his pipe and settling back against the railing.

Looking chastened for once, Morrison shook his head, his mouth crooked as he stepped aside so Glendower could see Sergeant Gunn slouching against the wheelhouse where he'd been pinned by a long dagger balanced for throwing.

Glendower pushed Morrison aside and tried to revive the sergeant, who breathed his last in the captain's face.

Cold fury roiled under the frigid tone of Glendower's voice. "Who are they?" he asked again

"I know how absurd it sounds—"

"On with it, damn you!"

"They're Assassins, Marion. The Syrian Hashishim: slaves of the forty-ninth Old Man of the Mountain."

On the train, Glendower and Morrison retired to a "ladies' special" sleeper compartment with only an exterior egress and a pass-through for meal services.

Captain Glendower sat brooding beside the window until the last lights of Constantinople had faded from sight and the window had become a perfect black mirror. He'd had precious little to say on the uneasy crossing and, leaping from the ferry to run into the market, had mutely returned with a suitable coffin. A hired wagon conducted them in tense silence to the Sirkeci terminus and the Saturday evening Simplon Orient Express train, impatiently puffing steam and giving full throat to its final boarding whistle. He had sat in morose contemplation of the retreating platform with his revolver cocked while Morrison tried in vain to make his friend let go of what couldn't be undone.

Once underway, they made short work of the only bottle of whiskey on the train until Belgrade. Both declined dinner. Glendower had no appetite, while Morrison pled stomach and kidney trouble. Plenty of fluids were in order, he insisted, to pass the stone.

By the time they had murdered a case of champagne, without feeling it, the pair had exhausted the old stories of comrades lost, but it was also then that Glendower finally saw nowhere else to go but forward. "Your invitation was vague enough," he said.

"You'll come to understand why I could spell nothing out," Morrison replied. "I'd heard you'd been cashiered and were seeking new opportunities, but three years in our line is a long time. . . ."

"Indeed, can't be too cautious. Three years is a *very* long time to be down in the arse-end of Christendom. Even before the war was over, we heard you'd met a bad end."

Morrison's grin never touched his eyes. "But you knew better, eh? After that beastly business at Ypres, those fools in Whitehall had to send me somewhere far out of sight. The Empire's crumbling, Marion. Rotting from the inside out."

"Go scratch," Glendower sneered, without much heat. Even now, the mere mention of Ypres, where half their regiment had met an end unspeakable, drove Glendower to touch one of the charms discreetly secreted on his person.

"You know it's true. They're content to let the Empire pass into history, the ones who'd never shed a drop of blood to keep it."

The only relief Glendower found from the bitterness of old wounds was digging into new ones. Taking out his briarwood pipe and loading it with a bowl of honest Georgian tobacco, he said, "Old Gunn never saw what killed him. Saved my life at Ypres and a dozen worse spots, only to stop a thug's knife on a ferryboat."

"Nothing could've been done. They're not just hired cutthroats. They're hell-bent on death in the service of their master."

"One wonders why *we're* still alive, then. If they're so inescapable, how'd you and I thin their numbers and get clear?"

"The ones we faced were bare initiates. They're not what they were eight centuries back, but if you could only see—"

"I've seen plenty, boyo. That explosion and fire. It wasn't their line of evil, now was it?"

Morrison nodded. "They prefer to strike in the dark, in silence. We foiled their plans, though."

"Didn't we, though?" Glendower absently cast about for a less-than-empty bottle. What were those plans?"

"To stitch up a delegation of Turk nationalists bound for the coast to shore up support for a Turkey without a sultan." From a false pocket in the lining of his conductor's coat, Morrison took out a chamois pouch and a small, curious dagger. The pommel of yellowed ivory was hollowed out for use as a pipe. "Dressed as they were, they must've hoped to provoke another diplomatic row, wedge the Turks against the meddling Triple Entente. The Assassins have been working rather unsubtly of late to keep their neighbors unstable."

"Rubbish! Whatever this lot call themselves, the *real* Assassins were wiped out seven hundred years ago, same as the Templars."

"Ah, Marion, I forget how no superior officer could ever lecture history around you for fear of that infamous Welsh memory." Into the dagger's shallow bowl, Morrison stuffed a pinch of a tarry, purplish brown *bhang*-like substance that looked unlikely to combust under the most strenuously applied flame. "But as anyone who applied oneself in the Scottish Rite might have adduced, the Templars and Assassins were not enemies. At worst, they were merely rivals for the same forbidden knowledge and power."

Striking a match off the flocked velvet wall, Morrison applied the flame to the nugget, causing it to bubble and hiss and emit an oddly heavy, silvery-blue smoke. "Furthermore," he added, "we know that the Templars fortunate enough to inhabit Great Britain were not exterminated but driven underground in the north, where they formed the first Scottish Masonic orders. What, then, did the Assassins become?"

"Gobs of goddamned lies and stories," Glendower said. "Mongols wiped 'em out, full stop. Mohammedans seem to split every time an imam drops dead. The Nizarites serve the Aga Khan, but they're no—what the hell is that horrible shite?"

Morrison let out a palpable stream of blue, fluidly twisting smoke. "You know so much of the history, I'm surprised you never tried their sacrament."

"Oh, pull the other one," Glendower sneered to cover his alarm. He opened the window to let the stupefying cloud of smoke out into the Turkish night. "That's the stuff that makes them think they've died and gone to Paradise. . . ?"

Nodding slyly, Morrison offered the smoking knife. "Like to try it?"

Glendower shook his head, but this afforded him a sad review of their compartment. The dining car had left them a meager fifth of Scotch. Being a French outfit, Wagons-Lits's selection tended to run to brandy, wine, and champagne, none of which seemed appropriate for the circumstances. *Damn it all. Good old Gunn . . . just like that. Damn it all, why couldn't I—?*

This whole mess, and his old mate from the Regiment, suddenly back from the dead just when it all threatened to boil over. . . .

"Give it here," he said. He struck a match with his thumb and touched it to the oily stuff, making it crackle and sweat before it burned. The gust of smoke that filled his lungs seemed to expand in his chest and flood his brain and burn the backs of his eyes. A surge of languid pleasure atomized him. He was nothing but a breath, and then he let it out and saw himself in the whorls of smoke that floated before him and then were sucked out the open window. Glendower thought, when he could finally form and hold onto one, that it was hardly mysterious that the stuff gave the Old Man of the Mountain such absolute control over his killers. "Seven hundred years is a long time, too, boyo."

Morrison closed the window and took the pipe from Glendower's absently trembling hands. Reloading it with long, adept fingers, he said, "After the Crusades, the League simply went underground. They never went away, and they never stopped exerting their will within their old territories in Iran and Syria."

The pipe came back to Glendower, who declined. "The stories we heard of your death were rather detailed."

"They had to be. I wouldn't have been much use as a faithful servant of His Majesty, otherwise. Did you believe them?"

"A few of us didn't. Two out of three from the old regiment gone and you sent away before the end. Maybe that was why some said you'd gone over . . ." Glendower's speech slurred and trailed off, but it was hardly because of what he'd drunk and smoked. Looking out the window, he left off talking and leapt to part the curtains and stare out into the dark.

"It's not just dark out there, is it, Morrison?"

"Very perceptive, old man. Yes, you're right. It's *gone*."

"And how long have we been stopped?" Now that he thought about it, he couldn't recall the train braking or even coasting to a stop, yet the compartment was still and silent.

Glendower groaned, a low, sad sound that came up from the toes of his boots. It never seemed to be the simple thing, the possible thing, anymore. He undid the latches on the window and threw his back into forcing it up a few inches before he jumped back, spitting Welsh curses.

The darkness poured in to pool on the carpet. Fine black sand, piled much higher than the window, it threatened to fill their compartment like an hourglass.

Morrison smiled like he'd heard a familiar tune in a strange place. "It appears we've reached our destination." He went to the door and jerked on the latch. It twisted and came off its hinges with a relieved squeal of rotten mahogany and crumbling rust. Black sand spilled into the compartment in a wave that soon came up to their ankles.

Glendower wrenched the rusted husk of the door aside. The wave of sand slowed and a ray of silvery moonlight cut through the clouds of dust.

"After you, old boy." Glendower stepped aside and stared into Morrison's hooded, deep green eyes. "You seem to know this country better than I."

"Indeed," Morrison said, barely hiding his bemused half-smile. He ducked under the doorway and crawled up over the dune that engulfed their car, then reached back to help Glendower up.

The Welshman scoffed at the hand and came up on his own, then stopped and whistled, looking about him. "Hardly Ploesti, is it?"

The train lay half-buried in a black desert under a too-full, too-large moon. Windows and doors hung open, but nowhere did he see any sign of the other passengers.

Glendower shook his head and considered punching himself. "What was really in that pipe?"

Beyond the abandoned train, the desert overran the horizon and a sky with only the constellation stars visible through the light of that overripe moon. Just over the next dune, there arose a mountain, but when they started to climb it, sand sifted away in great sheets, revealing the steps of a buried pyramid.

The view from the summit offered no comfort. Minarets eroded to tortured pillars, faceless colossi of luminous marble, crumbling ziggurats with great brass idols wreathed in thickets of human skeletons, polished to a dull gleam by the scouring simoom.

"None of this is real," Glendower said, hating the quaver in his voice. He started walking down the face of the next dune. Even if this were a nightmare, it felt real enough, and standing around wouldn't get him out of it. "We're still on the train, and you've slipped me a finn. Or else your friends . . ."

"You're most typically half-right, friend Marion." Morrison walked alongside him. "Marco Polo's stories of the Assassins' initiation, the garden of milk and honey and virgins and all that rot, fired the imagination, but no one ever found them. But they were real enough. You see, the *bhang* opens a door in the back of every human mind, one that leads to deeper dreaming. Under the spell of this particular smoke, the dreamer comes to this place. These are not the lands of Dream, but a memory palace, forged over centuries by fanatical adepts, until it has attained its own shadow reality. Our bodies are still on the train, but you and I are walking and talking here."

"And where is 'here'?" Glendower snapped.

"An Assassin's Heaven," Morrison said, "and Hell."

"I'm still waiting for my seventy-two virgins," Glendower growled.

The dreamlike landscape went on forever under the frozen silver moon, but past the graveyard of abandoned gods, he saw the gilded blossoms of minarets to dwarf the Hagia Sofia, Saint Peter's, or the Taj Mahal. Vast pleasure gardens spread out for miles in every direction, and the narcotic perfume of their flowers was wafted under his nose on the wind. Sparkling unnaturally in the darkness with the luminosity of a beacon, they promised pleasures unimaginable to mortal men, and wisdom unattainable in any earthly school.

"Ah, but temptations of the flesh are lost on you, aren't they, old boy?"

Glendower flinched, hesitating until his anger subsided. Any man who knew him less well would never dare . . . but Morrison had been at Ypres, and knew what happened to him there. "A man may lose the capacity for pleasurable distractions, but it sharpens his focus upon what truly matters."

"'What truly matters'?" Morrison nodded his head gravely. "Poor fellow, if only you were susceptible to such simple rewards," Morrison said, "how much simpler all of this would be."

A stiffer, colder wind drove them down into a narrow defile between a headless sphinx and a shattered Roman basilica, its vaulted dome broken like an eggshell. The walls were jumbles of crushed Corinthian columns and dismembered statuary.

"You seem to know enough about them," Glendower said.

"It's been a long few years, that's true."

"Once you tumbled to their game, they shared their *bhang* with you and fed you all this rot?"

Morrison started to open his mouth to pull the other one, but Glendower forestalled him. "How'd you get them to take you? You're hardly a practicing Mohammedan."

Now Morrison's grin broke out full on his face. His teeth looked long and yellow in the moonlight. "Neither are they, quite frankly. They never really were. They have need of men of all persuasions, now. They know the war of faiths is a Punch and Judy show. They've set their sights higher."

"The Ottoman Empire? They're welcome to it."

Morrison stopped and took Glendower by the arm, pulled him close and whispered. "You heard of that unpleasantness last year at the Hajj in Mecca?"

"More pilgrims trampled than usual, if memory serves. Some furor over the Ka'aba being defiled."

"That was *our* work, Marion. The pilgrimage came to bloodshed because the Black Stone at the heart of the sanctuary was stolen."

"Incredible . . . and absurd even if true, but to what end?"

"The Ka'aba was a holy site long before Islam. It was home to all the three hundred and sixty gods of the Arabs. When Mohammed retook Mecca, he smashed them all and replaced them with the Black Stone, which the Koran claims he received from an angel."

"Ah, yes. When he got it, the stone was white, but thanks to the sins of man . . ."

"Quite. And like most fables, this one had a grain of truth in it. The stone came from on high, all right, but no angel had a hand in it. We took it, Marion." He held out his hand, palm up, and half-clenched it. "It fit in my hand."

Glendower pulled away, but he still felt Morrison's fingers digging into his biceps. "What for? Just to provoke the Arabs to bloodshed?"

Morrison turned to walk on. "The Hajj went off the rails because the axle upon which it has turned is gone. We replaced it with a counterfeit, but the stone itself has been an object of ritual worship for nearly fifteen centuries. It's almost like the Curies' deadly radio-activity, really. It's absorbed a charge of faith that a clever adept could harness and use to do miracles."

At last, Morrison had given him something to push against. "You were always too clever for your own good, boyo." Glendower rubbed his burning, tired eyes. He'd had a bellyful of the scenery, and he couldn't bear to look at Morrison a moment longer. "They weren't after any 'Turk nationalists,' were they? They were hunting *you*. So now, you've returned to sell your new friends' mystical secrets to Whitehall?"

Chuckling indulgently, Morrison sauntered on down the path. "Nothing so mundane. I've learned things, Marion, that they'd happily go to war for. I've gone to places and learned things that even the current Old Man of the Mountain hasn't grasped. When the Templars and the Assassins first clashed in the Crusades, it was clear that they had more in common with each other than with anyone on their own 'sides.' The Assassins of old could move unseen through cities and strike at their enemies anywhere, at any time. At the final level of mastery, they could not be killed at all.

"In their mystical explorations, they came across a true deity who answered prayers and rewarded his faithful in this world and the next. All he demanded was a sacrifice of the very type soldiers are specifically trained to yield up on demand: kill in His name, and never die."

The shadows crept and waxed and waned under the guttering,

cloud-shrouded moon, giving a spark of fitful, unwholesome life to the deadfalls of ruined monuments. *Shattered idols*, Glendower thought with a sour glance back at Morrison, who had quite completely disappeared.

"*Cachau bant*," Glendower snarled in his native tongue, crude yet labyrinthine in its wealth of profanities. His holster and gun were gone, though he was quite sure he'd not removed them, but a short, curved fighting knife was sheathed in its place, and the stiletto in his boot was still there.

Their place—*memory palace*, he corrected himself—their rules. He didn't care for it, but worse was thinking of this nine-hundred-year-old nightmare as a *place*. Some deeply buried sense in the back of his brain made him suspect that it was acceptance of the dream that made it real to start with.

He tried to reject it and will himself back into his body on the couch in the special compartment on the Simplon Orient Express as it hurtled across the empty, bandit-haunted Thracian countryside. Morrison would be there, hanging over him like a cat and guiding his trance, hoping to bludgeon Glendower into pledging his allegiance to whatever abominable hedge-deity he'd gone native for.

Under the moaning wind, he fancied he could hear the metronomic clatter of steel wheels and the low, sonorous tolling of a bell. Brighter and flatter than church bells, more like a ship's bell, or a train . . . but it faded away when he tried to follow it.

Feeling eyes on the back of his neck, he whirled around and around, but saw no sign of Morrison or anyone else.

"You still doubt your senses, old boy. But this is bigger than nations . . . beyond life and death."

Glendower started at the booming voice, which seemed to come from directly overhead. He lifted his own voice to a shout that echoed through the sandy arcades of triumphal arches and headless emperors. "You'd bring us the same protection that serves them so well, and all we'd have to do is worship their god. I wonder: have you come to sell them to us, or us to them?"

Morrison's face hove into view. It was as big as the moon, leering down into the monument-choked canyon like a mischievous child over an anthill. "Will your masters in Whitehall mourn for you, old friend? Whenever they sit down to write themselves into history, they use soldiers' blood for ink. Well, we needn't die for their iron whims. We needn't die at all!"

His hand came swooping down, nearly the size of a Sopwith Camel and open wide to seize Glendower as it would a cowering mouse—if only Glendower could be made to cower.

Drawing his knife, he evaded the enormous grasping hand and drove the blade into the index finger's tip, burying it to the hilt under the great horny plate of the fingernail.

Morrison roared and tried to smash Glendower with his wounded hand. A torrent of blood left Glendower floundering blind in a red deluge.

He had only just crawled into a niche between two toppled caryatids when the downpour ceased. "You will see what He can offer those who are useful." Now the voice was a low, hissing whisper that seemed to come from all around him. "Such rewards as even a eunuch can appreciate."

Glendower lashed out with his other knife but found no target. And still he could hear Morrison, like the bastard was in his own head with him.

"Queen and country don't matter any more to you than they do to me. There's no East and West. Nations and faiths, kings and even gods . . . all are puppets."

Glendower itched all over. He raked his hair with his fingers and gasped with disgust. His hair was plastered to his scalp with cold, clotting blood, but it was also alive with wriggling things. Morrison's blood had coagulated into plump red larvae that squirmed from his grip or clung to his ruined suit. Clenching his teeth and squeezing his eyes shut, he brushed them violently off his body. He willed himself to awaken, for if this were a dream, surely he would have shocked himself awake. Surely he was still asleep and dreaming under the influence of that damned drug. He strove to feel the leather couch beneath his supine body and not the sensation of teeming, boneless bodies bursting under his hands and feet. This was nothing more than a hideous trick concocted by Morrison to drive him mad . . . but why? "You and your god have it all sewn up," he said. "What do you fancy me for?"

"Knights are needed—" the whispers came from every crevice in the ruins "—for a new Crusade. Men who would kill or die for

Britain, but who have no love for England. All who oppose us will fall like wheat before the scythe. We could be the ones who gather the harvest, old boy."

Glendower gave no answer. He lit a match and launched a few rocks at the largest of the creeping larvae wriggling among the ruins. He could see the sky was paler, but that meant nothing here.

"I took a great chance, trying to talk to you, for old times' sake. You were a lion in your time, and I could've used who and what you know at home to reconquer the Empire from the head down. But if you're going to be a—"

"Oh, I am."

"Right. You may as well know, then. Only initiates under the influence would be brought here in their sleep. They were promised they could return upon their deaths, but their oath of fealty was hardly enough for the Old Man of the Mountain. So they were ritually murdered here, as you will be."

Following the winding defile, Glendower ran into an ancient Christian temple. Shattered idols paved the aisle between crooked columns that bore white tapestries emblazoned with red crosses, and mosaic floors inlaid with images of the Holy Grail and the Crucifixion were encrusted with septic, ritually spilled filth. "You may as well wake us up, so we can have it out proper. Nothing you can show me in here will make me believe—"

"You needn't believe in any of it, you poor fool. You only have to die here to wake up. Every time you lay down to sleep, your dreams will bring you back here. Every time you close your eyes, you will be delivered to us . . . and it won't be all milk and honey."

Glendower scoffed, "It's hardly been anything at all, but cheap theatrics and yellow treachery."

He passed through chapels crowded with idols—of a headless man of red agate, with a golden hand outstretched; a toadlike, brazen giant with webbed claws holding out the small, charred bones of the last infants it had claimed as its just tribute. But all these false idols were arranged like serfs or slaves, an audience before the great central dais that was dominated by a small mountain of obsidian floating just off the floor and carved into the cruel, cold features of a god of war.

"Baphomet," said Glendower, "innit?" Hardly seemed prudent

to speak the god's true name aloud, in this unholy place. He had been lucky to survive encounters with the cult in its other incarnations, in Egypt and China. "You lot never do seem to pick a winner, do you?"

It made a measure of sense indeed, if one pried beneath the surface of that ancient travesty, the purge of the Templars. Captive knights confessed under torture to participating in a Mystery cult that spurned Christ and worshipped a goatish deity from the East whose idol was a great, black human head. The confessions were as vague and rife with contradictions as any testimony obtained under torture. No evidence of the wild orgiastic rites they described was ever uncovered in Europe or the Holy Land. But if Templars and Assassins alike had sinned and blasphemed in the fastness of this rotten old dream, then perhaps their wholesale elimination was not so rash a miscarriage of justice after all. With every step toward the dais, the flagstones shuddered and burst with gusts of charnel decay. Everywhere underfoot, the mummies of holy crusaders surged out of their crypts to split open and vomit torrents of overgrown grave worms. The incarnated greed of the grave, they boiled out of the tombs and reliquaries, devouring each other and growing larger even as they came writhing across the treacherous floor to converge on Glendower.

Leaping from the shallow rows of limestone pews that shattered under his weight, he came to crouch atop the wet red altar at the head of the temple.

"I did so hope you would see it my way." Morrison stepped out from behind the floating idol, wearing clerical vestments and holding a curling, serrated dagger like an ibex horn. "Baphomet was only one of His faces," he said, circling Glendower at a cautious distance, a patient smile on his face. "Of all the Outer Gods, only He has deigned to walk among men. He ruled over ancient Egypt as the Daemon Sultan, built and buried a capitol greater than Memphis for his tomb. As a god of the Mongols, he once accepted the blood sacrifice of thirty thousand men and women in a single day. On a thousand other worlds, he's worshipped by gents who can fly between the stars, do you understand? It's not just this world we gain, if we're on the right side. It's *everything*, you barbaric Welsh buffoon, and you have no idea how big that is."

Glendower lunged at Morrison but fell short, sliding halfway into a shallow crusader's tomb bubbling over with fat white worms. "I have some idea how big *you* still are," Glendower said in a low, defeated voice that drew Morrison a fatal step closer. Stumbling, he steadied himself by plunging his arms into the overflowing crypt. "And I reckon you're still not too big to kill, at least not yet."

Morrison grinned as he brought down the dagger. Glendower flailed backward, arms high above his head. The crude, curving blade sank deep into Glendower's chest. It would have pierced his heart, had he stood still for it.

Just as the knife pierced his flesh, Glendower laid into Morrison with the great two-handed bastard sword he'd found in the crypt. Its huge, wild weight smashed Morrison to his knees and clove his torso in half from the right shoulder down to the top of his sternum.

"Call Him now, boyo," Glendower said.

Gasping, flopping backward, Morrison tripped and fell into a crypt and sank out of sight in the churning sea of worms.

Glendower swore in ten tongues as he pulled Morrison's dagger out of his chest. It hurt as badly as getting stabbed ever did, but he wasn't coughing blood, for a mercy. The shredded sleeve of his coat served as a compress.

With his good arm, he took a wrought-iron candelabrum stand and used it to stab and sweep a path through the rising flood of bloated worms. After several near-disasters, he alit on the only apparent exit, a corkscrew staircase behind the dais that bored into the vaulted ceiling.

He raced up the stairs and entered a chill tunnel in the glassy black rock. Bouncing from wall to wall in his staggering exhaustion, he despaired of light and fresh air, and felt no relief even when the tunnel ended at the head of a narrow trail along the face of a sheer cliff. The chill, whistling wind of that great, empty sky was somehow more oppressive than the confines of a coffin.

I've got to wake up, he told himself. But for all its unreal atmosphere, this nightmare seemed quite resolutely real to his ragged, beaten body. Morrison had found some method of making this place his own, playing his games in a mad attempt to kill Glendower or force his fearful loyalty. Clearly, the mad bastard hadn't known him very well, after all. Funny how facing danger together could make one think his mates were more than brothers. He'd thought he knew Morrison a good deal better, too.

As if reflecting his tortured thoughts, the trail twisted and twitched to the top of the cliff, and Glendower sat gratefully upon a rock outcrop to take stock of the terrain. Looming on the distorted horizon, the Assassin's pleasure pavilions beckoned, but when Glendower turned his back on them, he caught sight of something he couldn't refuse so easily. The trail wound down from the dizzy heights to the shore of an inland sea. The depths of the sea were obscured by the moon's reflection and by leaden archipelagos of cloud, but as he descended, Glendower watched the play of moonlight on the strangely gentle ocean. He could only pray that it was fresh water, but he had no reason to expect any mercy.

When at last the trail ended in a spill of gravel that he rode down to the edge of the gray water, he felt some little gratitude to find the water brackish, but not salty. Certainly they'd have better refreshment at the pavilions of milk and honey, but he knew just enough about the true nature of Morrison's master to warn him against calling there.

Horrors from Outside and savage butchery he could abide if he had to, but temptation of any kind was something else again. Avoiding it made the worst places home for the Welshman, and his service something as frightening to his paymasters in London as he was to the Empire's enemies.

He'd hypnotized himself into a fugue of self-pity as he cleaned and bound his wounds while absently watching the horizon, the strange illusion of convexity to the great lake that made Glendower think he was seeing the curvature of this tiny, lost world.

Then the moon went behind a cloud, and Glendower got a glimpse of what he was drinking from. When the play of silvery light was doused, the gray waters revealed strange and hideous things skimming on its viscous surface and coils of red veins like submerged mangrove forests, and moving across the face of the waters like a phantom moon, like some predator bigger than any wave, was a great black whirlpool encircled by a gold-flecked brown corona.

Glendower retreated from the shore, climbing high enough to

confirm his initial, absurd impression. The circle of gold-rimmed blackness that swept across the great gray sea was the iris of a colossal eye.

Studying the craggy rocks, he belatedly saw the signs: the fluted black spires along the shore that he'd mistaken for charred trees or chimneys of lava rock—eyelashes—and the water he'd so gratefully drunk—tears.

He was certain enough that it couldn't see him. For all its impossible size, the eye had looked human. It wasn't the color of Morrison's eyes, which were a faded blue-gray. Perhaps he walked on the infinite face of Baphomet. If this were the true birthplace of the Assassins, then perhaps it was the original Old Man of the Mountain himself.

Fair enough, then. If this were the Old Man's mad dream, then one only had to figure a way to wake him up.

Morrison's voice came from on high again, but now it sounded weak and distant, a fading train-whistle on the wind. "My loyalty to the Crown was still a going thing. War between East and West is coming, inevitable . . . They know it. We could've led a new Empire to greater glory. . . ."

Shaking his heavy head, Glendower paced the cliff face overlooking the shore of the eye. "And with both sides worshipping the same greedy bastard god, the sacrifices would run on time, no matter who won."

He found a few stands of twisted, bone-dry wood and wedged the branches into the cracks in the stone. Morrison didn't answer right away. Maybe he was otherwise engaged, out there in the waking world with a knife to his old captain's throat.

The desiccated wood absorbed his water avidly, swelling like automobile tyres and widening the cracks in the lip of the cliff overlooking the eye.

"You'll live to regret this, old boy," Morrison said, just over Glendower's shoulder. The captain wheeled about, but Morrison was nowhere in sight. Instead, he faced a horde of tottering skeletons in the tarnished chainmail of Templar knights and the black embroidered rags and leather armor of Syrian Assassins. Their gnawed and polished bones were knitted together by knots of tomb-worms that clung to their limbs and animated them in grim parody of the flesh they'd devoured, wriggling in eyesockets and waving from gaping jaws in hideous imitation of facial features. Glendower dodged blind, halting sword thrusts, then lashed out with the sacrificial dagger, chopping through flimsy human wreckage and flinging the phalanx of decay back upon itself.

Clumsy as they were, he was pushed steadily back toward the edge of the cliff. Wherever their claws raked his unprotected flesh, the wounds blackened instantly and sent threads of infection coursing into his blood. His limbs began to falter, weakened by sickness as well as fatigue. He felt the edge of the cliff under his trembling heels and the oddly sweet sea breeze racing off the face of that awful ocean at his back. He tried to believe that Morrison had been lying when he fed him all that rot about this place. *Every time you close your eyes, you will be delivered to us. . . .*

A shrieking, concussive wind nearly hurled him into their teeth. All fell silent, and Glendower turned to see something like a waterspout erupt from the black vortex of the awesome eye.

So violent was its agitated ascent from the convexity that spawned it, that Glendower mistook it for a black cloud, but as it rose and drew nearer, he saw that it was somehow a thing of restless flesh, clawing its way up toward the gray emptiness of heaven. Wings seemed to sprout, wither, and disintegrate with each stroke, and its half-formed body was at once solid and gas, worm and bird, machine and demon. The only constant was the infestation of scarlet eyes casting a lambent glow from what served it for a head.

Glendower almost relished this fresh impossibility, but before his attackers could take advantage of his awestruck paralysis, the eye-born horror had vanished into the clouds, the uncanny echoes of its shrieking and an errant rain of tears tumbling down in its wake. Then all sound was drowned out by the cannonade of boulders fracturing. The cliff subsided and tipped to spill the worm-ridden horde toward him in a grisly avalanche.

With a last desperate burst of energy, Glendower leapt into the teeth of their tumbling swords, climbing over their helmets and shields as they fell, springing with arms thrown wide to catch the jagged lip of the new cliff-face.

He never reached it. Falling short, he watched in a kind of dilated, paralytic terror as the edge passed beyond his reach. Just below him, the plummeting rain of boulders struck the placid surface of the sleeping eye—

Curling in anticipation of impact, Glendower rolled and struck his head upon the polished teak paneling of his compartment aboard the Wagons-Lits car.

The shock of waking brought a series of seizures, mad, breathless laughter alternating with shivering and flashes of feverish nausea. His brain was a brick, his body clammy with tepid sweat, and his hand went reflexively to press at a stabbing phantom pain in his chest.

The compartment reeked like an abattoir. He looked for something to be sick into, then to open the window, but it was already open. In point of fact, it was gone. Frigid alpine wind gushed in the gaping hole, but did little to remove the stench that wafted from his traveling companion.

Lieutenant Morrison leaned back on his couch with the ivory-handled knife still resting in his hand. His chin rested on his chest as if he might wake up at any moment, or as if he were intently considering the ghastly trench in his torso.

The traitor had been opened from clavicles to crotch and inspected with all the diligence of a Bolshevik customs officer. All the major organs along the digestive and pulmonary routes were bisected and turned inside out like a smuggler's pockets, and a compact, swirling smear of blood on the curtain beside the missing window looked as if someone had wiped the gore away from something small and probably quite precious.

In its mad rush for answers, his disordered mind seized upon Morrison's preposterous story about the stone from the Ka'aba. *Kidney trouble*, Glendower thought.

Nothing could explain why they had stepped over him to do their grisly work, and hadn't troubled to cut his throat. Stranger still, the narrow window had been thoroughly smashed out to effect the murderer's escape, but no sign of entry, not even a sliver of broken glass anywhere in the compartment, remained. But that was mad, though no more nor less than the observation that the brackish dampness that saturated Morrison's clothing and the curtains had a horribly familiar odor.

Glendower closed the curtains and covered his old friend with a carriage blanket, then rang for the conductor. When the knock came, he cracked the door and studied the smiling Frenchman in the corridor before he ordered a bottle of brandy and requested a telegram to London the moment they reached Sofia.

The conductor was almost embarrassed to correct the captain, but they would be arriving in Vienna quite shortly. He had knocked to alert the travelers that the train's bar had been restocked in Sofia last night, but received no reply.

Biting his lip as he worked out the code from the cipher in his head, Glendower made out the message on the conductor's pad and passed it through the slitted doorway, mindful to block any view of his traveling companion.

Nose wrinkled, the conductor turned to leave when Glendower caught his arm.

"Scratch the brandy," he said, his eyes straying back to the corpse and the ivory pipe still resting in its blood-flecked hand. *Every time you close your eyes . . .* "Turkish coffee. Hot as hell and black as the Devil, and keep it coming till Paris."

A FINGER'S WORTH OF COAL

RICHARD DANSKY

IT WAS IN BRATISLAVA WHERE they put the fireman off the train, with the help of two burly passengers and a rather larger contingent from the local gendarmerie. The incident caused no small amount of scandal among the passengers, at least those who were aware of the disturbance, as it isn't often that a screaming, thrashing man covered in coal dust and blood is hauled bodily from his station by officers of the law. In an odd reversal of fortune, those impecunious enough to have purchased berths in the cars closest to the locomotive had the best view of the proceedings, which made them suddenly and briefly sought after by the curious among the wealthier travelers. Later, over drinks in one of the dining cars, more than one witness suggested that they'd seen the man, a thick-legged Magyar who'd come on board with the lumbering Hungarian 4-8-0 engine they'd acquired in Vienna, contorting in inhuman fashion and heard him screaming in a language that none of them could either translate or identify. This odd fact was later confirmed by those same two burly gentlemen, who after some delay had returned to the train and were now being feted like conquering heroes.

Graciously, the two—one a lawyer named Higdon with a London legal firm on his way to Istanbul on business; the other, Walters, the stolid personal assistant to a certain professor of natural sciences *en route* to a series of speaking engagements in Sofia—allowed the other passengers to purchase refreshing beverages for them in exchange for further details of their adventures.

It seemed, said the professor's assistant, that the fireman had abruptly begun acting as if he were *possessed*. When pressed for details as to what this meant, he rose briefly and demonstrated, flailing his arms, then commented that it was as if the man had somehow become unacquainted with the proper use of his limbs. In addition, he said, the man had been seen swinging a coal shovel about and generally screeching in what could be understood as no human tongue. His assistant had tried to restrain him and had gotten a vicious blow from the shovel in return. He, too, had been taken off the train, albeit on a stretcher, and it was doubtful as to whether he'd survive the night.

"Curious thing," interjected Higdon, clearly tired of having Walters relate the lion's share of the tale, "was that after they took the man to the police station, he just collapsed. No more screaming, no more of that damned animal talk. No, sir, out like a candle in a stiff breeze, that one was. Couldn't wake him up or get a word out of him, either." A bevy of young ladies traveling together heard this pronouncement and cooed in the lawyer's direction; their fluttered eyelashes told him how very impressed they were with this new tidbit. He flushed, and smiled, and wriggled up a bit straighter in his seat.

Walters coughed slightly, and all eyes turned to him. "Actually," he said, "there was one thing the man muttered after he stopped struggling. Under his breath, though, so I'm not surprised you missed it, Higdon." The lawyer stopped flushing and started glaring, but Walters ignored him magnificently.

"What was the word, dear boy?" asked the professor himself, a balding yet thoroughly mustachioed man named Madison. "You must share."

Walters nodded. "He said—well, whispered really—one thing. One word before he slipped away."

"Yes?" Even the lawyer was leaning forward now, and if the young ladies had been dewy-eyed before, now they were positively limpid.

"He said something that sounded like '*szen*.'"

"Ah," said Professor Madison, and sat back in his chair. "Of course he would."

"It's nonsense," blustered the lawyer.

"No," Madison countered. "It's Magyar."

"What does it mean?" twittered one of the young ladies. "Something dark and mysterious?"

"It means," Madison said, "coal."

"I suppose it wasn't entirely necessary to embarrass Higdon like that, was it?" asked Walters as he and his employer picked their way back toward one of the restaurant cars for their evening meal. Ordinarily, Madison had confided in his man, he would have disembarked for his evening repast, as he had quite been looking forward to a meal at *Traja Muskieteri*, and perhaps finishing his evening with a *pajgle* or two. The incident of the fireman, however, had quite put a pall on the day, to the extent that very few of the passengers had disembarked even with the announcement that there would be an extended stay while the police examined the scene for evidence. That they had found nothing in no way reflected on their thoroughness, nor on their enthusiasm, which was much remarked upon by the passengers. Indeed, they had taken so much time that it was now well past six, the train's departure having been delayed nearly half a day by the police investigation.

Now, however, it seemed that whatever conclusions there were to be drawn had been drawn, and the Orient Express had been released to seek its destiny farther down the line. At the front of the train, the lumbering 4-8-0 bellowed its discontent with the state of affairs. Clearly, someone had been found to feed it the coal it desired, and the engine was stoked and ready to travel.

Madison stopped to regard his protégé as the train lurched slowly into motion, jerking unsteadily forward as it restarted its long journey to Istanbul. "Embarrass Higdon? I supposed we did, at that. Not that he didn't deserve it, mind you—the man's a bully and a fool, only interested in making himself look more dashing to a gaggle of silly young things. Such habits are unbecoming, and should be discouraged wherever possible. I marvel that a reminder of the perils of this sort of behavior would be necessary after Boston."

Walters, whose thoughts had briefly drifted to the young ladies in question, shook his head. As for the brawl in Boston, he had the two twisted fingers on his right hand to remind him of that folly; they had never properly healed after he stepped in to silence a brute muttering obscenities at some schoolgirls.

The train had started moving, the *click-click* of the wheels coming faster and faster until they blended into a satisfying hum. And for an instant, the hum became something more, a buzzing that filled his brain; all around him was not the luxury of the finest passenger rail Europe had to offer, but rather a vista ancient and green and poisonously alive. Then it was gone, and all that was left was the train, and the professor, and a vague sense of unease.

"Is something wrong?" Madison asked, but Walters shook his head. "Nothing, I'm sure," he muttered.

"Dinner, then," said the professor, "and then I'll need to prepare for those talks a bit. You might want to spend the evening reading about the geology we're passing through. Fascinating stuff, really." It was not, Walters knew, a suggestion.

"Of course, Professor," he said. "To the dining car?"

"To the dining car."

Walters read until late into the night, long after Professor Madison had himself turned in. The minutiae of the fossiliferous coal swamps that dotted the region were less than enthralling, and yet he pressed onward, lest he fail to acquire the breadth of knowledge Madison required in his assistant. After all, the professor was a man of many and varied interests, some of them esoteric, and to apprentice under him was to need to know a veritable cornucopia of disconnected facts and call them forth at a moment's notice.

Twice more, as the train adjusted its speed for some curve or bridge, he had those faint, unsettling visions, but they vanished quickly. No doubt brought on by thoughts of the ancient landscapes he'd been reading about, he told himself, and eventually folded himself up for bed. The book he'd been attacking lay discarded on the floor, its impressive color plates of ancient insects and lumbering amphibians temporarily forgotten.

And it was only as consciousness faded that he remembered, dimly, that the buzzing and the first vision had come well before he'd read the first page.

❖   ❖   ❖

"Ahem."

Walters looked up; Professor Madison did not, instead choosing to concentrate on the *pfannkuchen* that comprised the largest part of his breakfast. Standing ostentatiously by the table was the lawyer, Higdon, whose piggy gaze was focused on the professor with an expression of triumphant contempt.

"Can I help you?" asked Madison.

Higdon's gaze swiveled over to where Walters sat, the demolished remains of his breakfast spread out before him. "Oh, I don't think you can. You certainly can't help that poor fellow back in Bratislava?"

"The fireman?" Walters asked. "Is there a new development?"

"More like a final one," Higdon puffed. "He's dead, you see." '

"Dead?" the professor interjected, putting down his paper and looking up from his apple pancakes.

"Oh, quite so." Higdon stopped for a moment, looking around as if to ensure the whole car could hear him dispensing a little tidbit of knowledge the so-wise professor did not possess. "Word just just came over the telegraph. Flung himself out a window in the hospital once he understood that the train had left without him. Shouting '*Szen, szen, szen*' the whole time, too. Loved his work a little too much, I guess, eh?" The last was accompanied by a buffoonish chortle, and then the lawyer turned to go. Walters rose to go after him, but Madison put a restraining hand on his arm.

"Let him go," the professor advised, but Walters pulled away.

"He's damned rude."

"As you noted, we did embarrass him. Only natural of him to try to get back."

"Yes, but to use a man's death to do so? Despicable!" Walters glared at the other passengers who'd been watching the drama; most of them had the common decency to flush and look away.

Madison raised a solitary eyebrow. "You're not going to get us thrown off the train, are you? The last time you thrashed a man in a dining car, it cost us two days' layover in Cincinnati."

"He swung at me first, as you may recall," Walters retorted. "And, no, I merely intend to express my dismay at his rudeness, and perhaps to call him a blackguard, a rake, and a cad."

"If you must." Madison sighed and hoisted himself to his feet. "As for me, I'm more interested in what Higdon said than in why he said it. *Szen* indeed."

But Walters was already gone, headed for the rapidly closing door at the end of the dining car. He passed through it and across the swaying gap, into the next car where he fully expected to see Higdon forcing his unpleasant company on some passenger or other.

Instead, there was nothing. Travelers sat here and there at tables, sipping drinks and playing cards or reading novels, but of the brusque solicitor there was no sign. Nor did the door at the far end of the car appear to be in any state of activation.

"You," he said, and wheeled to face a porter. "A man came through here just now. What happened to him?"

The man shook his head in confusion. "No man came through, sir. I'm sorry, sir, but you must be mistaken."

"But I saw him," Walters protested, to no avail. The porter was firmly polite but quite certain no one had passed him. In fact, the door hadn't even been opened until the young gentleman came through. If he wanted to ask the other passengers. . . .

"Very well," Walters said, perplexed, slipping the man a crumpled banknote by way of an apology. He thought about heading back to breakfast, but his irritation with Higdon's bad behavior had settled in his stomach like a knot, with no chance now to exorcise it. Better, he thought, to return to the compartment, retrieve the book, and resume his studies whilst the train chugged onward. His course decided, he nodded to the porter and made his way through the car.

But still, Higdon's disappearance nagged at him. Where could the man have gone? Surely he hadn't jumped from the train between cars, and yet, he'd evaporated as surely as water left on a hot stove. The whole thing felt unreal, the train and everything on it suddenly taking on the cast of ephemeral phantoms, as solid only as smoke.

The steady thrum of the train's wheels sang counterpoint to

Walters's internal debate as he passed out of the car and on to the next one, a buzzy hum that made stringing together complex thoughts impossible.

The new car was mostly empty, at least—the side route through Bratislava was not the most popular, he knew—and the absence of fellow travelers was a relief. Even the porter of this car had abandoned his station, no doubt for one of the innumerable cigarette breaks that were as much a part of Eastern Europe as crumbling signs of Turkish occupation.

A couple of old men drowsed at a table by a window, neither of them conscious of the scholar's passing. He gave them a nod as he trudged forward, bracing himself as the train threw itself around a curve and into a long, level straightaway.

As it did, the humming grew stronger, a low, insectile sound that persisted underneath the normal clank and bustle of the rolling stock. Walters could *feel* the sound now as well as hear it, could sense it climbing up from the carpet and through the soles of his shoes. Shaking his head, he took another step forward and immediately regretted it. His left foot felt leaden, his right tingled uncontrollably to the point where it went numb and he lost his balance. Pitching forward, he caught himself with a splayed right hand against the doorframe, which proved to be a mistake.

Instantly, the twisted fingers gave way and his palm felt as if he were grasping a handful of angry hornets. Sting upon sting upon sting bit into his flesh in rapid succession. The sensation crawled up his arm, climbing nerve to nerve until everything below the shoulder was a ball of agony. The force of it was enough to drop him to his knees, driving the breath out of him in a singular grunt. He held there for a moment, unable to make the muscles of his arm work well enough to pull his pained fingers away before the torment crept up his legs as well. Marching forward like jungle ants, the feeling crawled along every limb, meeting and twisting together in the space around his heart. Slowly he sank to the floor, his vision blurring as the buzzing grew louder and the pain crept up his spine to electrify the very base of his brain, and then . . .

Then suddenly he wasn't on the train at all. With no wall to brace against, he toppled down into a thick, oozing mud. The painful tingling in his arms and legs had stopped, however, and after a moment of wondering exactly what had happened, he pulled himself up out of the muck.

Kneeling—he didn't quite trust himself to stand—he wiped mud from his face with his good hand, marveling at the clingy qualities of the thick, black stuff. It was not the mud that truly startled him, though; it was what was growing out of it.

He saw now that he knelt on a small island or tumulus in the middle of a vast swamp, one that positively thrummed with life. Gleaming insects in iridescent green and blue and gold swooped and swarmed, dragonflies cutting the thick, steamy air with doubled wings and a steely sense of purpose. Everywhere, plants rose up out of the discolored water, an explosion of greenery reaching upward to a thick canopy that nearly shut out the sky. These were not trees, though; instead, they could only be titanic ferns or cycads, whose golden trunks speared up from black water to disappear in the canopy overhead. Some, he guessed, were over two hundred feet tall.

Which implied that the creatures swooping among them were huge as well—surely too huge to fly. And yet there they were, larger than birds, wings beating the thick, rich air.

Now that the visual shock was done, the sounds of his surroundings had a chance to assault his ears. And what sounds they were: the buzzing of those titanic insect wings, the thick sounds of muddy water flowing, the croaking of frogs, and in the distance, the wet bellows of massive beasts yet unseen. But just as disturbing were the sounds that he did *not* hear. There was no birdsong, no scuttling of squirrels in the "trees" or mice in the ferny undergrowth.

And, of course, no sounds of men. No thunderous engine, no clack of wheels over well-laid tracks, no voices calling or axes cutting into ancient, unfeeling wood. The entire scene sounded unfinished, absent so much of what Walters realized he took for granted. All evidence of mankind was absent, and he was utterly alone.

Or nearly so. He looked around at the island he stood on, a hummock a few hundred feet across rising up out of the muck and yet made largely of muck itself. Too many steps in any direction would lead him off its edge into the turgid waters, and his imagination quickly conjured the sorts of creatures that might dwell under the surface in a place like this.

Yet, in the mud he saw footprints—shod ones. They circled his position, he saw, then led away toward the water's edge. Treading carefully, he followed.

The prints were deep, deeper than his own, which implied a heavier man had made them.

Higdon had been larger than he, Walters recalled. His shoes might have made tracks very much like these.

Six feet from the water, the tracks stopped.

More accurately, they vanished, wiped out by a greater disturbance. The ground had been torn up here, obliterating any record of the man's passage. Instead, there were great, sharp gouges dug into the earth, ones that looked suspiciously like the work of massive claws. There was a familiar scent here, too, coppery but faint. He started to kneel down for a closer look, but some primal sense of danger stopped him, some unsuspected clue that told him he was in terrible danger.

The insects, it seemed, had found him.

He turned as a gleaming battalion of dragonflies plunged toward him, mandibles clacking with hunger. Questions of where he was became academic as he threw himself down to the ground, just under the first wing of swooping predators. They buzzed past as he rolled to his knees, then wheeled about in obscene formation to come around for another pass.

Then they were upon him, diving for his face and the tender softness of his eyes. Crouching down, he swung wildly at them, hoping to drive them away. One fist connected with a shocking *thwock*, the sound like that of wood on wood, and a monstrous bug spiraled down into the mud. Quickly, he smashed down with his fist and was rewarded with a satisfying crunch of chitin and a spray of foul-smelling innards. But that was just one of hundreds, and even as it twitched its last more swarmed to the attack.

One fastened on his forearm, its mandibles plunging down through the fabric of his shirt to pierce the meat underneath. He flung it away, but there was fresh blood in the air now, and more and more insects converged on him. Swinging, flailing, he was blinded by the cloud until inevitably he lost his balance, falling back into the warm, wet mud. He tried to escape, but the sucking, gooey muck held him tightly. The insects, sensing their prey was helpless, dove in for the kill. Walters shuddered as the ravenous jewels descended upon him.

And then, from somewhere very close, a monstrous, bubbling roar split the air.

The dragonflies reacted instantly. They stopped their aerobatics, holding position like a deadly curtain of the aurora while the roar sounded again. Then there was a sudden, sharp crack, and one of the dragonflies disappeared in a cloud of foetid vapor. A second sound, and another one burst, and then they were flying in all directions, a frantic explosion of vanishing color.

Desperately, Walters pulled free from the muck and scrambled to his feet to face the new danger. What he saw defied rational description. Rising up out of the water was a creature, green-skinned and rubbery, with a rough slash for a mouth that extended halfway around its bulbous head. Its front two feet rested on the island itself and they were heavy and clawed, barely supporting the beast's pendulous belly. It chewed, its lower jaw cycling in an odd, circling motion as what was undoubtedly one of the dragonflies crunched between its teeth. From nose to tail, Walters estimated, it was at least twelve feet long.

The real monster sat on its back.

It was huge, a wet gray cone that rose up to a series of four odd points. What only could be described as tentacles drooped from these, and Walters could not fail to note that the two extended in his direction ended in lurid claws clutching odd silvery objects. A third blossomed into a cluster of bright red mushrooms, while the fourth was festooned with bulging, inhuman eyes. They stared at him for a moment, during which time Walters got the shuddering sensation that the thing was studying him as he himself had studied amphibious specimens staked out in dissecting trays, pondering where to make the first incision.

The creature's mount opened its obscene mouth and roared, the sound echoing out of its fleshy gullet. Then, step by ponderous step it lurched forward. Its claws reached for him amidst a storm of excited clicking noises. He threw himself back as best he could as the horror plunged closer, until . . .

He found himself on the floor of the compartment he shared with the professor, who was staring down at him with raised eyebrow.

"Good heavens, Walters, you're filthy" Madison said. Walters tried to answer and found himself gasping for air, but Madison waved him off. "Go wash up and change, for God's sake. I think you've got a story to tell me."

An hour, one shower, and several brandies later, Walters found himself seated across from the professor, who gazed at him with keen interest. He'd been through the story of what he'd seen, or at least most of it: the swamp, the insects, the titanic cycads. The rest, though, he kept to himself. It was a vision too far—monstrous insects were one thing, actual monsters were another, and there was only so much a man of science such as the professor would accept.

"You're hiding something," Madison finally said, "But it'll be out in due time. Now this vision of yours—what do you think you saw?"

"I didn't see it, Professor, I lived it," Walters protested. "The mud, the blood—"

"The bites and the ichor all over your clothes, quite convincing, yes. So what did all that say to you?"

"It said to get home in a hurry," Walters replied, and took another swig of brandy. "That it was no place for men."

Madison nodded. "If pressed, I'd say it sounded like a swamp of the Carboniferous Era. Which, coincidentally, is some of what I'm having you study. Are you certain this isn't some sort of charade to get me to assign you more reading on the late Cretaceous?"

"Professor!" Walters was ready to rise out of his seat in protest until he saw that Madison was chuckling.

"Easy there, young friend. I have no reason to doubt your story. The evidence—" he pointed to the muddy footprints that now dominated the compartment "—is most compelling. Besides, even if you'd faked the other bits, your materialization on the carpet was most impressive. But it just adds another mystery to the ones we were already investigating."

"Other mysteries?"

Madison ticked them off on his fingers. "The fireman who went mad. The disappearing Mister Higdon, Esquire. And now your sojourn. I find it worrisome in the extreme."

"So you think they're connected?"

The professor nodded. "It seems likely. Speaking of which, what do *you* think really happened to the poor Magyar?"

Walters rubbed his aching head. "The conventional wisdom is that he went mad, yes?"

"You saw him. We're long past the conventional. But why mad now, and why on this train? He'd done the run, with that same fellow that he attacked, dozens of times before. And don't forget, he said something about the coal."

"I'm afraid you've lost me."

Madison smiled thinly. "Never mind. It may be time I made some inquiries. It's definitely time you lay down and got some rest."

"But I can help—"

"Rest," said Madison. "There'll be plenty of time to help later, I'm sure." He ushered Walters into his bunk, pulled down the shades, and then left. His footsteps echoed down the corridor as the young man sank back into his pillow, gradually merging with the relentless thrum of the train's progress.

Muzzily, Walters closed his eyes, counting in a dreamy four-four time as the wheels below rolled and clicked, eventually dissolving into a comforting, buzzing hum.

There was something about the hum, he realized. Something that he should recognize.

It was getting louder now, and he forced himself to open his eyes. All around him he could see the berth in the dimming light, the now-familiar brass fixtures gleaming with sunset glints. There was another world there, as well, a green haze settling over everything. Beyond the walls, he could see vast trees and vaster differences, could almost hear distant bellowing, and in his fingers and toes he felt a familiar tingling.

The shock of it jolted him to full consciousness. "Professor!" he shouted, and threw himself out of bed. The impact with the floor dimmed the vision for a second, but as he rose to his feet it returned with a vengeance. Half-guessing where the compartment door was, he staggered after Madison. Every step yielded the wet squelching sound of ancient mud. Every blink overwhelmed the ornate decor of the train with lush walls of primal green. "Professor!" he shouted again as he stumbled forward.

Dimly he could see other passengers diving into the compartments, alarmed at the madman who now lurched down the passageway toward the car's end. A figure stood there, perhaps Professor Madison. But the professor had never had claws, had never stretched forth welcoming tentacles, had never wished to—

"Here, my boy, take this!"

A hand reached out for him, or perhaps a snaking tentacle, and then something cold and metallic was pressed into his fingers. *Pocket watch*, he thought dimly as he clutched it. He could feel the wheels and gears within, the steady tick of the hands advancing. The sensation cut through the haze, and the green vision vanished.

"Professor," he said, and pitched forward.

Madison caught him as he fell. "Easy there. You'll want to keep that with you. It's the only thing that'll anchor you, at least as long as we're on this train."

"Anchor me?"

"To this era." Madison regarded him gravely. "I think it is time we put all our cards on the table."

Weakly, Walters nodded, then pushed himself upright. "There *is* something I didn't tell you." The professor, he saw, was headed toward the front of the car, and he followed. "When I was gone, I saw a . . . creature. Riding some sort of amphibious beast. I saw it again just now. It was reaching out for me."

They reached the end of the car, and a porter opened the door with a brisk salute and a surreptitious sign of the Cross. Madison stepped through, followed by his protégé, and they passed into another carriage. "Would this creature have been roughly the height of a man, possessed of four asymmetrical appendages?" The professor went on to describe the monster of Walters's vision so precisely the man's jaw dropped.

"Yes. That's it. That's it exactly. How did you know?"

"Not all of my researches are approved of by the Royal Museum," he said grimly. "There are certain books in my possession that my more rational peers frown on. Accounts of pre- and post-human civilizations, vast beasts from the gaps between the stars, ancient demon cults—not the sorts of thing that play well on Great Russell Street. And there are mentions of the creature you saw, vague hints at horrors out of time."

"What do they say?" They passed through another car, moving steadily toward the front of the train. "What do those things want?"

Madison laughed, a bitter sound. "What they want is to remain hidden. Anyone who has knowledge of them, or who might acquire it—such a man attracts their attention." He stopped and turned. "A man like you, now."

"Or the dead fireman?"

Madison nodded. "Quite possibly. Or perhaps he was merely an instrument, used to dispose of evidence."

"Evidence?"

"Think, Walters. You were drawn back to their time somehow. To the Carboniferous, when the vast beds of coal all around our route were laid down. What does this train run on? What did the man *do*?"

"Of course! It's something in the coal!" Walters sprang forward, and now it was Madison who hurried to keep up. "We've got to find the thing in the coal before they try again!"

"You've got to be careful, my boy," Madison puffed. "You've drawn their eye. They'll stop at nothing to silence you. Hold onto the watch. I got it at great cost from one of their other victims, a paleontologist from Brisbane who dug a little too deep. It's the only thing anchoring you to the now." Passengers and benches sped by as they ran headlong for the front of the train. "My best guess is that the vibrations of the train, mixed with some strange susceptibility of your own, is what flung you into the past."

"And Higdon?"

"Higdon, as well. You and he carried the fireman. Perhaps there was some sort of metaphysical contagion out of time."

"I'll take your word for it," said Walters.

And then, without warning, they were through the last car and into the cramped compartment at the back of the train's engine. The air hung thick with smoke and coal dust as two shirtless men shoveled away for all they were worth.

"You there!" Madison shouted. "You've got to stop. There's something in the coal, something terrible."

The two men straightened and looked at each other. One strode over to Madison, while the other shrugged and returned to his work. "Am sorry, sir. No passengers are allowed here."

"You don't understand. There's something wrong." Madison's earnest pleading was almost drowned out. The roar of the flames added hellish counterpoint to the chug of the wheels; the light from the furnace reflected luridly off the stokers' half-naked forms.

"What is wrong is that you are here," the man explained, less patient than before. "We are already behind schedule. The other passengers, they complain. If we stop shoveling coal, the train, it stops. It stops, they complain more. So you will go back to your seats, and we will keep the train moving, yes?"

"No," said Madison. "Look, if you'll just let me in the coal bin, I can—oh God, what's that?"

He pointed, eyes wide with horror. Walters and the stoker turned. The other man paused, the blade of his shovel half-buried in the mound of fuel.

Plainly visible hard by the shovel was something in the gleaming, unmistakable shape of a gun, gripped in the blackened fossilized bones of a human hand.

"There!" shouted Madison. "Do you not see?" And indeed they saw, gaping as the one man dropped his shovel. Disregarding the effect of the coal dust on his trousers, the professor dropped to his knees and gently extricated the find. Walters stood right behind him.

"Is not possible," said one of the stokers. "The bones—"

"The bones indeed! And what else—*szen, szen*! Of course. It was buried in the coal! This is what they were hiding, Walters, what they didn't want seen! Incontrovertible proof of their meddling in Earth's past!"

Walters stared. "The gun wouldn't burn. Even in the furnace, it would be found, and there would be questions. They possessed that poor fireman so that he'd destroy it."

Madison's voice was strained, but jubilant. "But they failed, and now—now we've found it, my boy. Oh, we'll blow their secret history wide open, we will!"

"There's more there," Walters said, and pointed. "The rest of the bones." And indeed there were: a radius and an ulna, both remarkably well preserved, leading back into the depths of the pile.

"Well done, Walters. There might be more artifacts back there, too! Hold this, will you?" Madison passed the hand and what it held up to his assistant, then leaned forward to dig at the distended arm.

Walters took the bundle without comment, and gave it a once-over. The gun, if gun it was, seemed poorly designed for the human hand. The grip was more suited for a claw than for fingers, and the hand that was wrapped around it, still held in place by bits of coal, was positioned awkwardly. Frowning, he held it up. The sight lines seemed off, and he rotated it until something about the shape clicked.

He'd seen the weapon before. Seen it held in that inhuman pincer reaching out for him. Seen what it could do.

"Professor," he said, leaning forward as his mentor burrowed busily into the coal.

"One moment," Madison replied.

Trembling, he stretched his right hand around the stony knuckle-bones.

"Professor, I really think—"

"I said not now!" Walters had never seen Madison like this, face pale, almost pleading. Sweat stood out on his forehead, a product of the coal chamber's intense heat. His eyes gleamed with excitement as his hands scrabbled in the detritus of the ancient strata. "We're finding . . . we're going to find . . ."

Walters closed his grip, his twisted fingers finding their twins. The fossilized bones and his were a perfect match.

"Professor!"

Madison turned, and Walters immediately wished he hadn't.

For the professor, it seemed, was suffering a seizure. Hunched over in agony, he screamed wordlessly. His fingers had twisted into claws, curled so tightly on themselves Walters could hear bones snap and ligaments pop. As for his face, it was a mask of horror. Eyes bulging, lips suddenly bloody where he chewed on them in frantic spasms.

"*Szen!*" the Madison-thing hissed, and then launched itself at his assistant. Walters barely had time to raise his arms in defense before Madison was upon him. Fingers crooked into claws raked his flesh, desperately clutching at the alien device. With a shout, Walters flung his attacker across the width of the car, sending him sprawling into the coal pile.

"You cannot fight in here," said one of the stokers. Madison turned to look at him, snarled, and then flung a fistful of coal dust into the man's face. He screamed and stumbled back, clutching his eyes, even as the other stoker fled the car.

"Professor! What are you doing?" It was a vain hope to think that any trace of his mentor remained in the creature that hurled itself at him, body contorting unnaturally. Its fingers found the punctures the insects had made in Walters's arm and dug in, causing him to gasp in pain. Involuntarily, his crippled grip loosened and the alien device tumbled to the floor. Coal and fossil bone splintered free as it hit, and the gun spun away.

"No!" Walters flung himself after it. The possessed Madison followed, a split-second later and a half-meter behind. The train took a curve, wheels roaring, and the device slid crazily toward the side of the car. Walters tumbled after it, blocking it from falling to the track below. A tug on his leg told him that his sudden opponent had grabbed a hold of him, and without a second thought he kicked. There was a gruesome crunch as his boot connected with the professor's shoulder, and then he could hear fabric tear as the Madison-shaped thing fell away.

Wheels screeching, the train pulled out of the curve and started accelerating. As it did so, the gun slid away once more, now toward the center of the car. Stumbling, Walters lunged for it. For an instant he thought it was too late, and then his fingers closed on it. He tightened his broken grip and turned, half-expecting to see Professor Madison lunging at him once again.

Instead, the professor stood there, blood streaming down his face. In his hand was the pocket watch.

"*Szen*," he said, and then the rising hum took Walters away.

The creature in the mud was dying, of that Walters was sure. He'd made certain of that, swinging a heavy length of wood at it from ambush and knocking it from the back of its mount. Six or seven more savage blows had followed, thoroughly pulping its star-shaped head and severing the odd tentacles that extended from it. Now greenish ichor oozed from the shapeless mass as it twitched and shuddered in its death throes. Rather than attempt to revenge its rider, the hulking amphibious mount had instead taken advantage of its freedom and plunged straightaway into the murky waters of the swamp. That left Walters and his victim alone, while all around them insects hummed and sang.

Professor Madison would hardly recognize him now, Walters thought with grim satisfaction. To survive in this place—no, in this time—he'd become a murderous savage, stalking his enemies and assassinating them one by one whenever the right moment arose.

Mud caked his hair and skin, the better to protect him from the ravenous appetites of the swarming insects. His clothes were in rags, but there was no need for modesty in this place. There was only survival.

And there was no way back, that he knew. It had been too long. Across the aeons, the train would have moved on, the peculiar vibrations of its wheels humming too far away to draw him back.

Or perhaps he'd been the one to range too far in his flight from star-headed hunters. He no longer knew where he'd first come back into this world, or where the train tracks would someday run. So there was no return to the future for him now, just black water and greenery and sucking mud.

Something shone in the muck at his feet. He bent down to examine it, and came away with a familiar prize. It was a gun, or something very much shaped like one. The creature had not had time to use it on him before he'd attacked. Now it was just plunder. Now it was his.

He'd long since abandoned the one he'd brought back with him. Ancient and useless, it was an unnecessary weight. But this one, new and deadly, was an entirely different proposition. He had long since resolved that he would not go down meekly. Let the monsters pursue him. He would make a home of the jungle. They would never take him from here, that he already knew. When his time came, he would be claimed by the thick waters, his bones sinking down with the rotting leaves and broken branches. And over the millennia he'd become one with them, as time and heat and pressure did their work, until someday, some poor train stoker's shovel would strike too close to where his remains lay, at the bottom of a pile of coal.

His twisted fingers closed around the gun. The circle would be complete.

"Are there any questions?" Professor Madison asked. The lecture hall was full of the usual first-year students, equal parts terrified and bored. Ten years on from the incident on the Bratislava train, seven years since he'd been released from the sanitarium, and still they flocked to the classes of the "mad professor."

For such blessings, he was occasionally grateful.

He looked back and forth across the room. Only one student raised a timid hand, a reedy young man with too much hair and not enough chin. One was good enough to start with, he supposed, and pointed. "Yes?"

"Professor." He hoisted himself to his feet and assumed a declamatory pose. "Today you told us about fossils forming in different strata according to the time period in which they evolved. What do you have to say to anomalous fossils, like human footprints next to dinosaur ones, or the human skeleton workers supposedly discovered in a coal car on a train? What about those?"

Rather than respond, Madison reached down into his pocket and pulled out a watch. It had seen hard use, as the marks of careful repair from some devastating accident attested. Carefully, he popped it open, feeling the reassuring whir of gears and wheels in the palm of his hand, the steady progression of time.

"I'm afraid we don't have time for questions after all," he said, and turned and walked away.

BOUND FOR HOME
CHRISTOPHER GOLDEN

THE LATE AFTERNOON SUNLIGHT GLINTED off of the rooftops of Vienna, casting long September shadows onto the cobblestone streets. Harry Houdini sat in the back seat, twisted slightly to one side to make room for the travel cases beside him. In the front, his publicist on this trip, an enterprising young man named Ned McCarty, rode with the driver. Harry listened to Ned's easy banter, so confident at the age of twenty-two, and wondered if he had ever been as light-hearted as that. Ned spoke almost as little German as the driver did English, but somehow the two had struck up an easy camaraderie that Harry envied. When the driver pulled up to the train station, Harry was glad to have that particular journey over, even as he felt such dread about the one he and Ned were about to begin.

The auto had barely rattled to a halt before Harry unlatched his door and clambered out, closing it behind him. The sun had slid farther toward the horizon and dropped just behind the train station's roof, silhouetting the building with golden fire and casting the street where Harry stood into deep shadow. Beyond the station, visible past the platform, the Orient Express awaited, hissing and smoking in preparation for departure, putting him in mind of a sleeping dragon. He took half a dozen steps toward that station and the platform and then hesitated, full of a trepidation he could not name.

Ned and the driver took the bags from the car and set them down. Harry glanced over in time to see Ned giving the man a tip and receiving a hearty pat on the back in return.

"Thank you," Harry said, touching the brim of his felt hat in a little salute.

The driver waved in reply and climbed into the car, which gave a full-throated roar as he started it up. A moment later it clattered away, a strange sight amidst the horse-drawn carriages and carts on the street. Harry turned his attention back to the train station, automobile and driver forgotten.

"You speak German," Ned said, frowning at him. "You couldn't bid him farewell in his own language?"

"I speak rotten German," Harry replied, "and not much of it. Besides, I'm an American. I speak English. We hired him to drive specifically because he spoke our language."

All during the exchange, Harry's gaze never strayed from the sight of the Orient Express, seething and steaming as it awaited them. He had admired machines and mechanisms of all kinds throughout his life—ingenuity intrigued him—and a machine as beautiful and powerful as this train impressed him. The handful of days he had spent in Vienna had been a pleasure thanks both to the loveliness of its architecture and to its near-constant gastronomic delights, particularly the tortes at Gerstner on Karntner Strasse. The night he had attended the opera with the city's mayor had been the one disappointment. The performance had bored him, and he had spent its duration wishing that he had been the one on the stage, playing to a packed house at the Wiener Hofoper. But it wasn't just the beauty of Vienna that made him reluctant to leave.

"Harry?" Ned said, nudging him.

"Hmm?" Harry glanced at him and realized that Ned had picked up his own valise and travel case and stood waiting, while Harry's own bags remained on the ground beside him.

"Do you want me to get a porter?"

"You're the publicist, kid. Do you want *the Great Houdini* to have his picture taken carrying his own bags?"

He smiled, just in case Ned hadn't caught the sarcasm. On stage he would always be the Great Houdini, and he played that up for the crowds on the streets and in the bars in order to feed his fame. But sometimes he grew tired from the effort it took to inhabit the role. Ned hadn't known him very long and he didn't want the kid who was supposed to be drumming up the Great Houdini's press to think that the Great Houdini *believed* his own press.

Ned studied him for a second or two, troubled and unsure. "You're right," he said. "Herr Diederich will have some journalists to see you off, for sure. Let me get the porter."

Harry shook his head and bent to hoist up his bags. "Forget it, kid. It's the Orient Express, first class. I won't have to lift a finger while we're on board unless it's to cut my steak. I can carry my own damn bags."

Weighed down with his cases, wishing he had packed fewer shirts, he started toward the front entrance of the station. He passed out of view of the platform and lost sight of the waiting train. A shiver went through him.

"You all right, Harry?" Ned asked as they approached the front doors, the people around them all in a hurry, whether they were arriving in Vienna or departing.

"Might be coming down with a cold," Harry replied.

"It's not that," Ned said. "You seem . . . well, I've never seen you nervous before. If I had to guess—"

Harry raised his chin a bit and gave the kid a hard look. "I'm fine."

An older man came out through the doors and was polite enough to hold one open for them.

"You know you don't have to do this," Ned said. "You're feeling ill, right? We can cancel."

Just inside the station, in the midst of echoing footfalls and the susurrus of voices, Harry paused to glare at him, using anger to hide the battle he was waging in his heart.

"How would that look? For Pete's sake, Ned, you're the damned publicist!"

For more than a decade, as he toured the world, Harry had been challenging local constabulary to lock him up in order to establish his reputation as an escape artist. In time he had begun to accept challenges from ordinary citizens. Most of them he ignored, because once he had publicly accepted such a challenge, anything other than success would be an embarrassment and a black mark on the image he had worked so hard to build. Sometimes, however, he simply could not resist.

182 ❖ Christopher Golden

Ned glanced around to make sure they were not being over-heard and then shuffled toward a wall, tilting his head to indicate that Harry should join him.

"You're on edge," Ned whispered. "If it's not the escape that's got you worried, do you mind telling me what the hell it is? Take me into your confidence. It's the only way I can do my job properly."

Harry took a long breath, fighting the tension in his back and arms, forcing himself to exhale. He glanced past Ned and saw Herr Diederich across the station. The Vienna banker stood with several others whose clothing and bearing marked them as similarly wealthy. They were surrounded by a small gaggle of perhaps half a dozen reporters, all of them hanging on Diederich's every word, save for a smartly dressed young woman with her auburn hair caught up in a tightly knotted bun. Of them all, it was she who spot-ted Harry, and she gave him a small, knowing smile, as if to say she didn't blame him for hanging back and delaying his exposure to the small circus that awaited his arrival. That smile charmed him, even from thirty yards away.

He turned to Ned, studying the young man's earnest blue eyes and the neat little mustache he had grown to make himself look not quite so young but which had had precisely the opposite effect. A young man, but smart and loyal.

"The reporters are coming over," Harry said quietly. "They've seen me now and will be upon us in moments. But you deserve an answer, Ned, and it's a kind of confession, I guess. I lived in Appleton, Wisconsin as a kid—"

"I know that."

"—but I wasn't born there. My real name is Erik Weisz. That's Hungarian, my friend. I was born in Budapest and spent the first four years of my life there. I remember almost nothing of that pe-riod, of course. The Orient Express, the journey we're about to em-bark upon . . . for me it's boarding a train that's bound for home, and it makes me feel like a charlatan."

Ned gaped at him. "Wow, Harry, I had no idea."

"Now that you do, you won't speak a word of it to anyone. I'm no charlatan, Ned. I've worked as hard as I know how and nearly died a hundred times to get to where I am. But you wanted to know what's gotten under my skin, and so I told you. It's Budapest, kid. It haunts me."

"You could have refused to—"

"But I didn't," Harry interrupted. "And we're here now, so let's give 'em a show."

Before Ned could reply, the reporters descended upon them, firing off questions that Harry ignored with a magnanimous smile until Herr Diederich pushed through them with his rich friends in tow and put out a hand to shake.

"Mister Houdini, what a pleasure," Diederich said in thickly accented English. "The train is to depart soon. I was afraid you would not make it in time."

"Not make it?" scoffed a gray-bearded man with spectacles and a ruby pin in his lapel. "You thought Herr Houdini had decided to break his word, that the challenge had frightened him away?"

Bristling inside, Harry managed a smile. "Not at all, my friends." He glanced at the charming woman with the auburn hair, saw the notepad and pencil in her hand and realized for the first time that she was one of the journalists. He liked that: a girl with pluck. "Just saying farewell to lovely Vienna, in case I never see her again."

The reporters exploded with excitement at this, as they always did whenever he dangled the possibility of his own death in front of them. The reaction never failed to elicit a strange combination of amusement and disgust in Harry. Only the lady journalist, in her smart suit with its buttons in a severe, slashing line down the front of both jacket and skirt, seemed to hang back, waiting for an opportunity to strike.

"Anna Carter of the *Boston Globe*, Mister Houdini," she said in the first lull. "Do you mean to tell us that a challenge this dangerous, circumstances in which most men would face almost certain death, doesn't intimidate you at all?"

The question quieted them all as they awaited his answer. Harry directed it toward the lady who'd posed it.

"My dear Miss Carter," he said. "The Great Houdini is not '*most men.*'"

❖   ❖   ❖

Harry enjoyed the rocking of the train and the way the candle on his table in the dining car seemed to stay still, only the flame wavering back and forth. The first class dinner menu had been extensive, but he had chosen the duck with traditional Austrian dumplings and cabbage. Ned had ordered wild boar and somehow managed to consume the entire dish. He had a prodigious appetite for so thin a man, and Harry envied him his youth.

"How do you find the duck, Mister Houdini?" Anna Carter asked, over the rim of a glass of Piesporter she had been nursing for half an hour.

"Delicious, Miss Carter. And your veal?"

"Very tender," the reporter replied. "Honestly, I never expected to experience a meal so fine in such circumstances. The cuisine onboard a train generally leaves much to be desired."

Harry smiled at her, but not only her—his gaze took in Ned as well as the four other journalists at the table. "Perhaps you ought to travel in better company."

Anna arched an eyebrow. "Duly noted."

One of the others—the gentleman from the *Times* of London—asked a question to which Harry only half paid attention. Ned jumped in to answer, giving Harry the opportunity to take a sip of water. He'd have preferred a whiskey, but drinking with his life on the line had never seemed a good idea. As it was, he had eaten perhaps more than he ought to have, in his effort to contribute to the convivial atmosphere at the table. Diederich and the others had gone along with Ned's request for them to dine with the reporters instead of their hosts, so he thought he ought to make the best impression he could muster. There was no point in having reporters around if he couldn't use them to the greatest advantage.

"So, Mister Houdini—" began Herr Kraus of *Wiener Zeitung*, an Austrian paper.

"Harry, please."

"Harry," Herr Kraus went on, his accent thick but not impenetrable. "Tell us: The escape you will attempt tonight . . . is it really a challenge for you, or merely something arranged to keep your name in the papers?"

"Herr Kraus," Ned began, but Harry held up a hand to forestall any protest on the publicist's part.

"No, it's a fair question," he said, noting the spark of curiosity in Anna Carter's eyes. He glanced at Herr Kraus before addressing the entire table. "I'll admit that some of the challenges I've accepted have turned out to be simple enough for one of my abilities. But Herr Diederich and his confederates have gone to great lengths to make this more complicated than escaping from a jail cell. They've bolted a platform on top of this train. I'm to have manacles placed on my wrists and ankles, the chains looped through clamps that are welded to the platform. I will be blindfolded, hands behind my back. There is a tunnel forty miles or so outside of Istanbul whose ceiling is quite low—low enough, in fact, that if I am still on that platform when we reach the tunnel, I will surely be killed."

No one at the table spoke. For journalists, this was a small miracle. It took Harry a moment to realize the reason—he meant what he'd said and that startled them. Of course he had a dozen ways to escape the trap, had trained most of his life for just that sort of thing, but he had never done anything like this on top of a speeding train before.

"Aren't you afraid of dying?" asked the man from London, after another moment's pause.

"My good man," Harry replied. "I have no intention of dying, but if tonight is the night death comes for me, fear will hardly save me."

A waiter arrived, a swarthy, thinly bearded man in wire-rimmed spectacles. He kept his dark eyes averted as he began to clear plates and glasses.

"Perhaps it's time to inspect the platform and the chains," Ned suggested.

Harry waved a hand. "I've done it already, while you were resting. We've an hour before the challenge begins. I recommend coffee and whatever pastries the chef has provided, though I myself must abstain in preparation."

Another waiter arrived to inquire as to whether they desired sweets or hot drinks. He had the dignified air shared by so many of the staff, that of one who found nobility in service, proud of his station. Something tickled the back of Harry's brain and he glanced around in search of the other man, the one who'd cleared their dishes. The dark-skinned man—of Middle Eastern descent,

he believed—had kept his eyes downcast in a conspicuously sub-
servient manner, nothing like the others. And yet, hadn't there been
just the hint of a smile on his face, as if he had taken some private
amusement from the moment?

Harry spotted him farther along the car, where Diederich and
the others who had funded the challenge sat, already enjoying
dessert. The strange waiter delivered a small metal pot—perhaps
of hot cocoa, a tradition in Austria—to the man beside Diederich,
and then made his way toward the far door of the car, where the
chef and his assistants were at work. As he passed through the
door, the man gave a single glance backward, and Harry frowned
deeply. Had he seen that face somewhere before, those dark eyes,
the long, thin nose, the brows with their almost diabolical natural
arch?

"Mister Houdini?" a voice whispered beside him. "Harry?"

He turned to see that Anna had shifted her chair nearer to his.
Ned had begun to pass after-dinner cigars around to Herr Kraus
and the reporters, who had all slid back from the table and begun
a loud conversation about the most extraordinary stories they had
ever covered for their respective papers—providing an opportunity
for Ned to amplify just what an amazing feat they were to see that
very night.

"You don't like cigars?" Harry asked Anna.

Her smile held a hint of admonition. "Why haven't you tried to
seduce me?"

She said it so quietly that for a moment he thought he had
misheard.

"I'm sorry?"

Anna's hazel eyes sparkled with a hint of green, the wavering
candle flame throwing suggestive shadows upon her face.

"Oh, it's not an invitation, just a matter of curiosity. Every other
man here has at least made overtures, but not so much as an inquis-
itive glance from you."

Harry inclined his head in a polite nod. "I never practice the
art of seduction before ten P.M., I'm afraid. In any case, I reserve my
earnest attentions for Missus Houdini."

The appreciative look she gave him held a distinctly American
frankness.

"A happily married man, huh?" Anna said. "I figured them for a myth."

"Not a myth, Miss Carter, though perhaps very nearly extinct."

They were interrupted by much shuffling and murmuring as Diederich and his associates rose from their table and came along the car toward them.

"The time has come, Mister Houdini," Diederich said in his wonderful accent.

"Now?" Ned said, brows knitted in consternation. "We're not scheduled to begin for three-quarters of an hour, at least."

The imperiously mannered white-bearded gentleman to Diederich's left sniffed dismissively.

"Our speed is greater than anticipated," he said. "If you are to have the agreed-upon interval before we reach the tunnel, we must begin in twenty minutes. Thirty at most. Surely if we are willing to give you more time to avoid being smeared along the ceiling of that tunnel, you do not object?"

The journalists all laughed good-naturedly, though the white-bearded man had not so much as smiled. *And I thought it was the Germans who have no sense of humor,* Harry thought.

"By all means, sir," he said, rising from his chair with an affectionate glance toward Anna. "By all means."

The blindfold posed no problem. Harry had spent countless hours practicing his craft in the dark, sometimes upside down, inside a tank full of water, or both. The speed of the train did not trouble him either, but its swaying and juddering did offer a challenge. He had a lock pick secreted beneath his tongue and several others in the lining of his clothing, including the cuff of his left coat sleeve. His hands were shackled behind him and the chains had been drawn taut enough that he was on his knees on the platform. In truth, if not for the fact that he wanted his challengers to feel as if they'd gotten their money's worth, he could have escaped in under a minute. Instead, he struggled and strained against his bonds, testing the chains, purposely crashing onto his side as the train jerked around a curve, when actually he was simply trying to adapt to the unpredictable shimmy and shudder of the Orient Express.

As the wind whipped past him, buffeting his face and making his coat billow around him, Harry heard voices murmuring in a strange sort of rhythm. A frown creased his forehead. He knew he was not alone atop the train car; Diederich and his associates had installed three platforms instead of just one, with Harry shackled in the middle and delicately-carved wooden chairs bolted to the other two, four each, so that the financiers of this feat could watch from ahead and behind. In the dark, with only the bright moonlight to illuminate the showman, they would not be able to see the finer elements of his escape. If he could hide lock picks from a theatre audience, he could do it atop a speeding train in the dark.

The journalists had not been afforded seats. Instead, they had been told they were welcome to view the event but would have to take their chances. Only Herr Kraus and Anna Carter had dared spend so much time exposed atop the train without any way to anchor themselves. Harry admired their courage and wished them well. For his part, Ned had returned to the dining car for a drink with the other journalists. He would handle the questions during and after the escape but Harry did not want him to take any unnecessary risks.

Now, though . . . that chanting . . . what in God's name were they up to, these men? Trying to break his concentration? If so, it wasn't very sporting of them.

The voices grew louder, all rough, guttural syllables that sounded like gibberish to him, and he realized they were indeed hoping to throw him off his game. A ripple of anger went through Harry. This might have been all in good fun were it not for the fact that they were hurtling at top speed toward a tunnel whose low ceiling would turn him into a red streak along the train's roof. Diederich and Wagner and the others would abandon their seats and retreat safely down the iron rungs between train cars, never risking their own destruction. Would they leave him up there, if their nefarious chanting achieved its purpose of distraction? Ordinarily he would have said no, but he seemed the type who might actually enjoy the notoriety of having posed the challenge that killed Harry Houdini.

To hell with them, he thought.

Working quickly, he pulled his wrists taut against his shackles and twisted his right hand so that he could snag the cuff of his left coat sleeve with his fingers. In a heartbeat he'd plucked the lock pick free of the lining, careful to keep his hands turned so that those behind him would not glimpse a glint of moonlight on the pick. He shifted his head, tossing it as if attempting to free himself from the blindfold but really only drawing their attention away from his hands and toward his face.

With swift precision, he slid the pick into the lock on the manacles around his wrists. He heard Kraus ask about the purpose of the chanting, but it only grew louder. It occurred to him, just for a moment, that he had heard it before. In the back of his mind, a memory began to rise. Harry pushed the distraction away, tugging against his bonds, hearing the chains clank against the hooks to which they had been moored. But he had stopped listening to the sounds of the train, stopped paying attention to the rattle and judder of the cars ahead of him, and so was unprepared when their car suddenly shunted to the right, switching tracks.

His wrists clacked together, twisting the lock pick from his hand, and he lost it.

"Shit," he muttered under his breath, his anger growing.

A dozen options presented themselves in his head, various ways in which he could still manage his escape. Some required physical contortions that would likely tear his jacket, for which he had paid handsomely. The chanting—the familiar, rhythmic chanting—infuriated him both because it was irritating and because it had achieved its goal. The bastards had distracted him enough that he had not only dropped his first pick but he had lost track of time. How long, now, until they reached the tunnel? He wasn't sure.

He opted for the quickest escape, which would also be the most painful.

Bracing himself on the platform, knees apart, he shifted his upper body, took a deep breath and exhaled, and then thrust out his right shoulder, dislocating it completely. Harry bit back a roar, allowing only a grunt. Trembling, breath coming in hitching gasps, he raised both arms and brought them over the top of his head, back to front. The damnable chanting faltered for a moment.

With a twist of his arm and another small grunt, he popped his shoulder back into the socket. His lips were stretched into a rictus grin to hide the pain. He'd dislocated both shoulders on occasion but had never learned to fully disguise the extent of his discomfort.

The chanting grew louder, but now Harry didn't care. On his knees, he rested a moment, shackled wrists hanging before him.

"Enough games," he muttered as he reached up to tear away his blindfold. The wind shearing across the top of the speeding train whipped at him and stung his eyes but he blinked them clear and then froze, shocked into paralysis by the scene that the moonlight revealed.

Diederich and two of his confederates sat on the chairs bolted to the platform ten feet ahead of him, along with a fourth observer—the swarthy waiter with the thin beard and wire spectacles. Confusion sparked in Harry's mind, but the others arrayed on the roof of the train ignited that confusion into a conflagration. In the space between his platform and the next, and arranged in a ring that encircled his position, were another dozen figures, cloaked and hooded in heavy black fabric run through with strands of moonlit silver. They were on their knees, palms upon the metal roof of the hurtling train, heads hung low so that their hoods hid any hint as to their identities. The chanting came from these hooded men, who it seemed had also hastily painted a scattering of arcane symbols on the roof around him.

Memory rushed in as if some barrier had been holding it back and now it flooded his mind. Two years past, on a visit to Egypt, he had endured a night of terror unlike anything else he had ever experienced. Lured beneath the sands, under the pyramids, he had been knocked unconscious and woken to find himself a captive, surrounded by creatures with human bodies but the heads of beasts, the intended sacrifice in a nightmare ritual that opened an aperture in the fabric of the world as some ancient, malignant presence—some dark god—attempted to slip through. Harry had escaped, of course. He had survived and immediately begun to obliterate the memory from his mind, doubting and undermining the experience, persuading himself that it had been a nightmare or drug-induced phantasmagoria, the result of some malicious attack by the guide he had hired to bring him safely on a tour of Egypt's most ancient sites.

His guide. Abdul Reis el Drogman.

Harry snapped his gaze back toward the platform, staring at the swarthy man beside Diederich. Take away the spectacles and the beard, account for the passage of time . . . Harry knew him now. *Abdul Reis, here.*

Panic set in.

Abdul Reis saw the recognition in his eyes and offered a sinister smile as the others continued their chanting. Harry stared past him and Diederich and the others, watching the nighttime horizon. There were low hills around them and many ahead. How far to the tunnel? He had no idea.

"Son of a bitch," Harry hissed, glaring at Abdul Reis.

Shoulder throbbing, he went to work, shifting his tongue around to force out the thin lock pick he'd hidden in the corner of his mouth moments before they shackled him. His heart hammered in his chest; this was no longer a game. He took the pick from his mouth, listened for the jerking and rattling of the train car ahead of them and managed to keep his balance like a sailor getting his sea legs. Barely glancing at the cuffs, he picked the lock on his manacles and slipped them off, allowing them to drop to the platform with a heavy clank.

Diederich slid forward in his chair, gripping its arms, his eyes lit up with alarm.

"Stop—" he began, but Abdul Reis clamped a hand on his wrist and gave a silent shake of his head, and only then did Harry truly understand who had been the mastermind behind this madness.

Abdul Reis raised his other hand and gestured. Behind Harry there came a scuffling and a cry, and he thought that over the wind he could hear someone calling his name.

Even as he sat down on the platform, working the pick into the lock on his ankle shackles, he twisted round to look behind him. The rest of the circle of hooded acolytes looked identical to their fellows, but toward the rear of the car, Diederich's remaining confederates stood in front of their chairs, restraining a pair of captives.

"Make no further attempt to escape, Mister Houdini!" Abdul Reis said, shouting to be heard over the wind. "Or they both die!"

Ned McCarty and Anna Carter struggled against the men who held them, but there was little they could do. Both had their hands bound behind their backs. Anna had been tightly gagged, but the gag on Ned had slipped down to his neck; he had been the one to shout Harry's name.

Anna had been stripped to her white underthings, baring her pale flesh to the moonlight. In the short time during which they had shackled Harry and he'd been feigning difficulty with his escape—while he had been putting on a show for them—these chanting madmen had painted her skin with the same bizarre sigils that had been drawn onto the roof of the train. She hunched slightly, grimacing as if in pain, and he realized that her bucking against them was not an attempt to free herself but a series of paroxysms caused by crippling pain in her gut. Bright, bloody crimson lines showed where the flesh of her abdomen had been cut and the skin peeled open in folds like flower petals.

"Anna!" Harry shouted. "Ned, don't let them—"

Ned lunged forward, fighting his captors, and wrested himself free. He turned and drove himself at one of the cultists holding Anna, trying to knock the man from the speeding train. The cultist turned to defend himself, holding an ornate, curved dagger. Ned collided with him and they both went down. Harry felt a surge of hope, before the cultist tossed Ned aside, the dagger jutting from his chest. Harry screamed his friend's name. Wide-eyed, Ned stared pleadingly at Harry for a moment, all of the strength leaving him . . . and then his killer hurled him over the side of the moving train. His body tumbled off into the night and was left behind in the wake of the rattling locomotive.

Harry sneered at the killer, ignoring the hooded men and their benefactors, Abdul Reis forgotten. Ned was dead, and Harry understood that the only chance Anna had of surviving to see the sunrise was if he were free. He bent to unlock the shackles on his ankles and one of the cultists rushed at him. Harry swayed with the rhythm of the train and when the man leaped at him, he twisted aside, grabbed the man's wrist, and used his momentum against him. The man sprawled across the roof, slid and tried in vain to get a grip before he, too, fell over the side and into the dark. As another cultist moved in, Harry unlocked his ankle shackles.

They clanked to the platform as he stood, facing Ned's murderer and his compatriots.

"Let her go!" he demanded, knowing even as the screaming wind stole his voice away that he could not intimidate them, not one man against so many.

Still, he intended to save her, whatever the cost.

Harry stepped off the platform, advancing toward the back of the train car, and two of the hooded acolytes that separated him from Anna and her captors glanced up, flinching at his approach. One of them was the Austrian journalist, Herr Kraus.

The other had the head of a tiger. Its black lips curled back from its fangs in a low growl as it began to rise.

Harry heard the ratcheting of the car ahead of theirs and braced himself as the train jerked to one side, following the tracks. Jostled, the tiger-headed man went back onto his hands and knees. Harry took two long strides and lunged between him and Kraus, landing just in front of the platform where Ned had just been murdered. The chanting increased in volume and speed.

He caught a few words on the wind and glanced back toward the front of the train. Abdul Reis had spoken.

"Not this time, Houdini," the Egyptian shouted. "This time, you will die."

Abdul Reis barked an order and the two men holding Anna drove her forward and shoved her at Harry, who caught her even as the collision forced him backward. He fell with her wrapped in his arms, the two of them sprawling past the hooded ones and crashing to the platform atop the coiled chains Harry had just shed.

Anna's eyes were bright with pain and she screamed against her gag. He tugged the cloth down and her words flowed in a frenzied, anguished torrent.

"It hurts. Oh, Harry, it's tearing me apart inside."

Harry shushed her as he worked her free of her bonds. On his knees now, holding her, he turned to glare at Abdul Reis.

"What did you do to her, you monster?"

Abdul Reis only smiled and gestured to the others. The chanting grew louder still, the acolytes lowering their heads so far they could have kissed the metal roof. The words had changed, and so had that guttural rhythm. Their ritual had entered a new phase.

Anna screamed and thrashed against him.

"Damn you, take me! You wanted me for your sacrifice!" he roared at the Egyptian. "Take me!"

The smile vanished from the Egyptian's features, replaced by open loathing and malice.

"You misunderstand, Houdini," Abdul Reis called to him. "You *are* the sacrifice. You have always been the sacrifice. You have escaped death again and again, and each escape has made your life force more powerful, more radiant. Your death will be a beacon, sure to guide the Old Ones into the world."

"Then let Anna go!" Harry shouted.

"No, you fool," the Egyptian said. "You are the sacrifice, but she is the *door!*"

Anna cried out to God and threw her head back, going rigid in Harry's arms as her eyes rolled up to their whites. She bucked, thrusting her abdomen upward, and he looked at her pale, smooth belly to see that a pulsing, bloodless slit had appeared there, a vertical mouth that began to open.

With a grunt of revulsion, Harry released her and tried to scramble away, but in the same moment a pair of thick tentacles slid from the pouting slit of her abdomen, probing the air like dogs seeking a scent. The chanting grew louder and Harry could hear the laughter of Abdul Reis as the hideous tendrils extruded farther, joined now by a third.

Jerked forward by the things forcing themselves from within her—*no*, he thought, *not within her but somehow through her; she is only a door into this world from some vast, chaotic other*—Anna looked down at her naked, obscenely split belly and began to scream as madness took her. She whipped her head around, eyes wild and searching, and locked her gaze upon him.

"Harry," she whimpered. "Please, Harry."

He twisted around, scanning the tracks far ahead in search of that tunnel, wondering how long before it would smash all of them from the roof of the train. He saw that they were approaching a bridge that spanned a deep river gorge. Regret and guilt swept him as a terrible decision presented itself. Harry tensed, crouched on the roof, balancing himself with his hands.

With wet, sticky sucking noises, the tentacles shot farther from

Anna's belly and seized him, slithering and coiling around him like serpents. Harry tried to fight them but his struggles only caused them to tighten. The thick, mottled tendrils dragged Harry toward her even as the slit in her belly grew, splitting her breastbone so that it seemed the entirety of her was opening to him, trying to pull him *in*.

A noxious, stinking gas exuded from that hole, the stench of some hellish otherplace, and as he gazed inside of her, the moonlight revealed nightmare things that had never existed in this world, other shapes that made his mind scream with their impossible geometry.

"No," he grunted, as the chanting reached a fever pitch.

His hands wrapped around Anna's throat almost of their own volition. Her eyes rolled back again and she jerked in his grip. Harry felt her life pulsing in the veins of her throat and he knew he could end it, knew that he had to end it, not just to save himself but to prevent the abominable others from being birthed into the world through the vast womb that her body had become.

Yet he could not. He thought of Ned, barely more than a kid and now dead because he had joined Harry on this journey. And then he thought of Bess, his sweet Bess, his best friend and staunchest ally, the foundation of his life. He had to get home to her, and to keep the world unmarred by the unimaginable malignance of the Old Ones.

Tentacles squeezed him, crushing the air from him, and he felt his body pressed to the moist, stinking gap in Anna's belly like some obscene lover.

The train began to rattle across the bridge. Beyond it he could see a low, narrow tunnel cut into the rocky face of a hill. Time had run out.

Harry counted to four, prayed they were over the river, embraced Anna Carter, and then pistoned his legs to hurl them both off the side of the train. He heard Abdul Reis scream in fury as they fell, and then he could hear nothing but the air whipping by his ears and the slippery squirming of the tentacles around him, pulling him into those sucking, wet folds.

The fall seemed to go on for eternity. Just before they struck the water he drew a ragged breath and held it, and then they plunged into the cold, deep river, the current carrying them swiftly away from the train bridge. Submerged, dragged along the river bottom, Harry fought against the tentacles and against Anna's flailing arms, but he did not strive for the surface. Instead, he struggled to stay down. The Great Houdini could hold his breath for a long, long time.

As they floated upward, he twisted in the water and kept her down, until at last Anna went slack in his arms and the tentacles loosened their hold and began to withdraw.

The river swept them into a shallow pool near its bank, scraping them against the rocks, and Harry dragged Anna up onto the shore. He could see the long slit that stretched from her groin to her throat, peeling her open. Nothing shifted in the dark, glistening cavity within her. He could see gray organs and pale bones, but whatever passage had opened inside of her, that door had closed with her death.

Harry wept into his hands, shaking with sorrow and fury.

When he could catch his breath, he lifted his gaze and stared upriver at the bridge spanning the gorge. The train would be far away by now. It would arrive in Istanbul without him. The homecoming he had imagined was not to be, and yet he had no intention of completing the journey. Home had taken on a new meaning for him, not his childhood home, or even the place he and Bess had made a home for themselves. He had caught a glimpse of what waited outside of his reality, and it had made him understand that the whole world was his home, and he would do anything to defend it. He would meet Abdul Reis el Drogman again. He would seek out every occultist and sorcerer, expose the charlatans and destroy the true practitioners, until he found Abdul Reis, and then he would kill the Egyptian.

For this had been no dream. He would never be able to persuade himself that it had been a nightmare, nor did he wish to. Anna's death demanded that he remember. More than that, he had seen the nameless things moving on the other side of the door that had opened inside her, and he knew those things could never be allowed to come through.

Harry Houdini sat bloody and bruised on the bank of an unknown river and pondered what would have to be his greatest escape.

He understood now that he was still a prisoner, bound by a future whose chains would continue to tighten around him until at last either he or his enemy, the diabolical Abdul Reis, was dead.

Only then would he truly be free.

ON THE EASTBOUND TRAIN
Darrell Schweitzer

It is an understatement to phrase it that some years ago my colleague Henderson encountered something *odd* on a train in the middle of the night, while hurtling through the wilderness of Eastern Europe. An understatement, because that's not the whole of it, though that much *is* true. It was a long time ago. He is retired now, albeit not for the usual reasons; but he was a young man then, a newly minted professional scholar. If the details are somewhat confused, that is because he volunteered them to me in a disjointed manner, with a great deal of effort on his part. His face went pale as he spoke, but was slick with sweat. This most well-spoken of lecturers stuttered and stammered. I cannot deny that it must have been more than *odd* to step out into the corridor of a racing, swaying railroad carriage and find oneself face-to-face with something so utterly *inhuman* that it might not even be accounted *alive* in the usual sense. That can only be described as terrifying.

But I am getting ahead of myself, as did he, when he told me this. Let me try to arrange things in their proper sequence.

George Henderson was, I say, a young man then. Having defended his thesis and taken his degree in the summer of 1912, only months later he found himself on the Orient Express, bound for Constantinople (as it was still called in those days) on a decidedly plum assignment to examine a unique medieval codex within his area of specialty, a bizarre volume that had been unearthed in an ancient, remote monastery and was now made, rather mysteriously, available to *one* selected scholar by invitation of the Turkish government. It may be true that certain relatives of his in the Foreign Service "pulled strings," as the expression has it, though there is no doubt that he was fully qualified for the job.

Did I mention that Henderson was—I mean, is still—a brilliant man, who was expected to rise to the very top of his field very quickly? Yes.

So there he was, as another expression would have it, with visions dancing in his head like a child on Christmas Eve, not of sugarplums, but of something more on the order of some fabulous piece of lost classical literature, something to make his reputation and career then and there and forever.

Of course he knew perfectly well that it could well turn out to be some dreadfully dull theological work in impenetrable, late Byzantine fustian.

He could hope, though. There was the *odd* detail, that the item was described in the papers sent to him as being bound in thick leather and clasped shut with an elaborate lock made of the bones of two human hands—which the Turkish excavator (one suspects, looter) had managed to smash. That did at least seem to promise something more exciting than theology.

He could also wonder why the Turks would only allow *one* Western scholar to see it, rather than just publish the thing.

As the familiar landscape of France, Germany, and Austria slid by, he could only putter with his notes and look out the window. He found it difficult to concentrate.

In Vienna he had the extremely pleasant surprise of being asked to share his second-class compartment with none other than Professor Augustus Lindsay, *the* Augustus Lindsay, whose own startling career had led him to considerable fame and even notoriety in scholarly circles.

At this point Henderson interrupted himself and went on at *great* length about what a remarkable man Augustus Lindsay was. Lindsay was quite a bit older. George had studied under him as an undergraduate, first ancient languages, then more recondite matters bordering on the metaphysical. For all his effusive praise, he was vague on the details. With increasing excitement, he described the man: a tall, gaunt figure with remarkable presence that was hard to describe—something in his manner, in his voice—to whom Henderson had looked up as a mentor, and, I think, a kind of father-figure. But I won't go into that. Suffice it to remark, as Henderson did, "If he were Faust, I would have been his Wagner—willingly."

"Professor? Good day, Sir!" Henderson said as the newcomer entered the compartment.

The other laughed and said, "Good day to *you*, Professor. Yes, I know I can call you that now. I am quite proud of you, George."

They greeted one another warmly, effusively.

There followed much amiable small talk, both over a meal in the dining car, and once more in their compartment: the usual academic gossip, catching up on old times and old friends and the like. Professor Lindsay was curiously evasive, though, about the reason for his own presence here. He wasn't merely on holiday, but something more like a sabbatical, for research purposes of his own. Henderson had heard from the faintest whispers back home that the university hierarchy expressed less than unreserved approval. But of course Professor Lindsay's position was such that he could not be seriously challenged.

All he could gather was that the older man had been in central Europe for some time, first in Prague, and had doubled back to Vienna before heading east again to the ancient, former abode of the caesars and basilei that was now, of course, synonymous with Ottoman sultans and the Sublime Porte.

Henderson was dying to know what Lindsay was working on, and when they got back to their compartment after dinner, he asked him directly. But it must be admitted that, particularly in his youth, Henderson was not an assertive fellow, and certainly incapable of forcing his will on his former mentor. Lindsay merely made a theatrical wave with his hand and remarked that their destination had quite enough mysteries, intrigues, and secrets for the both of them.

Henderson offered no resistance when Lindsay turned the tables and steered the discussion to the subject of *his* research.

"And I suppose you are hoping to discover an original manuscript in the handwriting of Homer, my boy . . ." said Lindsay.

Although Henderson was now, technically, a colleague, he so readily fell back into the student-teacher relationship that being called "my boy" did not even give him pause.

"That would be nice."

"Highly unlikely, you must admit, given the date of the thing."

"Late fourteenth century."

"The Paleologus period, then," said Lindsay, with disdain.

"That is the date it was written down, yes, but the content could always be far older. In any case, what of it?"

"I must admit," said Professor Lindsay, "that I have always despised the Paleologoi, cravens and villains the lot of them."

This caught young Henderson by surprise, such a conventional bit of judgmental morality coming from a man not noted for his intellectual conformity. "Surely this is just Gibbon's prejudice. I should think you would account at least Manuel the Second as noble and Constantine the Eleventh as decidedly heroic—"

"But their progenitor, Michael the Eighth sold his soul to the Devil. He put a curse on the whole damned line."

"Well he *did* restore the Byzantine Empire. It lasted another two centuries."

"There are some things, my boy, that are *not worth doing*, not after you have accounted the cost, whether they are reassembling shattered empires or translating forbidden books. It takes a larger context to understand if what we do is for good or for ill—"

This was the first thing to cast a pall over the otherwise holiday atmosphere of the excursion, like a cloud passing over the sun. Initially, Henderson thought the older man was joking, so incredible did it seem that Professor Lindsay would intone in the manner of some Sunday preacher that There Are Things Man Was Not Meant To Know, but he actually seemed to be in considerable earnest.

That was when the notion first occurred to Henderson, absurd as it might have seemed, that Professor Lindsay had something to hide.

This was reinforced a moment later when Lindsay looked up

with a start, and Henderson followed his gaze. Someone was standing at the door of their compartment. The door had a pane of semiopaque glass in it, so only a vague outline was visible. There was no knock. The figure just stood there in the corridor, as if peering in.

"Hello?" Henderson called out. "Can I help you?"

He rose to go to the door, but Professor Lindsay grabbed him by the wrist with surprising strength and held him fast in his seat, whispering, "For God's sake, *don't.*"

"What is it, Professor?"

"*Just leave it.*"

So they remained as they were for several minutes, while Henderson looked on, utterly bewildered, in silence, while the figure at the door was joined by a second, and a third, and it seemed to Henderson that something about these outlines was not right, distorted in some way.

Then they were gone. The door to the compartment next to them seemed to open and close.

Professor Lindsay let go of his wrist.

"I think I am due some explanation."

"Perhaps you are and perhaps you shall have it in good time." Then, despite Henderson's half-hearted protests, Lindsay launched into a seemingly ridiculous and irrelevant story about how the first Paleologan emperor Michael the Eighth had not only sold his soul to the Devil, but was so wicked that, when he died, the earth would not receive his coffin and, of course, Heaven could not, so it floated about four feet above the ground.

"What would you say," asked Professor Lindsay, "if I told you that I have *seen that coffin*? Would you believe me?"

"I don't know, sir."

"Well, my boy, you should at least think about it. There are more things in Heaven and Earth and all that. Mister Jedediah Orne, an American gentleman I stayed with in Prague, showed me quite a few things that you might find hard to believe."

"Should I know of this Mister Orne?"

"I hope not. Now, I have said too much. I think we should turn out the light and get to sleep."

Abruptly, Professor Lindsay shut out the light. There was nothing for it. Henderson undressed in the dark and crawled into his berth.

But he didn't sleep, not for a long time, and even after that, not well. He kept hearing noises through the wall, shuffling sounds as if several persons were perhaps dancing without music, and there were even rhythmic thumping. When he finally did get to sleep he had an unpleasant dream in which he entered—or was forced to enter—that compartment next door. Somehow it was much larger than seemed possible for a railway compartment, an almost-cavernous chamber, in the middle of which stood a strangely carven stone altar with candles set on it around an open book, a thick codex with a broken clasp made of human bones. Gathered around this were at least a dozen persons, one of whom he recognized by his height and by his clothing as Professor Lindsay, even if all of them wore something over their heads, not quite hoods, more like canvas mail sacks with holes crudely cut out for the eyes.

"Come, sir," someone said to him. "You must unmask, even as we do."

He was aware then that he had such a sack over his own head, and as he was hustled forward it fell out of position, so he couldn't see anything out of the eyeholes. He knew he was a prisoner then. He was suffocating inside the sack. Then someone yanked it off fiercely, even as the others removed theirs.

There was a flash of what might have been blinding light. He sat up suddenly in his bed.

Henderson saw Professor Lindsay in a dressing gown, seated at the small desk in the middle of their compartment. He had clearly been up for some time. When he noticed that Henderson had awakened, he said, almost curtly, "Oh, good morning," and quickly gathered the papers he had been working on into a briefcase, which he snapped shut and locked. "Did you sleep well?"

"No," said the younger man. "Actually I didn't."

"That's too bad—ah!" Professor Lindsay looked up. There was a knock at the door. Someone was there. Before Henderson could say anything or otherwise react, Lindsay was at the door. He opened it.

It seemed they had reached the Rumanian border. Outside were a conductor and a customs official.

"I am *so* sorry, sir," the conductor said. "If you're not dressed yet, we can come back."

"No, no, that is quite all right."

The two were admitted, tickets and passports inspected, and, as they were on their way out, Henderson asked of the conductor, "What is going on in the compartment next door, if I may ask? I heard . . . noises in the night."

"I am very sorry if you were disturbed, sir," said the conductor, "but I really could not say. That compartment is empty now."

When the two were gone, Henderson asked, "Did you hear anything in the night?"

"No. I can't say that I did."

"Do you suppose that compartment really is empty?"

"If the man said so, it must be."

Henderson himself was not so sure, and not sure why it troubled him. On their way to breakfast he fell a little behind his companion, then paused to try the door of the neighboring compartment as they walked past it. It was locked.

Most of the passengers must have gotten off in Budapest, because now, for all that there might have been several persons raising a racket in the night, the dining car was all but empty. Henderson noted a middle-aged German with an enormous mustache in imitation of his country's Kaiser, and what appeared to be a wealthy Russian couple; but as these made no attempt to mingle, he and Professor Lindsay otherwise had the car all to themselves. They breakfasted in a leisurely manner. There followed a delay of several hours as the engine was being exchanged for another one, and possibly the border officials took a while to be satisfied. Finally the train lurched into motion again, and throughout the day the view out the window was of the increasingly wilder forests and mountains of Rumania, although neither Henderson nor Lindsay had much opportunity to admire the scenery, because their journey descended into nightmare quickly thereafter.

They returned to their compartment. Once more Henderson pressed Professor Lindsay about the nature of his researches, and his reason for traveling to Constantinople at all. He may have been in awe of the man. He may have looked on him with almost juvenile hero-worship, but he was not stupid, and he knew when something was being kept from him.

"My boy, when it is time for me to make an announcement to

the world, I shall make it. Meanwhile, I am afraid, I must have my confidences. I'm sorry, but that is all I can say."

"But surely—"

"*Nothing* is sure. We know so very little. We drift like specks of foam in a vast sea of ignorance."

"This isn't making any sense, Professor."

"Then I am afraid I have nothing more to say."

In silence, then, they sat opposite one another for a time. Henderson got out and reviewed his notes. Lindsay actually did open his briefcase in his lap, and examine *his* notes, but he kept the lid up, blocking Henderson's view, even as Henderson made his best effort not to seem to be interested. As far as he could tell, some of Lindsay's notes were old, not on paper at all, perhaps medieval parchment. But he never found out. He never had a chance to retrieve that briefcase.

What happened was that a shadow fell over the both of them. Henderson looked up, and saw that Lindsay was staring at the door with an actual expression of dread on his face. Again, someone stood before the semi-opaque glass—two shapes, three, four. More passed behind the first ones. The door to the adjoining compartment very definitely clicked, loud enough that he could hear it unmistakably above the background noises of the train itself.

The silhouetted figures at the door appeared misshapen, as if, perhaps, they had bags over their heads.

Henderson made no attempt to go to the door. Lindsay sat absolutely still, then whispered to him, as faintly as he could, "I don't suppose you brought a pistol with you."

"No."

"Just as well. It probably wouldn't do any good."

"What is going on? Who are they?"

"I am very sorry, George, but something I have become involved in seems to have followed me and found me. I didn't want to expose you to any danger."

"Danger? What sort of danger?"

Just then a gloved fist smashed through the glass of the door, reached in, and undid the lock. Four or more hulking brutes, distorted or twisted somehow in the way they moved, invaded the compartment and seized hold of Professor Lindsay. Henderson couldn't see more than that. They did indeed have rough sacks over their heads. When he made to protest, then went to the other man's defense, one of them seized him by the lapels and shoved him backward against the wall so hard that he lost consciousness.

It might have been hours before he awoke. When he did, it was dark. He fumbled around for the light and turned it on. He saw Professor Lindsay's briefcase on the floor, the contents scattered, but he paid no attention to that.

He called out, "Help! Help! I need help here!" but there was no reply, only *silence*. That was, to overuse the term, very *odd indeed*. He could feel the motion of the train, but there was no sound at all. He heard himself moving around, his own gropings and footsteps. He could hear himself shout. He heard the door slam against the side of the compartment when he pulled it open and swung it to one side. So, no, he hadn't become deaf. Possibly he was injured. Possibly he had a concussion. There was some blood on his face.

He called out again, and made his way down the corridor, banging on one compartment door after another, but there was no response, and no sound at all but that he made himself. He reached the dining car, and it too was empty.

He thought that maybe he was still unconscious, dreaming. This was indeed like a dream, one of those drifting, slow-motion nightmares one has, in which time and distance aren't right.

He struggled back, in the darkness, to his own compartment, and then to the one next to it. He knew what he had to do. He had no idea how he was to rescue the professor, but he had to try.

He banged on the door. He shouted for whoever or whatever was in there to come out and fight, if they had to.

And the door swung inward, and he stumbled into the compartment, which, as in his dream, was much larger on the inside than it possibly could be, almost cavernous, as if—Henderson, telling me this, could not quite find the words for it—it occupied a "different kind of space."

Hands seized hold of him from every side. He confronted the dozen or more figures in strange garb, with misshapen sacks over their heads. He saw the book, and the candles, and he observed that the pages of the book were *blank* and that the whole assembled company looked on him expectantly. If Professor Lindsay were among them, he did not see him. That was a small comfort, but he hardly had time to think about it, because he saw now that whatever was under those sacks was so distorted, so strange, it could not be human at all. The way the lumps, the shapes *moved*—

"Come, sir," they all said at once, "*you must unmask!*"

And they unmasked, and his sight, his mind were blasted. What he saw revealed he could not entirely describe. Not human faces at all. Some of them bestial, some almost fish-like, some covered with tentacles like squids or cuttlefish, but always shifting, bubbling, like waxen masks melting and forming new shapes even as he watched. Once they were all faces like those of enormous bats, shrieking at him in a high-frequency tone that made his ears bleed.

Somehow—he never quite understood it himself—he was able to break free of their grasp. He said that the figures holding him seemed to dissolve, as if they were not quite solid, or made of matter as we know it. But he admitted it was only by what he tearfully described as an act of craven cowardice that he managed to escape. That is, he gave up all hope of saving the professor, and turned from that room and clawed his way back to his own, then threw up the window and hurled himself out, regardless of the consequences.

"And that is not a very satisfactory conclusion to my account," said George Henderson, as he told me this. He was calm now. But he seemed reluctant to say anything more.

No, it was not satisfactory. I already knew some of what had happened thereafter. He never got to Constantinople. The train must have, by sheer chance, slowed down just then, perhaps going around a curve, because he was found alive, albeit grievously injured, on a leaf-covered hillside. When those who discovered him rifled through his pockets and determined that he was an Englishman, not a Turk, they bore him up in an improvised stretcher made of a cloak, and took him to the headman of a village, who placed him in a cart and sent him to a priest. For Henderson, it was all pain and delirium. He could not report accurately where he had been or what happened. Much later, he ended up in a hospital in Bucharest, and later still was transferred into British custody and sent home on a steamer, via Athens. If he could not remember much of his adventure, it was merely taken to have been wild and terrible, but not unnatural, for he had a perfectly natural explanation for some of his predicament. He had coincidentally blundered into the start of the first Balkan War. Possibly the train was boarded by partisans of some sort, looking for Turks. It was never held against him that he had not completed his scholarly mission, and, of course, shortly after his return to England and his recuperation was complete, the Great War broke out, and there was no question of another trip to Turkey. His colleagues welcomed him back at the university, and he rose up the ladder of academic success at a considerably slower pace than once anticipated, but steadily enough.

It was only with almost infinite patience and tenderness, because I had been his friend for so long, that he eventually confided in me anything more.

First of all, there was an entire episode missing from his story as he had first related it. After he had returned from the dining car in the darkness, but *before* he barged into the compartment into which, he was certain, the abducted professor had been taken, he went into his own compartment, and sat down, holding his head in his hands, trying to think, to figure out what he should do next. Probably he did have a concussion. His head hurt terribly. He was bleeding from his nose. Therefore he could not be sure of anything he saw or heard. He became the most unreliable of narrators.

He said that he felt a hand on his shoulder, and looked up, and Professor Lindsay was before him. The light was still on in his compartment. He could tell that it was he, even though the professor wore a sack over his head, and peered out through crudely cut eyeholes, and the shape beneath the cloth bulged and moved strangely.

"You deserve an explanation, my boy," said Lindsay, and he did explain how he had been led astray, if that is the right word for it, by his own close textual studies of ancient languages, how he had discovered languages *beneath* other languages, roots within roots, unsuspected codes and ciphers within the most esoteric writings, until ultimately the meaning of meaning itself was deconstructed, and unfathomable chaos revealed. On this matter, he had first consulted a noted specialist in mental diseases in Vienna, as he grasped to understand how, as he put it, some people's minds—those of persons usually accounted insane—"vibrated" differently than most, and could perceive things others could not. But the Vienna man was obsessed with earthbound, carnal explanations, and was quite unable to follow the path of Professor Lindsay's brilliance. Therefore Lindsay moved more into occult circles, and eventually made contact with a very secret brotherhood that included among its members a certain Jedediah Orne, who claimed to be over two hundred years old, and who revealed to Professor Lindsay secrets of the universe itself that staggered his imagination.

It was no coincidence that Lindsay was on the train bound for Constantinople. The Brotherhood knew about that book. Henderson needn't have worried about a tedious work of theology. It was as he had speculated, transcribed in the late fourteenth century, but the content was incredibly ancient, older than mankind, and the key to everything. The title, only an approximation transmitted through half a dozen languages, was something like, perhaps, *The Book of the Undying Hands*. It was not deemed expedient that the Brotherhood should just steal such a thing. Instead, they proposed that *one of their number* gain access to it and translate it. Perhaps, once Henderson had started, he could even apply for Professor Lindsay to assist him. That was the plan, even though Lindsay had at one point broken with the Brotherhood, then come to view them as his rivals, then to fear them. He had tried to get away from them and obtain the book for himself, but that was all settled now. They were reconciled. He hoped, sincerely, that Henderson could be persuaded to join him in the endeavor, to whatever awesome and indescribable end it might lead.

That was why Henderson had actually entered that other railway compartment, not to rescue Professor Lindsay, but to *join* him, for he was indeed a willing Wagner to Lindsay's Faust. He all but worshipped the older man. He would have followed him anywhere.

It was only decades later, when the scandal finally broke, when something horrifying was found in the cellar of an old farmhouse that he maintained as a private retreat in Yorkshire, and *because of what that thing said before it was destroyed*, even as Jedediah Orne and other confederates around the world were systematically hunted down and destroyed, that George Henderson's academic career came to an abrupt end. It became all too clear how far he *had* followed in his mentor's footsteps. Professor Lindsay had disappeared in 1912, in the Balkans. No trace of him was ever found. But Henderson carried on. He even claimed that Professor Lindsay visited him in the night when he was alone in that farmhouse, and more secrets were revealed. Sometimes Lindsay brought with him his companions, who were not human at all and never had been, and who, on great bat-like wings, soared in the darkness between the stars into abysses beyond the capacity of even the most densely coded, secret language to describe. Always, Professor Lindsay wore a sack over his head. But he spoke with the same voice. That was how Henderson knew it was he.

"What about the book?" I asked him at last.

"It's all rubbish." Henderson laughed again, and again, harder and harder. "All lies. Everything I have told you is a lie! Do you know what that book was really about? It was a treatise by a fourteenth-century Greek monk who proposed to utilize the anti-gravitational properties of the coffin of Michael Paleologus to rise above the moon and visit the angels. Can you imagine that? I'd like to see the angels. I really would. If only the black spaces were actually inhabited by angels! Ha! Ha! I want to see the angels!"

His laughter became so intense that I thought he was having a fit and I called for help, and he was immediately taken away, as it is against practice in a madhouse to allow the inmates to become too excited.

I am afraid that in my several subsequent visits, I got nothing out of him at all.

THE GOD BENEATH
THE MOUNTAIN
JAMES L. SUTTER

THE WORLD IS BUILT ON patterns. From the shapes of rivers and coast-
lines to the fractal fronds of a fern, cycles repeat themselves, shifting
only in scale. It's part of what allows small things—a smile, a book
of matches—to have such a great impact. Tom taught me that.

And I wish to god he hadn't.

The ground trembled.

For a moment, it felt as if I were still on the train, the deck
rolling beneath my feet as it wound its way through mountain pass
after mountain pass. But no—there was the train behind me,
stopped at the last spur before the tracks entered the dark maw of
the tunnel. Was it merely my land legs returning after so many days
of travel?

A puff of smoke and dust from the tunnel mouth solved the
mystery. As it cleared, a line of dirty men in coveralls lit lanterns
and loaded onto motorized carts that carried them forward into
the darkness.

"Herr Cantor!"

The little man running toward me was as different from the
filthy miners as night from day. Blond, blue-eyed, and clad in a

spotless uniform, he could have been a recruiting poster for the Swiss military. He stopped a few paces from me.

"It's 'doctor,' actually."

"Of course." His English was flawless. "My name is David. Please, follow me." Without pausing for a reply, he lifted my bags and began leading me through the camp.

The Simplon builder's camp was a maze of muddy streets cutting between identical, flat-walled wooden boxes housing dormitories, cafeterias, and machine shops. Men crowded the streets, either coated in gray dust and dark oil or else freshly scrubbed clean.

Somewhere in there was my hospital. No doubt it would be a far cry from Saint Francis's, but given the circumstances, a shack with a few cots was better than nothing. A chance to start fresh.

I had presumed David would lead me straight into my exile, but instead, the building that rose up before us could only have been the director's residence—a miniature chalet, its smooth timbers and tall windows peering out over the shacks around us, none of which rose above a single story.

The inside of the building was significantly less elegant. The few pieces of furniture in the foyer and sitting room were expensive, but only emphasized the emptiness of the place—no art on the walls or rugs on the floor, no sign of anything approaching a personal touch. Even the angles of the furniture seemed awkward, as often facing the blank walls as each other.

We passed through the cold rooms and down a short hall, stopping before a door.

"The director is waiting." David showed no sign of entering himself. "Your luggage will be waiting for you in your quarters, and I'll let the hospital know to expect you."

"Thank you." When it was clear that no more words were forthcoming, I stepped forward and opened the door.

Inside, the office was the exact opposite of the rest of the house. Paper lay everywhere, with blueprints, diagrams, reports, and more tacked to walls or spread out across the desk and its single chair. Books of all shapes and sizes spilled off of shelves, from journal-sized notebooks to hefty engineering texts and a huge, leather-bound monstrosity that seemed more appropriate for a church altar. Behind the desk, a wall-sized topographical map of Mount Leone hung so cluttered with overlapping markings and arcane engineering diagrams that I had to blink back a moment of vertigo.

Director Hugo von Kager was a big man, neither fat nor muscular but simply large, with a lion's mane of black beard and unkempt hair. It was the sort of beard you saw in paintings of Zeus or Jehovah. A god's beard. And as far as the Simplon workers were concerned, this man *was* God. The Simplon Tunnel project had many backers and interested parties, but von Kager was the architect and crew chief, the man responsible for seeing it through.

He stood behind the desk wearing a gray waistcoat and matching trousers, ignoring the chair as he scribbled lines on yet another piece of paper. I shut the door behind me and stood, not wanting to disturb him. I needn't have worried. After a moment of being utterly ignored, I cleared my throat.

"Seven and a half years."

The voice that emerged from that thicket of beard was iron-hard, yet smooth as well, contradicting the barbaric visage.

"Excuse me?"

He looked up then, meeting my gaze. Immediately, I was forced to revert to my original impression. Those dark eyes burned, lending his face a fevered, furious intensity.

"It was supposed to be completed in five and a half. Five and a half years to bore through the roots of Mount Leone in the longest tunnel ever carved by man. A hole through the heart of the world." Thick brows like night-black caterpillars curved down and met above his nose. "But still we are not complete."

"You're close, though," I ventured. The man who'd offered me the position had emphasized that fact, not realizing that a potentially long stay abroad was the job's biggest appeal for me. "I'm sure your men—"

"The men are swine," von Kager snapped. "Italians, mostly, but that's no excuse. They're weak and cowardly, afraid to even enter the tunnel. I give them everything they could want: food, housing, medicine—" he gestured my direction as if I embodied this last "—and still they rise up against me in their ridiculous strikes. They force me to bring in the military simply to make them do their jobs."

"I see."

The truth was, I knew remarkably little about the job I'd signed on for. I'd heard vaguely of the project: a grandiose attempt to bore a rail tunnel for the Orient Express from just outside Brig in Switzerland all the way to Domodossola in Italy. Beyond that, though, I'd been focused on my own problems. There were men to be treated, and money to be made, all far off in the Alps somewhere. That had been enough.

Von Kager waved the matter away irritably. "None of this is your concern. You will be taking charge of the hospital on the Swiss side. Whatever supplies you need will be provided, but your objective is to keep the men healthy and working. If I believe that you are encouraging them toward sloth, you will be dismissed without hesitation." He waited, eyes boring into me.

"Understood," I said.

He nodded sharply. "Good."

There came a knock at the door, and a man entered.

He was beautiful. There was simply no other word for it. Taller than my own modest height by several inches, he was lean enough that corded muscles stood out on his bare forearms. Beneath streaks of gray dust, his hair was jet black, his eyes nearly so, and his skin a healthy olive. His features were sharp and angular, delicate without being effeminate.

God have mercy.

He stuck out a hand. "You must be Doctor Cantor, then. I'm Tom Halsham. Please to meet you."

His voice startled me so much I almost forgot to shake his hand. "You're English!"

The left half of Tom's mouth quirked up—a scoundrel's grin. The sort that made you feel like he was bringing you in on a secret.

"Several of your countrymen have taken positions in my operation," von Kager said. "Mister Halsham is our master of demolitions."

"Lord of the blast men." Tom's smile widened. "Chief banger and firebug." There was a smudge of grease along the left side of his jaw, as if he'd reached up to scratch his chin and hadn't bothered to wipe it off.

"Mister Halsham will help you familiarize yourself with the camp. After that, your role will be solely in the hospital unless you are called for. Understood?"

Angled slightly so that von Kager couldn't see him, Tom rolled his eyes.

"Perfectly," I said.

"Come on, then." Tom placed a hand on my arm and turned me toward the door. "Let me show you around."

Von Kager made no goodbyes.

When we were safely outside the house, Tom gave a loud laugh and released my arm, slapping me lightly on the back. "He's a barmy one, isn't he?"

The tension of von Kager's office left me in a rush, replaced by a new sort, and I found myself returning his smile. "He seems more like a prophet than an engineer. Or maybe an mad emperor."

"Around here, he's all three." Tom looked me up and down. "So you're the new doctor, eh? Tell the truth, I thought you'd be older."

Tom couldn't have been more than thirty himself, and I'd have been hard pressed to guess which of us was the senior. "You're not the first," I said. "You wouldn't believe how often an old woman's refused my treatment, demanding to see someone with spectacles and a beard."

Tom laughed again. It was such an easy sound for him, so natural. I felt myself standing up straighter in response, growing more confident.

"Well, you don't have to worry about that here. Most of the men will be happy just to have someone who knows what he's doing. The last doctor was a Swiss bloke who seemed to think laxatives were a panacea." He touched my shoulder again. "Come on, let me show you the dig."

We walked through the camp, toward where the rail line disappeared into the earth. Above us, Mount Leone was too close to see as anything but a hunkered mass of stone, but I'd seen it well enough from the train: a craggy, pyramidal blade that thrust into the sky like an alpine ziggurat, brooding and picturesque.

"There're about three thousand workers in total," Tom said, gesturing to the rows of boxy wooden barracks. "Most Italian, but some Swiss in there as well." He frowned. "More now that Kager's brought in the military to put down the strikes."

"He mentioned that. Have there been many?"

"A few," Tom admitted. "Excavation's a rough job, and this one more than most. Nobody's ever bored a tunnel this long before. It's dangerous."

"The dust?" I had no idea how long the workers' contracts ran, but it was easy to imagine that most of the men were afflicted with some degree of miner's phthisis—the dreaded "black lung."

Tom bobbed his head. "That's part of it. But this dig's had more trouble than most. A few years back, we hit a river—a goddamned *river*! The rock around it was all rotted out and kept collapsing on us no matter how much we timbered, and we only made it a hundred and fifty feet in *six months*. That was when von Kager started getting frantic. In the end, we had to encase that entire length of the tunnel in granite eight and a half feet thick."

"Good lord."

"You said it," Tom agreed. "And then we started hitting the hot spots. You know much about mining, Doctor?"

"Nothing at all," I said. "And please, call me William. Will's even better."

Another smile. "Will, then. Most folk presume that it's cold underground—water out of a well's cold, right? But once you get that much mountain on top of you, it insulates, trapping any geothermal heat, as well as heat generated by the dig itself. There are spots down there that hit a hundred and thirty. Some of the men think they're drilling into Hell itself. No joke."

"They're superstitious, then?"

"All miners are superstitious. Comes with the territory. Take the hot springs we hit earlier this year—a near-boiling system of streams that flooded the tunnels so badly we had to put in gates and start pumping out into the rivers. But that wasn't enough. Turns out there are big iron lodes down there, and the streams picked it up, turning the whole thing rust-red." His grin widened. "Imagine you're an Italian miner, Will. Suddenly the drill starts screaming and you're awash up to your waist in scalding, red, metallic-tasting liquid. What would you think?"

Of course. "Blood."

Tom chuckled. "Half of them were willing to face down the soldiers rather than go back in. 'The mountain's bleeding,' they said. 'We've wounded the lion.' Fortunately, the engineers were able to get the pumps in place before Kager got truly desperate, but still—it's a messy business, drilling through a mountain."

We had exited the barracks and were now in the structures closest to the tunnel itself, buildings that resounded with shouts and engine hums and the clang of metal. Tom led me up the ramp to one of the largest structures. "Here," he said, "you'll find this interesting."

Inside, the heat and humidity hit me like a wave. We were standing amid a forest of taut ropes—dozens of them, each padlocked to a bolt in the ground. Walkways and low benches cut through it at regular intervals. Looking up, I saw a series of large pipes running across the ceiling. The ropes were looped over these like pulleys, and from their ends dangled a tremendous number of shirts, trousers, and small bundles, creating a false ceiling of fabric several feet above our heads.

"What is it?"

Tom beamed. "It's the workers' clothes and possessions. Each of the shower houses has them. When a miner comes up out of the dig and rinses off the dust, he unlocks his rope, pulls down his clothes—all warm from the steam pipes—and sends up his wet mining clothes. By the time he comes back for his next shift, they're dry again. Plus, it makes theft far more difficult."

"Ingenious," I said, and meant it.

"Thank you."

I took another look at his smile, and it clicked. "You invented this?"

Tom nodded proudly. "Von Kager wasn't keen on it to begin with, but when I explained that wet clothes would make the workers sick, he came around quick enough." He laughed. "He's a strange one, but he'll do anything to make the tunnel go faster." He led me over to one of the large canvas flaps that opened into the rest of the building. "We've got both hot and cold showers so that the workers coming off-shift don't go straight from the heat of the tunnel to the chill of the alpine air."

He lifted the canvas, revealing a large, steaming shower room filled with men in various states of undress, the dust sluicing off them in thick gray rivulets. I struggled to maintain a purely clinical eye.

"Yes, of course," I said. "Very sensible."

"I thought so," Tom said, and let the flap drop. The corner of his mouth was still twisted up in a hint of a smirk.

He led me out of the shower building and turned me back toward the heart of the camp. As he did, I caught sight once more of the tunnels themselves, both the main bore and the smaller ventilation shaft to its right, both yawning like the throats of great beasts.

Tom followed my gaze. "I don't expect you're interested in touring the tunnels themselves? Six miles of dark is a bit much for some people."

I shook my head, relieved, then asked, "Only six? I thought the tunnel was supposed to be twelve miles long."

Tom nodded. "It is. We're only half the operation over here. The rest of the men are drilling from the Italian side. We should meet in the middle in less than a year." He extended a finger on each hand and brought their tips together. "Right smack in the center of the mountain."

"Ah," I said, embarrassed at my ignorance. "Of course."

Another touch on the center of my back. "No problem, Doctor. I doubt you'll so much as set foot in the dig while you're here. Like Kager said, your job is elsewhere. And having said that . . ."

He walked me back through the makeshift town, pointing out the mess hall, the commissary, and other notable landmarks. At last we stood in front of the hospital. Before entering, I paused to pull out my pipe for a smoke—and stopped short.

"Damn," I said. "My matches are in my luggage. David took them to my quarters."

"Here." Tom produced a pack and tossed them to me. I tamped and lit, then attempted to hand them back, but Tom put his hands in the air.

"Keep them." He pointed at his chest. "Blaster, remember? I've got more fire than I know what to do with."

"Oh," I said. "Thank you."

There was a pause.

"Right, then," Tom said. "Be seeing you around, I suspect."

"Be seeing you," I agreed, but Tom had already turned and begun walking away.

As the weeks rolled on, I got to know several of the other Englishmen in the camp. I was also surprised to find that David, the young Swiss soldier who had greeted me, was absolutely passionate about cards, with a good humor that remained intact even when he was losing terribly. Yet as much as these acquaintances flourished, I still found myself associating primarily with Tom, when I wasn't busy with the hospital.

The hospital: Two long rows of beds, with thirty-two in total. Thirty-two beds for fifteen hundred men. The medical supplies were well stocked, but my nurse and orderlies were all Swiss, and like von Kager did little to hide their casual disdain for the uneducated Italian workers. Not exactly a welcoming place to convalesce.

Fortunately, injuries had been light. I was given to understand that the early days of the dig had been terrible—a constant parade of shattered limbs and blackened lungs—but the five years since had given time for safety systems to be improved and ingrained, and the use of water with the drills cut down greatly on the dust.

Most of my patients spoke no English, forcing me to rely entirely on my Swiss orderlies to translate, yet on one particular day I had just taken over splinting a broken leg when the patient surprised me by thanking me in my own tongue.

"You speak English?" I asked.

"*Solo un po'.*" He gave a gap-toothed smile. "A little."

"Better than most," I said, and dismissed the orderly, happy for the chance to communicate directly for once. I cast about for some common ground, then noticed the old rust-colored stains smudging the lower half of his uniform. "Were you here when they broke through onto the hot springs? That must have been a sight."

His smile disappeared, and I realized I'd blundered straight into the Italian superstition Tom had warned me about.

"Is not right," the man said, shaking his head.

"What—the tunnel?"

He nodded. "Tunnel bad. *Mountain* bad." He reached for a word. "*Cursed.*"

"I see."

"*Leone* sleeps," he pressed. "Bad to wake. Tunnel wake."

"Were you one of the strikers, then?"

He frowned, then bobbed his head again. He pointed to the bridge of his nose, and I noticed the telltale bump of a poorly healed break. "We try. Kager no listen."

"So why stay?"

He looked at me like I was an idiot. "Contract," he said. "We—" Then he cut off, his expression contorting to one of unambiguous loathing.

I turned and found Hugo von Kager standing in the doorway, glowering.

"Doctor Cantor," he said. "I see you've already encountered the ingratitude of our workforce."

Behind me, the worker moved to stand. I put one hand on his shoulder and shoved him firmly back down. "They're just stories, Director."

"Stories have a way of causing delays," von Kager said. "Setbacks. I can do little to stop these . . . *people*—" he glared at the Italian "—from spreading their rumors, but I trust that you and your staff are above such things."

"You have nothing to worry about," I said honestly.

"That's for me to decide," von Kager said. Then he turned and disappeared out the door.

Four months in, I finally broke.

Tom and I had eaten dinner together as usual, and when a discipline issue among the soldiers removed David from the evening's plans, Tom and I had foregone cards in favor of splitting a bottle of halfway decent brandy. When all that remained in the bottle was the smell, we'd tossed it and gone for a walk up the side of the mountain, in search of a point where Tom said he often went to think and get away from the noise and stink of the other men.

We spent the better part of an hour following game trails and scrabbling up scree fields in a most undignified fashion—made even less dignified by the hot liquor sloshing in our bellies—but at last we reached the overlook. Here the trees stopped short of a little ledge, a solid slab of rock projecting up and out of the mountain's side. My natural—and in my opinion, sensible—aversion to heights kept me well back from the edge, but Tom would have none of it. He grabbed my arm and pulled me out till our toes fairly hung over the drop.

Below us, the mountain fell away. Down in the valley, the lights of the mining camp glowed like a fire died to embers, yet the sound of it was swallowed up by the night, the mountain catching it and reflecting it back. From up here, it was at once immediate and impossibly distant, like the stars themselves. As above, so below.

"Wow," I said.

"Amazing, isn't it?" Tom turned toward me, face a charcoal sketch in the starlight. "I thought you'd like it."

Suddenly I realized just how close we were standing—arms almost touching, close enough for me to smell the sweat of his climb up the trail.

Then we were kissing, hard, heedless of the empty space inches from our feet. My fingers buried themselves in that black hair, grabbing, pulling him in. His mouth was on mine, then on my neck, then my shoulder, then—

Mouths. Hands. Warmth. A release that peeled me inside out.

Afterward, we lay on a bed of our jackets, curled together with his arms wrapping me up from behind. The warmth of us radiated out into the alpine sky.

To my shame, I began to cry.

"Damn," I whispered, "damn damn *damn*."

"Shh." Tom's breath was soft and hot in my ear. He stroked the hair on my temple. "It's okay."

"I tried so hard." My breath came in little ragged hiccups. "How did you know?"

Tom laughed quietly, but it was a kind laugh. He leaned over me so that I could see his face. "You had the look of someone who was running from something. And, well . . . some things just don't stay buried."

"They *should*," I whispered.

"No, they shouldn't." Tom's body tensed. "Things are what they are, and just because you won't let yourself look at them doesn't mean they aren't there. You can't spend your whole life hiding from the truth." Then he relaxed and smiled. "Who was he?"

"A patient." The words were out before I could stop them, and even as they left my mouth, they tugged the rest with them—a long chain sliding up out of my gut. "At Saint Francis's, the hospital where I worked in London. I had never . . . but he knew, too." I closed my eyes, not wanting to see any of it. "He was a minister. The papers picked up on it. My family, the other doctors—everybody knew. The patient—Charles—took a position in India somewhere. I never saw him again. But I still had to live with it. When a friend told me about the tunnel project, it seemed like the best thing for everyone. A fresh start." The tears redoubled. "And now I've gone and done it *again*."

"No," Tom said firmly, taking my chin and turning my face toward him. "*We* did it. And what *we* do is no business of anybody but us. Do you understand? Out here, we're our own men."

Even through my tears, the word *we* sent a little shiver of excitement through me. I swallowed hard. "Do you really believe that?"

"I do," he said, and leaned down to kiss me. It was softer this time, without urgency or need. Just a kiss, but if anything it warmed me more, flooding my veins.

It went on for a long time. Finally he pulled back.

"Do you want this?" he asked.

I thought of the pack of matches he'd given me my first day, how I'd secretly refused to use them after that, instead carrying them around with me like a talisman. I felt the square of them in my pocket, pressing against my thigh, and knew I'd already made my choice.

"Yes." The rush of the word was so powerful, I said it again. "Yes." Then, more hesitantly: "But this has to stay between us."

"What, you don't want to notify the papers?" He chuckled, then drew me close again, pressing my face into his shoulder and his own into the top of my head.

"Between us," he said. "Just you, me, and the mountain."

Tom and I spent our nights together as often as we dared, which was as often as our shifts lined up—roughly every three days.

While we continued to eat together, either alone or with other friends for the sake of appearances, we didn't dare spend time in each other's quarters. Tom's bunk was one of several in a barracks shared with three of his men. As the head of medicine at the camp, my quarters were more private—a cramped little one-room cottage with a bed so close to the stove that the blanket was studded with spark burns—but my position meant that anyone might come knocking on my door in the middle of the night. We didn't dare risk it.

Instead, Tom was his usual resourceful self. As blasting master, he was the only person other than von Kager with a key to the explosives storage bunker, a cinderblock affair set on the tunnel side of camp but far enough way from any other structures to protect it from the threat of fire—and us from being overheard. There, in the midst of enough dynamite to bore a hole to China, he built a little nest of pillows and blankets stolen from the commissary. It was cold, and dark, and smelled of chemicals and cement.

It was wonderful.

Lying in the dark, or perhaps with a lantern turned to the lowest guttering flame, we would talk for hours—about our pasts, our families, our philosophies, or anything at all.

"Geology?" I asked one night, long after we'd snuffed the lantern on the pretense of going to sleep. "I figured you for chemistry."

"Why? Because I like to blow things up?" Tom laughed. He'd spent hours telling me about the blasting process, the placement of bore holes and careful timing of fuses. "There's something to be said for chemistry, sure—a blasting master ought to know what he's working with. But all these explosives are standardized, manufactured in factories somewhere." His body jostled, and I knew he was gesturing to the boxes around us. "What a blasting master really needs to know is rock. Recognizing the different types of stone, how it'll shear, how much shaking a tunnel's ceiling can take before it comes down on your head. It's not even enough to know the stone— you have to *love* it."

I laughed. "You love *stones*?"

His hand, splayed across my stomach, spidered its way lower, and I imagined I could hear his grin. "I thought that was obvious."

I batted at him. "No, really—what's so fascinating about rocks?"

He gave me a squeeze and reluctantly released his hold. His hands fluttered in the dark.

"It's the fractals—patterns that repeat themselves no matter how close you look. Like when you get up close to some trees, you see that each branch has its own smaller branches that look similar, and each of *those* has branches that look similar—"

"I'm aware what fractals are, Tom."

"Right," he said, embarrassed. "Anyway, that's what I love about stone. The patterns. Break a rock down, you get smaller rocks with similar shapes and properties. Push them together, you get a mountain, still with the same properties." He sighed. "Learn enough about rocks, you understand the whole world."

"Oh, you understand everything, do you?" I grabbed his hands and pushed my face close to his. "So surely you understand *this*?"

And then there were no more words.

Shifts never ended early—not under von Kager's direction. And so it was with great surprise that I looked out the hospital window and saw men streaming through the streets with the shift change still three hours off.

Fear gripped me. Despite the excitement of my midnight assignations with Tom, the last several weeks had found me filled with an increasing sense of foreboding, a creeping dread all out of proportion to any actual risk. My first thought upon seeing the crowd of workers was that there must have been some sort of disaster—a collapse, another subterranean river that flooded the tunnel, smashing men against the stone or boiling them alive. Tom's perfect body, battered and broken.

But no—while some of the men in the street looked confused, no one was racing to tell me to prep the surgery. Once it became clear that whatever was going on wouldn't require my services, I left the hospital in the charge of one of the orderlies and went to find Tom.

He met me halfway to his barracks, grinning wide. His hair was still damp from the showers.

"What happened?" I asked.

"The damndest thing," he said. "Not halfway through the shift, we broke through into a cavern. Crazy place—all these black crystals, like obsidian but in the wrong shapes, growing out of the stone in prism clusters like quartz. Almost like a geode."

"Sounds beautiful," I said. "But why's everyone come up? Von Kager will have a fit."

"That's the strange part!" Tom punctuated the point with a raised finger. "Every time we've run across a cavern or river in the past, all Kager's wanted to know is how much time it's saved or cost us. I swear, if we found Buckingham Palace down there, he'd expect us to cross the courtyard and keep drilling. So we send a runner up to let him know and keep working. But halfway through setting the next charges, in runs Himself with a dozen soldiers! He takes one look at the place and orders us all out. All work is suspended until he says otherwise. He wouldn't even let me pull the charges we'd prepped!"

Tom's wide eyes were eager for me to share the excitement. Von Kager never went down into the tunnel, and the idea of him halting the dig for anything less than the Second Coming was unbelievable.

"So what you're saying is that you've got nowhere to be for the next few hours."

A look of surprise, and then that easy smile again. "I guess you could say that."

Neither of us made it to the mess hall for dinner that night. Somehow, once we were tucked away in the bunker, the idea of leaving it for anything—even food—seemed like a terrible waste. So we talked, and dozed, and made love, and let the rest of the world fade away.

I woke to pitch blackness, unsure what had jolted me so firmly out of my dreams. Then the sound came again.

Footsteps on gravel. Coming closer.

"Tom!" I hissed, grabbing his shoulder and shaking him awake. "Tom, someone's coming!"

Tom jerked awake, and we both froze. Outside, the boots—one man, by the sound of it—continued to approach.

Tom was the only person who could approve the use of explosives, and all distribution of such equipment happened on his shift. There was no reason at all for anyone to be here.

No reason but us.

It was happening all over again. They'd find us, and then everyone would know. We'd be sent away—if they didn't just hang us. The Italians were devout Catholics, and everyone knew God's judgment on Sodom.

A match burst to life, and then Tom was on his feet, balling clothes and blankets around the dark lantern and flinging the whole mass behind a stack of crates.

"Come on!" He grabbed my hand and pulled me back behind a rack of blasting caps and dynamite packed in straw-filled boxes. He pulled me down with him, wrapping me protectively in his arms, just as the match burned down and went out.

Keys rattled outside. A surprised grunt at the missing lock. Then the door swung open, and light flooded in.

Von Kager stood in the doorway, one arm holding a lantern high, the other clutching the massive leather-bound book I'd noticed in his office. Instead of his waistcoat and trousers, he was dressed in some sort of dark robe, like a priest's cassock, but with a hood drawn partway up, leaving only the front half of his head exposed.

I held my breath as his eyes swept the room. I felt naked, exposed, the rack of boxes a laughably inadequate shield. At any second, his eyes would lock on mine, and then it would be over.

His gaze reached the gap from which I peered out—and moved on. Satisfied, he set down the lantern and stepped away from us, toward the coiled fuses. He selected several, slipping their loops over his shoulder. Then he recovered the lantern and left, closing the door behind him. Outside, gravel crunched once more, growing fainter.

Suddenly the darkness seemed crushing. My breath escaped in a rush, and struggled to sit up, Tom obligingly moving aside and lighting another match.

"He's gone!" I was grinning now, adrenaline filling me. Matchlight painted Tom's face in sharp lines, and in that moment there was nothing I wanted more than to pull him back down to the floor and make love to him again.

But Tom wasn't paying attention. He was inspecting the rack of fuses.

"Tom?"

"What was he doing?" Tom lifted up a coil like those von Kager had taken. "These are ten-second fuses."

"So? He didn't see us!"

Tom went to the door and cracked it, peering out. "He's going into the tunnel."

"Who cares? It's his tunnel!"

Tom turned and frowned at me. "*His* tunnel? He may make the plans, but I'm the blasting master. Nothing goes bang without my say-so. So what's he doing with fuses? And why was he wearing that robe-thing?" He began tugging on his clothes. "Come on, get dressed."

"Why?" The rush was fading, replaced by jitters at how close we'd come, and a growing resentment for Tom clearly not feeling the same way.

Tom looked at me, and at last gave a tight version of his usual grin. "Because you're going down the tunnel after all."

The darkness of the tunnel was at once claustrophobically close and unimaginably vast, at times threatening to smother me, at others to send me spinning off into an endless void. I clung to Tom's arm, him and the whine of the mining cart's motor the only things tethering me, keeping me from floating away into the nightmare nothing.

"There," Tom said, and killed the motor. Suddenly I realized that one of the phantom spots of light floating before my eyes was no illusion—up ahead, a pinprick of light must be the lamp von Kager's own cart. Tom had disabled ours before following into the tunnel, and now I understood why. Down here, even a candle would stand out like a signal flare.

Tom helped me out of the cart, and together we crept down the last of the tunnel, Tom explaining in whispers how to navigate by keeping one foot tight against the rails of the track. After a few minutes, we were close enough to clearly see von Kager's empty cart.

Beyond it, the tracks ended, the stone turning rougher, the walls less reinforced.

"Quiet, now." Carefully, Tom lit our lantern, banking it back to the softest glow, then took my wrist and led me down the last of the unfinished tunnel.

We didn't have far to go. As soon as we saw another flicker of light ahead, Tom set down our lantern, and we crept the rest of the way in the dark, moving by feel.

The light came from a huge crack in the wall, a jagged rent large enough for several men. Crouching on the pile of crumbled stone that had yet to be carted out, we peered through.

Inside, clusters of black crystals the size of police boxes caught the light from von Kager's lamp and reflected it around the room. The chamber was easily forty feet tall, a slightly recessed floor with a great glassy dome of a ceiling overhead.

Von Kager knelt on the right side of the room, before the largest of the crystalline growths, a faceted pyramid climbing twenty feet up the chamber's wall. His robes, dyed in strange swirls of purple and black, spread out around him in a puddle on the stone, and the massive book lay splayed open at his side. To his left sat the lantern, blazing brighter than it had any right to, as blinding and blue as a magnesium lamp.

He was manipulating something on the floor before him, and as he raised up part of it I realized it was one of the stolen fuses, un-coiled and woven into a loose knot several feet across. He shifted, and I felt a sudden pang as I recognized the knot's pattern of inter-locking lines from the giant map behind his desk.

Satisfied, von Kager sat back and touched a match to the end of the fuse. The cord burst to life, spitting and sparking, the flame marching steadily down its allotted path, tracing the burning sigil onto the floor.

"*The time for sleep has passed.*" Von Kager's words echoed off the crystals. The man's voice had always been strong, but now it was something more. The voice of a preacher.

"*Hear me, dreamer! You that fell from Chaos in the time before time. You that have lain beneath the mountain. You that have heard the piping of the blind god's court, and who bear his essence. You are the seed, and this world your garden. Awaken!*"

A crack reverberated through the chamber, followed by another. And another. Crystal splintered and fell to the floor like a rain of stars, chiming against the stone.

Something inside the wall was stirring.

"*Behold the seed!*" Kager intoned. "*Behold the scion of the Throne of Chaos!*"

With a sound like a thousand windows breaking, the crystal wall shattered, exploding outward in a blast of needles that knocked von Kager backward. He struggled to his knees once more, the blood of a dozen punctures clearly visible on his hands and face, and began to laugh.

"*He comes!*" he yelled. "*He comes!*"

And in front of him, something emerged from the wall.

It was huge—easily fifteen feet tall, and nearly as wide. It was humped and distended, a mass of red and yellow flesh like fatty tissue split by a surgeon's knife, and yet at the same time there was something weirdly familiar about its shape. It rose in a quivering ziggurat, expanding and contracting rhythmically like some hideous organ, and towered over von Kager, who continued to laugh.

"Master!" he called.

And that's when my hand slipped, sending a stone clattering down into the chamber.

Von Kager whirled, spinning to fix his gaze on the crack where we perched.

"You!"

"Bloody hell," Tom said.

Above von Kagur, the mountainous thing split open like the petals of a flower, half a dozen glistening lips peeling back and down. Attached to the inside tip of each was a long, thick tendril like a rope of intestine. As Tom and I watched in horror, the thing drew forth loop after twitching loop, writhing them high into the air.

"Run!" I shouted, shoving Tom backward into the tunnel.

A tentacle shot across the room toward me, its tip the bulging circle-toothed mouth of a lamprey, but with the hideous dark orb of an eye in its center. The ring of jaws slammed into my shoulder, shearing through cloth and into the flesh beneath, then yanked me forward into the chamber.

"*Will!*" Tom launched himself back through the cavern entrance, stumbling down the incline after me as my body hurtled through the air. Just when I thought the creature might be intending to slam me into the forest of crystals on the ceiling, the tentacle released me. There was the briefest moment of weightlessness, of gratitude for this small mercy. Then the ground rose up to meet me, and all my faculties were devoted to learning how to breathe again.

Somewhere, Tom might have been screaming my name, but my ears were too full of the sound of my impact to tell for sure.

My eyes refocused to find von Kager between Tom and me, his lips shifting in one imprecation or another. Above him, his monstrosity lurched, tentacles snapping downward.

Tom never missed a stride. Each time one of the horrifying mouths came slamming down, he jerked to the side at the last moment, the teeth tearing red furrows down his side but unable to find purchase. Still, his eyes refused to leave mine.

Von Kager moved to meet him, arms wide. Tom continued to run straight toward him—then at the last minute dropped low and to the right. He snatched up von Kager's lantern from the crystalline floor and spun.

The heavy steel lantern smashed into the big man's jaw. Blood and glass flew as the left side of von Kager's face crumpled around the object. He went down.

"Will!" My hearing returned in a rush as Tom dove for me, grabbing my hand. "We've got to get out of here. We—"

That's when it took him. Too nimble for the tentacles while running, Tom had stopped for me. His body shuddered and jerked as they slammed into his back, each impact the meaty *thunk* of a butcher's cleaver. His eyes widened. The tentacles lifted him off his feet.

It was impossible to tell where his scream stopped and mine began. A perfect union of sound, only gradually resolving into words.

"The charges!" he screamed. "Light the charges!"

Then the tentacles tore him apart.

Something broke inside me, then. As the blood of my lover rained down, his pieces drawn into that terrible, petaled maw, my mind refused to give way, to release me into the easy black of unconsciousness. Instead, it focused on his words.

The charges. Tom was setting the charges when von Kager called them out.

I lifted myself to my feet and ran.

There, opposite the cavern's entrance—holes drilled in the wall in neat intervals, each with a fuse extending from it. I grabbed the whole handful where they came together into a single fat fuse and pulled hard.

Dirty gray sticks of explosive shot out of their burrows, leaving me holding a tangled medusa's head of little cylindrical plugs. Ignoring the long safety fuse, I drew out my matches—Tom's matches—and scratched them to life. Flame kissed the fuses where the strands met and began the careful climb down to their individual ends.

Across the room, the monstrosity had lurched over to the burned fuse-symbol. As it loomed above the sign, the spent cord blazed back to life, this time with unearthly violet flame that grew steadily as it bounced from crystal to crystal, filling the room with a terrible glow. Above it, the tentacles began to weave themselves in a matching sign, humming with a high tone that buzzed in my bones. The creature seemed to drink in the light, growing larger.

One tentacle turned to look at me.

I wanted to say something. To tell the creature what it had taken from me. From the world.

I dropped the explosives and ran for the tunnel.

Behind me, the world exploded.

Nobody sits with me in the coffee shop. That's how I prefer it. Even after more than a year in Brig, I still don't speak the language. Some of the staff know English, but my poor German is a convenient excuse for us to ignore each other.

Across the street and the stretch of grass that separates us, the Orient Express makes its chugging way down the track, right on time. Brig Station is the last stop before the tunnel, and so it's barely picked up speed as it slides past, sleek and modern. The faces of the idle rich press against the glass in the carriage windows, staring back at the dour man in the coffee shop window, turning a worn pack of matches over and over in his hands.

The tunnel was finished, of course. The accident that caved in the crystal cavern and left me half-senseless on the floor of the tunnel was never really examined. When the workers threatened to strike once more rather than burrow through tons of treacherous—some said cursed—rubble, the new project head simply routed around it. On 24 February, 1905, the two tunnels met. Dignitaries shook hands. Champagne was popped.

Everyone has left. Even David, who stayed on with me a while after the tunnel's completion, has been recalled to his unit. I think he knew about Tom and me. Maybe he did from the beginning.

Tom. Sometimes I think about what he said on our first night together, about things not being able to stay buried, about not being able to hide from the truth. I'd wanted so badly to believe him then, despite my fear. Maybe I still do.

And maybe if I hadn't, I'd have more of him now than just a pack of matches.

Mostly, though, I think about the mountain. I look up at it, looming over the little town, and remember what Tom said about the fractal nature of things, how a part can be representative of a whole.

Because I know now why the shape of the creature seemed familiar. I see the same shape every day as I look out the window of my little flat. The same humped mass that is the silhouette of Mount Leone.

I want to believe it's over. That Tom, in his inexcusable bravery, sacrificed himself so that we could kill it. But as I stare at the mountain, the warm chocolate tasting like iron in my mouth, I wonder if perhaps the thing we killed was only a small piece. The heart of a greater living thing, which is the mountain itself. I think of the rivers of hot, rust-red water being pumped out of the mountain's depths and into the streams, carrying the mountain's essence with it. If the mountain has a heart, then we have given it veins.

And if the monster was the heart of the mountain, what is the mountain the heart of?

I watch the mountain.

And I wonder.

DADDY, DADDY
PENELOPE LOVE

Daddy, daddy, you bastard, I'm through.

—Sylvia Plath, "Daddy"

Why did he curse that his daughter wasn't a son? [. . .] what devilish exchange was perpetrated in the house of horror where that blasphemous monster had his trusting, weak-willed, half-human child at his mercy?

—H.P. Lovecraft, "The Thing on the Doorstep"

PARIS WAS ON STRIKE. THERE were no taxis and the metro was closed, so she ran all the way from the Gare du Nord. Her heavy nylon backpack banged painfully against her spine. Daddy always said she was useless and now she was going to miss the train.

Protesters filled the streets, stopping the traffic. They held placards with a red hand. *Arrête!* Horns blared and drivers cursed as she dodged between the cars. She gulped gasps of filthy air from the piles of uncollected garbage that filled the streets.

She arrived panting at the Gare de l'Est with her crumpled ticket clutched in her sweating hand. The station was built in the glory days of train travel, a vaulted cathedral-like space. She could not share its calm. It was bang on departure time, and she braced herself for one last mad dash through the ticket barrier and onto the train.

She arrived on the platform wheezing and pop-eyed, dragging her backpack, clutching at her half-cramped side.

Her heart soared as she spotted the handful of the gold and blue carriages waiting ahead. She had longed for a glimpse of something rich and beautiful all her life. Then her hopes collapsed. The carriages were dirty and dented, tacked onto the back of a long string of freight cars. There was one sleeper and no restaurant. The engine was an old workhorse. All glamor had long since fled the Orient Express. The general strike had crippled the remains.

Newspapers were preparing the great train's obituary: *Orient Express 1883-1977*. The future belonged to the Concorde.

The staff would not let passengers board and the hours dragged. Incomprehensible announcements filtered around the vast space. Dirty daylight seeped into the stain of night. She changed her last few pounds into francs, and bought a half-bottle of wine and some stale bread. She sat twelve hours on the station bench.

At midnight she went to the toilet, washed her face and gazed at her reflection in the cracked glass. She was slight and skinny with short-cropped fair hair. The harsh Australian sun had darkened her face but the pale skies of Europe had washed away the tan. Now her skin looked merely soiled. Her large eyes were pale blue. She wore dirty purple flares and a floral top whose once-bright colors had faded. Everything about her felt scraped and mean. The only thing with any weight was her backpack.

The staff finally let the passengers onto the train an hour before dawn. She got on at the first carriage and dragged her pack down the aisle. Hurrying passengers shouldered her aside in their rush to grab seats. She squeezed through a door between the cars and along a narrow corridor through the sleeper.

Everywhere were signs of faded grandeur. Frosted glass, etched with art deco designs, had missing panes plugged with paper. Graffiti was carved into the inlaid timbers. The leather seats were old and cracked. Everything was covered with gray dust. The staff were surly and indifferent, their uniforms ill-fitting. She could have wept with weariness and disappointment.

She reached her sleeping compartment at last. The upper half of the door was frosted glass so she could not see inside. She hauled it open. Four bunk beds were crammed into the narrow, stuffy compartment, but only two were occupied. The man on the top right bunk remained a stranger to her—a dim mound huddled under the blankets. The youth in the bottom bunk was thin and dark and French. He glanced up with a smile that died as he took her in. "*Ça va?*" he asked, eyes wide.

"Tired," she mimed. She tilted her head against her hands and closed her eyes. She dumped her backpack on the dirty floor, in the savage hope that someone would steal it, and thumped full length onto her own bunk on the bottom left. The sheets were dirty. A shudder passed along the length of the carriage. The train moved out. She stretched her weary limbs and slept.

She woke with a scream at an alien station. She found herself on her feet, so dazed with shock that she could not remember standing up.

The man on the top bunk was gone. The youth in the bottom bunk had pressed himself up against the wall.

What did he think? That she was mad of course. "I'm sorry, I'm so sorry," she implored. She touched her head. "Bad dream," she explained.

He surveyed her with frightened eyes then gestured at the door. It was ajar. He edged along his bunk, away from her. There was a chill draft swirling in the fetid air of the sleeping compartment and the floor was marked by wet, muddy tracks that stopped at her own feet. She had not been asleep. She had just come in from outside. *Where had she been?*

The train groaned and stirred like a wretched beast. It crawled painfully from the platform. She watched the rain-bleared station disappear from view. The spires of the Duomo pierced the night. She had just left Milan.

Memory returned. She had been to the Cimitero Monumentale. In that vast graveyard she had spoken to Others. The Others had spoken to her *and touched.*

Suddenly furious, she dropped to her knees, tore open her backpack, and hauled out the jar. She held it in both hands and shook it. "Daddy, you promised!" she shrieked.

The jar was heavy in her hands, most of the weight of her pack, with white lettering on a yellow and red label: *Vegemite.*

Daddy did not reply.

The youth slid from his bunk and fled.

She set the jar down with a vindictive thump. She sat on her bunk with head in hands and muttered to herself, rocking back and forth. "Daddy, you promised you wouldn't do that again, you promised you promised," she moaned in time with the wheel beats.

It was like this for as far back as she could remember. Daddy was sick all the time, but he never got better. Daddy was old, so old, but he would not die. She remembered the first lesson he ever taught her. "People get old," Daddy said, his eyes blazing with contempt. The hate was the only young thing in his aged face. "They get old and they die. Even Daddies have to die some time," he told her, but he would not. He would live on and on.

The house was a brick bungalow in a prosperous part of town. It looked sane enough from the outside. Within, things invisible stalked from room to room.

Daddy was furious that she was not a boy. A man's brain had unique and far-reaching powers that made it easier for Daddy.

She was not the last attempt. Her little brother—

She winced. Daddy forced the Unborn too hard. Mummy bore a crippled, clawed, wrinkled thing with a swollen head. "Fluid on the brain," the doctors said. It lived only a day and she was glad. She would have died of fright if they had brought it back home.

After that Daddy was very angry with Mummy. Mummy fell sick so she had to take to her bed. She grew thin and crippled. Her skin turned gray. She crumpled up like a question mark. Her gray skin slowly dried and powdered to a dust that sifted over the floors and furniture and filled the house.

She used to rest beside Mummy on the bed and stroke her crippled hands. Even when Mummy could no longer speak they could talk to each other with their eyes. They both knew that when Mummy was gone she would be left alone.

At last Daddy said that it was time for Mummy to go. He brought an oblong box into the house and nailed Mummy inside, ignoring his daughter's protests.

"Mummy's not dead. Mummy's not dead. Look! Her eyes still move," she had shrieked, until he lost patience and locked her in the shed. When he let her out after a day and night, the box was gone. She heard Mummy screaming in her head for months and months. But after a year the screams weakened. And then, after a long silence, she supposed that Mummy was dead.

That was when her training really began. She was Daddy's little girl now. For ever and ever. Daddy made her read aloud to him from books written in a language she did not know and which he did not bother to explain. She would not understand, he said, with her weak, female brain. Never had she been so terrified and so bored at the same time.

Daddy made her memorize the nonsense words and recite the meaningless sentences over and over again. If she forgot any he beat her, or worse. She was eager to obey, in dread of the final punishment. The heavy weight that bore down on her was not only physical but mental, crushing breath and spirit, until only a squeak, a scrape of herself was left; a writhing fragment that fought without thought to survive, like a half-crushed centipede.

Daddy made her draw the circles and make the signs then chant the Dho formula and sit inside the circles while he sat outside. Then she must sign and chant until their positions reversed; until she sat in Daddy's body on the outside looking in. Then Daddy sat in her chair and she watched his sly, rictus smile spread over her own face.

He drove her to it. She had no choice. His old body was failing so she knew he was preparing to make the switch. He would take her body but this time make the change permanent. She would be shut out, left to gibber alone in the Outer Dark.

She crept up on him when he was asleep. She stabbed him in the chest. The blade grated and bounced against bone. He woke and shouted and held up his hands. She stabbed, blinking and gasping as the knife finally cleaved the meat and blood spurted into her eyes. She kept stabbing and stabbing and stabbing and stabbing until she was sure he was dead. Then she buried him in a shallow grave in the back garden.

She told the people who came calling that he had gone on a trip.

For a few days she felt such exquisite light-heartedness and relief. She ate bread, butter, and Vegemite in a joyful feast. She had run off the tracks that he had laid down for her since before she was born. She was free and there was no one in her head but herself.

It did not last.

She should have known that death would not stop Daddy.

The third night after she killed him he came back, pounding on the walls of her mind with his fists. He threatened to drag her from her own body and thrust her into the rotting corpse buried in the dirt. That was when she used the carving knife on herself. But she was not thorough. She woke in the hospital with her wrists bandaged.

The hospital was a low pale brick building in a square of brown grass. The wards smelled of dishcloths and disinfectant. It was here that she met Nazir, with his gaunt face and scarred shoulders. He wasn't mad. He had tuberculosis. He smoked incessantly and hoarded the stubs in Coke cans. He gave her the hint. They watched TV together in the patients' lounge. She had never seen a color TV before. She told him her story. He laughed at her, then gestured at the screen. Women marched across the surreal colored glow, banners and placards high. They linked arms and sang "I am Woman, I am Strong." The police bore down with batons and riot shields and broke the protest apart, then pursued the survivors with fire hoses. Bloody water flowed.

"They made the same mistake as you. You can't confront the Man," Nazir scoffed. "You can't win. You need to pretend to go along then jump the rails at the last turn."

When she got out she did as Daddy said. She dug up the corpse, cut it up, and burned the pieces in the fire. She scraped up the ashes, crushing the bones that had not fully burned. She chanted the Dragon's Head Ascending, and turned the ashes into a fine, grayish dust that sparkled as she sifted it from hand to hand. Essential Saltes, just like Daddy called it.

She did not know if she could chant Dragon's Head Descending, or bear to see Daddy rise from the Saltes alive with dead eyes, sagging skin, and rictus grin. To her relief he did not tell her to do that. Instead he told her they were going on a trip together, they were going all the way to Europe. A train trip to Istanbul. They would take the Orient Express, for it stopped in a few cities where he wanted to get some things. He even allowed her to buy a return ticket to go to England to see the Jubilee. The train would arrive in Istanbul at six in the morning and depart at midnight, straight back to London. Imagine. There, she had said he wasn't a good Daddy, and all the time here was Daddy planning this nice thing. They had to take the Saltes with them but they couldn't be seen. She had to hide the Saltes.

Hide them.

She bought a large jar of Vegemite and scraped the black paste out. She poured the Saltes into the jar and then scraped the paste back in again. The smell made her retch—charcoal and brewer's yeast and death. It worked, though. Her passport was checked and luggage searched again and again, but no one questioned the Jar. Everyone accepted her explanation that she could not travel without it. Australians and their Vegemite.

She came out of her reverie. She was alone in the sleeper. The train had been halted for some time. There were guards in the corridor. Now the train lurched into life with a weary hiss and writhed on through two lines of concrete and barbed wire fences: the Iron Curtain. Gray hills rolled by outside the window as the train hauled itself along an incline through the border with Czechoslovakia. They had changed engines somewhere along the line. The diesel whistle was an exhausted wheeze.

With a prickle of her spine she realized Daddy was still absent. Lately, he had been gone for longer and longer periods. Perhaps death was finally wearing him down, weakening him like Mummy; or maybe he was off somewhere, *preparing*. His absence made her bold. Daringly, she allowed her thoughts to run from the grooves she forced them onto, the tracks that were ever-so-carefully fixed around the boundaries of her innermost self. She reached into the front pocket of the backpack. A crackle of paper rewarded her touch and she rolled her eyes in a kind of ecstasy.

She pulled out the map and unfolded it. It was a map of Istanbul, the end of the line, and so frequently consulted that the paper was tearing at the creases. Daddy had made her trace a route through the streets in bold red pen. She had done as he said, but it was in Daddy's crabbed handwriting. From Sirkeci Terminal she must turn right down Ankara Road to the shore, then catch a ferry across the Golden Horn. The train and ferry numbers were lettered in Daddy's Latin. Finally her path would lead to the abandoned cemetery below the Galata Tower.

Daddy said there was a surprise at the end, a present for Daddy's little girl. She could guess. This was the red-marked route to death.

Now that she was certain she was alone she thought openly, with a rush of implacable hate. She had stopped Daddy from transferring himself to her body directly. He had to travel to this cemetery to make the change, where the angles gave him the best chance of success. If she went there she would never come back. Her eye fell on the Jar and she gave an involuntary, horrified, despairing giggle. Daddy would have her body, and she would be lost in brewer's yeast and bone grit.

She stared lovingly at the map. Surely Daddy had decided she was beaten. He must no longer fear her disobedience if he used her body to leave the train in Milan.

Yet, what if she did not turn right toward the Golden Horn when she left Sirceki Terminal. What would happen if she turned left? She would do as Nazir had said and make a last-minute detour from Daddy's tracks. She eyed the map luxuriously, then traced the line with her finger. She would go left down Ankara Road to Yerebatan, past the Basilica Cistern to the Hagia Sophia. There lay her destination, not the great museum itself but the Shadow Sophia that lay beneath.

Daddy had made her repeat nonsense words in languages she could not understand, yet never realized that she was smart enough to work some words out. She had *learned*. The Shadow Sophia was her real destination. This was why she had so tamely tagged along with Daddy, and endured his midnight stops, on his European vacation.

The Shadow Sophia was not safe, of course, and she must offer living sacrifice. She zipped the Jar back into her pack. She had a sacrifice—Daddy was alive all right. The books said there would be ripples from the Act. The ripples would spread outward in a circle through time, so some of the ripples traveled away from her and some toward her. The ripples would be traveling even now, she hoped, from that longed-for point in future time and place.

She didn't know what shape these ripples would take, or what price she would have to pay. She only thought that it could not be worse than the price she was paying already.

❖   ❖   ❖

Daddy took her body again in Zagreb, and this time it was worse. She woke at the bottom of the six thousand steps, in utter darkness, with something wet and sinuous nuzzling her face. The heavy weight of the pack ground against her spine. She knew not to speak. She clapped both her hands over her mouth to prevent a shriek and ran back up the steps.

The stairs were uneven—cold, clammy stone, worn with countless treads. They got steeper as they rose. She climbed until a gray light assaulted her eyes. She ran out into the misty rain of a Czech graveyard.

She ran as if on rails, following the trail of her own footprints in reverse. She tried not to look at the amorphous marks beside her own tracks. At last she came to a proper road and flagged down a car. She spoke wild English to baffled foreign faces, traced a circle with her arms to mimic a train, and hitched a ride back to the station.

The train whistle sounded to depart as she arrived. She bolted along the platform, brushing past guards who tried to stop her, and threw herself aboard the last carriage as the wheels turned and clacked. She fell face-first to the floor. The passengers turned in silence in their seats to regard her. They had all changed since the last time she had been here. She knew none of them.

She picked herself up and hurried along the aisles to the sleeping car. She needed quiet to gather her scattered self. The backpack zip was broken, and the flap gaped with each step, like a mouth. A black glob of Vegemite was smeared on the lip.

She burst into the compartment. The blank faces of four total strangers confronted her. "But—but—this is mine," she told the girl in the lower left bunk, whose soft, damp face was perched incongruously on top of a vast kaftan.

The strangers were puzzled. She showed them her ticket. Then they were sympathetic. They pointed out the date. She thought she had been gone only overnight. She had been in Zagreb five days. Her train had left without her.

They were Londoners, with stiff, blank faces and clipped voices. The girl was Alice. The men wore tie-dye T-shirts, denim bell-bottoms, and Chelsea boots. They were going to Istanbul to smoke hashish and then head farther east. Oh, how she envied their straight-forwardness. They laughed and sang. They had friends in the compartment next door. They shared joints and a battered paperback of *The Lord of the Rings*. They drank gin. They befriended her. Whenever they saw the conductor coming they sent her to the toilet to hide.

The toilet was horrible. It stank. The cubicle was a dark, enclosed space. The window was boarded up but a little light reflected from the tarnished mirror. The toilet had no seat. Some boards were missing from the floor and she watched the gravel of the train tracks roll hypnotically beneath. The door would not lock. She kept it closed by bracing herself against the handle, with one foot wedged against the base of the toilet, one against the basin stand.

That night Alice let her share the bunk. They slept head to toe. The train ran beside a road. The streetlights filtered in racks through the slats of the thin blinds, over and over again. Even in her sleep the thin, repetitive, winking light mesmerized her. It was like an epileptic dream.

When she woke before dawn she was alone. She thought her companions had left the train but then she saw their packs and belongings were scattered around the compartment. A bottle of gin lay spilled by the door.

The Londoners came back once it was light. They entered the compartment in a huddle, as though numbers gave them strength. Their faces were white and strained. They would not look at her directly. They grabbed their belongings and returned to the compartment next door.

Alice lingered in the doorway.

"Did I scare you?" she asked Alice.

"I am not scared of *you*," Alice said, softly.

What had they seen last night? She could guess: Daddy sitting upright on the bunk. That rictus grin.

One of the men came back and caught Alice's arm. He spoke softly. She heard "crazy bitch" and "bad trip" before he led Alice away. She was alone again but she was used to that.

Rain fell endlessly, blurring the windows. The train ran through wild mountain peaks and steep valleys where trees had been felled and left to rot where they lay. Then the tracks ran across a desolate plain with concrete outcrops where cement factories poured filthy smoke into the gray sky.

At midday, Bulgarian customs guards boarded on the train.

She rushed for the toilet but a guard stood in front of it. "Passport please," he said. He was a thickset, ugly man with a pockmarked face and a spotless uniform of shiny, green serge. A machine-gun swung at his hip. She turned to run the other way, but guards blocked the passage behind her.

She walked slowly to her compartment, the guard behind her. She handed her passport over. He looked at it and frowned. He had a peasant face, suspicious and bewildered. He carried a clipboard that he laboriously consulted. He spelled his letters aloud as he wrote. He picked up her pack and rummaged within. He drew out the Jar.

"Vegemite," she said. Useless. She was behind the Iron Curtain. He had never heard of the breakfast spread. He looked at her blankly then his face closed over in suspicious stupidity. She mimed eating. "Yum yum," she said.

He set down his papers and unscrewed the Jar. He took a sniff and reared back, wrinkling his nose. What if he took a taste? She bit back a wild, hysterical laugh.

There were loud voices from the next compartment. "You can't do that. We're British!" There was the sound of a scuffle and a heavy thump. Alice screamed, shrill and high.

Her guard dropped the Jar and left the compartment, heading to her neighbor. She did not wait for him to return. She grabbed her belongings, fled to the toilet, and braced the door. She heard more shouts, in English and Bulgarian, and then the sounds of a fight. More guards piled in, then a line of heavy bodies thumped past the toilet and onto the platform. She did not venture out until the train started moving again.

She slid into her own compartment. She wondered if the guards had taken all the Londoners away. After she sat down she heard a muffled, continuous moaning through the thin timber partition between the compartments. Someone was still there. She rooted through her pack for something to help but found nothing to give.

The train traveled across Bulgaria in fits and starts. It was shunted aside for hours not once but twice. The moans and sobs continued from next door. At last the wretched day darkened. She lay down and closed her eyes, willing for time to pass quickly.

She wished the moaning would stop. Surely the injured man must sleep.

Yet the moans sounded so near, as if he were lying with her in the bunk, his hoarse breathing whistling in and out. She stiffened. Rank breath poured over her. She was sure that a thing crouched over her, one bloody hand on her shoulder, moaning softly and constantly in her ear.

She woke with a start. Moonlight came through the slats in her thin blinds. Nothing leaned over her. She gave a great gasp of relief, swung herself upright, and switched on the light.

There was nothing in her compartment, and no sound from next door.

Her mouth was dry. She headed for the toilet. The cubicle had got worse in the night. The stench had redoubled. The bowl was clogged and overflowing with filth. Stinking liquid crept across the floor. She turned on the tap. Brown fluid trickled out. Gagging, she looked up. A huge, bloody palm-print was smeared on the polished glass of the mirror, three times her own hand-span.

She reeled out and staggered to her compartment. A glance at the compartment next door revealed a figure standing behind the frosted glass, a bulky, shadowed shape with hanging head.

She had slipped inside her own compartment before she realized the shadow was too large, and had stood too still, to be a living human being. Her mind flew back to the bloody handprint. She mustered all her courage and stepped into the corridor. The shadow was gone. She raised a hand to knock on the glass then bit her lip and backed off. She had nothing to give them. They would not want to see her again.

The train reached the Turkish border in the night. The next morning she opened the blinds to blinking brightness. Minarets greeted her dazzled sight, and a great swathe of blue sea shone along the horizon. With a final, weary wheeze and whistle, the train shuffled into Sirceki Terminal five hours late. She had reached Istanbul, the end of the line.

She heard a stir from next door; a sickly scuttle. She couldn't let the injured man fend for himself. She slung her pack over her shoulder and stepped into the corridor before the pane of frosted glass. She braced herself for rejection and knocked.

There was no response.

"Do you need any help?" she asked. No answer.

A conductor hurried past behind her, a lanky man with dapper hair. She stopped him.

"The people—" she pointed "—here."

"They were taken from the train in Bulgaria," he said, in perfect English.

"What—all?'

"All." He unlocked the door. The compartment was empty, the bed stripped and luggage gone. There was a bloodstain on one pillow but it was old and brown. She stared, befuddled.

"Was it locked all the time?" she asked stupidly.

He was eyeing her carefully, clearly failing to recognize her as a fare-paying passenger. "Were they friends of yours?" he asked.

"No. No," she shrank backward. If the Londoners had all left, then who had moaned in her ear and stood with hanging head behind the locked door?

She ran from the train.

The solidity of the platform felt unreal after the constant rocking of the wheels. The air was full of an unfamiliar softness and warmth. She could smell the sea, and see the salt glitter in the air. The amplified roar of a thousand minarets called the faithful to mid-morning prayer.

Sirkeci Terminal was a grandiose dream built in the style of an imagined Orient. Its red and white patterned walls were inset with arches topped with round windows, and its clock tower resembled a minaret. She rushed down the platform without pausing to buy a drink, although her throat was tight with thirst. She hurried through the bustle of the departure hall, and stumbled out into the bright light of Ankara Street.

Traffic ran in every direction between the canyons of buildings. The streets were a maze. A motorcyclist turned in front of her with a startling horn blast, forcing her to stumble back to avoid being struck. The cyclist mounted the pavement then roared off the wrong way up a one-way street. Pedestrians hustled past her. Turkish pop music blared from every shop front.

Here I am in Istanbul, she thought. *Just like Daddy wanted.* Then she braced herself, and turned left.

She walked down the street, dazed at her own daring, at every step expecting to be thrust back on her proper track. Nothing happened. She saw a café and went in, hoping her handful of francs would buy her a drink.

She realized as soon as she was inside the cool dimness that she had made a mistake. Turkish men sat over coffee and hookahs and glared at her in surprise and contempt. Clearly only a Western infidel slut would ever dream of venturing into this sacred masculine space. The café was a long, low, dark room, with a beaded curtain at the back. Beyond the curtain she could see soft green light and hear a tormenting trickle of water. A garden and a fountain lay out there.

"Drink," she appealed to the waiter. He shook his basilisk head.

The sound of water was torture. She stepped through the curtain at the back. The beads rattled against her face. She shut her eyes as she passed through and for a moment she was blind. When she opened her eyes she found herself in a small green oasis surrounded by a high brick wall. A long timber table was set amid green ferns and roses. In the dim green light strange birds were singing.

At the table sat a skinned man, an écorché, a flayed figure, seven feet tall. She could see every exquisite detail of bone, muscle, and sinew. The scent of roses could not hide the reek of formaldehyde. On the table before the flayed figure lay a mummified crocodile.

She thought they were anatomical figures until the crocodile twitched its tail. Then the flayed figure smiled and held up one huge, wet, red palm.

She fled. She ran the length of the long, dark room, straight past the outraged men. She hurled herself from the doorway. She saved herself from flying into the traffic only by seizing hold of a lamp post, so that her force and velocity flung her around to face the café again. She was in time to see the door slam closed.

She turned onto Yerebatan Street. It was downhill all the way. She hurried past old timber houses that had once been beautiful but were now derelict. Hungry machines were clawing them to splinters and combing through their timber bones. Bleached apartment blocks rose amid the rubble. The blocks were inhabited but unfinished, with wire mesh and struts poking from the crumbling concrete. Whole faces of the new buildings eroded away into dust. Dust blew in the hot wind and plastered her cracked lips.

Two domes soared ahead, one rusty red, one cool and blue. The Hagia Sophia and the Blue Mosque. She quickened to a jog.

She dreaded at any moment to be suddenly stopped, or worse that Daddy knew what she was doing and had devised a suitable punishment. She ran past the locked entrance to the Basilica Cistern. *Discos Here Nightly*—a gaudy, torn sign flapped in the hot wind. She found herself in a garden of parched trees and dust-covered grass.

The great rust-red dome was now directly before her. It was surrounded by four smaller domes, each topped with azure copper and the slender spires of four minarets. She headed up the steps, through the great doors, and into the Hagia Sophia.

She was stunned by a sense of vast architectural tranquility. She stood in an immense space bathed in distant, ethereal light. The soaring vault of the dome dwarfed the whispering crowds of tourists and touts. On the walls were gold-washed mosaics of Mother and Son, and six-winged Seraphim; the emperor Justinian held a mosaic model of the church while the empress Zoe, in gilt robes encrusted with jewels, held out a gilded scroll.

For a moment she halted, awed. Peace everlasting. Then her neck cricked. She rolled a dry tongue around a dry mouth. She remembered. She hurried on.

She climbed the stairs to the immense balcony that ran around the sides of the dome. A corner of the gallery was screened with temporary wire builder's fencing, faced with orange plastic. She looked around to ensure she was alone, then tiptoed to the fence. She found a rip in the plastic and peeped within. Writing was carved into the stone wall, low down and to the left: *Enrico Donaldo.* Her heart soared. She had found the right place. It looked like a grave but it wasn't. It was an eighteenth-century folly, a memorial to the blind and vindictive Venetian Doge who led the Fourth Crusade. It was built over a secret entrance but the architect had left clues for the initiated to follow. *Take that, Daddy*, she thought triumphantly.

She tugged aside the concrete-weighted iron leg of the temporary fence and slipped inside. She knelt by the grave and pressed the corner of the marker. With a grating rumble the tombstone moved, pivoting vertically into the ground. She laid herself flat, thrust her pack through the gap, and gently let it drop. It landed below with a soft thump.

The gap was just wide enough for her to slip through. She crawled in backward, feet first, hands clutching at the stone lip. Her feet groped for ground, but found none. She lowered herself carefully until her body was hanging from her hands. Then her grip slipped.

With a shriek she fell half her own length. She landed on a smooth surface and rocked on both ankles, then collapsed to her knees. She slammed her hands down to stop her forehead smacking the stone.

The stone slab overhead pivoted shut. All light was quenched. She slung her pack over her shoulder and groped her way down a narrow, circular set of stairs. It was claustrophobic, like descending a gullet, although there was a source of light below, faint and green. The circling stairs inspired dizziness as implacably as a whirling dervish. She stumbled, rather than stepped, down and down until she reached the bottom.

A poisonous green luminescence came from fungus growing on the walls. The foxfire gave off just enough light to see by. A vast hall spread out before her. She took one step forward, then threw herself backward as the floor fell away into emptiness. She knelt and groped to find a vast pit. The glow of decomposition filled it like water. Foxfire lapped against the walls, revealing an expanse of mosaics.

The mosaics were old, faced with porphyry and jade and gold; men and women. Giants. They were naked and their bare feet dangled, toes pointed, poised and confident. In their hands they held models of buildings, dungeons, and torture machines. They held tiny figures of the dead. They grinned implacably above the murdered, the staked, the tortured, and the skinned. She looked away. She had seen enough. She was in the Shadow Sophia all right.

She skirted the poisonous green pit, warily, crawling. She squashed pulpy fungus beneath her palms and knees. Putrescent slime smeared her skin. She crept around the gulf, her back aching, her knees and palms raw. Slowly the weight of her pack grew, crushing her, bearing her down until she slithered with her chin barely clear of the floor.

Daddy had realized what she was doing at last. It was his weight pressing down on her from above. But he did not call a halt or order her to turn back. After the first agony of discovery, faint hope crept into her heart. Perhaps he could not. There was a bitter taint in her mouth. She tasted it, puzzled, a long time before she realized what it was.

It was fear.

Daddy was afraid.

There was something in this place that even he could not face.

She almost turned around and crawled straight back out. If Daddy was afraid she had no chance. Then she reached the far side of the pit. In the giddy rush of her relief she made the mistake of looking down. The mosaics on this side of the pit were recent. She saw a grinning man in Western suit and bowler hat holding a model train. There were the blue and gold carriages; she saw the rich people cavorting within. These were not the dalliances she had always imagined but the writhing contortions of the damned. She glanced at the last figure; just a look. The last figure had no skin or face.

She turned her back to the pit and saw that she had reached the end of the hall. Floor, ceiling, and walls all converged and twisted into a monstrous corner, an angle that was at once obtuse and acute. It made her eyes ache and her brain burn just to look at it. At this angle all humanity ended. Tentacles of stone writhed. Fanged maws snarled open. Globes of leprous fungus hung from the jaws like slime, and dripped. One petrified tongue jutted from the corner, the center of a vision of cosmic chaos, with galaxies writhing around it. The root of the tongue fell away into the darkness of the utter abyss. She looked up, just once, to see that the glistening stone cacophony rose for as far as she could see. Then she looked down, grimly. She dropped her pack. She rummaged for the Jar and held it up, in offering.

She hoped for one final triumph, for Daddy to plead and beg. She was disappointed. She thought she heard one whimper, far off. That was it.

She placed the Jar upon the upward curve of the Tongue. The

black and yellow gleamed incongruously amid the glistening green-tinged gloom.

Then it was gone.

She had placed it square. It could not have slipped. The only way for it to vanish was for the Tongue to writhe, to arch, for the stony jaws to gulp.

Time collapsed inward. The corner and its carvings were swallowed in an angle she could not comprehend with a sound beyond sound, a vast, fathomless, maddening roar. She understood at the last possible moment, turned and ran. This Shadow Sophia existed only for her. Now that it was no longer required, it was imploding into the Void. The bottom of the pit rose to meet her racing feet. Mosaics, gold, porphyry, and foxfire crumbled and collapsed. She fled back up the stairs. The stone gullet closed behind her, ceiling, steps, and walls crushed silently together like rotten teeth.

She reached the top and leaped for the pivoting gravestone with a breathless gasp of despair. To her relief, her clawing fingers held and the counterweight swung. She hauled herself up over the edge. Her feet dangled over wet stone fangs that snatched at her toes. She threw herself from the brink.

The gravestone swung closed behind her. She lay on her back, legs sprawled, gulping for air. She was so certain it was still day outside that it was a shock to realize it was night. Moonlight shone through the windows above. The interior of the Hagia Sophia was dark. The crowds were gone.

She pattered down the stairs and across the shadowed nave to the great doors, one small being beneath the immensity of the dome. She hauled at the doors, breaking her fingernails, until she realized they were locked. She darted to a small side door, pulled the bolt back and slipped outside. The night air was warm and scented with roses. A lamp post stood in a brave pool of light, gilding the dusty grass.

She ran straight to the lamp post and embraced the cold metal, rejoicing in the brightness.

The Hagia Sophia stood behind her, calm and eternal, no matter darkness or light. At last the numbness of the gulf fled. Exultation filled her. She had done it. Her sacrifice was accepted. Daddy was gone, for ever and ever. She had escaped. She had survived.

She slumped, boneless, and slid down the lamp post to lie at its iron foot, bathing in the pool of light. Daringly she let her thoughts leave the groove of years, jump the iron rail, and run wild in any direction they liked.

A distant, thin wail reached her ears: the whistle of a train. She remembered that the Orient Express departed Istanbul at midnight. She climbed to her feet. She was going to catch that train. She was going to see the Jubilee.

She trotted past the surreal, colored glow reflecting from the Nightly Disco thumping in the Basilica Cistern and along Yerebatan Street. It was uphill all the way and very steep. At first she moved from one lamp post to the next, bathing in each pool of light. Then she gained confidence and went steadily in a straight line.

The train whistle sounded again. It was later than she thought, and she could not miss this departure. As she turned onto Ankara Street she found strength for the last flight. Her arms were pistons, her legs were circles of steel. Each gasp of breath was an engine rasp.

She reached the white and red brick walls of Sirkeci Station, no longer her terminus, but the platform for her new beginning. The departure hall has dark and silent. There was no bustle, no one to take her ticket. Puzzled, she hurried onto the platform. The carriages gleamed blue and gold as kindly darkness hid their rusted age, but they were locked.

There were only two passengers on the platform. Waiting for the train. *Waiting for her.*

Her legs buckled but the paralysis of nightmare seized her and forced her upright.

The books said there would be ripples from the Act, spreading outward in a circle through time; some into the past and some into the future. Now the future was her past. It had always been too late.

The Skinless One gave her a loving smile and extended a wet red hand in welcome. In his other hand he held the Mims Sahis. The crocodile stood on its hind legs. Its black pebble eye surveyed her, unblinking, with all the brute, mindless indifference of the universe.

She opened her mouth to scream. All that came out was the shrill, demented whistle of the train.

STAINED WINDOWS
JOSHUA ALAN DOETSCH

I USED TO BE INSANE.

I got better.

The cure is worse than the disease. Cures are terrible things. They're not chicken soup or twelve-step programs. *Hello, my name is John and it's been seven months since I last flayed a vagrant to see if monsters were hiding under his skin.* I also have a drinking problem, but it's not my worst trait, and it's not the point.

This is the point:

I used to be mad.

But I got better.

The Orient Express rocks. I'm in a corridor. Must have lost myself staring out a window into the rushing black. I shake my head, humming the tune to a half-forgotten song that might have gone something like: "The fireflies jarred us all up." How did I get here? The scenes of my life always just begin, but I fumble for what came before. Lost transitions. Fugitive hours.

The woman. The girl in green. Half a carriage ahead. Every step is a sway of her dress, the green of the deep sea, and a defiant bounce of her scarlet hair, cut in a flapper bob. How long have I been following her? I find a notepad in my pocket, but can no longer decipher the scribblings, the pages traced over with spirals, the nib of my pen stabbing, bleeding black ink through—page on page—the echo of spirals.

"Hey, aren't you—?" A man squeezing by in the corridor. Australian from the accent. He uses my name, not the one on my passport. With a wink, he introduces himself as a fellow scoundrel in the brotherhood of larceny. If we had a secret handshake, this is where we'd perform it. We don't.

"Pulled a few jobs myself," he croons with onion breath. "But nothing like you. Can't believe it. The man himself. The gentleman thief."

He rambles on as she rambles away. He's followed my career: the famous diamond in London, the bird statuette in San Francisco, the paintings from the impenetrable mansion of a French nobleman. Amazing! Brilliant! He even saved a few newspaper clippings. He asks for my autograph. We both chuckle. She's getting away.

"What's the secret?" he asks.

He means the big cons, the grand jobs—the flare and panache, being both famous and anonymous, a celebrity shadow—and vanishing from jail the one time it managed to embrace me. I try keeping the girl in green in view as she enters the next coach. All these encounters feel repeated, rehearsed. Everything is *déjà vu*. The universe teeters on the tip of my tongue. I mutter something about misdirection.

"Ah, right, too right," my fan says. "You studied with them magicians and escapists, eh?"

"Escapologists," I correct. I also studied with a voice actor, a contortionist, a professor of Japanese wrestling, a chemist, a forger, an art historian, and a pearl diver who could hold her breath for eleven minutes—all part of my methodical apprenticeship, years of self-discipline to be in all ways different from the thug looming before me. All he ever studied was the requisite force to make a club crack a skull.

I extricate myself from the brute. He nods, pointing at his nose conspiratorially. He'll tell his friends he now knows the secret. "Misdirection," he'll say, which isn't any more insightful than saying, "I know how it works: it's a trick." I smile encouragingly. He'll be sleeping in striped pajamas within a month. He's the guy they always catch to make society feel better, because they can't catch me.

Misdirection is a truth, but it's a tiny truth magicians let slip to feed the brains of laypeople, to make them fat and content. The dupe who thinks himself clever ceases the effort of being clever. See? The illusion's the thing.

The real secret isn't sleight of hand. It's timing. To have the maneuver done before they perceive it's doing—in the casual moments before: an opening joke, an introduction, or while taking off a jacket. Then comes the heightened instant. They hold their breath, cease to blink, knowing your hands are moving too fast for them to perceive. They try to figure how you slipped the poison into the lunch in front of them, when you've already put it in their breakfast. All that gaudy patter, pageantry, and spectacle—they just drown in that, and it does not matter how sharply they dissect it. Their intelligence is being used against them, in a circular motion, as they concoct complex plots and skullduggery to decipher.

But it's already done. Already too late.

There are other secrets. Deep secrets. In my most recent performance, I stole a book in Istanbul. A special book. There are people after me. I really should not have opened that book. I saw the nighted worlds lurking in its pages. How, then, can I be sane?

I found the cure. I saw something. What did I see?

Cures are horrible things. *Cures* is an anagram for *curse.*

But please understand: I used to be as insane as they come. I used to stick thumbtacks through my tongue so that I could better explain the Truth to the weeping children whose beds I hid under.

I quicken pace in the wake of the girl in green.

Down the corridor. So many doors.

I like trains. All these disparate people—the diplomats, gunrunners, and spies; the somebodies, everybodies, and nobodies—from the world over, nothing in common but a rocketing roof for a mayfly moment.

Every door is a window, every window a story. Some leave their doors a hair open, and I feel obliged to look. Voyeurs. Aren't we all?

A cracked door. A young couple argues. Newlyweds? A secret affair?

Another door. A woman sprawls in a chair, head thrown back with opiate moans, syringe gleaming in her hand like a dead pixie.

A closed door. Behind it, someone mutters, "The anachronisms. Oh, the anachronisms are compounding."

A door opens. A dwarf peeks out, the metal submarine shape of a kazoo held between his lips. He looks one way, then the other, before his head flashes back inside. The door closes. The clicking of locks always sounds like a whispered dare to me. I can hear the membranophone nocturne playing within, ridiculous and sad.

I like windows. Fragments without context. *In medias res*. I remember my dream-plagued childhood, the hours staring out the passenger window of automobiles. But never stained windows—no—I recall the long Sundays at church, and how I hated the colored glass—pretty and opaque and stifling. I longed to hurl my hymnal through the painted panes and see what lay beyond.

A porter knocks on a door and delivers a carafe of mineral water to an old, regal woman in furs.

"This train, it goes in circles, always in circles," she says in a thick accent. Exiled Russian nobility?

"Madame, I assure you, our train runs in a straight line," says the porter with a congenial smile. The old woman takes her water and slams the door in his face. I give the porter a sympathetic nod.

"Do you have the time?" I ask.

"It is eleven past eleven, sir."

"A.M. or P.M.?"

"Sir?"

"Never mind. Travel is playing havoc with my sense of time."

"Perhaps my time piece is malfunctioned, sir. Chronography is not our specialty." His smile never changes, his facial muscles like pressed glass.

I move on, following liquid green memories.

An open door. Inside, a squat, old man in a tall top hat. A German doctor. Have we met? He opens a large, mysterious cabinet, revealing a gaunt, pallid young man, eyes closed and hands folded, sleep-standing. The doctor urges, and the sleeper speaks in a somnambulist trance, "*Wir ertrinken alle in der Flüssigkeit, die uns nicht sterben lässt.*"

A sluicing sensation, behind my eyes. I shake my head. What is happening? Things used to be easier. I used to be insane. I used to stare at piles of feces, for hours of monomanic fascination, finding all the hieroglyphic secrets of the cosmos in the coils and bumps.

Down the corridor. More doors. Lots of windows. Lots of stories. No clocks, but there is a countdown, and I don't want to be on the other side of the chime. Yet curiosity is my oldest vice.

Into the dining car, crowded and opulent. The infamous and the anonymous fill large, cut-velvet armchairs. A famed Dutch dancer draws admirers closer with the slow, exotic motions of a carnivore plant. A Brit pins and mounts the specimens of a butterfly collection right at his table. I barely catch the meaningful glance between the collector and the dancer.

All those arthropod limbs and wings give me an inexplicable shiver, so I turn to admire an art deco frieze, Bacchanal figures worked in glass—a man in the center and a woman on each side, all nude. The man plays a flute to the sky. The women hold great clusters of grapes.

Sitting beneath the frieze, the lady in green smiles at me.

"From your wanted poster, I thought you'd be taller," she says.

"Well, I try to be," I say, taking the opposite seat.

I tell her my name. She tells me hers.

"Pretty name," I say. "Unusual. Reminds me of the Latin word, *ululare*."

"Oh," she coos in three syllables. "Latin. You're a fancy flimflammer. What does it mean?"

"To howl or shriek."

"I like that."

"I like your eyes. They're the same color as your dress."

"I like your eyebrows, they arch sly like wary black cats." She reaches across the table to stroke my right eyebrow. It arches.

"Maybe we should run a tally, then let each other borrow our best parts."

She bites her lower lip. My toes curl. "Maybe we should have a drink first," she says.

"Don't know if that's a good idea. I'm in AA."

"Is that your room number?" She looks confused.

"No," I chuckle. "Alcoholics Anonymous."

"Never heard of it."

"Really? They started a few years back and . . . I'm an alcoholic."

"I pegged you as a Scorpio."

I lean in closer, over the table. "I have the oddest feeling," I say. "Like we've known each other a long time."

She leans in closer still. "I'd say that's a line, but—"

"But you feel it, too."

"Yes."

"We're dancing around it."

"What?"

"The point."

"And what is the point?" she says like a dare, like a clicking lock.

We take each other's hand. The momentum is too strong now, a centrifugal force pulling us together. I use both eyebrows.

"I used to be insane," I say.

She squeezes my hand. "Me, too."

"But I got better."

"Me, too."

"That seems . . . unlikely." I grin.

"It does." She smirks.

"I mean, I was deranged. I used to shove mirror shards into my eye sockets, like razor monocles, so curses would reflect back on others."

Her foot pokes mine playfully, under the table, as she says, "Applesauce! I was crazier than a shit-house rat. I used to eviscerate Teddy bears with a scalpel, yank out their fluffy innards. Then I'd fill the cloth husks with grave worms, sewing it all up. I hoped the bears would rise and walk and keep me company on lonely nights."

We both release a long-held breath with a hiccuping laugh.

"It's not the worst thing I've done," she says, playing with a steak knife.

"Same here."

"We have so much in common."

"There's something else," I say. Our eyes wander over the rest of the dining car. The collector methodically eats the specimens from his mounting board; a colorful wing hangs from his mouth as he crunches. The dancer is gone, as are her admirers, though their clothes remain in neat piles. We both hold onto something ticklish in our throats, like a private joke.

My lips hover over her ear. "I think everyone else on this train is loosing their mind."

"And they're getting worse."

"While we get better."

"Inverse curves."

"Sounds sexy when you put it like that."

"Does erudition coax you to barneymugging?"

"I like brains and legs when they're attached."

We release our giggling fits, then catch our breath.

"Something awfully bad is about to happen on this train," she says. We grin at each other like teenagers. "We should be more afraid than this."

"We've already been mad."

"It's strangely calming."

"'*The worst had fall'n which could befall—He stood a stranger in this breathing world—An erring spirit from another hurled—A thing of dark imaginings . . .*'"

"What's that?"

"It's from a Byron poem. My father liked rhymes. He'd have me memorize them. A sort of game."

"Oh? That sounds nice."

I remember the *bump-scrape, bump-scrape* up the drunken, dizzying stairs, the rhymes oozing from his reeking lips, the rapping at the red, red door. "No," I say. "It wasn't."

"I am not afraid!" screams a man at the head of a dinner party on the other side of the car. "I can never be afraid!" Thick strands of spittle punctuate his words. The others answer, first with words, than with screams, cursing the International Sleeping-Car Company—then laughing at the grotesque faces they make at one another.

"I get to feeling like the thing that's about to happen," says the girl in green, "is inescapable."

"No such thing," I say with no small amount of professional pride. Something a little like hope and a lot like audacity swells between us. Nevermind the nightmare slow-blossoming around us like a maggot bouquet.

"Let's discuss this further over that drink," she says, and all the universe is her green eyes. "You can tell me how you lost your mind. I'll show you mine if you show me yours."

"You're an enabler."

"No, I'm a Taurus, and I have a flask of pretty good rye in my room," she says, getting up. "Compartment C-19."

"Really? That's the room adjoined to mine. All this time and the only thing separating us was a communicating door. The latch is broken. I was going to get a porter to fix it."

"Don't bother," she says, leaving in a swirl of liquid green.

I'm nearly out of the dining car when I look again at the glass art frieze. The man is now sitting on an altar, playing his flute to the sky. The women, on either side, are now holding ornate daggers instead of grapes.

"Admiring the Bacchanals?" says the deep grind of a tectonic voice. A fat man in a red fez overflows from his luxuriant chair like a greedily poured drink. "Fine work, very fine."

"By Rene Lalique himself," I say. "Very avant-garde."

"You know your art, but then, it pays to in your line of work, hmm?"

"Weren't the women holding grapes instead of daggers a moment ago?"

"I don't believe so. I do have reason to believe that you possess a certain book and are in need of a buyer."

I take a seat with the corpulent man. He gives me his name. I give him mine. I notice the bluish silver medallion he wears, pressed with the likeness of the god Neptune. The corpulent man notices my notice.

"Oh, this? A keepsake bauble, a reminder of home. You look pale, friend. When was the last time you saw the sun?"

"No date comes to mind. You said something about a buyer?"

He nods. "Indubitably, friend. I represent parties interested in acquiring your tome." He gives me a figure.

"That's generous," I say. "Do you know what the book is actually worth?"

"That, my friend, I refuse to even speculate." The corpulent man picks at his food, one pinch at a time

"I have a buyer. Just have to make it to the end of the line."

"I have reason to believe, dear friend, that you will not make it that far."

"Is that a threat?"

"No, heavens no, friend, not from me," he says, shaking his head. His jowls quiver with hypnotic plasticity in a face that barely contains him. "I have reason to believe that there are other interested parties aboard the train, more zealous, less interested in making offers."

"Tell me about your buyers."

The corpulent man regales me with stories hatched and cross-hatched with cloaks and daggers, with clandestine encounters, with aliases, cryptic leads, globetrotting chases, near misses, dust-shrouded tombs, back alleys, words whispered from dying lips, convoluted plots, Tarot decks of archetypes, and whole pantheons of MacGuffins. As he talks, the corpulent man feeds, one finger-pinch of food at a time. I try to pretend not to notice that the tiny morsels he picks go not into his mouth, but into his right ear. It is the ear facing away from me in his profile, so I cannot see the food dribbling out, can assure myself that I do not hear chewing under the words, can assure myself that it is a trick of the lighting, that when he talks, there are no odd undulations beneath his shirt.

The corpulent man stops, mid-sentence, tripping over a detail and then another. "No . . . rather . . . I . . . I have lost my place." He takes my hand, looks to me with watery eyes, voice suddenly higher. "Have we met before, friend, my dearest friend? I feel we have known each other for several lifetimes. Could I induce you to hide within the folds of my coat?" A thick fluid salivates from his ear.

I take back my hand and stand. "I have a prior engagement, but I'll think about your offer."

"Yes. Do. But think quickly. Time and tide wait for—"

"Do you have the time?"

The corpulent man pats his pockets. "Eh, no. My apologies, friend. My fob watch stopped."

In the glass frieze, the women have plunged their daggers into the man on the altar as he plays his flute to the sky. I slip out of the dining car. There are no clocks, but there is a countdown.

❖　❖　❖

Down the corridor.

Muffled fragments of a man's voice from compartment B-67:

". . . experiences few men have ever had . . . plenty of nourishment . . . nothing to fear . . . All transitions are painless . . . When the electrodes are disconnected . . . especially vivid and fantastic . . ."

The door opens, and a young, urbane man, fashionably dressed, with dark mustache, emerges.

Down the corridor. Static and feedback hiss from the door on my right. A familiar voice swims in the static. The Mocking Voice says:

"Yesterday, upon the stair,
I met a man who wasn't there."

My mouth tightens. I quicken pace. Two doors down, on the left, the static hisses and the Mocking Voice continues:

"He wasn't there again today
I wish, I wish he'd go away. . . ."

I run. The Mocking Voice follows. How long has it chased me? Every door is its mouth:

"For though my rhyme be ragged,
Tattered and jagged,
Rudely rain-beaten,
Rusty and moth-eaten,
If ye take well therewith,
It hath in it some pith."

Down the endless corridor. Rhymes and rhymes and the Mocking Voice calling my name. One thousand years later, I knock on the door of C-19.

She pours our drinks, while I try and fail to recall the opening of the door. She puts a record on a phonograph, and something jazzy plays out of its blunderbuss mouth.

"Coffin varnish?" she says, handing me a glass.

"I really shouldn't."

"Don't be such a Missus Grundy!"

"What decade are you from?" I ask.

She smiles and shrugs, and the rye burns good all the way down.

Then she sways. Oh gods. The way she sways—so elementally ever-present in her skin, reveling in every molecule. Some people go their whole lives without enjoying their own body half so much as she delights in a single sway. She takes my hand, and then we're both swaying to the music.

I twirl her, and she leans into me, back to chest, carrying me away on the tide of her hips, and I ask, "So, what was yours?"

"Mine?" she says. "Mine was a cult."

"A good cult or a bad cult?"

"Ba-a-a-ad," she brays like a she-goat. "Every last one of them was a wrong number."

As we dance, she tells me about her roaring days, and falling in with a crowd seeking starry wisdom.

"I gazed into a stone, in the dark, and something the size of a planet slid greasily into my skull. And that was that."

My hand finds heaven in the inches of the small of her back, as I pull her closer, she whispers to me, voice vibrating against my neck, "And what was yours?"

"Mine was a book."

"That how it goes with you?"

"Yeah. It's either women or booze or books."

"*Booze and the blowens cop the lot,*" says the Mocking Voice in the static of the phonograph.

I flinch.

"What was that?" the girl in green asks.

I shrug. We sway. I tell her of my love of books, leather and spine—how my brain claptraps every little factoid of the rare editions. Of all the treasures I pilfer, I prefer the rustle of pages to the clink of coins. One day, I dared to filch the rarest of tomes. In a hotel, in that choking room with yellow wallpaper, I opened the book like a door, and brain pathogens in its grammar opened an event horizon in my head.

"And that was that."

I remember that first night perfectly. An officer of the police came into my room, and I sang a prehistoric lullaby that ate him in the dark. I tore into the night, into the geomancy of the city streets. I came upon a man working the graveyard shift of a newsstand. I slaughtered him. Sobbing, I begged his severed head to make it all make sense again. He looked sympathetic. All the howling nights after that bleed together.

"I still have the book," I say as we sway. "There are people after it. After me."

"I think mine are after me, too," says the girl in green, with a semi-embarrassed scrunch of her face.

"And here we are dancing."

"I'm no canceled stamp."

We let the motion of the train grind us together. I wonder what she was like in her bedlam nights. Had she ever degloved someone's face?

I dip her and say, "Two recovering lunatics romancing each other."

"Tale as old as time."

"The Gershwin Brothers should write it as a musical."

"Who?"

"Nevermind."

"You ever feel guilty about your line of work?"

"Misers live in terror of losing their hoard, and I liberate them from their fear."

"You rationalize even better than you dance."

"The criminal is the creative artist, the detective only the critic."

"You even stole that line, didn't you?"

"Everyone's a copper."

She laughs, and it sounds like victory.

"*Booze and the blowens cop the lot,*" repeats the Mocking Voice from the phonograph mouth.

"That's not supposed to be on that record," she says.

"It's just a voice that's been giving me the tail."

"Oh," she says with a nonchalance that makes me wonder what's been haunting her on this train.

The Mocking Voice straddles the music, saying:
"*Suppose you screeve, or go cheap-jack?*
Or fake the broads? or fig a nag?
Or thimble-rig? or knap a yack?
Or pitch a snide? or smash a rag?
Suppose you duff? or nose and lag?
Or get the straight, and land your pot?

How do you melt the multy swag?
Booze and the blowens cop the lot."

I try to ignore the voice, to talk over it. I tell her how I inherited the entire estate of my father's disease with drink—how alcohol, when combined with the accelerant of certain kind of women, made me combustable.

The Mocking Voice continues:

"It's up-the-spout and Charley-Wag
With wipes and tickers and what not!
Until the squeezer nips your scrag,
Booze and the blowens cop the lot."

I yank the record and dash it against the wall.

"Sorry," I say.

"S'alright," she says.

And then it calls my name, the Mocking Voice, says my name, over and over in the static-hiss of the emptied phonograph, says my name the way my father used to.

"A man of words and not of deeds—is like a garden full of weeds," it says. I shiver. That deadly rhyme. I hear father's footsteps limping up the endless stairs—*bump-scrape—bump-scrape*—the pounding at the red-red door. My hands find my face. I feel lampreys wriggling in my veins. I—

The Mocking Voice chokes to a comic muffle. I look up. A rag is stuffed in the phonograph mouth. My green-eyed girl winks at me with cartoonish exaggeration.

"Jeepers creepers, but I was getting sick of listening to him," she says, and, just like that, everything is impossibly all right.

We sway again, and she hums her own music—amidst all this, she can just hum her own music. We neck and giggle at the Muffled Voice. She twirls and her dress swishes around her in a slow, underwater swirl.

"I like the way you do that," I say.

"And here I was hoping you'd love me for just my brain."

"Gouge out my eyes let's see where the night goes."

"Fuck-a-vous! Who says romance is dead?" We kiss, hard. She gives me a dangerous look. "Oh, I'll cop your lot."

❖   ❖   ❖

Down the corridor and up the spout.

Where was I? Oh, right. We agreed to escape. We'll meet back at her room. We each have something to check out first. We each have our own scabs to pick.

A man stands, like a wax museum display, in front of the door of that imperious Russian woman. It's the conductor himself. They all look the same to me, the conductor and his porters—mustache, waxen face, and never-changing smile.

"Have the time?" I ask

"It's eleven after eleven, sir, on the button."

He tips his blue hat and we make small talk.

"How long have you been a conductor?"

"Since they took my wings, sir. Now I ride the train. My accommodations are the same as the passengers. I do miss my wings. . . ."

"When was our last stop?"

"Some time ago, sir."

"Where?"

He tells me the name, but his words buzz like cicadas. I stumble away, assaulted by chitinous vibrations on the inner ear. From behind her door, the old woman shouts, "We're going in circles!"

I hear knocking and the conductor saying, "I must ask you to please be calm, Madame. Don't make me take off my face."

The dinning car is empty.

Trains are the only confined spaces I enjoy. Claustrophobia and freedom in a speeding paradox. I've paid more than one writer to give me a thinly disguised presence in the mystery pulp pages. My reputation says that it was bravery that released me from all those handcuffs, tight spots, and the felon's cell. But that's not true. It was fear.

Windows are important. I have to look through them to reassure myself. Objects flicker-flash by in the ever-looping night, like rattling film over the projector lamp. I stare freely outside, yet I feel the noose tightening. I think I know why.

I find what I need on the table. I pray that it will give me answers, but I don't pray too loud, because you never know who's listening. An abandoned newspaper. I open it. I turn the page. Nothing. I crumple it and throw it away.

Useless.

I look at menu after menu. I rip each one up.

Useless.

I tear all the paper I can find, cursing. This used to be easier. I used to be insane. I used to be taunted through invisible holes in my walls by incomprehensible demons that weren't there or woken in the night by rats with human faces.

But I got better.

I found the cure.

Now I'm taunted by newspapers and menus.

In the glass frieze of the Bacchanals, the man is laying on the altar. The women have opened him with their daggers. One pulls out his insides, the other is doing things to his remains that would make a cadaver blush. The man still has his face and hands, still plays his flute to the tentacular sky.

Sitting on the floor, the abandoned red fez with a crushed crown offers me no answers.

Why do they all leave their doors open?

Another door ajar. Ululating, infant gibberish from within. I peek inside. An old, wrinkly man stares at me, nakedly, from a large bathtub with clawed feet. Water sluices onto the floor with the rocking of the train. He splashes, smiling, the high-pitched baby jabber coming out of his whiskered face.

I close the door.

Another room. Empty. On the desk, a bible, a proper book, leather and spine, hefty and full. That will do. It's weight feels reassuring. I flip the pages. I flip a few more. I tear out the pages, page after page.

"No, no, no!" repeats a voice in the room, and the mirror over the fold-out washbasin informs me that the voice is mine.

Crackle-bzzzzt-hiss, says the large radio in the room. Crawling out of static thick as reptile afterbirth, the Mocking Voice says:

"A man of words and not of deeds

Is like a garden full of weeds."

My father's favorite rhyme. After a night's debauch, it was always a race between the rhyme and his heady reek to announce Drunk Daddy slamming up the steps.

*"And when the weeds begin to grow
It's like a garden full of snow.
And when the snow begins to fall
It's like a bird upon the wall."*

Bump-scrape. He'd limp-lurch up the stairs. *Bump-scrape.* The drink turned him into a hopping, bulgy-eyed frog-man. *Bump-scrape.* I'd clutch my blankets and pray.

*"And when the bird away does fly
It's like an eagle in the sky.
And when the sky begins to roar
It's like a lion at your door."*

There would be a pounding at my red-red door. Sometimes he finished the poem. Sometimes the red-red door gave in.

"And when the door begins to crack—"

I tip over and slam the radio down. "Jiggers, fellers!" whines the static. I kick the radio. I flip it over, face up.

"What's up, Doc?" says the Mocking Voice.

"Who are you?" I interrogate the machine.

"*Vampyroteuthis infernalis.* Ain't I a stinker?"

"Who are you?" I punch the machine.

"Don't kill me, Doc. I'm just the message."

"You mean messenger."

"That, too. And you are all the enclosed. You are all just ghosts drowning in meat."

"Who are you?"

"You know me, Doc. I'm the rhyme, and I'm coming up your steps." The Mocking Voice laughs, and all of the Orient Express laughs with it.

And I'm running, and I'm running, and I'm running.

Room B-68. When did I come in?

"I've been wanting to talk to you," says a bearded, grizzled man.

On the desk is a ghostly bust of Milton, a phonograph with a dictaphone attachment, and several waxen cylinders of the kind people once used to make voice recordings with. He tells me his name. I tell him mine.

"You're an escapist?"

"Escapologist. Actually, I'm a thief."

"You break out of systems. Very good. Please, sit."

I get comfortable. The train rocks. Red drops pitter-patter on the floor.

"I used to be insane," I begin. "And now I'm not."

"You want to know why?"

"Yes."

"What would knock the sane mind mad and the mad brain mended?" He shifts thoughtfully in his armchair, his handsome robe sliding enough to reveal the red spirals etched into the flesh of his body—I imagine they cover every inch. As he talks, he carves a new spiral into his forehead with a penknife.

"Tell me the first early memory that comes to mind now," he says.

"Catching fireflies."

"Go on."

"I'd put them in mason jars. I'd carry them with me on summer nights, till their lights went out. The cicadas were so loud."

"Cicadas?"

"Yeah. I'd nearly forgotten. My mom had this thing. She didn't like me sitting out too long, at night, listening to the cicadas. She didn't think their buzzing voices were entirely . . . wholesome. She'd nag the way some mothers nag their kids to get out of the bath before their fingers prune. It was hard not to hear the cicadas. They were as loud as gas-powered chainsaws."

He asks me about my vocation. He begins a new spiral on his left cheek. Lines of red form in his white beard. He hands me maze puzzles on sheets of paper stained red. I take out my fountain pen and solve them all with a rapidity that excites him.

"Very good, very good," he says. "Maybe you are the one to escape. I suppose it doesn't matter in the end. There is nothing beyond the train."

"You sound like the institutionalized. Nothing outside the joint, eh?"

"And you think your brain is free?"

"I believe that reality is just the high-water mark where some other asshole's audacity gave out."

My mind was always free. I was always good at getting out of things. I could escape ruts, obligations, and self-identity traps—all the *I-dos* that map out a person's life from birth to death. I deftly stepped out of commitments, some of them I regret, but I'm good at escaping regret, too. I just slip out of the noose. I escaped them all and dashed across the world, pissing in the eye of the tyrannous stars.

The man with the stained beard nods.

"So you, you're some kind of shrink?" I ask.

"An alienist? Oh, no. I'm a folklorist from Vermont."

I lean forward in my chair. "You said something about the whys."

"Oh yes. The spirals."

He points to all the spirals he's scribbled about his room, explains that the shape of the universe is the spiral. The spiral repeats, from snail shell to hurricane, from galaxies to the tinniest building blocks of all matter. It is the flight path of carrion birds. Everything is the spiral. What if, posits the man with the stained beard, the spiral is a pictogram, drawn by the universe, under manic compulsion, over all reality? The runic story, the only story, of how everything tries in vain to escape the gluttonous gravity of the horrible thing at the center of all. The decaying orbit. The tightening circle.

"I don't understand," I say.

He taps the dripping penknife against his teeth. His eyes loose focus. "I . . . uh . . . That is . . . rather . . . It's getting harder to . . . You . . . Certainly you've noticed the anachronisms. I, for one, don't have the foggiest notion of what a gas-powered chainsaw is."

"What? What is this train? Are we all dead?"

"Of course not. We are . . . rather . . . all alive . . . or . . . uh . . . what theoretically and mentally amounts to alive. I'm sorry. I just. The orbit decays! I can't . . ." He trials off and holds his head for several moments. "It was good to talk to you again."

"Again?" I leap out of my seat. Nostalgia flows through my ventricles as deadly as air bubbles. The universe teeters on the tip of my tongue.

"Do you think this is the first time we've had this discussion?" asks the man with the stained beard.

"What—what are you talking about?"

He stabs the penknife into the center of his forehead. "I would like to think that if we drew a radial line outward—" he rends the line through the spiral in a gory gash of exposed bone "—we would find an encounter where I was the lucid one, and you the gibbering madman."

I want to shake him like a radio, make him make sense of it all. But, with perfect suavity, he bites out his own tongue and spits it at me. He sings a song, but I'll never know the words. It's all blood and vowels.

Down the corridor. I can't hear my own footsteps. I get to my room, and notice the door is just a hair open. Trained senses scream a warning. I kick hard—my legs are well muscled—and the door swings open, slamming something with a wet *umph!* It swings back again, dangling on one hinge like a hanged man's neck. Liquid red pools on the floor.

A yellow-robed cultist lays behind the door, sad as a broken Jack-in-the-Box, an obsidian dagger driven between his ribs. A red circle spreads through the yellow fabric. He had been hiding in the shadows, because that is what cultists do. Everything is entirely too archetypal. I think I know why.

"There's no true excuse yet made for the bungler at his trade," I taunt down to the dead man. Oh, the familiar rhymes. I'm becoming my father.

Under the robes, the cultist's naked flesh is wrapped in strands of barbed wire. A short, spastic tale extends from the end of his spine, still curling and uncurling posthumously. Nothing in his pockets but space and questions.

Was I too late?

I yank out my large trunk and open it. Beneath the clothes, inside the false bottom, I find the book. I sigh. The book that started it all. It's as heavy as I remember. I have to use both hands to lift it. Ancient, of course, it smells like a dead pharaoh's taint, bound in leather that feels like no cowhide I ever touched. It promises chthonic wisdoms. The night I stole it, when I first riffled the pages with my thumb to listen to the quality of the vellum, I heard the distant moan of omnipotent mollusks like the sea in a shell.

My hand shakes.

The book that drove me insane.

I open it . . .

My mouth twitches. This shouldn't surprise me. I mean, I already knew. But the rage comes on all the same, and with a strained curse, I lift the weighty tome over my head and bring it down on the dead cultist. I slam it down again and again, with a meaty squelch, until all that remains is the rhythm and a memory and a stain.

Panting. Now.

"I used to be insane," I say to what's left.

My violence must have knocked my pocket watch, hanging from its special hook on the wall, because it swings like a descending pendulum.

11:11

   11:11

11:11

The book lies open like an accusation

"Nothing," I spit. Nothing! No answers, no wisdom, not even any madness. None of the Mesozoic calligraphy that stretched the suture-cracks of my skull and boiled my brain in cuttlefish ink. No words! Just empty pages and perdition, just like the bible, just like the newspaper, the menus, and all documents on this train. In this place, text does not exist. Sunlight does not exist. Glass friezes move more regularly than the faces of clocks and conductors.

My mind sloshes. None of these plots track. I think I know why. I—

I look about the room. It is a mess, but all the mess is mine. The cultist did not so much as overturn my pillows. My trunk's false bottom is clever—true—but he didn't even search. Maybe he wasn't here for the book.

I leap up and tear open the communicating door adjoining my compartment to room C-19.

❖   ❖   ❖

The girl in green is handcuffed to the pipe of her sink. Black tendrils of mascara slither down her face. A fresh spiral is cut, angry and red, just beneath her collarbone. I think she's gone, like everyone else, but she looks up, and her green eyes are clear.

I say her name.

She says mine.

"You came back?" she says. "There's no way out. No way out. No way."

"Really?" I say. With a flourish that Philistines might call overdramatic, my fingers dance over her manacles, and they come undone. It can take up to six seconds for me to get out of that particular make and model, but I really want to impress her.

"This is screwy," she says. "You don't even know me."

"I know that we're riding the raggedy edge, and all you wanted to do was dance," I say, wiping the inky tendrils off her cheek. "I know that all of our collective damage and fuck-ups fit together like key teeth on tumblers."

She hiccups a laugh and says, "Yeah, I'm goofy about you, too." And everything is impossibly all right.

Then two vice grips crush my shoulders and slam me into a wall. The conductor has me by the scuff, looking at me with his waxen smile. "Sir, you are being a disruption, and we must have a modicum of calmness for this journey."

I slip from my jacket, like a snake out of his skin, but before I can get away, another hand—where did it come from?—grabs my throat and lifts me off the ground.

"Be calm, sir," says the conductor. "Please don't make me take off my face."

That's when the bottle caves his head. Full wine bottles don't break like they do in the movies. But skulls do. He crumples to the floor. My girl in green stands behind, bottle held like a cudgel, the look on her face is . . . well, many are the fights I saw in school, and the scariest scraps were between the girls.

I want to say something clever, but the conductor crawls toward us. His smiling face hangs off him, and something writhes beneath. "Sir!" he says. "Madame!" The voice is a buzzing drone.

"Let's dust!" she says.

I take her hand. And we're running, and we're running, and we're running.

Down the corridor.

There are pleasure sounds, in the long night of the train, and what might be construed as muffled screams. Lots of stories. Lots of paths. No matter where each began, they all go bad on the vine. It comes down in waves. In synchronized patterns. The countdown is done.

Flashes of images. Smiles. Blood. Hair. Leaking fluid from an open eye. Whispers. Chewing. Ragged nails, dark and dripping in the moonlight. Hair covering a jabbering face like a creep show curtain.

The girl in green and I run. Coach to coach, to the back of the train. We'll leap off the caboose if we have to.

All the compartment doors are open. All these windows.

An open door: A room crowded with people surrounding a paralyzed man in bed. They pass around a dripping knife like a party favor. Everyone has a turn.

An open door: A man holds a severed woman's arm, injecting it with a green fluid from a large syringe. The dead hand twitches, stroking his cheek comfortingly.

An open door: A young debutant tearfully scrubs at the outbreak of pimples upon her face and shoulders. Each one pops, hatching a new eye.

They are gaining on us. I can hear their footsteps, only they don't sound so much like footsteps as horn scraping hard rubber or splintery wooden shoes shamble-rattling over a polished floor. We run, but the train is endless—carriage after carriage.

An open door: A mother picks the last stubborn strand of flesh from a little boy's head. "There," she says, "was that so bad?"

An open door: A man sits up in bed, pale flesh pocked with barnacle sores, wriggling growths, and sea cucumber discharges. He watches as competing colonies of coral battle for primacy of his chest, spitting up their digestive enzymes in time-lapse warfare.

The train never ends. Ten thousand years later, we arrive in front of the door to my room.

"Impossible," I say.

We duck inside, close what's left of the door, and barricade it with my trunk. The conductor and his porters batter the red-red wood, and through the jagged cracks, I see too many sets of limbs, segmented and crustacean-like, and trembling stumps that may have been wings at one time. Their voices buzz in a cicada cadence.

"We're getting out of here!" I yell.

I lift the heavy, bloody book and hurl it through my window. The glass shatters. Everything shatters. The girl in green screams.

I think of the pickled punks you can see at nickel sideshows. I think of fireflies in mason jars. I remember the cicada voices whispering to me in the darkness, one summer night. I see stars. The gulfs of space. The wells of night. Green sloshes over everything.

Their great wings catch the aether. Pink crustacean bodies. The arthropod angels carrying us. Their faces are not faces, but masses of tendrils that glow in alternating colors, and I can see the syntax in their blinking, a never-ending string of Christmas. Beyond counting. Flying in formation, an endless train. Several pairs of arms each, and in each arm, a cylinder of strange metal, and in each cylinder: a brain. I see them, through their little windows, floating in the green nutrient soup. Some cylinders contain organs of a non-human shape.

The fireflies had jarred us all up. They carry us through the mindless void, past time and matter, into the idiot vortices.

The closest cylinder to me is marked C-19. I'm glad I get to be close to her. She dances and twirls with impossible liquid slowness— so graceful—my girl in green.

I hear her scream my name. I hear them all, through the network, but their voices sound metallic and flat. The conductor says, "Istanbul! Budapest! Vienna! Munich! Strasbourg! Chalons! Paris! Istanbul!"

We're going in a circle, a ring around a nuclear chaos at the center of all. It mutters. Its radiation poisons the dream train and all of its dreamers. The closer we get, the madder they get, the more lucid I'll become. I found the cure.

We must get closer. The gravity is irresistible. Our orbit decays. The spiral is absolute. Louder and louder—the thin whining of cracked flutes.

Right now, I'm just going to look out my window on the night drive. I'll eventually go back to sleep. I'll rejoin my fellow guisers on the dream train, our little plots repeated in each rotation, our follies in endless loop. They're mummers plays, a shadow puppet show, a Punch and Judy delight for the audient void. I can almost hear the silent, mocking applause of the thousand-thousand hands that are not hands.

CONTRIBUTORS' NOTES

ELAINE CUNNINGHAM is a *New York Times* bestselling fantasy author whose publications include over twenty novels and three dozen short stories. Most of her novels are set in licensed worlds such as the Forgotten Realms, Star Wars, EverQuest, and Pathfinder Tales. *Shadows in the Starlight*, the second book in her urban fantasy series Changeling Detective, was included in the 2008 *Kirkus* list of 10 Best Sci-Fi Novels. Her short fiction explores most of fantasy's subgenres, from Arthurian fiction to sword & sorcery. She does not usually write horror, but finds that getting into an Elder Evils mindset is a lot easier than it used to be. For more information about her stories and upcoming projects, please visit elainecunningham.com.

Writer, game designer, and cad, RICHARD DANSKY was named one of the top twenty videogame writers in the world in 2009 by Gamasutra. His work includes bestselling games such as *Tom Clancy's Splinter Cell: Conviction, Far Cry, Tom Clancy's Rainbow Six: 3, Outland*, and *Splinter Cell: Blacklist*. His writing has appeared in magazines ranging from *The Escapist* to *Lovecraft Studies*, as well as numerous anthologies. He was a major contributor to White Wolf's World of Darkness setting, with credits on over one hundred RPG supplements, and will be developing the upcoming twentieth anniversary edition of *Wraith: The Oblivion*. His most recent novel, *Vaporware*, is available from JournalStone. Richard lives in North Carolina with his wife, statistician and blogger Dr. Melinda Thielbar, and their amorphously large collections of books and single-malt whiskys.

Dennis Detwiller is a writer, game designer, and illustrator, who works as design director for a major video game company. He writes and illustrates for many publications, is creative director and co-founder of Arc Dream Publishing and Pagan Publishing, and updates his website (detwillerdesign.com) regularly with games, fiction, and art.

Joshua Alan Doetsch was grown from an experimental pumpkin patch by Monsanto scientists in a top-secret biotech project known only as "Agent Orange." He was genetically designed, honed, and perfected to do only two things: write stories and strangle kittens. Please, please encourage his writing career at joshuadoetsch.com. His previous publications include the novel *Strangeness in the Proportion*.

Geoff Gillan is the lead author of the first edition of Chaosium's *Horror on the Orient Express* for the *Call of Cthulhu* roleplaying game. He has also contributed a Dark Ages adventure and a Gaslight-era sourcebook and adventure for its second edition. His other game credits include many *Call of Cthulhu* adventures, some for *Elric* and *Pendragon*, and the *Corum* sourcebook (penned many moons ago). He has published a fantasy novel, *Envious Gods*, in the U.S. and in his native Australia has worked as a writer for television and film. He has a degree specializing in Southeast Asian and Australian history. His second job at age fifteen was at Wyong railway station north of Sydney, which might explain his unhealthy interest in trains. He moves a lot but is currently residing in Brisbane with his wife Cathie and daughters Lucille and Abigail. This is his first published piece of short fiction, but not his first brush with Madness.

Christopher Golden is the *New York Times* bestselling, Bram Stoker Award-winning author of such novels as *Of Saints and Shadows, Snowblind, The Myth Hunters, The Boys Are Back in Town*, and *Strangewood*. He has co-written three illustrated novels with Mike Mignola, the first of which, *Baltimore, or, The Steadfast Tin Soldier and the Vampire*, was the launching pad for the Eisner Award-nominated comic book series, *Baltimore*. He is currently working on a graphic novel trilogy in collaboration with Charlaine Harris entitled *Cemetery Girl*. His novel *Tin Men* will be released in 2015. Golden was born and raised in Massachusetts, where he still lives with his family. His original novels have been published in more than fourteen languages in countries around the world. Please visit him at christophergolden.com.

CODY GOODFELLOW has written five novels—his latest is *Repo Shark* (Broken River Books)—and co-written three more with John Skipp. He received the Wonderland Book Award twice for his short fiction collections, *Silent Weapons for Quiet Wars* and *All-Monster Action* (both Swallowdown Press). He wrote, co-produced, and scored the short film *Stay at Home Dad*, which can be found on YouTube. He was a contributing editor at *Substance*, the world's first CD-ROM zine, and cofounder of Perilous Press, a micropublisher of modern cosmic horror by such authors as Michael Shea, Brian Stableford, and David Conyers.

KENNETH HITE has designed, written, or co-authored more than eighty roleplaying games and supplements, including *GURPS Horror*, *Call of Cthulhu d20*, *The Day After Ragnarok*, *Trail Of Cthulhu*, *Qelong*, and *Night's Black Agents*. Outside gaming, his works include *Tour de Lovecraft: the Tales*, *Cthulhu 101*, *The Nazi Occult* for Osprey Publishing, and a series of Lovecraftian children's books. He has several published Cthulhu Mythos short stories, writes the "Lost in Lovecraft" column for *Weird Tales*, and covered the High Strangeness for ten years in his "Suppressed Transmission" column in *Pyramid*. Half the podcasting team behind *Ken and Robin Talk About Stuff* and an Artistic Associate at Chicago's Wild-Claw Theatre, he lives in Chicago with two Lovecraftian cats and his non-Lovecraftian wife, Sheila.

ROBIN D. LAWS is the author of the recent fantasy novel *Blood of the City* and *New Tales of the Yellow Sign*, a collection of weird works. Other novels include *Pierced Heart* and *The Worldwound Gambit*. As creative director for Stone Skin Press, he has edited such anthologies as *Shotguns v. Cthulhu* and *The Lion and the Aardvark*. He is best known for his groundbreaking roleplaying game design work, as seen in *The Esoterrorists*, *HeroQuest*, *Feng Shui*, and, most recently, *Hillfolk*. He comprises one-half of the Golden Geek Award-winning podcast *Ken and Robin Talk About Stuff*, and can be found online at robindlaws.com.

PENELOPE LOVE was one of the original contributors to 1991's *Horror on the Orient Express* roleplaying campaign and has returned for the revised edition. Her short stories have appeared in numerous anthologies including *Cthulhu's Dark Cults*, *Made in Goatswood*, and *The Year's Best Australian Fantasy and Horror*. In 2009 she and Mark Morrison retraced the Orient Express route, traveling from London to Istanbul by train, although not, alas, on the Simplon-Venice Orient Express. She used her experience of the train ride on the delightful, but aging Bosphorus Express through Turkey as background for her story in this collection, which focuses on the last days of the original Orient Express. The real train is far more charming than the one depicted here.

JAMES LOWDER has worked extensively on both sides of the editorial blotter. He has directed book lines or series for both large and small houses, and has helmed more than twenty critically acclaimed anthologies, including *Curse of the Full Moon*, *Hobby Games: The 100 Best*, *Beyond the Wall*, and the Books of Flesh trilogy. As an author, his publications include the bestselling, widely translated dark fantasy novels *Prince of Lies* and *Knight of the Black Rose*; short fiction for such anthologies as *Shadows Over Baker Street* and *Sojourn: An Anthology of Speculative Fiction*; and comic book scripts for DC, Image, and Moonstone. His work has received five Origins Awards and an ENnie Award, and been nominated for the International Horror Guild Award and the Stoker Award. He can be found online at jameslowder.com.

ARI MARMELL would love to tell you all about the various esoteric jobs he held and the wacky adventures he had on the way to becoming an author, since that's what other authors seem to do in these sections. Unfortunately, he doesn't actually have any, as the most exciting thing about his professional life, besides his novel writing, is the work he's done for *Dungeons & Dragons* and other

roleplaying games. His published fiction consists of both fully original works and licensed/tie-in projects—including works for the
Darksiders and Magic: the Gathering lines—for publishers such as
Del Rey, Pyr Books, Titan Books, and Wizards of the Coast. Ari
currently lives in an apartment that's almost as cluttered as his subconscious, which he shares (the apartment, not the subconscious,
though sometimes it seems like it) with George—his wife—and a
cat who really, really thinks it's dinnertime. You can find Ari online
at mouseferatu.com and on Twitter @mouseferatu.

LISA MORTON is an award-winning author, screenwriter, and Halloween expert whose work was described by the American Library
Association's *Readers' Advisory Guide to Horror* as "consistently
dark, unsettling, and frightening." Her short fiction has most re-
cently been seen in *The Mammoth Book of Psycho-Mania*, *Dark
Fusion*, *Shadow Masters*, *Danse Macabre*, and *Zombie Apocalypse:
Fightback*, and her acclaimed non-fiction study *Trick or Treat: A
History of Halloween* was released in trade paperback in 2013. Other
recent and forthcoming books include the novellas "Smog" (part of
Double Down #2) and "Summer's End," the novels *Malediction* and
Netherworld, and the tie-in novel *Zombie Apocalypse: Washington
Deceased*. She lives in North Hollywood, California, and online at
lisamorton.com.

DARRELL SCHWEIZTER is the former co-editor of *Weird Tales* (for
nineteen years), a four-time World Fantasy Award nominee (and
one-time winner, for *Weird Tales*), and the author of three novels:
The White Isle, *The Shattered Goddess*, and *The Mask of the Sorcerer*. His novella "Living with the Dead" was a finalist for the
Shirley Jackson Award. His over three hundred stories have appeared in numerous magazines and anthologies, and have been
gathered in eight collections so far, the most recent of which is *The
Emperor of the Ancient Word*. He has published books about H.P.
Lovecraft and Lord Dunsany, and is a critic, reviewer, poet, and
one of the few people ever to rhyme *Cthulhu* in a limerick. He has
edited anthologies, including two in the Cthulhu Mythos, *Cthulhu's
Reign* and *That is Not Dead*. A collection of his own Mythos stories
is forthcoming.

Lucien Soulban, a veteran of the games industry for both tabletop games and videogames, with over twenty-one years of collective experience. Or as he puts it: he's a professional geek who loves making a living at being a nerd. Lucien is a BAFTA-nominated videogame scriptwriter and lead scriptwriter at Ubisoft Montreal, who has worked on *Far Cry 4*, *Far Cry 3*, *Far Cry 3: Blood Dragon*, *Deus Ex: Human Revolution*, *Rainbow Six: Vegas*, and *Warhammer 40K: Dawn of War*. That's not counting the dozen-plus handheld games he's written, including adaptations of *The Golden Compass*, *Enchanted*, and *Kung Fu Panda*. He's contributed to numerous anthologies including HWA's comedy-horror anthologies: *Blood Lite I*, *II*, and *III*. He's also written five novels, including *Warhammer 40K: Desert Raiders* and *Dragonlance: Renegade Wizards*, and worked on over ninety roleplaying books as writer and editor. All this he does from Montreal, Quebec, the city he loves.

C.A. Suleiman has contributed scores of books for some of publishing's top properties, including *Dungeons & Dragons* and the World of Darkness. Along with being the creator and developer of the award-winning occult horror RPG *Mummy: The Curse*, he is the creator of the Hamunaptra fantasy setting, co-creator and editor of The Lost Citadel shared world, and the co-author of *Vampire: The Requiem*. He is especially proud to have shepherded development of the world's first fantasy campaign setting—Dave Arneson's Blackmoor—until its storied creator's passing in 2009. C.A. lives in the Washington area, where his band, Toll Carom, has either just released or is busy toiling away at its latest concept album. Despite the many and varied protestations of his better judgment, he finds himself a regular contributor to the Facebook.

James L. Sutter is a co-creator of the *Pathfinder Roleplaying Game* and the managing editor for Paizo Publishing. He is the author of the novels *Death's Heretic* and *The Redemption Engine*, the former of which was ranked #3 on Barnes & Noble's list of the Best Fantasy Releases of 2011, as well as a finalist for both the Compton Crook Award for Best First Novel and a 2013 Origins Award. James has written numerous short stories for such publications as *Escape Pod*, *Apex Magazine*, *Shattered Shields*, *Beneath Ceaseless Skies*, *Geek*

Love, and the #1 Amazon bestseller *Machine of Death*. His anthology *Before They Were Giants* pairs the first published short stories of science fiction and fantasy luminaries with new interviews and writing advice from the authors themselves. In addition, he's published a wealth of gaming material for both *Dungeons & Dragons* and the *Pathfinder Roleplaying Game*. For more information, visit jameslsutter.com or follow him on Twitter at @jameslsutter. The Simplon Tunnel and the problems described in its construction are real. What may reside at the mountain's heart remains unknown.

SELECTED CHAOSIUM FICTION

ARKHAM TALES

#6038   ISBN 1-56882-185-9 $15.95

STORIES OF THE LEGEND-HAUNTED CITY: Nestled along the Massachusetts coast is the small town of Arkham. For centuries it has been the source of countless rumor and legend. Those who return whisper tales of Arkham, each telling a different and remarkable account. Reports of impossible occurrences, peculiar happenings and bizarre events, tales that test sanity are found here. Magic, mysteries, monsters, mayhem, and ancient malignancies form the foundation of this unforgettable, centuries-old town. 288 pages.

CTHULHU'S DARK CULTS

#6044   ISBN 1-56882-235-9 $14.95

CHAOSIUM'S *CALL OF CTHULHU*® IS AN ENDLESS SOURCE of imagination of all things dark and mysterious. Here we journey across the globe to witness the numerous and diverse cults that worship Cthulhu and the Great Old Ones. Lead by powerful sorcerers and fanatical necromancers, their followers are mad and deranged slaves, and the ancient and alien gods whom they willingly devote themselves are truly terrifying. These cults control real power, for they are the real secret masters of our world.

ELDRITCH CHROME

#6052   ISBN 9781568823898 $17.95

UNQUIET TALES OF A MYTHOS-HAUNTED FUTURE: during the decades since H.P. Lovecraft first wrote of the Cthulhu Mythos, many authors have crossed his themes into other genres, enhancing his original vision with stories taking place in the distant past, in the far-flung future, and in myriad places in-between.

Cyberpunk tales are written in dark, gritty, film-noir styles. Their protagonists live and die at the bottom echelon of an electronic society gone awry. They may be seedier, poorer, and less inclined to make moral judgements than stoic Lovecraftian New Englanders, but in Cyberpunk-Cthulhu tales they encounter the same horrors as their more-genteel predecessors.

Confronting monstrous entities and fiends from beyond space and time, the Cyberpunk-Cthulhu hero may wield high-tech weapons and have other advances at his or her disposal. To beings where time has no meaning and whose technologically is so advanced that their actions seem supernatural or powered by magic, no human finds an advantage.

This is the Cyberpunk-Cthulhu world—mythos horrors lurk at the edge of society, mythos-altered technology infects human beings, dark gods lurk in cyberspace, and huge corporations rule society while bowing to entities inimical to humankind. 272 pages.

ELDRITCH EVOLUTIONS

#6048   ISBN 1-56882-349-5 $15.95

ELDRITCH EVOLUTIONS is the first collection of short stories by Lois H. Gresh, one of the most talented writers working these days in the realms of imagination.

These tales of weird fiction blend elements wrung from science fiction, dark fantasy, and horror. Some stories are bent toward bizarre science, others are Lovecraftian Mythos tales, and yet others are just twisted. They all share an underlying darkness, pushing Lovecraftian science and themes in new directions. While H.P. Lovecraft incorporated the astronomy and physics ideas of his day (e.g., cosmos-within-cosmos and other dimensions), these stories speculate about modern science: quantum optics, particle physics, chaos theory, string theory, and so forth. Full of unique ideas, bizarre plot twists, and fascinating characters, these tales show a feel for pacing and structure, and a wild sense of humor. They always surprise and delight.

FRONTIER CTHULHU

#6041   ISBN 1-56882-219-7 $14.95

AS EXPLORERS CONQUERED THE FRONTIERS of North America, they disturbed sleeping terrors and things long forgotten by humanity. Journey into the undiscovered country where fierce Vikings struggle against monstrous abominations. Travel with European colonists as they learn of buried secrets and the creatures guarding ancient knowledge. Go west across the plains, into the territories were sorcerers dwell in demon-haunted lands, and cowboys confront cosmic horrors.

MYSTERIES OF THE WORM

#6047   ISBN 1-56882-176-X $15.95

Robert Bloch has become one with his fictional counterpart Ludvig Prinn: future generations of readers will know him as an eldritch name hovering over a body of nightmare texts. To know them will be to know him. And thus we have decided to release a new and expanded third edition of Robert Bloch's Mysteries of the Worm. This collection contains four more Mythos tales–"The Opener of the Way", "The Eyes of the Mummy", "Black Bargain", and "Philtre Tip"–not included in the first two editions.

By Robert Bloch, edited and prefaced by Robert M. Price; Cover by Steven Gilberts. 300 pages, illustrated. Trade Paperback.

NECRONOMICON

#6034   ISBN 1-56882-162-X $19.95

EXPANDED AND REVISED — Although skeptics claim that the *Necronomicon* is a fantastic tome created by H. P. Lovecraft, true seekers into the esoteric mysteries of the world know the truth: the *Necronomicon* is the blasphemous tome of forbidden knowledge written by the mad Arab, Abdul Alhazred. Even today, after attempts over the centuries to destroy any and all copies in any language, some few copies still exist, secreted away.

Within this book you will find stories about the *Necronomicon*, different versions of the *Necronomicon*, and two essays on this blasphemous tome. Now you too may learn the true lore of Abdul Alhazred.

STEAMPUNK CTHULHU

#6054   ISBN 9781568823942 $18.95

"We live on a placid island of ignorance in the midst of black seas of infinity, and it was not meant that we should voyage far. The sciences, each straining in its own direction, have hitherto harmed us little; but some day the piecing together of dissociated knowledge will open up such terrifying vistas of reality, and of our frightful position therein, that we shall either go mad from the revelation or flee from the deadly light into the peace and safety of a new dark age."

So said H.P. Lovecraft in the first chapter of his most famous story, "The Call of Cthulhu" (1926). This is also the perfect introduction to Steampunk Cthulhu, for within these stories mankind has indeed voyaged too far, and scientific innovations have opened terrifying vistas of reality, with insanity and worse as the only reward.

The Steampunk genre has always incorporated elements of science fiction, fantasy, horror and alternative history, and certainly the Cthulhu Mythos has not been a stranger to Steampunk. But until now there has never been a Steampunk Cthulhu collection, so here are 18 tales unbound from the tethers of mere airships, goggles, clockwork, and tightly bound corsets; stories of horror, sci-fi, fantasy and alternative realities tainted with the Lovecraftian and the Cthulhu Mythos. Here you will discover Victorian Britain, the Wild West era United States, and many other varied locations filled with anachronistic and sometimes alien technology, airships, submersibles and Babbage engines. But the Victorian era here is not only one of innovation and exploration, but of destruction and dread. 310 pages.

TALES OUT OF INNSMOUTH

#6024   ISBN 1-56882-201-4 $16.95

A shadow hangs over Innsmouth, home of the mysterious deep ones, and the secretive Esoteric Order of Dagon. An air of mystery and fear looms... waiting. Now you can return to Innsmouth in this second collection of short stories about the children of Dagon. Visit the undersea city of Y'ha-nthlei and discover the secrets of Father Dagon in this collection of stories. This anthology includes 10 new tales and three classic reprints concerning the shunned town of Innsmouth.

THE THREE IMPOSTORS

#6030   ISBN 1-56882-132-8 $14.95

SOME OF THE FINEST HORROR STORIES ever written. Arthur Machen had a profound impact upon H. P. Lovecraft and the group of stories that would later become known as the Cthulhu Mythos.

H. P. Lovecraft declared Arthur Machen (1863–1947) to be a modern master who could create "cosmic fear raised to it's most artistic pitch." In these eerie and once-shocking stories, supernatural horror is a transmuting force powered by the core of life. To resist it requires great will from the living, for civilization is only a new way to behave, and not one instinctive to life. Decency prevents discussion about such pressures, so each person must face such things alone. The comforts and hopes of civilization are threatened and undermined by these ecstatic nightmares that haunt the living. This is nowhere more deftly suggested than through Machen's extraordinary prose, where the textures and dreams of the Old Ways are never far removed.

THE WHITE PEOPLE & OTHER STORIES

#6035   ISBN 1-56882-147-6 $14.95

THE BEST WEIRD TALES OF ARTHUR MACHEN, VOL 2. — Born in Wales in 1863, Machen was a London journalist for much of his life. Among his fiction, he may be best known for the allusive, haunting title story of this book, "The White People", which H. P. Lovecraft thought to be the second greatest horror story ever written (after Blackwood's "The Willows"). This wide ranging collection also includes the crystalline novelette "A Fragment of Life", the "Angel of Mons" (a story so coolly reported that it was imagined true by millions in the grim initial days of the Great War), and "The Great Return", telling of the stately visions which graced the Welsh village of Llantristant for a time. Four more tales and the poetical "Ornaments in Jade" are all finely told. This is the second of three Machen volumes to be edited by S. T. Joshi and published by Chaosium; the first volume is The Three Impostors. 294 pages.

EXTREME PLANETS

#6055   ISBN 1-56882-393-2 $18.95

Introduced by Hugo and Nebula Award-winning author David Brin. Featuring stories from David Brin and Gregory Benford, Brian Stableford, Peter Watts, G. David Nordley, Jay Caselberg and many more.

"A stellar line-up of writers presenting the most exotic worlds imaginable—prepare to have your mind blown!" — Sean Williams, Author of Saturn Returns and Twinmaker

TWO DECADES AGO ASTRONOMERS CONFIRMED the existence of planets orbiting stars other than our Sun. Today more than 800 such worlds have been identified, and scientists now estimate that at least 160 billion star-bound planets are to be found in the Milky Way Galaxy alone. But more surprising is just how diverse and bizarre those worlds are.

Extreme Planets is a science fiction anthology of stories set on alien worlds that push the limits of what we once believed possible in a planetary environment. Visit the bizarre moons, dwarf planets and asteroids of our own Solar Systems, and in the deeper reaches of space encounter super-Earths with extreme gravity fields, carbon planets featuring mountain ranges of pure diamond, and ocean worlds shrouded by seas hundreds of kilometers thick. The challenges these environments present to the humans that explore and colonise them are many, and are the subject matter of these tales.

All titles are available from bookstores and game stores. You can also order directly from **www.chaosium.com**, your source for fiction, roleplaying, Cthulhiana, and more.

9 781568 823997